ILLC☤NCEIVED

M K TURNER

D1496449

Acknowledgements
Edited by Sharon Kelly
Cover by ebooks-designs.co.uk

CHAPTER ONE

October 2011

The doorbell rang and Derek Christie looked up at the face of the grandfather clock and tutted. He was going to be late again. He pulled open the door.

"Yes?" he barked. His eyes opened in amazement as a gloved fist flew towards him. Blood spurted from his nose as it made contact. He took two steps backward and then sat heavily on the hall rug. His hands flew to his nose and attempted to stem the flow of blood as he watched two men hurry into his home, slamming the door behind them.

"Don't panic, old chap. The boss wants a word that's all." The shorter of the two men bent forward and squinted at his face. "No harm done, it's not even broken I don't think." He straightened up. "Help the gent to his feet then Tony," he instructed, and the taller man pulled Derek up.

"Think you'd better wash your face. We don't want the neighbours talking, do we?" Tony jerked his head towards the cloakroom. "Go and wash up."

Derek couldn't move. His feet felt as though they were held in place by some unseen force. Instead he twisted his body towards the door. How could they know which one was the toilet? He twisted back only to be prodded in the chest by the smaller man.

"Move," he spat.

Derek staggered backward, and using the momentum, he made the journey to the cloakroom. After splashing water on his face several times, he stared at himself in the mirror. Tearing off a strip of toilet tissue he dampened it and dabbed at the remnants of blood. He could see the reflection of the two men standing in the doorway behind him, and he gripped the basin to steady his nerves.

"Is this about the money? I can pay, you know that. I always do." His voice sounded calmer than he felt. He watched the smaller man shake his head.

"Just get a move on. You can chat all you like when we get there."

"Get where? I can't go anywhere, I have appointments this morning." He turned to face the men. "I don't know who you are, or why you're here, and much as I'd like to help, not this morning." He shook his head, and glanced past them at the clock. "No, not this morning."

Tony grabbed him by the shirt collar and dragged him into the hall.

"You'll do as you're told," his voice was menacing. "Now get a coat on. We need to make a move before your missus gets back from dropping the kid off." He shoved him in the direction of the coat hooks, but still Derek tried to resist.

"I'm not going anywhere until you tell me where we are going, and who it is I'll be meeting."

Tony stepped forward and head butted him. Derek yelled and fell to his knees as blood spurted from his nose once more. The shorter man tutted and grabbed him by the collar from behind.

"Now look what you made him do, it's definitely broken now. Get cleaned up again, put a coat on, and let's get this done."

He put his foot into the centre of Derek's back and pushed, sending him sprawling onto the rug. Derek crawled towards the toilet. His ears were ringing and his lip trembled. He pulled himself up using the door frame, and closed his eyes at the bloody fingerprints he left there. She would start nagging again now, as if he didn't have enough to deal with. He snorted as he realised that despite his predicament, the thought of his wife nagging him was never far away. He needn't have worried though. The shorter man tore a strip of toilet tissue and wiped the prints away.

"Now be careful. We don't want to worry anyone, do we?" He gave a short laugh, and winked at Tony. "Well, not yet anyway."

Half an hour later Derek was dragged from the back of their car, and taken into what appeared to be the rear entrance of a café. He was then pushed into an empty room. He looked around. Apart from a desk and three chairs the room was empty and it stank of cat's pee. He wrinkled his nose as he looked at the stains that patterned the threadbare carpet.

"Hello, Derek, glad you could drop by."

Startled he spun round towards the voice. His gaze was met by a smartly dressed, middle-aged man of average build. Michael Brent was tanned, good looking and smiling. If it were not for the threat that Derek detected in his cold eyes, Brent looked as though he had just stepped into a boardroom, not the stinking rear room of some seedy café.

"Oh no," groaned Derek, "what do you want? I did what you asked and I paid up. I don't owe you anything." Derek pulled his shoulders back a little, hoping it would show he could stand up for himself.

"Didn't you know that your other debt now rests on my books, and my rate of interest is a little higher than Hitchens'?" Brent smiled kindly, for a brief moment, before his face fell and his eyes narrowed. "I have to say Derek I have been most upset that you haven't been responding to me. I nearly came to visit you at work, but thought better of it. Just so we can be sure that never happens again, you take this and keep it safe, and never ever ignore it." He jerked his head. Tony stepped from behind him, and tucked a mobile phone into Derek's pocket.

"I can pay, I always pay." Derek was confused as to how Brent thought the mobile could help.

"I know, but this time it's not money that's required." Pulling out a chair on the other side of the desk, Brent sat and nodded, indicating that Derek should also sit, and he did so gratefully. Tony stepped into the room and shut the door behind them. Derek shivered involuntarily.

"What do you want? I don't understand what it can be if it's not money? I don't have anything else, not really."

Derek watched as Brent threw his head back and laughed, and then calming himself he waved his finger at Derek.

"Now that's not true, is it? I just want to use your talent again, that's all."

"What? Derek raised his voice. "No, not again, we agreed."

Tony stepped forward and slapped the side of his head. The force and shock of the blow caused Derek to fall from his chair.

Derek sniffed and swallowed. The metallic taste of blood made him retch, his nose was bleeding again. The two men sniggered. He blinked and a tear escaped from each eye and travelled slowly down to his ears.

"Oh for God's sake, the fat bastard is crying now." Tony rubbed his hands wearily over his face before turning to his boss. "What do you want me to do? I don't think I've ever met such a chicken shit before."

"Leave him. I'll come over."

Brent stood and walked to where Derek lay staring at the ceiling. He pulled the chair Derek had vacated closer and sat on it, leaning forward, elbows on knees, so his face obliterated Derek's view of the cracked ceiling.

"Let me tell you what I need. Then we can get you home." He smiled as Derek nodded, and then he quietly told Derek what was required of him.

Derek's eyes grew wide, first in amazement then in fear. He began to shake his head. "I can't, and even if I could, I wouldn't." There was desperation in his voice. "You can't be serious. It wouldn't work."

Brent leaned a little closer. "I think it would, and I'm rarely wrong. I don't think you're contradicting me, are you? Now that wouldn't be wise."

"Shall I show him how unwise?" Tony asked, stepping closer to Derek's body. "I think I would enjoy that."

He prodded Derek's ample stomach with the toe of his boot, and Derek whimpered. Brent waved him away.

"Calm down now, I'm sure there's no need for violence, is there Derek?" He smiled as Derek quickly shook his head. "I was going to threaten you with this. . . now, where is it?"

He patted his pockets in search of something, and smiled again as he pulled out a photograph taken earlier that morning. He held it towards Derek. Derek took a deep shuddering breath as his eyes focused on his daughter waving goodbye to her mother outside the school. His leg jerked violently for no apparent reason, and he heard Tony snigger. The photograph was placed back in the pocket.

"I don't think I need to use that," he leaned closer. His eyes were cold and he had a look of distaste on his face. "I think you're a coward, and just knowing what we will do to you will be enough to. . ." he looked up at the ceiling and back down at Derek, "to ensure your cooperation." He smiled. "And look on the bright side, once this is done your debt, as it stands at the moment, of course, is wiped out."

He clapped his hands together and stood abruptly, the chair falling backward onto the threadbare carpet. "We'll be in touch."

Derek reached out and grabbed his trouser leg. Brent stopped and looked down at him.

"What if it doesn't work? I don't think it will, I don't think I can." The man shook his leg and Derek let his hand fall to his side.

"Don't worry, we'll give it a trial run, a couple if you like." He smiled briefly then turned and strode away. He paused as he opened the door, "As I said, I'll be in touch shortly." He left the room.

Michael Brent grimaced at his driver as he climbed into the car and Derek's roar of pain reached their ears. "Tony loves to kick them and it's rarely necessary." He shook his head and pulled the door shut.

CHAPTER TWO

January 2012

Andrew Short shoved his hands deeper into the pockets of his hoodie and hunched his shoulders against the cold. His face contorted into an unattractive yawn. He had been up and out of the house so early this morning, he hoped it had been worth it. Pulling one hand from his pocket he glanced at the large garish watch on his wrist. His bus would arrive in less than ten minutes. He quickened his pace and turned into John Street. Stepping around the road sweeper's cart, he turned up his nose in disgust. He didn't care that he didn't have a job, he got by. He would never do that for a living. What a loser.

Short squinted at the person entering the other end of the street who was dressed much like himself. He pulled his shoulders back to assert his authority. As they neared each other his brow creased in partial recognition. Didn't he know that face? He refused to wear the glasses needed to correct his short-sightedness, and couldn't cope with contact lenses. His face broke into a smile as the penny dropped, and he slowed his pace. The smile was returned and a warm greeting issued. His eyes widened in appreciation as the other person pulled him into a hug and held him; he hadn't expected that. Then his mouth fell open in surprise, he leaned back against the wall of building behind him and slowly began to slide down it.

He was dead before he reached the ground.

DI John Meredith gazed down at the body for a moment longer. The man was in his early twenties and looked like every youngster around. Trainers, skinny jeans, crap tee shirt and a grey hoody, which now had a large red stain that made its way to the puddle on the floor. The knife was still in the wound.

Frankie Callaghan stepped forward as he rolled the gloves off his hands. "The knife obviously hit the spot. He would have died very quickly. We'll get him back to base and I'll confirm later."

"Thanks, Sherlock." Meredith looked over at the uniformed officers taking the names and addresses of the witnesses and sighed. He had been hoping for a quiet day. He looked at his watch again. "Do we know him?" he asked as he hugged himself, and rubbed his hands on his upper arms to warm them.

"Yes, I thought they would have given you his wallet. His name was Andrew Short," Frankie answered, and then nodded at his colleagues, who stepped forward to remove the body.

Meredith rolled his eyes at DC Seaton. "Not know *who* he is, Sherlock, I mean do *we* know him?" He looked to Seaton for a response.

Seaton smirked and nodded. "Small time dealer, that's all. He lives, or should I say lived, over on the Homemead estate, and as far as I know he was limited to selling marijuana and the odd pills in town. He's been pulled in on numerous occasions, but always got away with possession." Seaton sniffed and blew warm air into his cupped hands. He nodded across the street. "Anyone fancy a coffee? I need something to warm me cockles."

Frankie shook his head and made his excuses, before walking away towards his car.

Meredith called after him, "Thanks, Sherlock, and give me a shout if the post mortem throws up anything odd." He turned to Seaton. "Come on then, I'm buying, but it has to be a takeout. I have to get home sharpish tonight."

Seaton raised his eyebrows and smiled knowingly.

"No, no," Meredith shook his head, "well yes, but also Chris Grainger is coming round, says he has news." He looked up at the CCTV camera on the corner of the building. "Who's dealing with the cameras?"

"Travers is on it. He said he'll meet us back at the station." Seaton lifted the police tape to allow Meredith through. "Should be easy, there are loads of cameras around here, and it was broad daylight." He looked up at the grey brooding sky. "Murky daylight anyway. So, Chris reckons he knows who Patsy's stalker is then?"

Meredith nodded as he pulled open the door to the coffee shop. "Seems like it. Don't know why he couldn't just tell her on the phone, or why he didn't call me. Still, all will be revealed." He gave his order to the girl behind the counter. "Two large Americanos to go and a couple of muffins please." He held out a ten pound note.

Seaton placed his hand on Meredith's arm. "Don't go shooting from the hip, Gov, take it steady. You don't want to screw up any possible arrest by being charged yourself."

Meredith turned to him and attempted to look indignant. He slapped his hand against his chest. "Me?" he protested. "I can't believe you would suggest such a thing." He took his change from the waitress and picked up the bag of muffins. "Come on, let's get back to the ranch."

Seaton shook his head and wondered if it would be wise to give Chris Grainger a call; after all, forewarned is forearmed. He sighed, knowing that whichever way he called it, it would be wrong.

Meredith rapped the table with his knuckles, and then sat on it, facing his team.

"Right, listen up you lot. We've had a fatal stabbing on John Street. Just around the corner from the courts, so loads of CCTV. Hopefully, it will get put to bed quickly." He paused as Travers entered the incident room carrying a box. He held his hand out. "And here's the man himself. Sherlock is doing the honours down at the morgue, but looks like a clean blow to the heart and I doubt he will turn up anything more interesting. Name of the victim is Andrew Short." Meredith nodded at Seaton, "Take us through what we know."

"Still waiting for all the eye witness accounts but it seems a youngster, probably male, but wearing a hood, so open minds people. Anyway, this person just walked up to him shortly after one o'clock. Did the deed and strolled away. There was no scuffle and no shouting, even from the victim. Took the public a while to realise what had happened, and by the time the alarm was raised they had disappeared towards Corn Street. So, as the Gov said, CCTV should give us what we want."

He paused as Jo Adler raised her hand.

"Is this lad from Homemead? Early twenties, shaved head and stud in his eyebrow?" she asked.

"The very same, do you know him?"

"Yes, picked him up a few times when I was in uniform. Pain in the arse to the locals, gobby little sod he was. Perhaps he's rubbed one of the players down there, up the wrong way?" she suggested.

Seaton shrugged. "Possibly, I'm going to pull his records now. It maybe he's stepped up a gear, who knows? Like the Gov said, hopefully those will help us,"

Seaton nodded to the box which Travers had placed on his desk.

Meredith slid off the table. "Right, let's get on with it. Travers work with Adler. If she knows Short, she may know who did it. Jones and Collins take the other half. Until we have anything else the rest of you get on with whatever it was you were working on." He paused. "It may be worth getting some of the community boys up here early on. Give me a shout when you find something. Mine's black with sugar, whoever's doing the honours." He strode away towards his office.

"Nice to see you without the plaster, Gov, I bet that was a relief. When does Patsy get back?" Rawlings called to Meredith as he opened his office door.

The whole team knew that their boss was now unofficially living with one of their colleagues, DC Patsy Hodge. It had been played down. They had been told that the arrangement was due to Patsy first having a stalker, then getting shot during their last investigation. Meredith breaking his leg had also been thrown in for good measure. The few that had been to see Patsy at Meredith's home could see there was more to it than that. Gossip was rife and there was more than a little concern as to how that would affect the dynamics of the team.

Meredith turned back to face them. "Due back in two days." He eyed his team. "Why?"

"Just asking, it will be good to have her back." Rawlings turned away and picked up a file.

Meredith simply nodded and went into his office. Taking a muffin out of the bag Meredith placed it on the centre of his desk and slowly peeled away the paper case. He sat spinning it as he pondered his best course of action. He was totally committed to his relationship with Patsy. She had bowled him off his feet when he was least expecting it, and he wasn't going to let anything get in the way of what they had, and what they were building together. He knew that one of them would be leaving the team, and it wasn't going to be him. He was hoping to find her a post based at this station in a different department.

The Superintendent was all for it. Patsy had raised his public profile during the last case, and let him think it was all his own doing. Meredith smirked as he remembered the Super's smug grin when he got back to the station after appearing on *Crimebusters*. He sighed again. The pickings were thin though, and he couldn't see Patsy going for any of them, which meant she would have to transfer out, and then he wouldn't be able to keep an eye on her. Patsy was a good detective, but she was prone to going it alone until she was sure of what she had, and he didn't want her putting herself in danger again, ever.

Meredith was also concerned about the meeting he and Patsy were due to have that evening with Chris Grainger. Patsy had picked up a stalker during the last investigation, and had received indirect threats on her life. Whoever the stalker was, they had only made contact twice since she had left hospital, so they were either getting bored or they knew Chris was on to them.

Chris Grainger had been Meredith's first boss when he joined the CID, but had left to take over his father's private detective agency. Given how close the team were to both Meredith and Patsy, Chris had been given the job of tracking down the stalker. Patsy was convinced it was something to do with Meredith's previous love life, and wanted to keep it well away from work. Chris had made little contact since taking the job and had kept his cards close to his chest on the few occasions that they had spoken. Meredith knew that was probably for the best, but it still irritated him.

Tonight all would be revealed. Chris had told Patsy he would be handing over the file, and telling them who was responsible. Meredith had no idea why he couldn't have told them on the phone, and the waiting was becoming unbearable. He sighed and looked at his watch again. He could probably shoot off in an hour or so, provided the results from the CCTV footage the team were looking at didn't throw up anything too soon. He knew Patsy would be as impatient as he was for the results. She had little, if anything, to keep her mind occupied. He picked up the muffin and took a large bite as Rawlings walked into his office. He looked at him expectantly.

"Any luck?" he asked.

Rawlings shook his head. "Not really. A few partial facial images from who we think it is. We're going to have to get some of the witnesses in to confirm we have the right person and take it from there. Might have to do a local news thing," he shrugged. "We're still waiting for Bob to get back in. He used to work the estate so he might know, but I don't think it's going to be as cut and dried as we were hoping." He looked around as Seaton walked in behind him.

"You're going to love this, Gov. We've got Short's mother on the phone, demanding to speak to you and get an update on what we're doing about it." Seaton let out a bitter laugh. "I wonder where she was when she should have been doing something about him," he sniffed. "I'm assuming you're out?"

"No go on, put her through, I'll sort her." Meredith took another bite of the muffin. "And where's that coffee got to? I'm dying of thirst here."

Seaton and Rawlings left the room, exchanging surprised glances. Meredith rarely spoke to the relatives at this stage. He tended to leave them to the family liaison officers until there was a need, so this was an unusual turn of events. Meredith, however, needed something to keep his mind occupied. His phone rang and Seaton told him Mrs Short was holding on line four.

"Good, I'm assuming the coffee is on the way then?"

Meredith took a deep breath and pushed the button to pick up the call.

Patsy flipped the door to the dishwasher up with her foot and switched the machine on. She glanced up at the clock again. It had only been fifteen minutes since she last checked, but it was almost six o'clock and Meredith would be home soon. She smiled as she still didn't have an alternative name for him. She called him Gov when speaking to workmates, and Meredith to the few friends they had in common. When speaking to him personally calling him John just didn't sit comfortably, so she avoided using any name, unless of course she wanted to irritate him, and then she called him Johnny.

Glancing at the newly replenished wine rack she considered pouring herself a glass, but shook her head and walked away. Chris and Sharon Grainger were due to join them for dinner at seven thirty, and that would be soon enough to start drinking. She walked to the hob and lifted the lid on the curry she had made earlier and stirred it. Replacing the lid and licking the spoon, she stretched and yawned. Today had dragged by so slowly. She was bored, worried, and expectant but most of all she was concerned. Whatever news Chris had to give them, it paled into insignificance when compared with what she had to tell Meredith. She threw the spoon into the sink and walked back to the wine rack. Selecting a bottle at random she collected a glass from the cupboard and sat at the kitchen table. She poured herself a small measure and sipped it. He might take it well, of course, but that was unlikely, very unlikely, and she had been bracing herself all day for the fireworks that would surely come.

Meredith opened the door and ushered Sharon and Chris Grainger into the hall. Patsy hugged them and took their coats and admonished them for the two expensive bottles of wine they had brought. Meredith showed them into the sitting room and poured them a drink. Patsy knew he wanted the business element out of the way and hoped it wouldn't ruin the evening. She thoroughly enjoyed the Graingers' company and had been looking forward to seeing them. Meredith waited until everyone was settled.

"Right, I reckon you reveal all and then we eat." He eyed the folder that Chris had placed on the coffee table. "I'm hoping that we can leave off any arrests until tomorrow as I also really fancy a serious drink tonight."

Patsy closed her eyes momentarily. He would probably need one once she shared her news. Chris exchanged a glance with Sharon that she couldn't quite read and she leaned forward.

"Come on then, Chris, let's get this done quickly." She tapped her fingernails against the side of her glass as though calling the room to order. "Over to you, Mr Grainger." She held her arm out towards him, giving permission to speak.

Meredith walked over to the bay window and, having looked out at the street for a few moments, turned to face them as Chris opened the file.

"Okay, you gave me several suggestions and we followed up on all of them," he tapped the folder. "One of them turned up something I'm sure you'll be interested in, although not related to the matter in hand." He paused as Meredith cleared this throat to indicate his frustration. Chris rolled his eyes. "And in reverse order, so we cover everything, I'll start with those not involved."

He ignored Meredith's sigh. "Tanya Jennings and latterly Kirsty Marsh had nothing to do with it. Our friend Dawn Jessop also had nothing to do with it. Although, and this is what will interest you, she is abusing her position on the *Crimebusters* team."

"What does that mean?" Meredith interrupted.

"I was just getting there." Chris patted his wife's knee. "Sharon here followed her for four days, and she met with the same man several times, and when she showed me the photographs I knew who he was." He paused and inclined his head. "In fact, you might know him, Tommy Sealy?"

Meredith frowned. "Name rings a bell." He thought for a moment but then shook his head. "No, enlighten me."

"Tommy Sealy is a photographer, bit of an ambulance chaser. You know, takes the shots the tabloids want on the front pages. I knew him both from the job, as he was always there at a murder scene or when somebody had bobbed up in the docks, but also from our investigation work," Chris explained. "He quite often takes a cut from private investigators that have an open and shut case but want the right photos to prove it."

Meredith was nodding his head. He had remembered.

"What's he got to do with it?" Patsy asked, confused as to the connection.

Sharon answered in place of her husband. "He's a weasel, and she, Dawn Jessop, was giving him information she picked up from making the *Crimebusters* programme. This enabled him to get candid shots of family and victims. Anyone involved really that would enhance her exclusive stories. Cost of each photo varies from twenty quid to hundreds apparently, depending on the story of course." Sharon shrugged, "I suppose it's a living."

"So she sells them for him? Why doesn't he just do it himself?" Patsy questioned.

"Because she writes a story to go with the photograph, and sells it on to whoever will pay. She uses a pseudonym, Danny Cryer," Sharon explained.

Meredith clapped his hands together and pointed at her. "That's why I could never track the bastard, or should I say bitch, down. A couple of times the Cryer bloke, as I thought him to be, wrote stories on current cases. Never did any real damage but caused a bit of upset to victims and relatives alike and I wanted to mark his card. Could never get to him though, as he never actually broke any laws and the papers wouldn't give him up. So how did you get Sealy to tell you all this?" Meredith had left the bay window and had perched on the arm of Patsy's chair. "I can't see he would want to boast about it."

"Well, you will remember that I'm allowed to be more devious than you, so I called him and told him I had a job for him. I thought he had probably taken the photograph of Patsy with your ex." Chris was aware that everyone in the room had stiffened, and Meredith circled his hand encouraging him to move on.

"And had he?" Meredith didn't want anyone dwelling on anything but the matter in hand. He rested his hand on Patsy's shoulder and gave it a squeeze.

"Nope, but when I told him that I'd been hired to find out if a couple of coppers were bent and gave him your names and this address he looked very confused, which I think is a common state for him."

Meredith grunted and slammed his eyes in impatience at the unnecessary commentary. "Because . . ." he encouraged.

"Well someone else already had that case, so he asked me if Brenda had failed."

"Brenda, who's Brenda?" Meredith asked, shaking his head.

"Brenda Allerton." Chris leaned back and folded his arms across his chest as though that were enough explanation.

Meredith rubbed his hands over his face. "Brenda Allerton took the photo then. Who put her up to it?"

"Hang on a minute, let's just put Dawn Jessop away first. Long story short, Sealy told me what he knew about Allerton and then we got talking about the police, about *Crimebusters*." He paused, "Will you stop winding your finger at me, all in good time." Chris shook his head and Meredith allowed his hand to drop into his lap. "Sealy tells me about this nice little earner he's got going aside of his normal jobs for *Crimebusters*. She's not breaking the law as you have already said, but it can't be good, betraying the trust of the police when they are trying to solve a case. What you might call biting the hand."

Meredith nodded curtly. "Yep, got it, and I will have a think about that, but back to Brenda."

"Can I ask who Brenda is?" Patsy piped up in a quiet voice, and everyone knew she thought that Brenda was probably one of Meredith's previous conquests.

"She's a second rung private investigator," explained Sharon. "She just deals with cheating spouses and missing cats and the like. She's not good at it either. She's taken a couple of hidings when caught at the end of a lens." Sharon wrinkled her nose in distaste.

"And Brenda Allerton was involved how?" Meredith made no effort to mask his irritation.

"Well, Brenda was employed to follow these two coppers, but concentrate on the woman as they were believed to be bent and no one could prove it. So Tommy Sealy, or do we mean the mythical Danny assumed she'd cocked up again and we'd been given the job. He didn't know who the client was though, so I sent Sharon to see Brenda, and she told her."

"What, just like that?" Patsy asked. "I know there is probably little client confidentiality and all that, but surely you must have some standards?" Seeing the look on Chris's face she quickly apologised, "Sorry, I meant her, not private investigators generally."

"Of course, but we were talking shop, and as I told her I had been asked to do a similar thing, we compared notes. She thinks our client was someone Meredith had fitted up." Sharon winked at Meredith. "Sorry, John, it was needs must."

Meredith sighed and closed his eyes before looking up and saying wearily, "No offence taken, and her client was . . ." He paused and sighed again, "Just tell us. All this background stuff is very nice, and much appreciated. It's sure to come in useful at some stage, but would one of you simply spit it out. Who's the stalker?"

"Peter Branning," Sharon said abruptly.

Patsy's mouth fell open and Meredith clenched his fists. Peter Branning was Patsy's former fiancé and, other than to acknowledge he existed, Patsy had never spoken about him.

"Peter? No, he wouldn't be so stupid," Patsy threw her hands up, "would he?"

"Why not?" Meredith asked curtly.

Sharon and Chris exchanged a concerned glance, hoping this wasn't going to lead to an argument.

"Why not?" Patsy looked at Meredith as though he had gone mad. "Because he's a police officer, and forget the messages and flowers and what have you, but breaking and entering, or just entering, smashing windows . . ." Patsy shook her head. "No I just can't see it."

Meredith chewed his lip for a while. "And if he wasn't a copper? What then? Would you still be saying, no not Peter?" He pinched the bridge of his nose as Patsy considered the question. Eventually she nodded. Meredith's eyes widened a little believing she was going to continue to defend her previous lover.

"Yes," Patsy confirmed and nodded again.

"What?" Meredith had raised his voice.

Chris leaned forward as though to intervene. Meredith held his hand up and Chris stilled. "Explain that." Meredith's face had hardened and Patsy was confused.

"Why are you getting angry? Yes, I think he would be capable if he wasn't a copper. But I don't think he'd risk it because he is. I can't understand why that's so difficult for you to get your head around." She reached up and squeezed his hand, "You explain, please."

Meredith closed his eyes and shook his head sighing. When he opened his eyes, he shrugged, "I'm sorry, I thought you were going to say you just couldn't see it either way, which would have been stupid and naïve. I misunderstood, sorry." He raised his eyebrows and gave her the 'I've done it again, haven't I?' look.

Meredith was renowned for shooting from the hip when he felt passionate about something. Patsy bit her tongue as having this out with Meredith now would solve nothing, and she wanted more detail. She smiled and shook her head.

"Okay, well that's sorted then." Patsy looked across to Sharon who was waving her hand.

"Can I just interrupt before this turns into a domestic?"

Patsy smiled at her, Sharon was not one for subtlety, and Sharon returned her smile before continuing.

"I understand what you're saying, Patsy, and the logic is right, but it is him." She and Chris nodded in unison. "However, he didn't break in. Brenda did that, but he did get the keys or a copy of them anyway. I went back to the agent and spoke to the young girl they have there again, and she confirmed that a policeman came in and asked to see the records for the keys to the block. He then wanted to check they were all present and correct as per the key log and asked for a cup of tea so she left him to it. My guess is he pressed them. She didn't see him again. Her boss was a right cow when she found out, she didn't half lay into her about it. She sacked her afterwards."

"But Brenda admitted going into Patsy's flat, so what did she think the purpose was?" Meredith's frown had returned.

"Well, I asked that of course. I said something like, so you went in and messed it up a bit did you, and she laughed and said she had done the opposite. That was all the copper, that's Branning, wanted. She was to spook the woman into making a move. As she wasn't breaking anything she didn't mind and he was a good payer."

"He broke Meredith's window then?" Patsy asked, still shaking her head in disbelief.

"Possibly, he used to come down and follow you too." Sharon gave a sympathetic shrug as Patsy's mouth fell open. "As far as I can make out, if he thought there was something he wanted to know about going on, and he had to get back to Southampton, he'd call her and she would take over. She sent the flowers when you came out of hospital. She didn't like doing it, but she thought you were bent so it eased her conscience. She didn't mention Christmas though, so that could have been him."

Sharon took a deep breath and held her shoulders back. "So, it is him. The question now is what you want to do about it?"

A silence filled the room as Patsy thought about this. Meredith and Chris

Grainger exchanged glances which Sharon saw, and she made a mental note to warn them off. Patsy missed this and held her hands up helplessly.

"I don't know. . . I just want it over. Perhaps I should call him. If he knows we know, he may back off." Her eyes travelled across the three faces, looking for their opinion.

Meredith stood up and stretched. "I think you need to think about it. I have no idea what happened between you two to make him do this, and I can see you're struggling with it. If you make a complaint he's a goner, and that might make him very dangerous. My vote is you think about it, sleep on it. I don't know, perhaps you should take a couple of days. Then, when you know what you want, that's what we'll do. If anything happens in the meantime at least we know what we're dealing with."

Chris was nodding his agreement. Sharon showed no opinion.

Patsy sighed deeply and stared at her feet for a while before agreeing. "Yes, you are probably right. A knee jerk reaction could backfire on us." She smiled at Meredith, "Good thinking Batman."

"Right, that's that done then." Meredith smiled, "Where's my dinner? I'm starving!"

Patsy rolled her eyes at him. "You pour some more drinks and I'll get onto it. It'll be about twenty minutes."

She stood up and raised herself onto her toes and kissed him on the nose before leaving the room. Sharon called after her that she would give her a hand after she'd paid a visit. She waited until she could hear Patsy was busy in the kitchen and pointed at her husband.

"I know I don't need to say this, but I'm going to anyway. Just don't." She turned and her finger was now aimed at Meredith. "That goes for you too."

Meredith nodded in agreement and Sharon went in search of the toilet. Meredith looked at Chris Grainger and winked, then held up his hand showing his fingers were crossed. Chris buried his face in his hands and groaned.

The topic was not discussed over dinner, and the two couples had a pleasant meal with much banter. The feeling that something had been left unsaid hung in the air on occasion but they all chose to ignore it. It was a little after eleven when they waved their guests goodbye, and Meredith sat at the kitchen table and had a final night cap as Patsy took a call from her father. It was clear that all was well and Meredith breathed a sigh of relief, glad that that was one area that she didn't need to worry about.

"Well, that was pleasant," Meredith stated as Patsy came to join him.

"Hmm, not a great start but we got there in the end." She reached across the table and squeezed his hand. "Thank you for giving me some space, I think sleeping on it is for the best." She sipped the drink Meredith had poured for her and smiled at him. She could see he had something to say. "Come on spit it out, I can see there is something."

Meredith shook his head. "No not really. We've never discussed Branning though." Meredith shrugged and finished his drink. "It's not a problem. Come on, let's go to bed, I've got a murder to investigate tomorrow."

He walked to the dishwasher and put his glass in. Patsy stood to join him.

"We can talk about it if you want, it's not that long a story," she said quietly.

Meredith shook his head, and pulled her into his arms. "Nope, when you're ready will be soon enough. I have no idea what you did to him, which is a little scary given his reaction. But," he kissed her forehead, "I'm sure he deserved it, and I'm glad he turned out to be a little deranged. After all, if he hadn't been we wouldn't be standing here now." He turned her around and pushed her towards the door. "Although I would rather be in bed, so get a move on."

He slapped her backside and Patsy yelped and hurried up the stairs. She was pleased as she didn't want a long conversation, not tonight. She had enough to think about, but she knew Meredith wouldn't let it go. She resolved to speak to him the next day once she had decided how to deal with Peter Branning. She sighed as she realised the other thing hadn't been dealt with either, but for sanity's sake she was shelving that for now.

CHAPTER THREE

Meredith sat on the edge of Dave Rawlings' desk, and shuffled through the photographs. He dropped the pile on the desk despondently.

"No clear face shots then, and I thought this would be a quick one. Have you got someone to go round to the family, just in case?" Rawlings nodded and Meredith slapped him on the back. "Right, let's widen the search on CCTV. This lot stops at the centre opposite the Hippodrome. We need to find out where they went then. Onto a bus, into a taxi, you know the drill. Take Bob Travers and do all the cameras on the other side of the centre. If that doesn't help, we may have to get in touch with the local news to do a slot. They'll jump at it I'm sure. So, get on with it, and give me a shout if anything occurs."

"We've got uniforms in town with the best of these, to see if any of the shopkeepers etcetera, remember anything." Rawlings stood and looked at Meredith. "We could try *Crimebusters* too. They run the last Monday of each month, might be worth considering," he suggested, as he pulled his jacket off the back of the chair.

"Yeah, maybe, let's see how we get on today first."

Meredith walked briskly to his office. He still hadn't decided on what to do about Dawn Jessop. He had a meeting with the Superintendent about Patsy in an hour. Not surprisingly, the news about Peter Branning being her stalker had thrown things out of kilter, and he had yet to broach the subject of her transfer. He glanced at his watch and wished the meeting was sooner as he had another appointment at midday and the Superintendent was on the verbose side. Few meetings with him ever ran to time.

Meredith had hardly sat down at his desk when Seaton called for him. He looked out into the incident room. Seaton was holding the telephone in one hand and beckoning Meredith with the other. Meredith went to see what all the excitement was about. He and the rest of the team listened to Seaton respond to the caller with a few grunts, and begin to make notes on his pad. Meredith held his hands up to the team in a gesture questioning Seaton's initial excitement. They shrugged in response. Eventually Seaton hung up.

"Got a shooting, Gov. The victim has been taken to the General. Happened in the coffee shop at the bottom of Christmas Steps. Uniforms have got the area taped, armed response have been and gone, but they have the gun. Who you taking?"

Meredith was already striding away towards his office. "You, get your coat. You're driving. Adler ring the Super and tell him I'll be late." He lifted his overcoat off the hook. "Tell him I'll call him, promise." He winked and followed Seaton out of the room.

Meredith and Seaton stood as the surgeon came into the family room where they had been awaiting news of the operation.

He nodded at the coffee table. "Is that going begging? I'm starving."

Meredith told him to help himself. He picked up the muffin and took a bite as he sat down. He held up a finger whilst nodding and chewing and then took another bite. Meredith bit his lip. When the surgeon had finished the second mouthful he smiled at them.

"Sorry about that, I haven't had any breakfast. Right, the bullet entered here," he pointed half way up his ribcage, on his right-hand side, "and stopped just about here." He twisted and pointed at his back. "Sorry forgot to bring it with me, but I have it bagged in recovery for you. No major damage done. I think it will take her longer to get over the shock than it will the injury. She's also in recovery. She has woken up and is still drowsy, but you should be able to see her," he glanced at the clock on the wall, "in maybe an hour? They're getting a side ward ready for her." He took another bite of the muffin as Meredith shook his head.

"No sooner than that? It wasn't a long op, are you sure we can't get in sooner?" he asked and held out the bottle of mineral water. The surgeon took it with a nod of appreciation and washed down the last of the muffin.

"I doubt it very much, but that will be up to Sister once she's down there, but unlikely."

"Okay, so take us to the bullet then. You do realise we don't want to set her recovery back but the sooner we speak to her, the more likely we are to get whoever did this. We have to assume that they intended to kill her, so might want a second pop at it."

Meredith was now standing, and he stepped over the coffee table to leave. He had to step back as a nurse pushed open the door. She looked relieved when she saw the surgeon.

"Ah, Mr Billings, this is Anna's mother and sister. They've just arrived and I said you'd be able to update them." She ushered a middle-aged woman and a girl, whom Meredith guessed was about nineteen, into the room. Henry Billings stood and turned to the woman. Taking her by the hand he led her to the seat recently vacated by Meredith and helped her to sit down. She was holding a shredded tissue to her mouth.

"Will she be all right, doctor? They won't let me see her." She gulped in breath and the young girl knelt by the side of the chair and took her hand.

Billings smiled at her. "She'll make a full recovery, don't worry. I've removed the bullet and repaired what damage there was, so other than being a little sore and having a small scar she will be absolutely fine. She'll be taken to a side ward soon and the nurse will come and get you. Now, if you have any more questions just ask the nurses, I must dash I'm afraid." He smiled as the woman nodded then turned to Meredith and Seaton who were standing next to the door. "As I say, the bullet is waiting for you in recovery, operating room four, when you're ready. I have to get on." He jerked his head towards the door, then opened it and left.

The woman looked up at Meredith. "Are you police then?" she asked and Meredith and Seaton nodded confirmation.

Seaton pulled his ID out and sat on the chair opposite the woman. "I'm Tom Seaton and this is DI John Meredith. Whilst we wait to speak to your daughter, would you mind if we ask you a few questions?"

The woman shook her head. "No, of course not."

"What's your daughter's full name?" Seaton flipped open his note book.

"Anna Marie Carter."

"And her age?"

"Twenty-four, last Thursday."

The woman sniffed and screwed the remains of the tissue into a ball and dabbed the end of her nose. Meredith picked up a box of tissues from the window sill and handed them to her.

"There you go, love. Can I get you a drink or anything?" He looked from one woman to the other, but they both shook their heads. "Well, just let me know," he smiled kindly at them. "Let's start with your name, and when you last saw Anna?"

"I'm Betty Carter, I'm her mum, and this is her sister Gill." She pulled one of the tissues from the box and blew her nose. "I suppose it must have been about seven this morning, she came out of the bathroom as I went in. She had left to catch her bus by the time I came downstairs. I hated her opening up," she paused and frowned, "actually that's not true, I hated her being there on her own. They take it in turns to open and shut the diner, and dressed like that they get a lot of attention. I kept telling her to take something to change into, didn't I, Gill?"

She waited until Gill had nodded in agreement. "Mind you, that's why she went for the job, she likes all that glamour stuff, and it suits her. Her dad calls her his little Marilyn." Her hand flew to her mouth. "I hope they've managed to get hold of him, he had already left the office when I called him."

Seaton stopped writing and raised his eyebrows to question that information.

"He's a copier repairer. He covers Bristol and Bath, so he could have been round the corner, or the other side of Bath. He never answered his mobile, he keeps leaving it in the bloody van. I have told him." She sighed and looked up at Meredith who was still leaning against the wall. "Can you find out?"

Meredith nodded and smiled. "Of course, but just give us a little more information on Anna first. What did you mean about the clothes?" He stepped forward and perched on the back of a chair.

"Well you know, it's an American dinner style café. It has those lovely big red leather booths, and an old-fashioned juke box, even got a little dance floor, although I don't think it gets used. Kids these days don't know how to dance to that music. But the girls all dress in fifties style, big skirts with petticoats, bobby socks, tight tops, pedal pushers." She looked from Meredith to Seaton. "Do you know what I mean?" The two men nodded. "Well our Anna loves all that, got the Marilyn hair do, and always looks the business, and that attracts attention. Attention that causes her grief sometimes, she's quite shy you know. Girls these days go out almost naked, but Anna still got the attention."

"I think I might have been there once. Did Anna seem okay this morning?" Meredith watched as Mrs Carter's head drooped and she shrugged.

"Perfect. The same as always, she's as bright as a button in the mornings," she nudged her other daughter, "not like us."

Gill Carter smiled back at her.

"Has she mentioned she was worried about anything? Was there anyone in particular bothering her? Or perhaps she's been acting a little strange or different lately?" Seaton prompted. But the two women shook their heads.

"Everyone loves Anna," her sister announced, "and anyway she was shot! She wouldn't know anyone with a gun. I thought she was just robbed." She looked across at Meredith. "Do you think this was someone she knew then?"

Meredith shook his head. "I don't know, but the more we find out the easier it will be for us to catch whoever did this."

"But why would anyone rob the café first thing in the morning? That's daft, they would only have a small float in the till at that time of day. Anyone would realise that it would be better to do that later in the day, wouldn't they?" Betty Carter looked to Meredith for confirmation, and he shrugged.

"You would think so, but we shouldn't assume that whoever did this would think like that. If this wasn't personal, then it could be as simple as her being in the wrong place at the wrong time." He looked at his watch. "The quicker we get to speak to her the quicker we will have a better idea. It shouldn't be long now."

"Did she have a boyfriend?" Seaton asked, and watched as Betty Carter shook her head.

"No, not at the moment. She was seeing some chap for a few months last summer, but nothing recent." She looked at her daughter, "Was there?"

Gill glanced at Meredith and shook her head. "No, there was some bloke she fancied that used to come into the café, but she didn't even know his name, she was too shy to ask. When do you think we can see her?"

Meredith stood and walked to the door. "I'll go and check. You just answer DC Seaton's questions, I won't be long."

Meredith left the room and went to the reception area where the nurse that had brought the Carters to the family room was directing some visitors to their destination.

She turned to Meredith and smiled. "How are they doing?" She looked up the corridor towards the family room.

"As you would expect, but they are asking to see her. Have they settled her yet? It's important we speak to her as soon as possible." Meredith watched as she leaned over the reception desk and picked up the phone. She pushed the extension she required and waited. There was no answer, so she chose an alternative. This time she was more successful and established that Anna Carter was now in bed five of Ward H, and was doing well if a little drowsy. "So you can go and see her now, but the Sister up there is a tyrant. She won't let you stay long."

Meredith thanked her and hurried back to the family waiting area.

"They have settled her in," he smiled, "we can go up and see her now." He paused as the two women jumped to their feet and he placed his hand on Betty Carters shoulder as she reached him. "Apparently, she is still very drowsy, so once you've said hello, I'd be grateful if you would let us take over. The sooner we get on with finding who shot her the better."

Betty Carter smiled her agreement and Meredith led the way to the lift.

Anna Carter opened her eyes and gave a brief smile as her mother rushed to her side.

"Hello Mum, someone shot me." It sounded more like a question than a statement.

Her mother leaned over and kissed her forehead. "I know baby, but you're going to be fine." Mrs Carter gestured over her shoulder. "These two are policemen and they need to ask you a few questions. Is that okay?"

Anna nodded and her mother picked up her hand and sat in the chair next to her. Gill Carter pulled a chair from a stack of three in the corner. She took her position on the other side of the bed, and she kissed her sister's cheek before she settled herself.

Meredith stepped forward until his legs were leaning against the bottom of the bed. Despite her condition the girl was strikingly beautiful. He smiled warmly.

"Hello, Anna, I'm John Meredith and this is Tom Seaton. We know you're not quite with it, at the moment, but we do need as much information as you can give us to help us get whoever did this to you."

Anna took a deep breath and groaned with pain, causing her mother to glance at her, and nodded.

"Good girl, now rather than ask you questions why don't you tell us what happened this morning from when you left the house. If we need more detail we will interrupt, is that okay?"

"That's fine, but there's not much to tell. I caught the bus as usual, got off at the centre and walked to the diner. I opened the shutters and unlocked the door."

"What time was that?" Seaton asked.

"Probably got there about five past eight. We open at eight thirty on Wednesdays."

"And you weren't aware of anything out of the ordinary? There was no one on the bus you thought was odd or anyone hanging around the café when you got there?"

"No, I sat upstairs on the bus and it was empty when I got on." She frowned, trying to remember her journey. "A couple of people got on near the Downs and came upstairs, but they weren't odd." She blew out a breath and Seaton could see she was trying to breathe without too much movement of her ribcage. "I didn't see anyone at the café." She shook her head. "I just went in, turned the alarm off, put the lights on. You know, the normal stuff."

Seaton nodded his head in agreement. "According to our records, you called the incident in at eight forty-five. What happened between you getting there and opening up and you making that call?"

Anna took too deep a breath and her face screwed up. Meredith and Seaton winced with her. They waited whilst she regulated her breathing.

"Nothing happened. I set the coffee machines up, put the specials up on the board, chose some music on the juke box and filled the cake stands." She shook her head. "It was just a normal day. We usually get a couple of customers at least as we open, but there was no one until he came in."

"Can you describe him?" Meredith asked softly. He watched as Anna closed her eyes. When she opened them she looked directly at him and blinked. A single tear travelled towards her ear and disappeared into her hair. She raised her shoulders slightly as though she were going to shrug but thought better of it, and shook her head instead.

"Not really, I had my back to him when he came in and I told him to take a seat. He sat with his back to me, so I could only see the back of his head, and he had a hat on. You know one of those beanie type things, and a dark coat, navy, I think."

"Did you notice his hair colour? Was it sticking out beneath or around the hat?" Meredith held back a sigh as once again Anna shook her head.

"No." She grimaced. "I'm not much use, am I? I'm sorry."

"Don't be, it might come back to you." Meredith smiled again. "So, he sits with his back to you and then what?"

"I picked up my pad and pencil and went to take his order. Because he was sat with his back to me I went to the seat opposite him, turned to take his order and he shot me."

Her mother gave a little gasp and lifted her daughter's hand to kiss it. Anna smiled at her and blinked. Meredith watched her chin tremble and waited whilst she controlled the need to cry.

"He didn't speak? Can you remember anything else at all about him, scars, glasses, what he was wearing, anything like that?"

"I remember looking up to take the order, and then this movement of his hand. I felt like I'd been punched. I was spun around by the shot and then staggered back and fell over the seat behind. I ended up sort of lying across the table. I remember thinking I'd probably put my back out again, but realising that it was my shoulder that hurt. When I put my hand to my shoulder it was bleeding and I understood then what the noise was. I realised that I'd been shot. Then I don't know what happened. I don't know if I fainted or if it was just seconds, but I realised he'd gone. I got up and went to call an ambulance."

"Well done, Anna, this is really good," Seaton encouraged. "So you didn't hear him leave, or see him walk past you?"

Anna shook her head.

"Did any other customers come in whilst this was happening, do you know?"

Again she shook her head,

"Okay, so when you . . ." Seaton stopped speaking as the door opened.

The ward sister entered the room, and took in the scene quickly. "Hello, Anna, I've brought your jewellery back for you. Perhaps Mum can take it home to keep it safe."

She placed a paper kidney bowl on the table across the bed from Meredith. It contained a pair of hoop earrings, a string of what Meredith assumed to be fake pearls, and a large dress ring with an amber stone in a plain setting.

"How are you feeling? If you've had enough, these gentlemen can wait." The sister took her hand from her mother's and felt her pulse whilst looking at her fob watch. She placed Anna's hand back on the bed. "Well, that's all normal. Now shall I ask them to leave?"

Meredith rolled his eyes at Seaton and answered in place of Anna. "We're almost done here. A few more minutes and we'll be out of your hair." He smiled his most charming smile. "I know Anna needs her rest, we won't push it, don't worry."

"As long as you don't. I'll be back in ten minutes and you'll be gone I hope." She nodded and smiled at Betty Carter to enlist her help. "Don't let them outstay their welcome they can always come back later." She turned and left the room.

"Sorry, Anna, we won't be much longer," Seaton confirmed. "Any other customers? Can you remember seeing anything outside? When you got up from the table what did you see?" He pushed for as much information as possible before they were ejected.

"I didn't. I stood up and knew I had to get to the phone, which was behind the counter. I saw the gun on the table where he had been sitting and got past it as quickly as possible. Once I'd called the ambulance I sat on the floor behind the counter in case he came back. No one came in until the police, or perhaps it was the ambulance men, I don't know. I can't remember who came first." She sighed and caught her breath as her ribcage moved.

"Okay, that's fine," Seaton said soothingly. He lowered his voice, "Is there anyone you think may want to hurt you, in any way? Have you any jilted boyfriends or perhaps someone whose advances you have rejected?"

Anna frowned and shook her head. "No. He was just a nutter, wasn't he?" Her frown remained as she indignantly added, "I don't know anyone like that."

Meredith straightened up and stepped away from the bed. He pulled some cards from his jacket pocket. He placed one on the table and handed a second to her mother.

"We'll leave you in peace, for the moment, but call us if you remember anything else. Even if it seems really trivial or unlikely. It's best we check it out." He looked at Seaton and jerked his head towards the door. "Now, until I'm sure you're safe I'm going to get one of our colleagues to stay with you," he smiled at them. "Any questions for us?"

Betty Carter raised the hand holding Meredith's card. "You will keep us informed, won't you? You know, let us know what's going on and everything?"

Meredith confirmed that they would as he and Seaton left the room.

"Right, get a uniform up here now. I doubt it's necessary but let's be sure." Meredith paused and looked down the corridor. "Here comes the father." He nodded at a man hurrying towards them, a short nurse scurrying along behind him. "Look at his shirt."

Seaton looked at the man's shirt, where two lines of black finger prints started at the centre of his chest and slowly faded as they reached the edge of his body. He had clearly been rushing and used his shirt to clean his hands rather than wash them.

"Leave him for now, we can catch up with him later if necessary." Meredith stepped to one side as the man rushed past. "Right, you get the bullet and we can find out how we're doing elsewhere" He looked at his watch. "I was supposed to be meeting someone today. I'll make a call and postpone, then meet you at the car.

Meredith pushed open the door to the cramped office and squinted at one of the screens. Fuzzy figures were walking past Joey's Diner. Patsy hit the pause button and turned round, shortly followed by Jo Adler. They looked at him expectantly. "I heard you were back." He nodded towards the screen, "Anything?"

"The Super called me. He asked if I could come in as you're shorthanded now you have a murder and a shooting. And Tanya's replacement has yet to arrive." Patsy looked back at the screen. "We don't have anything yet. Tom said all we had was a dark coat and a beanie. These were taken from the building society across the road. I'm doing the ones on Christmas Steps next, but there are only two cameras, which are both static and easy to avoid." She shrugged. "Jo may have something though."

Meredith nodded. "What's that then, Adler?" Meredith sighed as Jo Adler rewound the recording. Patsy was due back tomorrow anyway, but he had yet to speak to the Super and he was irritated that she had become involved in the investigation if she were to be moved on. Knowing Patsy, she would get the bit between her teeth and there would be words.

"Here you go, Gov. I'm not even sure if it's our man, but the timing's right." Adler paused and sat upright. "Here, now, getting onto the number seventy-eight bus."

She tapped the screen with her pencil and Meredith watched one bus pull away and a queue of people start boarding the bus behind. Third in line was someone wearing a hoody, jeans and trainers. The hood was up and obscured the face. "Not much but some of the buses have cameras. I've put in a call."

"Nothing yet then." Meredith shook his head. "Anything from the Homemead estate?"

Jo Adler grunted and turned back to him. "The usual chest beating crap from his mates. None of them could name anyone though. And, of course, he was loved by everyone, a regular charmer. Why would anyone do that, and so on. If we didn't know him we'd have put him forward for an award." She gave a short laugh. "His mother chucked the family liaison out this morning when they turned up. Said they'd be better off out finding the bastard that did it." She shrugged and tapped a box at her feet. "Only another six to go. Let's hope that the boys doing the door to door come back with something."

Meredith grunted and left the room without further comment. He walked briskly back to the incident room.

"Anything new?" he asked, heading towards his office. He received only negative replies.

Sitting at his desk he picked up the telephone and dialled out. "It's me, sorry about earlier, we had a shooting as you may have heard on the news. I called but you were engaged. I assume you got my text?" He stretched his legs out under the desk and leaned back in his chair staring at the ceiling whilst listening to the response. "Hmm, well it's a 'with or without you' deal I'm afraid." He held the phone away from his ear a little. "I know but there you have it. Am I picking you up or not? Good. I'll meet you at the Harvester then. Bye." Slowly sitting upright, he replaced the receiver, and wondered what excuse he could find for his absence.

CHAPTER FOUR

Michael Brent parked his Range Rover on the zigzag lines outside his son's school, and he hushed his wife as the news came on.

"...and still no news on either the stabbing of twenty-three-year-old Andrew Short yesterday, who died at the scene, or on the shooting of twenty-four-year-old Anna Carter, who is said to be comfortable and out of danger this afternoon. Police have been out in force in the city centre, questioning commuters and local businesses. A police spokesman has confirmed that there is nothing to link the two incidents and are appealing for. . ."

Brent turned the radio off and shook his head, a smile playing around his lips.

"It's terrible, Mike, isn't it? I saw it on the news at lunch time. It's not safe to go out. They were so young too. Do you reckon it was drugs?"

Michael Brent turned to look at his wife and shrugged. "I don't know, and it sounds like the police don't know much either." He tutted.

"Janine next door reckons it was bound to be drugs. The police say that poor Anna Carter wasn't robbed or anything, so why shoot her? Mind you, I always thought she looked a bit of a tart. They had a picture of her all eyelashes and big boobs plastered on the news." She opened the car door. "I'd better go and get James. You've parked on the lines again, and you know what Mrs Hitchings told you."

Michael Brent's top lip curled up as he watched his wife make her way towards the school gate, teetering on heels that were too high. She was still something to look at, but nothing like as good as Anna, and she was just so thick. He used to think her naivety was cute but that had worn off years ago. She would have been history if it wasn't for Jimmy, whom she insisted on calling James. He groaned and rubbed his temples in a circular motion with his middle fingers, wondering how old Jimmy would be before he could get rid of her. His son would be six next year; was that too soon?

He pulled his mobile from his breast pocket and dialled out. "Hello, Tone, it's me. I take it you've heard the news." He sighed as he listened to the response. "Yeah, well, it was close enough. Meet me at the club tonight. We need to talk, and bring that redhead with you, what's her name, Bianca." He hung up and waved at his son who was dragging his mother towards the car and waving a painting at him with his free hand.

CHAPTER FIVE

Meredith ran towards the man as he approached the building. Grabbing him by the shoulder of his jacket with his left hand, he threw his weight behind his right arm, and pinned the man against the brickwork with his right forearm. The man called out and Meredith leaned forward until his mouth was directly above the man's ear.

"Keep it down, pal. You don't want me to have to shut you up, do you?" he snarled through clenched teeth. He then slid his forearm up the man's back and pushed his face onto the red brick with his hand. The man groaned and tried to look around at his assailant. Before he could do so Meredith had lifted his hand away, made a fist, and then punched the man with all the force he could muster into his lower back. The man's body arched backward before he leant forward, resting his head against the rough brickwork. He attempted to catch his breath, but before he could recover Meredith had kicked his legs out from under him. The man hit the floor heavily, the gravel crunching beneath his body, and he instinctively covered his face with his arms.

Meredith tapped the man's elbow with his toe. "Get up, you piece of shit. Don't judge everyone by your own standards," Meredith growled and stepped back. "You're going to buy me a pint now." He leaned down and yanked the man to his knees by pulling on his coat.

The man looked up at Meredith, and recognition flared in his eyes. He sighed and put his hands flat on the wall, then used it as a support to get to his feet. Once upright he touched his cheek, and gently ran his fingers along the angry graze.

"Evening, Branning, walk this way." Meredith put his arm around Peter Branning's shoulder and pulled him in the direction of the entrance. Chris Grainger followed silently behind.

Meredith pushed Branning up against the bar.

"What will you have?" he asked as the barmaid approached. Meredith smiled at her, "Two pints of lager, one whiskey chaser and . . ." Meredith looked at Branning through cold uncompromising eyes.

"The same." Peter Branning ran his tongue around the inside of his mouth in an attempt to create moisture and held Meredith's gaze.

Meredith looked back at the barmaid. "Make that three and two then. He's paying." Meredith jerked his head towards Branning, and pursed his lips as Branning reached into his pocket for his wallet. Having paid, the three men made their way to the furthest table. Branning was encouraged to sit in the corner, hemmed in by the other two.

"We meet at last," Meredith announced. Then he leaned forward putting his elbows on the table and, clasping his hands together, he rested his chin on them and stared at Branning. "Tell me why you came here today."

"You know why," Branning snapped. "The question is why you wanted me here? Are you going to have a pint then give me a good hiding? No, I wouldn't think that was your style."

Meredith raised his eyebrows and cocked his head towards Chris Grainger. "Now, how would he know what my style was do you think? Maybe it's because he's no better than a peeping tom. Watching what other people get up to, peeping through curtains and playing with himself whilst he watches them." He sat back suddenly and banged the table. "Or is that when you break in and go through their knicker drawer, is that what does it for you? Either way, you're a wanker."

Branning gave a short laugh and clapped his hands twice. "I bet you've been rehearsing that." His smile was short-lived as Meredith raised his foot and thrust it into his crotch. Branning gasped and doubled over, and Chris Grainger pulled him upright by the scruff of his neck. He then leaned forward and whispered in Branning's ear.

"Brave words, Branning, but don't upset him, there's a good chap. He's a pain in the arse when he's upset, and he's not even drunk yet."

Grainger and Branning watched as Meredith emptied his pint, quickly followed by the whiskey, and then called to the barmaid for a refill.

Meredith looked at the other two. "You aren't drinking then?" He waved his finger at the full glasses in front of them and shrugged. "Let me see, I need a drink. A stabbing, a murder and a stalker all in one day, and despite my well-honed skills," he nodded and smiled confirming this information, "I only have the stalker banged to rights."

Meredith handed the barmaid a ten pound note as she put his drinks on the table.

"Keep the change, love." He picked up the whiskey, drank it down and handed the empty glass back to the barmaid as she left, then smacked his lips together. "That's better. Now, as I was saying, I've had a bastard of a day." Splaying the fingers on each hand and tapping them together he stared at Branning. "My problem is what to do with the stalker." He lifted his foot to cross his legs. Branning flinched and brought his knees together. Chris Grainger snorted.

"What do you want, Meredith? Spit it out. You can't enjoy being here anymore than I do." Branning wanted whatever was going to happen to be over with, and he would rather it was now before Meredith got drunk.

"What do you think I want?" Meredith asked and pursed his lips.

Branning shrugged.

"Come on, come on, you must have some thoughts on the matter?" Meredith encouraged.

"I have been stupid and impetuous, and things got out of hand, and I know that. For what it's worth, it's over," Branning said quietly.

Meredith leaned forward on the table again and drew in a deep breath.

"The thing is, Branning, I want to know why? Why did you put your job on the line? What was it that made you do that?" He held Branning's gaze for a while before Branning looked away, and Meredith smirked at his small victory. "I have all night," he taunted, and saw the white of Branning's knuckles as he clenched his fists. He picked up his pint and took a sip. "Are you not going to drink that?" Meredith nodded at the whiskey.

Branning stared at it for a moment then picked it up and drank it in one gulp, banging the empty glass back down on the table. He leaned towards Meredith. "She ruined my life, and she knackered my career. I was pissed off, okay? I'm not proud of what I did."

"Ruined your life and knackered your career, did she? Well, when I asked around I heard you were caught with your old man in the wrong Assistant Chief Constable. Now correct me if I'm mistaken, but that sounds like you did all the ruining and knackering." Meredith inclined his head and silently challenged him.

Branning swallowed then took a deep breath. "I wanted her back, okay? I got Brenda whatsit to just mess about in her flat hoping to unnerve her. You know, make her a little jumpy." Branning saw Meredith raise his eyebrows, and shrugged, "Okay, vulnerable. I wanted her vulnerable so that when I turned up I could rescue her and take her home with me." He sighed, "Then she started seeing that pathologist and staying over at your house, and I just saw red. Things escalated."

He looked down into his lap and shook his head before looking back up at Meredith. "I loved her and I made a mistake, a huge one, but a mistake none the less. I wanted her back and when I saw her with you I knew I'd lost her." He swallowed and cleared his throat. "I just lost it, wrong I know, but it was over. I had lost everything." His features hardened a little, and he sniffed. "I've done some asking around myself. I reckon you've been where I am, but you just controlled it better."

Meredith and Branning stared at each other and an uncomfortable silence developed. Meredith actually felt sorry for Branning, knowing that he had indeed walked in those shoes. Branning hoped Meredith would let him walk away in one piece. He had humiliated himself enough for one night and Meredith could obviously handle himself.

Chris Grainger leaned forward and rapped the table. "Right, which one is going to draw first?" he asked sarcastically. "All this posturing and staring, it's like a spaghetti western. What happens now?"

Meredith grinned and turned to look at his friend. "Well, that's up to Patsy."

Grainger nodded solemnly and Branning sat upright and demanded, "What do you mean, up to Patsy? Doesn't she know you're here?" His heart sank. He had thought Patsy had sent the heavies in. Meredith slowly shook his head.

"Afraid not, she would never have allowed it. I'm here on my own account as I don't like being spied on either. Patsy's still making her mind up as to what to do. I'm content for my part that your card is marked and noted. I know you know not to even think her name anymore, and if you do, I'll be waiting. But next time I won't be talking." His look was menacing and Branning ran his tongue around his lips. Meredith relaxed his shoulders and shrugged before adding, "So I can only suggest you go home and keep your fingers crossed. She's a decent sort, I'm sure she'll make the right decision." He picked up his pint and finished it before standing. "Right I'm off home, and I suggest you do the same. No diversions, just straight back to Southampton and no looking back."

Meredith winked at Branning, and followed Chris out of the bar. Branning picked up his own pint in a hand that trembled now the threat had gone. He finished half of it and placed it back on the table before walking quickly to the car park.

Meredith slammed the door and tapped the dashboard. "I think that went well, don't you? I actually felt sorry for the bloke for a fleeting second." He looked at Chris who nodded in agreement. "He held himself well. I thought he would be a jabbering wreck like most cowards are when the tables are turned." Meredith shivered and turned the fan up on the heater. "What do you think Patsy will do?"

Chris pulled out of the car park before answering. "I don't know, but I agree she's a decent sort, she'll probably let it drop." He nudged Meredith with his elbow. "I was quite surprised he was so handsome. I thought Patsy only went for blokes that had been hit with a shovel."

Meredith threw his head back and laughed. "Just get me back to my car. I have something I need to get home for."

He smiled as Chris grunted and put a little more pressure on the accelerator.

Patsy scooped her wet hair into a band and fixed it loosely on the top of her head. She blinked at her reflection in the bathroom mirror. Being back at work had focused her mind, and helped her finalise several decisions. She wanted Meredith to get home so she could tell him. She walked naked into the bedroom and pulled on some sweatpants and a baggy shirt. Glancing at the clock on the bedside cabinet she saw that it was almost eight o'clock. He hadn't said he'd be this late. She frowned and her eyes drifted down to the drawer beneath the clock. She knew that Meredith had been planning to ask her to marry him less than a month ago, he had told her father as much, but for some reason he hadn't.

A small box sat in that drawer; she had found it a few weeks before. He had buried it under a couple of books and some boxes of indigestion remedies, but she had not opened it. Although she was in no hurry to be married, it concerned her that he'd not mentioned it. She sighed, switched off the light and closed the door.

As she got to the top of the stairs Meredith opened the front door. He looked exhausted, and she quickened her pace and threw her arms around his neck in greeting.

He pulled her to him and inhaled. "Mmm, you smell good," he murmured into her hair.

She pushed him away and looked up at him. "You don't. Who have you been drinking with?" She tapped him on the nose, "No, don't tell me yet, go and shower you can tell me over dinner."

Meredith did as he was bid, and returned fifteen minutes later. He pulled her into his arms. "Is that better?" He slid his hands up under her tee shirt and she smiled and kissed him on the chin.

"Much, now sit down, it's ready."

Meredith grumbled and made his way to the kitchen, but the table was bare. He turned to ask her why, when he noticed the light on in dining room. He pushed open the door and found the table was set for two. He frowned, wondering what the occasion was. The dining room had only ever been used when they had guests to entertain. He didn't ask, deciding to wait for all to be revealed. He went in and took his seat. Patsy followed moments later holding two plates in napkins so as not to burn her fingers.

"Only lasagne, I'm afraid, but I thought it would be nice if we ate in here for a change. I'll just grab the salad out of the fridge."

Meredith waited for her to return. "This isn't for a special occasion then?" He waved his hand in a circle above his head, and pursed his lips as she shook her head. "Why don't I believe you?"

Patsy rubbed her forehead as though trying to remember something. "Okay, I think we need to talk about a few things, and I just thought that this would be more comfortable. Anyway, let's eat. Who did you have a drink with?"

"Does it matter?" Meredith wondered if somehow she knew about his meeting with Branning, and was testing the water.

Patsy took it that he was deliberately being awkward. "What does that mean? I'm making conversation, or trying to. Have I done something specific to irritate you other than come back to work a day early?" she snapped.

Meredith held his hands up. "Blimey that was a bit sharp, and no, nothing specific." A smile danced at his mouth and he held his hand across the table. "We do need to talk about work though."

Patsy squeezed his hand and put her fork down, then releasing his hand, she picked up her glass and took a sip of wine. "Me, first," she said quietly.

"You first what?"

Again, she saw the promised smile. It disappeared as she took a deep breath and looked down at the table. Meredith knew he didn't want to hear what she was going to say.

"I'm leaving." She blew out a breath. "There, I've said it."

Meredith swallowed but didn't speak.

She looked up at him. "Well, say something then."

With all the control he could muster, Meredith said, quietly, "When?"

Patsy had a look of incomprehension on her face. "When I've served my notice. Unless, of course, they want to put me on garden leave, which as I'm a good girl, I doubt. What an odd question." She shook her head. "You are certainly in a weird mood tonight."

Relief flowed through Meredith, so much so that his toes tingled. He cleared his throat. "Ah, work."

Patsy's head shot up and she looked at him aghast. "Work. . . you didn't? Did you? For God's sake, what does go on . . ." She stood and rushed around the table to him. Meredith swung his legs out from underneath the table, and she sat on his lap taking his face in her hands. "Johnny, Johnny, what am I going to do with you?" She planted little kisses all over his face, and he pulled her to him, burying his head in her chest.

"I think my heart stopped then. I might need resuscitating," he murmured and looked up into her eyes which glistened at him. "Oh no, don't cry or I might join you." He kissed her tenderly, and she clung to him. "Come on, let's get this finished and get to bed." He pushed her away and reluctantly she went back to her seat. He rubbed his hands over his face. "Right, let's start again. Tonight, I went for a drink with Chris Grainger. How was your day at the office?" He smiled, but noticed Patsy start at the mention of Chris's name. "What? I saw that look. What did I say?"

"Did he say anything? Did Chris mention me at all?" Patsy avoided his eyes by fussing with her cutlery.

"Only in passing, why?"

"Because I think I've made up my mind that that's where I'm going."

Patsy gasped as Meredith raised his hands a little, and then deliberately dropped the cutlery he had just picked up back on to the table. His knife clattered to the floor.

"What? Do I need to go out and come back in again?" He closed his eyes and shook his head. "I could have sworn that having established that you are not leaving me, you told me you are going to become a private investigator, and I know that can't be right."

Despite his choice of tone, Patsy saw his anger. His eyes bore into her.

"Why? We both know I can't go on working with you. I don't particularly want some crap desk job, and I don't want to be stationed elsewhere, not when

I've hardly settled here. I've spoken to Chris and Sharon and they have agreed to let me buy into the business if that's what I want. And I think that is what I want." She gave a slight shrug, "I thought you would be pleased."

"In what way pleased?" Meredith snorted. "Pleased that you will go out alone without the backup you get being a copper? Pleased that you are going to be dealing with the dregs of humanity wanting you to do dirty little jobs for them? Pleased that you will be sat freezing in your car waiting to catch some bloke climbing out of a window in his undies? Pleased that you will go out on a limb, on your own, as you have done before, over and over again? Pleased . . ." He stopped as Patsy held her hand up.

"Enough. You know that's not true, you heard what they said at Christmas. This is about you trying to protect me. Wanting to sit me in a nice little cotton wool chair at a nice little cotton wool desk. Well it's not going to happen. Chris said -" It was Patsy's turn to be interrupted.

"Chris said what? Because he said bugger all to me whilst we waited for an hour for Branning to turn up, not a word!" Meredith had raised his voice and he held his hands up. "Sorry, I didn't mean to shout, but I'm struggling with this. Why would you want to do that?"

"You're the one asking questions? I think it's my turn to do that, Johnny." Patsy returned his sarcasm then calmed herself a little before continuing. "What did you mean by waiting for Branning to turn up? Did he turn up? Explain to me, please, because I'm struggling to understand this bit too!"

Patsy placed her knife and fork together carefully to the side of her untouched lasagne, and she reached over and picked up the wine bottle to top up her glass. She held it up to Meredith who sighed and nodded.

"I was going to tell you this evening." He put his elbows on the table and cupped his face in his hands. "There's not much to tell really. We met Branning, he told us why, we warned him off, and I doubt he will do anything stupid again."

Patsy gasped and Meredith added quickly, "And before you say it, I told him his invasion into my privacy was dealt with, but that whether you reported it was a whole different kettle of fish."

Meredith decided to stop speaking before he dug a deeper hole and he picked up his glass. Patsy was shaking her head, her bottom lip clasped between her teeth. She drew in a deep breath through her nose and he watched her chest rise and then fall before she spoke.

"Did you hurt him?" she asked quietly, willing herself to keep her voice steady.

Meredith shrugged and shook his head.

"What does that mean?" She mirrored his action. "Did you do anything to him?" This time she failed in her attempt at control. There was an edge to her tone and she was no longer speaking quietly.

Meredith rolled his eyes and held his hands out, questioning the relevance. "Yes, I roughed him up, in a minor way. He's in one piece, nothing broken. Are you really concerned about him?" Meredith sounded incredulous that that could be the case.

Patsy was so annoyed with his attitude and his lack of understanding that she suddenly banged the table with the flat of her hands. This caused the crockery and Meredith to jump. The near empty wine bottle rocked from side to side before settling back on its base.

"You *need* to ask me that? I don't understand you, how could you ask me that?" She put her hands on her head, linked her fingers, and closed her eyes for a moment before looking back at Meredith. "Of course, I'm concerned, why risk your job over him?" She was shouting now, but she paused to take a deep breath and added in a more moderate tone, "There is nothing I would like more than to see someone beat the whatsit out of him, but not you."

Patsy stood up and began to clear the table as noisily as possible just to be sure that Meredith was aware of her displeasure. Having returned from taking the first load to the kitchen, she stood in front of him.

"Bring your glass and bring the wine. We have to get this sorted before it spirals out of control, and I want to sit comfortably."

Meredith eyed his plate of lasagne longingly but left it on the table. As he followed Patsy through the kitchen he picked up another bottle of wine and the corkscrew, knowing that this might be a long conversation. He smirked as he noted that Patsy had chosen to sit in a chair rather than share the sofa.

"I thought I didn't smell anymore?" He fell heavily onto the sofa, and the two wine bottles clashed against each other. He placed them carefully on the coffee table and laid the corkscrew next to them. Patsy took a sip of her wine. Meredith put his feet up on the table and leaned back, his arms folded on his chest. "Come on then, spit it out."

"I don't want to row," she said quietly.

"Well, I'd never have guessed."

"Don't be like this, please. You're a control freak, I accept that. But you have to accept that I'm a grown up, I have a mind of my own and I'm not always going to do what you want me to, whatever it might be. It doesn't mean I'm wrong just because you don't agree with me." She sighed. "I made two decisions at work today. The first was that I was going to get Chris to warn Peter off." She paused as Meredith coughed and rolled his eyes, "BUT without violence, without it being personal. Just show him the file of evidence and tell him once more and it goes upstairs. That would have sorted it. You do see that, don't you?" She watched Meredith sip his wine, then twirl the glass by its stem and watch the red liquid rise and fall in the bowl. "Please answer me. We're going to get nowhere if you sit in silence."

"Well, in essence that's what happened. I just went along to make sure he knew how I felt about it. It was all done to scare you, I know that. But you have to remember that for the best part it was my home he targeted. I couldn't even protect you here. I have no feelings or loyalty to the man. I wanted him scared. I wanted him to know that . . . well, he needed to be told. He's been told. You have what you wanted only via a different route." He emptied the glass and leaned forward and poured the remains of the first bottle into it. "Can we drop that bit now? I've had my wrist slapped, I think that's unjust, but it makes you happy so let's move on." He looked at Patsy's glass and opened the second bottle whilst she considered this.

"Okay, it's done. Now we have to discuss me joining the Graingers." She held out her glass and he topped it up.

He didn't reply until he had returned to his previous position. "Is it worth a discussion? I didn't think I was allowed an opinion because I was a control freak."

"Sarcasm? Again? I thought you would want to discuss this, but if you're happy for me just to get on with it, I will." Patsy huffed and leaned back in her chair.

Meredith put his hands behind his head and looked at her for a while before speaking.

"Let's pretend that we're not *we*," Meredith waved his finger back and forth, "but by chance you happen across the Graingers and you have the conversation that was had at Christmas. Everything else that happened, still happened," he paused, "except us. Would you still want to dump your career to join them?" He watched as Patsy wrestled with this question whilst tapping her glass lightly with her fingernails. Eventually she looked at him.

"That is such a good question." Then she shrugged and went back to tapping the glass.

Meredith chewed his bottom lip to contain the grin.

She looked up again. "How did you know?" she shook her head and tapped.

"I'm going to have to press you for an answer."

Patsy heard the amusement in his tone and immediately her irritation resurfaced. Once again, his perception had astounded her. He was right as he usually was. If she wasn't with him she wouldn't have considered leaving the police force. But she was with him, she had considered it, and she was excited by the prospect of joining the Graingers, although Meredith had managed to dampen that excitement. But what was it about being with Meredith that made the difference? She smiled slightly and gave a little sigh as the understanding set in.

She looked across at Meredith. "Why, do you think it was?"

"Oh, so we're going to play the 'answering a question with a question' game, are we?" He raised his eyebrows. "Can you not answer my question?"

Patsy tutted, "And there it is, right back at me. Yes, I think I can, but before I answer I'd like your take on it." She lowered her chin and fluttered her eyelashes at him. "Please," she smiled as Meredith grinned at her.

"Okay, my take on this is that for some weird woman's reason," he paused, "not to mention your past experience, you think it's not possible to work with me." He smiled, "But that's not going to be a problem. I don't want to keep our relationship a secret. I'm happy for the world to know. It does, as you mentioned earlier, mean you have to move from my department, but that's not the end of the world and it doesn't have to be a crap desk job. I know it will be difficult working for someone who is not as charming, rewarding or motivating as I am, but I'm sure you'll soon find you can cope without my expertise to guide you." He patted the sofa, "Come here, you look lonely over there."

"I will, let me just answer that first. I have to say you're almost there, but I think it's because I want to be your equal." She gave her shoulders a little shake. "Which granted is nigh on impossible with someone as illustrious as yourself, but, and please don't take this the wrong way, I don't want to be controlled by you." She shook her head, "No, that's not quite it."

She paused. "You have a tendency to over-react, over-compensate, over-everything really and that makes you break things you care about," she looked up at him, "and I won't let you break us." She swallowed and looked away. "If I stayed on the force you would interfere wherever I was or whatever I was working on." She met his gaze, "And I would resent that. Then one day you would overstep the mark, because you do, and that would be that. You can't control me, I'm not made that way." She looked down at the empty glass for a while. "It's not that I won't ask for and of course take your advice. I will want your input into what I do, but the only thing I want you to know you absolutely have to do," she blinked, "is love me."

Patsy waited for his response, Meredith simply looked at her. She cleared her throat, "Is that too much to ask?"

"But you don't want my advice on this? That bit comes later, I suppose." Meredith watched Patsy nod at her empty glass. "Then I guess I'll just have to love you, now get your ass over here."

Patsy put her glass down and leaped across the room jumping in to his lap. She kissed him, then pulled away and looked into his eyes. "Thank you," she whispered, and he kissed the end of her nose.

"You're welcome. Now before I love you, because I'm allowed to do that apparently, can I please have something to eat so I have the strength to show you just how much?"

The next day Patsy handed in her notice. The Superintendent was not best pleased. He had been planning to use her as the "Face of the Force" as part of their next local recruitment drive. She closed his door quietly and breathed a sigh of relief. Grinning, she made her way back to the incident room. She had thought that he would make her serve her notice, but it was a small price to pay for escaping that humiliation.

CHAPTER SIX

I t had been two weeks, and Meredith was no nearer solving either crime. He was frustrated and getting a hard time from the Super who also blamed him for Patsy's departure. He looked at his team shuffling useless paper around their desks. They had wasted hours following up leads that turned out to be fruitless, and they were now becoming restless. He walked across the room and stood in front of the board re-reading the scant information logged there.

He turned around. "Travers, Rawlings, Adler and Hodge, my office now."

He strode to his office as they exchanged glances and picked up their notepads before following him. There were only three chairs so Dave Rawlings leaned against the filing cabinet. They watched as Meredith sifted through some photographs. Selecting two of them he held them up to face his officers.

"Right, we've hit a brick wall again. There is apparently no reason why these two got what they did. But my gut tells me they are in some way connected. Different assailants and I know they moved in totally different circles with nothing to connect one to the other."

Meredith noted the change in body stance of Travers and saw the quick glance exchanged between Adler and Patsy.

"And I can see you are questioning my judgement here, but luckily for me I call the shots." He looked at Patsy and she stifled a grin, "Don't I, Hodge?" She nodded quickly. "So what I want you to do is ask the Short family if they know Anna Carter, and hers if they knows him. Any link, however tenuous. Did he ever eat at the café, had she ever seen him on the bus?" He looked up and they nodded their understanding. "Good. Right Hodge and Adler take Anna Carter and you two others take Short's parents and anyone else you think might know something."

He hushed them as they made to leave, "And before you go, we'll all be in the Dirty Duck tonight, six thirty sharp. Seaton will need someone to celebrate with."

He held his hand up halting any questions. "He doesn't know yet, the Super is telling him at close of play when he gets back from his meeting with the council. Keep it under your hats and don't let on." He nodded and his smiling team knew they were dismissed.

Jo Adler pushed the doorbell, stepped down off the doorstep, and pulled her ID from her pocket. Patsy looked up and saw the curtains twitch in the bedroom window, before they heard footsteps on the stairs. The door opened and Anna Carter put her head around the door. They had only seen photographs of her before and both were taken back by her natural beauty, and a little envious of it.

Adler stepped forward. "Hello, Anna, I'm DC Adler, Jo, and this is DC Patsy Hodge. Can we ask you a few questions please?"

The two officers held open their IDs and Anna let them in without really looking.

"Yes, of course, come in. Do you mind coming up to my bedroom? Mum doesn't like leaving me on my own, so Gramps is here, but he's asleep on the couch." She grinned at them and led the way upstairs. "Have you found anything out?" she asked as she pushed open her bedroom door. She walked in and sat cross-legged on a beanbag in front of the window.

Patsy shook her head as she sat on the stool in front of the dressing table, leaving Jo to perch on the bed.

"Sorry, Anna, nothing yet I'm afraid. We want to ask you a few more questions." Patsy looked around the room. In one corner, a chrome clothes rail was adorned with colourful outfits with shoes neatly lined up beneath. On one wall a large frame held a collage of photographs. She stood and went to look at it.

"All me, I'm afraid," Anna informed her. "My mates did it for me for my twenty-first. The one in the bottom corner was my party."

Patsy followed Anna's progress from a baby in her mother's arms, to shapely beauty in a tight pencil skirt and polka dot blouse in a night club. She tapped it lightly with her fingernail. "That's fabulous. You really do look like Marilyn here, you've got the pose off to a tee." She turned and smiled at Anna. "Where was that taken? Everyone is certainly having a good time."

"The Lodge, down on the waterfront, and yes, it was great." She watched as

Patsy returned to the stool and her smile fell away. "I was hoping you were going to tell me who did it and more importantly, why."

Jo Adler pulled several photographs of Andrew Short from her bag. She handed them to Anna.

"Do you know him?" She watched Anna shuffle through the photographs. There were four different compositions. The first showed Andrew Short at home with his family the month before he died; he was holding up a pint glass to the camera and smiling. The second was a pose for the photographer at school when he was sixteen. The third showed him bare chested on a beach and the final one was a shot of him on the day he died walking towards the street in which he had been stabbed. The image was a little blurry as it was a still from one of the CCTV cameras.

Anna looked up at them and shook her head. "I recognise him of course, he's been all over the news, same as me," she grimaced and shrugged, "but I don't think I ever met him." She shuffled through again, and paused a while with a little frown on her face as she looked at the last photograph, but she shook her head and held them out to Jo Adler. "No, I'm sorry, why do you ask? Do you think that the same person that shot me also stabbed him?" Subconsciously she rubbed her ribcage where the wound had almost healed.

"No, we think it was very unlikely to have been the same person. The descriptions are totally different."

Patsy exchanged a 'didn't we already know this would be the outcome' glance with Jo Adler.

"Both incidents happened within twenty-four hours and less than half a mile away from each other, so it was just an end that needed tidying up." She shrugged, "I don't suppose you have remembered anything else about that morning, have you?"

Anna shook her head again, and Patsy stood and smoothed down her jacket.

"Well, we'll let you get on, thanks -"

Patsy was interrupted as the door opened and Gill Carter rushed into the room. She stopped abruptly.

"Sorry I didn't know someone was here, I just had these printed at Asda and ..." She peered at the two women. "Are you police? Has something happened, have you got him?" she asked excitedly. Her shoulders slumped as the women shook their heads.

"We were asking your sister if she knew this chap."

Jo Adler slid the photographs out of her bag and held them out. Gill Carter placed those she had been holding on the bed and took them from Jo. She too shook her head as she leafed through them. Patsy picked up the photographs from the bed. The two sisters were dressed up in fifties clothes and posing for the camera. Gill was not as stunning as her sister but still carried the look well. They had obviously had a good time as in the last one they had collapsed on each other, laughing.

"These are wonderful, what was the occasion?" she asked as she looked again. "That's a lovely ring, I don't think I've seen one like that before." Patsy turned the photograph round for the others to see. Anna was posed with her head bent forward a little, pouting up at the camera through long eyelashes, the fingers of her right hand were splayed on her chest and a large diamond shaped stone covered much of the length of her ring finger.

"That was before I was shot. Joe wanted some shots of the staff to put up on the walls, and I convinced Gill to join me. She hates those clothes," Anna grinned at her sister, "but she looks fab, don't you think?" She pointed to the dressing table. "That's that ring, it's a one off. I bought it from the jewellery stall in St Nicholas's market. It is lovely but it catches on everything."

Gill handed the photographs back to Jo Adler, who had opened the door.

"Well thank you, girls. Have a nice afternoon, and call if you think of anything that may help." Patsy followed Jo down the stairs and they let themselves out.

"Well, that was a waste of time. She is stunning, don't you think? If I was wearing leggings with a loose shirt over them I'd look like a sack of potatoes," Jo grumbled as they walked to the car. "Let's hope the boys get something, though I doubt it."

Six miles away, Travers and Rawlings were sitting uncomfortably on a two-seater settee in the living room of Andrew Short's parents because his mother had insisted on sitting between them.

"Do you think she's got something to do with it then?" she asked as she looked at the photograph.

"No, as we explained, Anna was shot the day after Andrew was stabbed. There is no obvious link, but we have to cover all angles, so we needed to ask," Travers explained patiently.

"I'll have to ask his dad, he's down the pub again. Been drinking a lot since . .

." she sniffed, "well he's been drinking a lot. Can I keep one of these?" She fanned herself with the photographs.

"Of course, take your pick." Rawlings prised himself off the seat by using the arm of the settee. "We'll be off now and leave you to it, but if your hubby knows anything, or Andrew's mates, come to that, give us a shout." He held his hand out and helped Mrs Short to her feet as she was struggling to get up.

She stared at him for a moment, and leaned forward, her voice low. "I didn't say anything before because his dad won't have a bad word said," she glanced over her shoulder as though to check that no one else had entered the room, "but I know he was no angel. But he wasn't bad either, not in one of them gangs. I did hear him on the phone about two or three weeks before this. Just after Christmas it was." She blinked rapidly and got lost in her own thoughts.

Rawlings put his hand gently on her shoulder. "What was the call about?" he asked quietly.

She shrugged and looked at him, tears forming in her eyes. "I don't know but he sounded scared." She blinked and dabbed at the corners of her eyes with her knuckles.

Travers stood to join them, and glanced hopefully at Rawlings. "What was he saying, love? Can you remember why you thought he was scared?"

Pauline Short pulled a tissue from her sleeve, and dusted a football trophy which sat proudly at one end of the mantle. When she was satisfied, she used it to blow her nose before she sat back down on the settee and looked up at the two men.

"He was pacing up and down outside the back door. He was having a smoke, I don't let them smoke in here, it makes the paintwork mucky. I had brought some dishes out to wash up and I heard him say something like 'I'm sorry, I didn't know'. He stopped walking as whoever it was spoke to him. I know I shouldn't have, but I stayed to listen, it wasn't often our Andrew said 'sorry'." She looked up at them again and they nodded in agreement.

"That's kids these days though, never think they're wrong," Travers shrugged sympathetically. "Then what happened?"

"Well he just said, 'I know I'll sort it, it won't happen again', or something like that, and he flicked his butt out onto the grass. I was going to give him what for because I've put a flower pot out there filled with sand, you know like you get abroad on the beach?" The two men nodded. "But when he came in he was white. Looked like he'd seen a ghost he did, so I asked him and he said he was fine. Next thing I know the front door slams and he goes out. He was all right the next day though so I forgot about it. It was only the other day I remembered it. When I was cleaning the pot out." She shook her head sadly, "I'm glad I didn't shout at him." Her chin trembled and Rawlings leaned down and patted her shoulder.

"I know, but he would have known how much you loved him, whether you had or not." He paused a beat, knowing that they had Short's telephone records at the station. "When do you reckon this call was?"

He watched as she counted silently on her fingers. She looked back up at him.

"Fourth or fifth of January. I know because I'd gone back to work, but my decorations were still up and I always take them down on the sixth. Twelfth night and all that. It was just after tea."

"Thanks love, we'll look into it. We'll get off now and leave you in peace, but as I said give us a shout if anything comes up. Don't get up. We can see ourselves out, you stay there."

Travers rubbed his hands together as they hurried to their car.

"Bloody brass monkey weather again, we going straight to the pub?" Rawlings looked at his watch.

"Yeah, why not? It's a lead of sorts and we haven't had many of those, certainly not enough time to sort it tonight. Good old Seaton, aye?"

Meredith and his team sat at several tables they had arranged in front of the fire. Two bottles of champagne in ice buckets awaited the arrival of Tom Seaton. Travers and Rawlings had updated them on their meeting with Short's mother.

"Well, you can get onto that tomorrow, first thing. I doubt we would have picked that up on a one-off call," Meredith told them. "From little acorns and all that." He sipped his pint and looked towards the door as Susan Seaton walked in. She looked around anxiously. He waved and called her over. "You're all right, Susan, he's not here yet. Has he called you?" He stood and embraced her.

"Yes, about five minutes ago, but I ignored him," she laughed. "I bet he's so cheesed off, does he know about this?" she nodded towards the ice buckets as she slipped her coat off and took the chair next to Meredith.

"Nope, we left a note saying we were off to the pub if he fancied one." Meredith waved in the general direction of the team. "Do you know everyone?" He paused as she looked around the table, "Everyone, this is Susan. Susan, this is everyone.

I'll let those you don't know introduce themselves while I get you a drink. Any more for any more?"

He took orders from a few people and went to the bar. He watched Patsy get up and go and sit next to Susan to introduce herself and winked at her as he caught her eye. He had been pondering her departure on and off all day. She was going to be around for another week and although he had a weekend away planned before she started at the Graingers', he was already missing her.

Susan waved her phone at him. "He's texted to say he's popping to the pub for a pint but won't be too late as he has news," she called to him beaming. Meredith picked up the drinks from the bar and returned to the table.

"Well then, we'd better keep it down a little, he'll be here in a minute."

Meredith gave out the drinks and left Patsy with Susan. He took her seat at the other side of the table. A few minutes later the barman called out to them.

"John, love, he's on his way. I just saw him hop over the wall." He winked at Meredith who tutted.

Patsy giggled and raised her eyebrows at Meredith who shook his head in a disappointed fashion. The door to the bar opened and Tom Seaton stepped in.

"EVENING SARGE!" they shouted in unison, and a startled Seaton stopped in his tracks.

His wife ran over to him and he swung her around. "You minx, I wondered why you weren't answering. Come here." Seaton planted a noisy kiss on her lips and hugged her, and the team cheered him on.

There followed a lot of back slapping and Seaton received many congratulations. When things had calmed down Meredith asked him if he wanted a pint and Seaton nodded.

"But first you must meet the new member of your team."

Seaton turned and beckoned a smartly dressed man leaning on his elbow at the bar and watching the festivities. He stood upright and walked towards Meredith, his hand out. Meredith had noticed him come in behind Seaton, but had assumed he was another punter. He sized him up as he approached. He was wearing a sharp suit, expensive raincoat, and highly polished shoes. His reddish coloured hair fell in a wave across his forehead. Meredith knew before he opened his mouth that he would have a plummy accent. He braced himself, knowing that he shouldn't prejudge the man, but realising that was already too late.

He held out his hand. "DI John Meredith. And you are?" Meredith forced a smile, aware that the noise level from the team had dropped a little as they tried to work out who the man was.

"Louie Trump. DS. I joined your team at about," he looked at his watch, "yes, about thirty minutes ago. Nice to be aboard." He pumped Meredith's arm up and down and slapped him on the arm. "I think it must be my round," he looked at the team. "I'm buying, what's everyone having?"

Meredith's heart sank; a fast tracker. The man was probably twenty-five at most, and hadn't spent the last seven or eight years working his way up. Meredith was old school, and he preferred his team to have done it the hard way. He maintained his smile and Louie took orders from the team as they came up to introduce themselves. After being polite for what he felt was long enough, he pulled Seaton to one side and shook his hand.

"Well done, Tom, you deserve it. Where did you pick him up then?" Meredith nodded towards Trump.

"He was waiting outside the Super's office when I went up. The Super told me the news and then called the new boy in. Apparently, he's been transferred from Bath due to the loss of Jennings and Patsy, what with us having two majors on the go." He smiled and nudged Meredith.

"What are you grinning at?" Meredith asked.

"Guess who's just walked in?"

"I don't like guessing games." Meredith made to turn as the Superintendent's hand slapped his shoulder.

"Meredith, I thought you lot would be here tonight. I kept young Louie back so he could get to meet the team in a more relaxed atmosphere."

Meredith dug out his forced smile once again. "Sir. We don't often see you over here, can I get you a drink?" He stepped back as Louie Trump handed two pints across to Travers.

"Don't worry about that, I'll get Uncle David a drink. The usual?"

Meredith bit his lip as Tom Seaton choked on his beer. He closed his eyes for a second. Had he really just been lumbered with the Super's nephew? He leaned towards his boss and said quietly in his ear, "I'd have a word if I were you, Sir. If he wants to settle in quickly it won't be good if the natives know he's related to top brass. Seaton and I won't mention it."

The Superintendent's eyes flared a little, and he nodded curtly. He caught hold of his nephew's arm and pulled him away from the bar.

"Louie, two minutes. A quick word to the wise." He repeated Meredith's message and Louie put his finger to his lips.

"Enough said, they're sealed."

Meredith and Seaton exchanged glances before Meredith growled and walked away.

The Superintendent only stayed for one drink, and once he had gone the team began to let their hair down. Meredith leaned against the bar and smiled at the banter that was flying in every direction. They would all probably regret it in the morning, but they needed nights like these. He looked across at Patsy. She was doubled up in laughter and holding on to Susan Seaton who was dabbing her eyes. Tom had obviously told one of his funnier jokes.

He stiffened slightly as Trump came towards him, but nodded acknowledgement. Trump's eyes were now ever so slightly looking in different directions, and Meredith smirked. The boy couldn't yet hold his drink, but he knew he would learn. Trump slapped Meredith on the back with a familiarity he wasn't due. Meredith let it go without comment. Tonight was Seaton's; he would deal with Trump tomorrow.

"Wonderful team you seem to have here, Meredith. Are they any good?" Trump took another sip of his drink, "They certainly know how to party."

Meredith stilled and pursed his lips then he turned slowly to face Trump. "A couple of things, Trump." Meredith took Trump by the arm and walked him further up the bar. He positioned himself so that his back was to the team. "First, you are only a DS, and you might be the Super's nephew, which I appreciate is not your fault, but to you I am Sir or Gov, take your pick, but never Meredith. Not to my face." He screwed his face into an unpleasant smile before adding, "The second and most important thing you should know is that they," Meredith nodded backward at the raucous crowd behind him, "work for me. Therefore, they have to be good. The question you should be asking yourself is not how good they are, but whether you are good enough to join them." He returned the slap he had received earlier. "Now buy me a drink and then go and mingle. Some of it might rub off if you're lucky."

Trump was staring straight ahead unsure whether or not he should speak.

Meredith leaned in, "And, Trump."

"Yes, Sir?" Trump replied quickly.

"Smile, it's a party."

Trump smiled, and asked Meredith what he wanted to drink. Meredith was impressed that the man hadn't taken offence, which was good, as none was intended.

The men had started singing rugby songs and the girls clapped along and joined in when they knew the words. The landlord had replenished the sandwiches and everyone was having a good time. Meredith felt good, and more surprisingly he didn't feel drunk which was probably a first on such an occasion. Two of the uniformed officers arrived, and Meredith bought them a drink and told them to join the party. When they asked what the occasion was, Meredith called Seaton over so they could congratulate him.

Trump was leaning against a fruit machine trying to engage anyone that would stay put long enough in conversation. Rawlings came over to speak to him.

"How are you enjoying your baptism of alcohol?" Rawlings joked.

"Splendid. I'm having a really good evening. What's her situation," Trump nodded at Jo Adler, who noticed and waved at them. "Bugger, she's married," Trump cursed as he caught sight of her wedding ring. He nudged Rawlings, "Mind you, she's far more my type. What's her name? Patsy?" He cocked his head to one side and watched as Patsy handed out metal trays to three of the men to bang on their heads. "I like this one, we used to sing this at my club. I could never bang the tray in time though." Trump tapped his foot and joined in with the chorus.

"She's leaving next week," Rawlings informed him. "Oh yes and she's taken."

"Shame that, she seems like a great girl," Trump observed eyeing the laughing Patsy.

"She is," Rawlings agreed. He raised his eyebrows watching Trump make his way across the bar towards Patsy, as the boys sang the final line of the song.

Patsy had collected the trays, and was attempting to press the dents out before she handed them back into the bar. Rawlings shot a look at Meredith, who was busy chatting, as Trump asked Patsy if she needed any help. Patsy nodded and handed him the stack of trays. Trump leaned in and said something to her and she smiled and nodded. Trump took the trays and stood with Patsy, watching a yard of ale get handed out from behind the bar. Seaton took it, and began to drink as the others clapped and cheered. Trump stood close to Patsy and rested his arm across her shoulder, his fingers dangled dangerously near her breast.

Rawlings checked Meredith was still busy and began to walk towards them. This was definitely a situation that needed heading off at the pass. He saw Patsy whisper something to Trump, who nodded and removed his hand. Rawlings relaxed until he saw Trump had simply placed it on her backside. He saw Patsy stiffen, and quickened his pace. He frowned as he watched Trump's face contort in pain, and he looked down. Patsy had hold of two of Trump's fingers, which she had bent backward so that his hand was almost at a right angle to his wrist. Rawlings smiled and slowed again. He came within earshot and heard what Patsy was saying.

"You see, Sarge, no always means no. Now smile at the nice people or they will realise what a prick you are."

Rawlings grinned and slapped Trump on the back. Patsy released his hand and he shoved it in his pocket as Meredith looked over. The trays were still in his other hand.

"Right then, I'll get these back. Catch you later."

Trump walked away. Rawlings and Patsy burst out laughing. Meredith nodded towards them and Patsy waved back believing he had not seen the exchange, but Meredith had, and was pleased at how Patsy had dealt with Trump without making a scene. It was a black mark for Trump though, who had now reached him and had placed the trays on the bar.

"How's it going, Trump?" Meredith turned towards the new member of his team.

"Splendid, Gov. Thank you. We have a little firecracker over there," Trump looked towards Patsy. Meredith nodded in agreement. "I hear she's leaving so that gives a chap hope, you know not mixing business with pleasure. What does she drink? I think I'll buy her one."

"She's taken Trump," Meredith said pleasantly.

"Ah well, there's taken and taken. What does she drink? I think she likes me."

"Really? Well, in that case, she's probably drinking house red. But I assure you, she is taken."

"Yes, but she hasn't had the Louie love yet."

Meredith had just taken a sip of his pint and spat it out before coughing violently.

"The what?" he spluttered. "Did you just say 'Louie love'?"

"Watch," Trump announced confidently, and he ordered a glass of red wine.

He didn't notice Meredith give a slight incline of his head to Patsy, who then made her way towards them. Nor did he notice her arrival and almost bumped into her as he turned.

"Ah, Patsy, for you," he blinked, attempting to align his thoughts. He hadn't anticipated having to perform with his new boss standing next to him. He cleared his throat, but before he could speak Meredith nudged him.

"Go on then, show her the Louie love."

This time it was Patsy's turn to spit out her drink, and unfortunately all over Louie's jacket. She apologised and mopped at it with a bar towel as she tried to keep a straight face, but she didn't manage.

Louie shook his head. "That was a tad unfair, if you don't mind me saying." Trump sounded wounded but smiled broadly. He had a sense of humour, and one little blip wouldn't make him give up.

"Do you want some loving, DC Hodge?" Meredith asked and Louie raised his eyebrows. He was aware from Meredith's tone that the question was serious. He watched Meredith from the corner of his eye hoping Patsy would floor him with some serious repartee.

"Yes please, DI Meredith." Patsy stepped forward and put her arms around his neck.

Meredith leaned down and kissed her. "In which case, take me home now, while I'm still capable."

Meredith threw his head back and laughed as Trump turned back to the bar and buried his head in his arms groaning.

CHAPTER SEVEN

Derek's wife Rebecca replaced the receiver in the cradle and walked through to the dining room frowning. He looked up as she entered.

"Who was it?" he snapped. He hated dinner being interrupted and he had told her to let it ring.

"I have absolutely no idea. All they said was tell him to answer his phone. Do you know who it was?" She watched her husband closely.

Derek's pulse quickened and he felt a wave of heat run through his body. He placed a forkful of food into his mouth, and held up a finger asking her to wait. Having finished his mouthful, he looked at his wife and shrugged.

"How would I? Was it male or female?" He took another mouthful.

His wife remained in the same position and her eyes narrowed. "Male." She arranged her napkin on her lap. "Have you been, or should I say, are you up to something again? Because I warn you, Derek, I'm not living through that again. You know what Daddy said the last time he bailed you out. There is no more money."

Her face had hardened, and she studied the overweight, middle-aged man sitting opposite her with distaste. She blinked as she thought about the warnings from her late mother that she had ignored. She watched Derek's fleshy jowls wobble as he chewed, and wondered what had happened to make her think she was in love with this man.

He looked up from his food and seeing her expression put his cutlery down carefully. "I am not up to anything, as you put it. I am simply trying to eat my dinner, and quite frankly the look on your face is enough to make even the hungriest man lose his appetite." He pushed his plate away from him and stood, tutting and shaking his head. "If you'll excuse me." He walked swiftly to the cloakroom.

Locking the door, he sat on the toilet and took the mobile telephone from his inside pocket. He always set it to silent when he was in Rebecca's company.

He looked at the screen and noted he had missed three calls in the last hour. One text sat unopened; he opened it, and read the scant message. Looking at his watch he took a deep breath and pulled his shoulders back. He needed to orchestrate an argument to get out of the house. He snorted, realising that would take little effort. He pulled the flush and slipped the phone back into his pocket. He returned to the dining room but his wife was not there. He went through to the kitchen and found Rebecca stacking plates in the dishwasher.

"Well, that was yet another exquisite dining experience," he announced, and walked to the back door. He turned the key in the lock, and stepped into the garden. He pulled a cigarette from the packet in his hand and cupped his hands around the flame of the lighter. He pulled in the nicotine. He turned to look at his wife who was studiously ignoring him. "Would you like one?"

Rebecca looked at him briefly and shook her head with a sigh.

"Oh dear, tell me you're not going to get sozzled again tonight. A cigarette will calm you, and you won't have a headache in the morning. You really are drinking too much, you know."

Derek watched his wife bite her lip to halt her natural response. He raised his eyebrows; she was very controlled tonight, it was clear he would have to step up a gear.

"Is that another new dress?" he asked, pointing at her with the hand that held his cigarette.

That did it. His wife spun to face him, her nose wrinkled and her nostrils flared.

"I have had this rag for over three years. I can't remember the last time I actually bought anything I wanted rather than could afford, and we know why that is, don't we?" She spat the accusation at him.

Derek closed his eyes momentarily in a silent prayer of thanks. This wouldn't take long now. He looked at his wife and inclined his head.

"Rebecca, please. I was attempting to give you a compliment, the dress suits you. I have no idea why you have to be so vile all the time." He took another drag on his cigarette. "And as for what we can afford," he waved his hand in a circle towards the house.

Rebecca watched the trail of smoke disappear into the cold night air; she had one arm across her body which the other elbow rested on, and she tapped her chin with her index finger.

"You were the one that wanted all this. You are the one that feels you are too superior to actually go out and earn a living," Derek pointed at her again, "and don't bring Sasha into this. She's ten now, and most of her friends' mothers work. Perhaps if you want to afford more up-market clothes you should consider making some effort to actually do something about it yourself. Instead of this constant complaining about how tough you have it, do something about it. Despite my past misdemeanours, which you know were all about trying to keep up with your constant demands, I work hard for our family. What do you do?"

Derek took the last puff of his cigarette and dropped it into the planter next to the back door. He looked at her and could see the tension in her rigid body. "Exactly what do you do?"

Rebecca was incensed. She dragged a breath in through gritted teeth, and before Derek knew what was happening she had walked back to the dishwasher and launched a wine glass at him. It shattered on the door frame. Rebecca picked up another, and another, until there was nothing left to throw.

Derek had protected himself by stepping to one side of the door, and had pressed his back against the outside wall. For a fleeting second, he felt guilty, perhaps even sorry for his wife. Cautiously, he leaned forward and put his head around the door. Rebecca had picked up the wine bottle, and in the absence of anything in which to pour the wine, was drinking straight from the bottle. She pulled it away from her mouth and pointed it at him. He flinched thinking she might launch it.

"I must have been drunk every single day right up to the point that I married you." She looked at him in disgust. "No one, but no one, would have taken you on if they were sober." She took another swig from the bottle, "And yes, Derek, I am going to get drunk. That way I might forget for a few blissful minutes that you really are my husband."

Any pity Derek felt dissipated, and he stepped back into the kitchen. The broken glass crunched beneath his feet. He stopped a few feet away from his wife.

"And all I wanted to do was compliment you," he shook his head. "I'm going out, because if you think I'm staying here to watch you get drunk and insult me for no good reason, well, you can think again." He twisted and looked back at the broken glass. "Try and get that cleared up before you're too far gone, or you will have to explain to Mrs Hancock how it got there." He snorted. "That's an expense we could save, Rebecca. Let's get rid of her and you do the cleaning."

Rebecca ignored him and took another swig from the bottle.

He tutted, walked out of the kitchen, through the hall, and grabbing his raincoat from the coat rack, he slammed the door as he left.

Once in the street Derek blew out a breath of relief. He checked his watch. He still had an hour before the meeting. He would have time to go into the bar next door for a drink first. He walked to the end of the street, and as he turned the corner he was pleased to note that there were two taxis at the rank. He quickened his pace to ensure he got there before they moved off.

Derek walked into the lobby of the casino and waited to sign in to behind two young men. He looked them up and down from the back. They were wearing jeans, and he shook his head in distaste. He had much preferred it when one had to dress up for an evening out. They moved away from the counter. He placed his raincoat down and pulled his membership card from his wallet.

The cloakroom assistant looked at him and smiled. "Hello, how are you?" She placed her hand on his coat. "Are you sure I can take this? The last time I saw you, you told me never to let you in again, remember? I'm sure you'll be lucky tonight though." She put his coat on a hanger and slid a ticket onto its neck before handing Derek his receipt.

He smiled at her. "I doubt it," he said as he put his wallet back into his inside pocket, "but I live in hope."

Derek pushed open the doors to the gaming room. He paused for a moment and scanned the area. It was still early, and only half the tables were open, but he knew that within an hour they would be full. He stepped in and decided to wander around until they found him. He couldn't afford to play so he would have to make do with watching others enjoy themselves. He walked down the stairs to the lower level that contained the card tables, and which circled the roulette tables sitting in the centre of the vast room on a raised platform.

Three Chinese men sat at the first blackjack table, and one had obviously been lucky. He had a tray full of dark coloured chips with silver inserts sitting on the table in front of him. In this casino that represented the higher value chips. Derek guessed he had several thousand pounds sitting there. He caught the eye of the croupier who nodded recognition as he finished dealing the hand. The man in the middle slapped the table as the croupier scooped away his money, and chattered in his native tongue, obviously not best pleased. The croupier asked if Derek wanted to join the next hand, but with great restraint he shook his head and moved on.

At the next table a large black woman had just won and was dancing in her chair as the croupier paid her with chips containing the silver inserts. She laughed joyously and told her smaller companion that she was now winning funny money. Derek smiled at her warmly, he enjoyed it when people appreciated their luck. He was about to walk on when somebody stepped up behind him and spoke quietly in his ear before walking away again.

"Go to the final table, please, Derek."

He recognised the voice as that of the thug Tony. He resisted the temptation to rub his ribs, and walked slowly around the circle towards the requested destination, repeatedly clearing his throat as he did so. As he approached the table he saw there were three men sitting at it, only one of whom he recognised. There was a vacant seat next to him. He walked towards it, but before he reached it a young croupier rushed up to him.

"You left these on the table sir. You shouldn't be so careless." She smiled a dazzlingly white smile at him. "Be lucky, and don't forget you don't know Mr Brent." She moved away quickly.

Derek looked down at the rack of chips she had placed in his hand. He knew each rack contained one hundred chips, and he knew from their burnt orange colour that they were worth ten pounds each. A smile twitched at the corner of his mouth as for a few seconds he forgot why he had been summoned.

He stepped forward towards the vacant space and, placing the rack on the card table, he clambered awkwardly into the chair. He placed a single chip in the yellow box marked on the green baize in front of him; it was the minimum bet for this particular table. The dealer dealt the first cards. Derek's was the queen of hearts. He scanned the table. There were no other picture cards, and no aces. The dealer dealt his second card and it was an ace. "Blackjack," the dealer called, and paid Derek.

He dealt the next hand. Derek was dealt two nines. "Eighteen split nines?" he queried, and Derek nodded, adding two chips to the box. The dealer dealt two more cards. Derek won both hands. He went on to win eight out of the next ten hands. His rack was full and next to it stood a further stack of chips. Once more, he forgot why he was there, until a new dealer approached the table.

"New dealer after the next hand," the current croupier announced, and Derek was aware of the shuffle next to him.

Michael Brent turned to shake his hand, indicating his winnings with the other. "Well done. I don't suppose you want to join us for a hand of poker?" Brent asked loudly, ensuring all, on or around the table, could hear. "House rules, we've booked a private table. It starts in ten minutes, if you're interested."

Brent thanked the croupier, picked up his chips and walked away.

Derek played two more hands with the new croupier before standing and giving his chair to one of the men behind him awaiting a space. He glanced at his watch as he noticed that the room was now full and buzzing with noise. It was ten past eleven, and the poker game started in five minutes. He walked back around the circle until he reached the steps that would take him to the raised platform on the left of the casino. This was the area where private tables were available.

He waved a waitress over. "Diet coke please. I'll be at table six."

Derek knew that table six sat at the far end of the facility. It was where the house placed the big money; he'd not been that far down before. He swallowed and climbed the steps, knowing Michael Brent was watching his approach, but he kept his eyes down as he walked forward. Brent stood as he reached the table and walked forward to greet him. He again pumped Derek's hand up and down, a broad smile on his face. To anyone watching, this was simply an enthusiastic greeting. Only Derek could hear what he was saying.

"Right, put your chips down opposite me, make your apologies and go to the gents. Read the note in your pocket and get back out here pronto. I don't want you to hold the game up," Brent instructed Derek through his smile. "And smile, Derek, you're on a winning streak."

Derek followed Brent's instructions and walked quickly through the doors to the toilets. Once there, he locked himself in a cubicle and searched his jacket pockets. He pulled out the paper and read the information. He swallowed and re-read it. The paper began to flutter as his hand jerked involuntarily. He dragged the paper into the palm of his hand with his fingers, and screwed it into a ball. He brought up his other hand and sat for a while with both hands clasped around the paper. When his nerves had settled, he threw the paper into the toilet pan and pulled the flush. He waited to ensure it had disappeared before making his way back to the table. Taking his seat as instructed, he nodded at the other men sitting at the table. He was unsure as to which, if any, of them other than Brent knew why he was really there.

He threw some chips into the centre of the table. Brent nodded and the croupier dealt the first hand. After four hands a comfort break was called and Derek was up three hundred pounds.

As he walked to the door that led to a smoking area on a small flat roof to the rear of the casino, Derek wished with all his being that he could enjoy this rare run of luck he was experiencing. He shivered as he stepped out onto the terrace. It was empty with the exception of one man pacing up and down in an attempt to keep warm whilst speaking quietly into his mobile. Derek lit his cigarette as the door opened behind him, and Michael Brent stepped out and lit a cigar. Brent nodded at the man on the mobile, who crushed his cigarette with his foot, and went back into the casino.

"Hello, Derek, did you understand?" Brent asked blowing out a stream of smoke. Derek nodded.

"You get that we are going to do a trial run?" He held his hand up as Derek opened his mouth. "I know what you're going to say, but I want to make sure that's all. My problem is who to use." Brent shook his head, absently. "You'll get a text next week letting you know who and when. So keep the bloody phone on. Then we can give it a go to see how it pans out. We have to get this right, and practice makes perfect."

He nodded as though to leave. Derek stepped forward and put a hand on his arm. Brent looked down at it, and then slowly raised his eyes and stared at Derek. Derek pulled his hand away as though it had been slapped.

"I need to know that this will end." Derek's voice revealed his desperation. "You must understand that, my nerves are in shreds. I need to know it will end."

Brent smirked at him. "You have my word, old chap." He slapped Derek's arm. "Now finish your cigarette before you come in. Play two more hands, then excuse yourself and leave." He paused and added, "And I mean the casino, not just the table. You can keep what chips you have. We'll call that a bonus."

Derek watched him leave and lit another cigarette with shaking hands. He turned and gazed at the river which glinted in the gap between the buildings opposite. He wondered how much money he would need to set himself up abroad. He shook his head knowing he could not raise enough, and that he would never leave Sasha.

CHAPTER EIGHT

Travers knocked on Meredith's open door and walked in waving a sheet of paper. Meredith was on the telephone, and he nodded towards the chair. Travers sat clasping the paper, and tapped his foot restlessly as Meredith brought the call to an end. He jumped up as Meredith replaced the receiver. He waved the paper at him again.

"Here's hoping, Gov." He stepped forward. "We've only gone and got a result on the Short call. You know the one his mother mentioned?" He beamed as Meredith nodded. "It hadn't been checked out, you were right. It came in on the 5th January, at six thirty. Only call from that number and it lasted just under two minutes. The phone is registered to Anthony Wilson. We have his address in Redfield. I've run a check and he's got one conviction for GBH and one for causing an affray. I've asked around but no one knows that much about him. Shall I go and have a word?"

Meredith grinned at him and pulled his jacket off the back of his chair as he stood to join him.

"Indeed you should, and I'm coming with you. I've been itching to get out of this bloody office. Your car or mine?"

As they walked towards Wilson's house, Meredith looked at the BMW parked on the drive.

"That's only two years old, top of the range by the look of it. What did you say our boy did to earn a crust?"

"I didn't. Let's go and find out, shall we?" Travers opened the gate to the side of the drive and walked purposefully towards the door. He pushed the doorbell then stepped back and looked up at the house. The red brick end-of-terrace looked much like any other house in this part of town. It was neat and tidy and his mother would have been pleased to note that the net curtains at the window were white. The door opened and a boy of about ten stood before them. He didn't speak.

Meredith smiled at him. "Hello, son, is your dad in?" The boy shook his head, so Meredith tried again. "What about your mum, is she here?"

"She's down the shops. She's buying me some new stickers."

"Which shops? Will she be long?" Meredith watched the boy shrug. "Are you on your own? Where's your dad then, is he at work?"

"Probably. I'm ill so I just got up." The boy nodded, a serious expression on his face.

"Oh dear, do you think we should wait with you until your mum gets back?"

The boy shook his head vigorously. "I'm not allowed to let anyone in, or talk to strangers." He looked past them and pointed up the road. "Here comes my mum now."

The two men turned and looked up the road. A harassed looking woman in her mid-thirties and carrying two bulging shopping bags was hurrying towards them.

"Ah, that's good. Where does your dad work?"

"Down the club."

"What's it called, this club?" Meredith smiled as the boy shrugged again. It had been worth a try. He turned and walked towards the gate and held it open for the woman to come in. Both he and Seaton noticed the bruise on her cheek.

"Mrs Wilson, sorry to trouble you, we're looking for your husband," Meredith explained as she walked past them.

"Why, what's he done?" Wendy Straker knew instinctively that they were policemen. "And he's not my husband." She stepped over the threshold and put the bags down, then turning, she wiggled the fingers on her left hand at them. "We're not married."

"Why do you think he's done something?" Meredith asked from the doorstep. He watched her slide her coat off and hang it on the bannister. She had a row of bruises on her upper arm that disappeared into the sleeve of her tee shirt, and he nodded towards them. "You've been in the wars," he observed.

"Yeah, well it's this door, it keeps getting in the way." She stepped forward and made to close it. Meredith blocked it with his foot.

"Now, that's not nice, is it? Where's your bloke? It's easier to tell us now or we'll have to wait, and I think she's had enough for one day." He nodded to the bay window of the neighbouring house and the curtain twitched and fell back into place.

Wendy Straker stepped outside and raised two fingers towards the window next door. "Nosey cow!" She stepped back into the house. "I don't know where he is, but at this time of day best bet is a pub or the bookies." Again, she made to close the door but Meredith's foot was still there. She sighed, "Come on, you're letting all the heat out and he's not well." She nodded at her son who was sat on the stairs anxiously awaiting his stickers.

"I know, he said. He also said his dad worked down the club. Which club would that be?" Meredith smiled at her, and she shrugged indicating she didn't care what the boy had said.

"Sensations, I'm sure you know it." She gave the door a shove and Meredith moved his foot so it almost closed. He leaned forward.

"Thanks very much." He nodded at the door, "Do you know love, you want to get this sorted. Living with a door that causes bruises like that is asking for trouble. Oh yes, and just in case we don't find him, tell him we called." He pushed a card towards her and she rolled her eyes as she took it. She then pushed a little harder and Meredith allowed the door to close.

Meredith looked at his watch as they walked back to the car. "What time do these joints open? I'm not sure I can cope with Sensations stone cold sober, and on an empty stomach."

Travers laughed and shook his head. "No idea, but we're about to find out."

They drove to the club and were disappointed to find it was shut. A plaque on the door gave the opening hours as seven until late on week days. They banged on the door for a while just in case there were any staff inside, and then they went around to the rear of the building. The gates were chained shut, and it was clear that there was no one around.

"Bugger! That means someone needs to come back tonight," Meredith cursed and then he shrugged at Travers. "Let's get back to the station and find out who wants some overtime?"

Back at the station Meredith updated the team on why they wanted to speak to Anthony Wilson. He asked for volunteers to attend the club that evening. Most of them pleaded prior engagements. The only person to volunteer was Louie Trump. Meredith wondered if he was keen to get involved or just keen. He hadn't got the measure of him yet and he looked at Seaton.

"I reckon that our two new sergeants should get this one then. Tom, I'm away this weekend and I've got a stack of paperwork to go through for the CPS. Any chance you could swing it with Susan?" Meredith held back a smile as Tom Seaton cast a sideways glance at Trump and sighed.

"Go on then, but I want next Saturday week off, and guaranteed. I don't care if the Super's kidnapped. There are tickets for Twickenham with my name on, and I've never seen the All Blacks live." He crouched down and slapped his thighs attempting to imitate a haka, much to the amusement of the team.

Meredith held his hand up laughing. "Done. And no tips for the girls and, absolutely, no private dancers. Our budget is buggered already. Now, who's making the coffee?"

Meredith walked to his office grinning.

Patsy walked into the dining room with a mug of coffee for Meredith and looked at the piles of files surrounding him.

"Is there anything I can do to help?" She pushed a pile to one side to make a gap for the mug, and ruffled his hair as he shook his head.

"No, nearly done now. I am just going to have a quick look through those again though. I know we're missing something" He nodded towards the files on Andrew Short and Anna Carter. "Then you can get me something much stronger than this." He pointed at the coffee with his pencil, then looked at his watch. It was nine o'clock. "The boys should be there by now; they went home for dinner and a change first." He smirked. "I hope Trump doesn't get carried away and try to dish out some Louie love." He laughed and Patsy started giggling.

"I never thought of that," she dabbed at her eyes with the back of her hands. "Can you imagine? I hope Tom can cope with him."

Patsy started towards the door, and looked over her shoulder, still grinning. "Correct me if I'm wrong, but I'm still owed some Meredith love. Once I've had a shower, I'll help you go through those last two, and then you can pay up." She winked and left the room.

Seaton and Trump walked into the lobby of Sensations and a busty brunette smiled at them from behind the counter.

"All right chaps, I'm Janelle, that will be a fiver each. You got one of our flyers?

Drinks are half price until ten with them." Her face fell as Seaton pulled out his warrant card.

"I don't think we'll be paying, love. We just need a quick word with Anthony Wilson." He smiled and slid his ID back into his pocket.

The girl looked confused. "Who's that then? We don't have any Anthonys." Then the cloud lifted and she rolled her eyes at them. "You mean Tone. Tony Wilson. He's not due in until ten so you got nearly an hour to waste. He's never early."

Seaton sighed and nudged Trump as he nodded to the entrance to the bar.

"Come on then, you're buying." They walked into the club leaving a confused Janelle wondering if she should have charged them.

They quickly scanned the sparsely populated club. It was dimly lit and reeked of stale beer and sweat. There was a bar along one wall, behind which two scantily clad barmaids were drying glasses. They were talking to a middle-aged man, who was sitting on one of the chrome bar stools on the other side of the bar. They assumed he was a customer. A long narrow stage jutted out into the main floor space, and two girls dressed only in thongs were gyrating on poles for two men sitting at a table to the left side of the stage. Around the edge of the room were several semi-circular booths. Heavy curtains were draped to each side, ready to be closed for privacy. All of the booths were empty.

"This is a shit hole. I'd have to be paid to have her lap dance for me." Tom Seaton nodded towards one of the girls on stage, "It was a train, not a shovel, that did that to her face."

"I quite agree, but she does have magnificent bazookas," Trump replied. "What's your poison?" He took ten pounds from his wallet and having reached the bar waved it at one of the barmaids. She put her towel down and walked towards them. "Now she's a little better," Trump said quietly to Seaton.

"Yes, Sir, what can I get you?" The girl had an eastern European accent, and when she smiled the saw that one of her front teeth was gold.

"Two pints of your finest, please," Trump smiled kindly at her, and leaned forward to watch as the girl prepared their drinks. "I've never seen it done like that before."

The girl had positioned her feet slightly apart and several feet away from the pump. Each time she pulled on the pump, she bent from the waist, her back arching forward, and licked the top of the phallic shaped pump suggestively.

Tom Seaton nudged Trump.

"Don't buy her one, and don't tip her, you won't get it back on expenses," Seaton advised and Trump smiled at him even though he was about to totally disregard the advice.

He nodded appreciatively as the waitress returned.

"Twelve pounds please."

"How much? I didn't want the barrel, that's highway robbery," Trump exclaimed.

Seaton snorted and picked up his pint. He walked to the table furthest away from the stage and sat down. Within seconds two girls appeared from nowhere. The first was a tall blonde and had a scar that ran the length of her very long thigh. The other had jet black hair and tattoos which covered half her body. Both wore skimpy bras and thongs. Seaton guessed that neither had seen their twenty-first birthday yet, and wouldn't for some considerable time. The tattooed girl leaned forward ensuring that her cleavage blocked his line of vision.

"You want private dance?" she asked, clearly another eastern European. Seaton shook his head and shooed her away with his hand. The other girl stepped forward and rested her ample bosom on his shoulder. She drew a long finger nail across the back of his neck as she did so.

"You can have the two of us for sixty quid mate, it'll be worth it," she advised in a broad Bristolian accent.

Seaton shifted awkwardly so that he could both pull out his ID and look her in the face, but not before his nose had brushed her bosoms. She smiled thinking he had taken out his wallet. He opened it and she looked at his warrant card. She jerked her head at the other girl.

"Come on, love, we ain't getting nothing here. He's a copper." She nodded acceptance at Seaton and turned to leave. Without warning she bent to touch the floor, and looked at him from between her open legs. Her hair trailed on the filthy floor. "If you change your mind give us a shout." She laughed as she stood upright and pulled the other girl away.

"Cheeky bugger," Seaton grinned as Trump sat next to him.

"Did I miss all the fun?" he asked and Seaton shook his head.

"I reckon I'm old enough to be their dad and then some. Too skinny for my taste, I like a bit of meat on the bone." He looked at his watch and sighed; they still had half an hour to waste. "I'll text the Gov and let him know."

Meredith picked up his phone and smirked.

"What's tickled you?" Patsy asked, pulling the final pile of photographs towards her.

"Seaton and Trump are held up awaiting Wilson's appearance. Ten at the earliest, so they say." He punched in a response, and then smiled once more as Seaton replied.

Patsy ignored him as something had caught her attention. She lifted the photograph up and turned it around to view it from different angles. She then placed it back on the table, stood up, and looked at it from a distance. Meredith put the phone down and watched her.

"Are you on to something?" he asked as Patsy put her hands on her hips and took a step back.

She waved him towards her. He went to stand behind her, wrapping his arms around her waist, and resting his chin on her shoulder.

"What am I looking at?" He peered down at the photograph. Whatever it was had clearly been caught by a light as there was an explosion of rays reflected onto one side of the photograph. He squinted in an attempt to bring it into focus. Patsy was nodding. She stepped forward to retrieve the photograph and turned it over. Meredith shuffled forward behind her, unwilling to release his hold.

"What code is five five seven two, from?" Patsy queried, and leaned across the table to reach a file.

"Mmm. Is it wrong that I don't care?" Meredith murmured pressing his hips forward, and sliding his hands underneath her shirt until they found her breasts.

"Get off," Patsy wiggled, which did nothing to deter him. "All in good time. I think I know what this is, but I don't know where it's from so . . ." She flipped open the file and ran her finger down the list, then banged it against the table. She forced Meredith to step backward and turned to face him. "I know what this is, and now I just want to know why. Are there any more from this batch?" She pecked him on the nose. "I'm leaving tomorrow, so this is my last chance to make my mark on this case. Are there any more photographs from the bus? I promise I will reward you later."

"You certainly will. Tell me what you think it is," Meredith replied, turning her back round, and stepping forward to stand beside her.

Patsy tapped the photograph. "This is a photograph from the bus. You will remember that they only had the one camera that was a rapid shot rather than video. It was angled incorrectly so it only took photos of the coin tray, and a little bit of midriff, so totally useless. But it did take three or four of each passenger depending on how long they took to board." She looked at him, and he shrugged and nodded. Patsy rolled her eyes. "So we should have the other shots of this hand, because that's what it is. But it was moving and caught the light, hence the bad quality. I reckon I know what this is." She drew her finger in an outline of the rough shape behind the rays. Meredith picked the photograph up and peered at it closely. He held it away from his face, and then up to the light, mirroring Patsy's earlier movements. Patsy grinned at him, "If I'm right, the only thing I don't know is -"

Meredith interrupted her. "The only thing you don't know is, why Anna Carter appears to be boarding the bus that we think carried Andrew Short's killer?" He finished her sentence and she pouted.

"How did you know that?" she demanded. He smiled slowly and pulled her into his arms.

"Because I'm intelligent, observant, handsome, and lucky," he murmured into her neck.

She pressed her body against him and held her head back. "Lucky, why?" she asked softly.

"Mainly because I am now about to have my wicked way with you, and also because I was at the hospital when they returned her jewellery." His hands had started to unbutton her shirt. "No bra, so knickers or no knickers DC Hodge?" His hands skimmed down to her sweatpants, where she caught them before he pulled them down.

"Do we have the rest of the photos here or not?"

Meredith had no idea, but knew they wouldn't do anything about it before the next day, so he shook his head, and tried to continue with the task in hand.

"I'm not convinced about that, but you've convinced me on the other." She released his hands and jabbed him in each side with her fingers. He jumped backward and she made a dash for the hall. "But only if you can catch me," she yelled behind her as she started up the stairs.

Meredith walked slowly from the room grinning. He already had.

~ ~ ~

Meredith groaned as they heard his mobile ringing downstairs.

Patsy stroked his face. "Well DI Meredith, you certainly deliver on your promises. Go and get it. We have to clear up anyway." She giggled. "I need another shower now, but first a drink."

Meredith circled the scar on her shoulder with his finger and leaned down to kiss it. "I might join you for that." He smiled briefly before his face became serious. "Patsy, I am almost coming around to you becoming Patsy Hodge PI, but I am worried. Promise me, and I mean promise, that you will never put yourself out there like that again." He pulled her back into his arms as the land line started ringing. He gave a sigh and pushed her away. "I'll get it." He hopped out of bed and ran down the stairs naked. He caught Seaton just before he hung up.

"Were you in bed?" Seaton accused him. Meredith grinned into the receiver. "Because I've been sat in some skanky club, then had to speak to the most obnoxious prat, and I'm still not home. Although, the gallant Sergeant Trump is dropping me off first. I'm knackered, pissed off, and -"

"Get on with it, Seaton," Meredith snapped, still smiling. "Did you get anything or not?"

"We did. Because he said he left the phone with his fags at the end of the bar, and when he realised he came back in to get it and some bloke had picked it up and was using it."

Meredith interrupted him. "And that's something because . . ."

"Because it took him a while to remember who could have made the call. If his story was to have any credence it couldn't be the club as it doesn't open until seven, *and* we were reliably informed he never gets in before ten. I asked him which bar and it took him a further while to remember it was The Plough. Absolutely, and definitely lying. He was very uncomfortable, and far too friendly, do you know what I mean?"

"I do. When you get in tomorrow get hold of his phone records and let's see who he's been speaking to. Well done, Seaton. How was Trump?"

"Yes, thanks Gov. I'll speak to you in the morning then." Seaton evaded the question and hung up, and Meredith frowned into the phone as Patsy held out a glass of wine.

"Right, let's take a second look at those photos." Meredith walked back to the dining room.

"I thought you said they weren't here," Patsy accused, as she followed him.

"I rather think I said I didn't know if they were here or not." He walked into the dining room, and leaned across the table pulling a pile of photographs forward.

Patsy slapped him on the backside. "If we're going to do this, you are at least putting knickers on, that was not pleasant Johnny." She skipped out of his way before he could grab her.

CHAPTER NINE

Meredith paused and looked at his team. He eyed Trump suspiciously. He had yet to find out what Seaton had been unable to tell him the night before.

"To summarise, Hodge and Adler have gone to pick up the girl, and when Seaton receives those records it's all hands to the deck to find out who Anthony Wilson has been speaking to. Start with last night and work backwards. As we got this lead from a single phone call I want the identity of one off calls listed too. Run whoever you find through the system as a first resort." He picked up his pad. "Right, anything else?" He surveyed the room. "Good. Then someone get the kettle on. Seaton, my office please."

Seaton ignored the calls asking what he'd been up to the night before, and went to Meredith's office. He closed the door and took a seat. Meredith looked at him expectantly.

"Well?" Meredith raised his eyebrows and held his hands out.

Seaton played dumb. "Well what?"

"Well, what was it that happened with Trump last night that you couldn't tell me?" He pursed his lips and watched as Seaton struggled with what to say.

"It was something and nothing really." Seaton looked down and brushed imaginary fluff from his trousers.

"What was?"

"We had finished questioning Wilson, and Louie went to the gents. He was gone a little while and I got concerned. There weren't that many in the club, but they all knew we were coppers. So I went to investigate." He shrugged, torn between his loyalty to Meredith and telling tales on a colleague. "It was something and nothing really."

"What was?"

"When I entered the lobby leading to the gents, Trump was with this bird. She threw her arms around his neck and snogged him."

Seaton saw the smile twitch at the corner of Meredith's lips. Meredith nodded for him to continue.

"He said it was all perfectly innocent on his part, and that she had been asking for his help. She spoke little English so it was proving difficult to understand exactly what her problem was, hence the length of time he had been gone. When I showed up, he thinks she kissed him in case it was one of her bosses come looking for her. Anyway, he gave her his card and told her to call him." He shrugged again. "That's all, nothing for you to worry about."

"I think that's for me to decide, don't you? What was her name?" Meredith leaned back in his chair and stretched his legs out beneath the desk. Seaton frowned wondering what difference her name made.

"I'm not sure, something like Natalia I think. What's the relevance?"

"Not sure there is any," Meredith grinned. "Did she have any clothes on?"

"Not so as you'd notice, no," Seaton returned the grin.

"Okay, get on with the phone records then. Let me . . ." He paused as his telephone rang. He snatched up the receiver. "Okay, settle her in. I'll be down in a minute." He looked at Seaton, "Anna Carter is here. I'll catch up with you later."

Meredith picked up a file containing the photographs and his note pad, and made his way to the interview room.

Patsy and Jo Adler were talking in the corridor as he opened the door leading to the interview rooms.

"Have you settled her in?" They nodded confirmation. "Did she say anything?"

"Nope. We said we had a few questions and would she mind coming in. Sad really, she jumped at the chance to get out of the house. We just exchanged pleasantries on the way here," Jo Adler informed him.

"Right, so she's not been read her rights then? We'd better start with that." He shook his head at the two women. "Jo, you're in with me, Hodge you make the coffee. I think we have a drought upstairs, and then get in there and observe. There's no point in you getting any more involved now."

Patsy nodded in agreement, opened the door to the interview room, and took an order for white coffee from Anna Carter. Meredith and Jo Adler went in and sat down opposite Anna. Meredith made small talk about her injury whilst he awaited the arrival of the coffee. Once that was done, he gave Patsy a few minutes to get into the observation room. He then leaned forward and smiled at Anna.

"Anna we've asked you in as a few oddities have come to light which we need to discuss with you. Because they are odd I'm going to caution you first, and advise you that you are able to have legal representation present if you wish. Would you like a solicitor?"

Anna Carter was bemused. She thought perhaps they had asked her in to look at photographs or CCTV footage. Why would she need a solicitor?

"Why would I? Is this normal?" she asked.

Meredith didn't answer the question. He pushed some buttons on the recorder and her eyes quickly glanced behind him at the camera. Meredith announced the time, date, and those present for the purpose of the recording. Then he opened the file and took out three photographs

"You don't want us to call your solicitor or get the duty chap in here then?" He smiled at Anna as she shook her head.

'No.'

Meredith then cautioned her, before beginning the interview.

"Do you recognise anything in any of these photographs?"

Anna leaned towards the table and squinted at the prints laid out before her. At first, she shook her head, and then she shrugged and looked up at Meredith.

"I think it looks like my ring. Can I touch them?" She picked up a photograph as Meredith confirmed that she could. She held it away from her nodding. "Yes, that looks like my ring." She placed it back down on the table.

Meredith tapped the right-hand corner. "These numbers tell us these were taken at the entrance to the number seventy-eight bus, at one thirty on the thirty-first January, the day before you were shot. Why were you catching the bus on that day and at that time?" He smiled kindly at her.

"I didn't. I was off work that day. I stayed home because it was so cold." Anna shook her head. "Are you sure this is the thirty-first?" she asked, and watched as Meredith reopened the file and took out seven more photographs which he laid on the table above the others. The table was now full of images.

"These are taken from the camera at the corner of Colston Street. They show the people boarding the bus at one thirty to one thirty-three on," he tapped the bottom of the photograph in the centre showing the date, "the thirty first."

Anna leaned forward again. Her eyes scanned along the queue of people boarding the bus until it had just one man stepping forward. She looked at Meredith and shrugged.

"I don't understand," she shook her head to emphasise the point. "If you can see that I'm not there, what am I looking for?"

Meredith pursed his lips and looked into her eyes; she didn't look away.

"Am I missing something?" she asked. Her eyes searched his face for a clue.

Meredith leaned forward and chose the photograph of the hooded youth. He picked it up and pushed the others to one side.

"Who's this then?" He placed it down in front of Anna. Once more she shook her head and shrugged. "For the tape, Anna Carter has shaken her head indicating she does not know the person in photograph 3736a." Leaning forward he tapped the photograph of the hooded character and then the ring. "The timings from two cameras show that it was this person wearing the ring."

Anna looked up at him,

"I don't know what you want me to say." She raised one hand helplessly and let it fall back into her lap.

Meredith drew in a deep breath and inclined his head. "Do you know the route for the number seventy-eight?"

"Of course. It goes from the centre, up Whiteladies Road, across the Downs, and there's a stop near the end of our street. I catch either the seventy-eight or the thirty-nine every day." Anna Carter's beautiful face now carried a worried frown.

Meredith looked at her hands which were screwed into fists on her lap; she was not wearing jewellery. He nodded towards them. "You don't wear your ring every day then? But you do agree that this is your ring?" He shuffled through the photographs he had pushed to one side, and pulled back the clearest shot.

"No, I don't wear it all the time. Like I told your two police ladies, it catches on stuff and I don't want to damage it. But I agree that looks like my ring." She looked up at Meredith who was pinching the bridge of his nose.

He knew that her choice of phrase indicated it might be her ring but she had yet to agree it was. "Have you let anyone borrow it? Or could anyone, like Gill for instance, have borrowed it on the thirty-first?" He slid his fingers up and down his nose as he spoke, and continued to do so whilst she considered the possibility.

Finally, she shook her head. "No, I don't think so. Well, that is she could, but she doesn't like my taste." She looked at Jo. "Does she?" She pressed for Jo's agreement, "You know, you were there."

Jo smiled at her warmly. "She did say she didn't like your choice of clothes. She didn't mention jewellery, but that doesn't mean she didn't borrow it, does it?" Jo smiled at Anna who was still frowning.

"No I know but . . ." Suddenly Anna smiled, and her whole being seemed to light up.

Meredith drew in a sharp breath. He had been caught off guard by her beauty, and he wondered what she was doing working in a diner on the centre.

"She might have borrowed it on the thirty-first, but she couldn't have been on that bus." Anna shook her head. "She'd been to London to see some friends and she didn't get home until after tea. She caught the train and then Dad picked her up from the station."

"So we are agreed this is your ring, and that you believe this to be a one-off design. How then did it appear on someone's hand on that day?" Meredith, now recovered, pressed her a little harder.

"I don't know. Perhaps it's not my ring. Perhaps she lied, the girl that makes the jewellery, perhaps she has made loads of them." Her face fell and she looked at Meredith with sad eyes. "What do you think? Because I'm getting worried now, and you haven't even told me why you're asking." She swallowed and blinked.

Meredith stared at her for a while and decided not to tell her. All his experience in interviewing told him Anna was telling the truth. She didn't seem to have the wherewithal to be smart enough to fool him.

He shook his head and smiled. "I don't know, but I'm going to find out." He stretched out his arm. "Interview over at 11.45am." He pushed the button to stop the recording. "Now you tell Jo here where you bought it, when, and for how much et cetera, then she'll give you a lift home. I'm sorry we bothered you, but we just need some ends tidied." He stood. "Take care, Anna."

A troubled Meredith left the room and walked quickly next door to consult with Patsy.

"What do you reckon?" he asked as he entered and closed the door behind him.

Patsy shook her head. "I don't think she has a clue. I don't think it was her, but if it was she should be an actress." Patsy walked to one of the two screens on the desk and rewound the recording. "Look at her reaction here."

She pressed the play button and Meredith's voice filled the room, "The timings from cameras show that it was this person wearing the ring." Patsy stepped forward and stopped the tape.

"There, look at her face, she seems totally bemused," Patsy shook her head. "I just can't see it, Gov."

Meredith smirked. "Me neither. I was just checking." He trailed his finger down the side of her face, across her neck and down to her cleavage. He then hooked the front of her sweater and pulled her towards him. "I like you calling me Gov." He leaned forward to kiss her. Patsy pushed him away.

"Well, make the most of it, it's my last day." She laughed as the door opened.

Seaton rolled his eyes at Meredith and jerked his thumb behind him. "We've got the first two months' analysis on Wilson's phone available if you want to look."

"I do. I'll be up now. Hodge take Anna home with Adler. Then get down to the jewellers and see what you can find out. When you take her home, ask to have a look at her shoes," he paused, "and the sister's as well if possible. See if either of them has a pair of those trainers." He walked towards Seaton, and paused to look over his shoulder. "And keep in touch," he winked as she scowled at him.

Seaton had listed all twenty people who had either made calls to Anthony Wilson or received calls from him on a white board in descending order of number of calls. He had then listed the total call time. Next to four of the names he had drawn an exclamation mark. Meredith scanned the board as he walked towards it. He raised his hand and pointed at the marks as he perched on the side of Dave Rawlings' desk.

"What do they represent then?" he questioned the three officers also looking at the board.

"Those with records."

Rawlings stood and walked to the board, then pointed at the first name to be marked. "John Prescott, yes his real name. Four convictions, three for violence. He did six months for GBH and one for possession." Rawlings moved to the next. "Samuel Obyeo, two for possession with intent to supply." His finger tailed further down the list. "Toby Samson, no convictions but he's been arrested more times than I could list. Mainly for violence and drunk and disorderly." He tapped the board.

"And finally, on a whole different playing field, one Paul Wilde. An accountant who did three years for fraud. We've looked at him on a forgery scam too, but didn't get anywhere. Our boy is on speaking terms with some great blokes."

"Isn't he just. But then I suppose that could go with the territory." Meredith looked towards the bottom of the list. "So, there's the one call to Andrew Short, and one to Michael Brent. Who's he? Why do I know that name if he's not got form?" He turned to Tom Seaton who picked up the commentary.

"He was on the peripherals of that fraud last year. Local entrepreneur," Seaton rolled his eyes at the euphemism. "Property developer, club owner, part racehorse owner, has shares in a gym. You name it, he has a finger in the pie. Never had anything on him, though I doubt he's whiter than white. You don't make that kind of money without shortcuts. But nothing suggests he's a bad boy, unless of course he is very clever. He also owns Sensations so that is probably why he called him."

"Hmm, okay, well check out his partners too. It's a long shot but we might pick up something useful." Meredith pushed his fingers through his hair and nodded. "Okay, talk me through the rest."

"Top of the list is one of the dancers at the club. Most of the calls go to rather than come from her."

Meredith held his hand up to stop him speaking, and asked in a loud voice. "Natalia Comanawhatsit? Why do I know that name?" he asked and Seaton's eyes narrowed at him. Rawlings and Travers shook their heads. Meredith raised his voice and shouted to the rest of the team. "Anyone know Natalia Comanawhatsit here? She works at Sensations, and the name rings a bell."

Meredith watched as Louie Trump held up a finger and walked to join them.

"I don't know her exactly, but I believe I may have met her last night," Trump advised as he reached them.

"So soon, Trump? You've only been in Bristol two minutes and you have a lap dancer on the go? That's mighty quick work," Meredith commented and raised his eyebrows awaiting an explanation.

"Not on the go. No, Sir," Trump replied evenly. "I think the girl is in trouble, I think she was asking for help. She came up to me at the club last night," he began to explain.

"What did she want, Seaton?" Meredith turned to Seaton, who shrugged in response. "So no dancing or touching then, just gave you a message that you didn't understand." Meredith turned back to Trump who sighed.

"Well, she did touch me, and not the other way round." He paused as Rawlings and Travers laughed. He shook his head, "I swear it. She was trying to explain what was wrong, it was difficult, and when Seaton came out she kissed me. That was it. I left my card of course."

"Well, Trump, just be careful. You don't want to make a habit of kissing strange lap dancers, it means they love you if they let you kiss them," he smirked, "at least that's what I've heard. You don't want to give her any Louie love or you'll never get rid of her. Then you'll have her and three shot-putting sisters to support." Meredith nodded at Trump and the rest of the team fell about laughing.

"Yes well, you lot can laugh, but when I crack an international human trafficking ring you'll all be sorry you doubted me," Trump grinned.

Meredith nodded approval; the man had a sense of humour which was needed on this team. He waved in the direction of the board again. "Right, take me through the rest then."

"Second highest call rate is to Wendy Straker, his other half, we met her yesterday," Seaton continued. "Then we have Sensations, the bookies, his dentist, the local Chinese, and his brother and mother," Seaton tapped the board, "and this one is untraceable. A pay as you go. Most of the calls are incoming to Wilson, a few of which he has returned, and you can bet your last sixpence that if Wilson is involved that's the one we want."

He completed the commentary and Meredith nodded whilst he studied the list.

"Right, let's get this moving then." He turned and pointed at Trump and Rawlings. "You two find out who the other members of these syndicates are, and run them. You two get mug shots of Wilson and his four known buddies up there and get around to Short's home and find out if they recognise them. Track down the father if he's not there, it's more likely he will know than the mother." He stretched as he completed his instruction to Travers and Seaton. "Oh, and while I think about it, get hold of the driver of the number seventy-eight, and show him a picture of Anna Carter together with the shots of the queue. You never know, it might pay off."

Meredith walked to his office and picked up the pile of files he had been working on the night before and made his way to the administration centre. Pushing open the door with his shoulder he walked across to place them for collection in the corner of the office. As he turned to leave again, one of the public relation girls was waving to catch his attention. She was unable to call to him as she was listening to a caller on the telephone. Meredith gave thanks for small mercies and tapped his watch indicating he didn't have time, and was about to promise to call when she hung up.

"DI Meredith, so glad I caught you. I need a word about *Crimebusters*. We need you to get down there as soon as. We've got a slot for the Andrew Short stabbing." She smiled at him, "How soon can you sort it? The show goes out next week so the sooner the better."

Meredith could think of nothing worse, and this time it would be unlikely he could palm the job off on someone else. He still had to deal with the revelations about Dawn Jessop but hadn't decided how. He forced a smile.

"Andrea, nice to see you. I'm very busy at the moment and away for the weekend, but I'll get something sorted for Monday. Will that do? If not, you're going to have to get someone else to do it." He paused. "When you say 'slot', what do you mean, just the photo gallery stuff?"

He sighed as she shrugged and waved her hands in the air.

"Not sure yet, the Superintendent was pushing for a longer slot, but we haven't got much to go with. Unless you're going to tell me differently, it's a two maybe three-minute thing. You know, this man, photo of Short was minding his own business et cetera, et cetera. Then it will move on to police are keen to identify. . ." She shrugged apologetically.

"So why do you need me? If there's no interview and no need for some berk to stand there and stammer, why don't you do it?"

"Because the Superintendent asked that you to deal with it." She grimaced, "And I am pushed at the moment."

Meredith winked at her. "I have just the man. I'll send him down later."

He whistled as he made his way to the incident room. Sitting back at his desk he flipped open his diary and turned to the telephone numbers scribbled on the inside of the rear cover. He picked up the phone and dialled out. He was somewhat relieved when the answer service cut in.

"Meredith, here, I'm going to be sending one of my chaps over on Monday to sort out a slot for this month's programme. You will not give him a hard time, in fact you will be help personified. If you want to know why, give me a call."

He replaced the receiver and touched his desk for luck, hoping that he had made the right decision. He stood and tapped the window which overlooked the incident room.

"Trump, my office now," he bellowed.

Trump closed his eyes for a moment before standing and making his way to Meredith's office.

"Come in, sit down, I have good news for you." Meredith held his hand out towards the chair.

"Really?" Trump was hesitant in his response. His mobile rang and he hit the reject button. "Sorry, Sir, you were saying." He smiled at Meredith as he sat to face him.

"You're going to be a star, Trump." Meredith nodded knowingly at him. "Well, perhaps anyway. You need to work on the *Crimebusters* slot we've been given on Andrew Short. I'll arrange a meeting on Monday for you, but you'll need to get down to Andrea and sort out what the brief is first."

Trump was horrified. This was usually a coveted task and he was the new boy. Surely Meredith could see the folly in sending him. He began to shake his head and tell Meredith just that, when his phone rang again. Once more he rejected the call.

"I am honoured, of course, but I do think that you should do this, and if not you, then one of the others. I don't want to step on any toes, I've not settled in yet. So, thank you, but no." He smiled his charming smile at Meredith, who leaned forward on his forearms.

"It wasn't a choice, Trump. It was an order." Meredith waited whilst that message registered and then added, "Just think how happy Uncle David will be." He leaned back in his chair and linked his fingers behind his head. "Leave Rawlings to it, get downstairs, and liaise with Andrea."

"But really, I do . . ." Trump's second attempt at rebuttal was interrupted by a knock at Meredith's door.

Rawlings motioned to Trump. "You've got a lady downstairs to see you, won't speak to anyone else. Name of Natalia." He grinned and walked away.

"So, Trump, the Louie love is working," Meredith observed, "but don't bring it to work. I'm being serious now, get rid of her."

Trump jumped up and muttered his agreement before rushing off to find Natalia. Five minutes later he called Meredith.

"Sorry to bother you, Sir, but she is hysterical, and I can barely understand her. I'm going to bring her up to the interview room, would you sit in with me?"

Trump breathed a sigh of relief as Meredith agreed, and he patted the girl's hand.

"Come on, Natalia, let's get you a cup of tea." She smiled at him and he punched the code to allow him to lead her into the main police station. He took her straight to the interview room and then asked her to wait whilst he got her a drink.

Knocking on Meredith's door, he half stepped into the office. "She's in number three, Sir. I'm just going to get her some tea, so would you like a coffee?"

Meredith nodded and closed the file on his desk. Picking up his note book he went to sit with Natalia. He smiled at her as he walked into the room but she shrank back against her chair. She was obviously petrified, and large eyes followed Meredith as he came to sit opposite her. He maintained his smile as he took in her appearance. Natalia was, to Meredith's mind, severely underweight. Her skin was pale, and black circles made her eyes look too large for her small face. Her jet-black hair needed washing, as did the clothes she wore.

"I'm DI Meredith, I'm here to help you. Would you mind if I recorded this conversation?" He spoke slowly and pointed at the recorder.

Natalia's large eyes followed his finger to the machine then back again.

"Where is Louie?" she asked, her eyes darting towards the door.

"He is coming with tea," Meredith mimed, and was grateful the recorder was not yet running. He was relieved when Trump kicked the door and called for him to open it.

Trump placed the three mugs he had balanced together between his hands down onto the desk and took a seat next to Meredith. He smiled at Natalia.

"Now, Natalia, how can we help you?" Trump asked. Natalia eyed Meredith and nodded towards him.

"Who's him?" she asked and her accent made it sound as though she were throwing an insult.

"He's a good man. My boss." Trump patted Meredith on the back. "Good man," he repeated. Natalie relaxed a little, but continued to monitor Meredith as he switched on the recorder, and then gave the time and date.

"We are about to commence a meeting with Ms Natalia Comaneci." He knew he had mispronounced her name when her eyebrows rose, but he ploughed on regardless. "Natalia has asked to see us and we have yet to ascertain why. We are therefore recording this interview as it may be necessary to use the services of an interpreter at a later stage." He paused and smiled at Natalia. "Natalia, please tell us why have you come here today?"

Natalia shrugged, signifying her inability to understand. Meredith sighed and Trump leaned forward.

"Why you here today?" he asked loudly.

Meredith closed his eyes and wondered what had possessed him to sit in on the interview. He was surprised when Natalia leaned forward and rested her forearms on the table. She looked at them both and blinked.

"They want to take baby," she announced solemnly. The two men exchanged concerned glances.

"Where is baby?" Trump asked loudly.

Meredith elbowed him. "I think she has problem with the language not the volume," he observed.

Trump nodded and tried again in a normal speaking voice. "Natalia, where is baby?"

Natalia smiled and nodded. Meredith pursed his lips as Trump sighed.

"No Natalia, WHERE is baby?" Trump tried again, this time holding his hands up to demonstrate he needed an answer. Natalie smiled again.

"Ah," she nodded and smiled, "there." She patted her flat stomach. Trump smiled at her.

"You are pregnant?" He turned to one side and made a circular motion over his own stomach and then pointed at her. She grinned and nodded.

"When it due?" he asked, and heard Meredith snort at his use of broken English.

Natalia shrugged again, and Trump drummed his fingers on the table for a while trying to work out how to communicate the question. He smiled as he pulled a small diary from his inside pocket. He placed it before her and opened it on the page showing the year. He circled the current month, and looked up at her, tapping the date.

"Today." He then waved the pen at the calendar before pointing it at her stomach and asking, "When?"

His heart fell as she shrugged again. Then she reached out and took the pen.

"Maybe," she shrugged as she circled October. She then circled November and repeated, "Maybe" and then followed September, "Maybe."

"Good." Trump smiled not knowing where to go with this next. He looked at Meredith who was rubbing his thumb and forefinger along the length of his nose. "What now, Sir? I'm not sure where to take this."

Meredith sighed and leaned forward. "For the purposes of the tape Natalia has indicated that she is pregnant, and that the baby is due sometime between September and November. I am hoping that she has not come expecting us to be able to effect a termin . . ."

He stopped speaking and looked at Natalia.

"Men want to stop?" He had taken up Trump's style of communication, and made a definitive sideways move with his hands.

Natalia nodded slowly, the corners of her mouth drooped a little, and big eyes stared into his.

"For the purposes of the tape Natalia has indicated she may be forced to terminate her pregnancy. What men?" he asked giving an exaggerated shrug.

She shook her head. "He kill me," Natalia stated simply, "so you help."

"We will help, but we need to know who," Meredith asked again. Natalie shrugged and shook her head. "We can't help you, not if you won't tell us," Meredith insisted, and knew that he had spoken too fast, and she hadn't understood a word that he had said.

Natalia looked at Trump.

"You help me, no?" she nodded.

Meredith rubbed his hands over his face. He turned to Trump. "This is getting us nowhere, get us an interpreter. What nationality is she?"

Trump didn't know so Meredith leaned forward.

"Where are you from?" he asked slowly, but Natalia shook her head.

"Russia?" Meredith pointed at her and she shook her head. "Poland?" he tried again. "Ukraine?"

Suddenly Natalia understood what he was asking. "Croatia," she said proudly.

Meredith turned to Trump. "Good luck with that. I've got to have a cigarette. Ring down to admin and see what they can sort out. I'll be back in a moment."

When Meredith returned, Trump explained that the only person suitable was not available until Monday as they were on holiday. Natalia's eyes moved from one to the other as they spoke but it was clear she had no idea what they were saying. Trump sat down opposite her and pulled out his diary again. He underlined Monday.

"You come back then?" He tapped the date and she shrugged. He pointed at her. "You come back here." He waved his arms then pointed at the floor. "THEN." He tapped the date again.

Natalia leaned forward and tapped Saturday and Sunday. She looked at him as she said simply, "Why?"

Trump leaned forward and buried his face in his hands,

"Oh God, it will be Monday by the time I explain this." He groaned. "Do you think I could get social services to help out? Are there any hostels around here?"

"What, on a Friday afternoon? Don't talk rubbish. We don't even know she's in real trouble, so see if you can find out who the father is," Meredith suggested. "You don't know, he might not even know about it. Sorry, Trump, I can't waste any more time. Hang on a minute." He sat back at the table and scribbled something quickly on the pad and turned it to face Natalia.

Natalia looked at the three matchstick people. The middle one had an arrow pointing to it with her name printed above it. Meredith nodded at her, and pointed to the representation of her.

"Natalia." He pointed to her and back to the drawing. "Baby." He pointed at the smallest figure and then at Natalia's stomach. She smiled at him. He then pointed at the largest figure and said, "Father" before drawing a question mark above its head.

"Tony," Natalia announced.

Meredith pushed back his chair and stood up. "I'll be back. Stay here," he muttered as he left the room and rushed to the incident room. He picked up the photographs of Anthony Wilson and his four law-breaking friends and took them back to Natalia. Her eyes widened as she looked along the row.

"Father?" Meredith asked, and she pointed to the photograph of Wilson.

Meredith slumped back in his chair. Having seen the bruising on Wendy Straker he didn't fancy her chances if Wilson found she had been to the police station. His problem was what to do with her.

"Trump, get back on the phone and see if there are any places for a couple of days in one of the women's hostels. There are a couple about, I really must-" He stopped speaking as Natalie leaned forward and tapped the photograph of Toby Samson.

"He take baby," she said quietly. Meredith stood up and his chair scraped the floor noisily.

"Oh for God's sake, this goes from bad to worse. Does she mean has taken or will take? Get her down to the Doc and have a pregnancy test sorted. Then you make sure she's safe for the night, and we'll see what we can sort on Monday," he looked at his watch. "I have a plane to catch tonight."

"Oh right, going anywhere nice?" Trump enquired.

"Paris. In February, can't wait." Meredith left the room, then remembering something he walked back and put his head around the door. "And don't forget *Crimebusters*. I'll let you know what time you have to be there, but sort out with downstairs what you need to have."

As Meredith walked back into the incident room Seaton looked up, and walked purposefully towards him.

"A word, Gov." He nodded to Meredith's office and once they were both in he closed the door.

Meredith frowned. "What's the problem?"

"Dawn Jessop, she rang about twenty minutes ago, said she was returning your call. Please tell me I haven't got this right." He shook his head in disappointment.

"Sit down, Seaton, stop being dramatic." Meredith sat and glanced at his diary. He called Dawn Jessop again, this time she answered.

"Dawn, I'd say it was nice to hear your voice but I'd be lying. I'm sending a chap over to you on Monday, Louie Trump. Help him sort this slot we've got for the Andrew Short stabbing and no buggering about."

Meredith grinned at Seaton and held the receiver a little way away from his ear as she responded. He then waited for a moment, and once she had stopped ranting he replied, "Because if you don't help me, on this, and any other case we have on the show, you will lose your job. Not a threat, just a promise. You really don't want me to take the gossip about Danny Cryer and how he obtains witnesses addresses and the like any further, do you? Oh and by the way, that will stop too." This time he didn't have to hold the receiver away, Dawn Jessop was silent. Eventually she spoke and he nodded as he signed off. "Glad to hear it." He then replaced the receiver and Seaton shook his head.

"I'm not even going to ask." He stood to leave. "The girls are back, let's hope they got somewhere." He watched Patsy and Jo remove their coats, and turned back to Meredith. "I also hope that little stunt doesn't backfire on you." He pointed at the phone before calling out to the two women. "Any luck, ladies?"

CHAPTER TEN

July 2011

Stella Young tapped on the door and entered. Her doctor smiled as he greeted her. "Ms Young, come on in, take a seat." He nodded at the chair to the side of his desk. "We have the results of the tests back."

Stella sat and crossed her legs. "Tell me it's something easy to sort out. I have two new branches opening next week." Her smile was smug. "Although, I have to say I am feeling a bit better now, but as you've called me in I have assume there is something wrong." She looked at him expectantly and he beamed at her.

"Well, it's congratulations all round then." He continued to smile as he spoke. Stella frowned wondering what he could mean. He leaned forward and patted her arm. "You are pregnant, Ms Young. We will need to arrange a scan, but looking at my notes from our last meeting it would appear you're about five months gone." He beamed again but his smile fell away at the look of utter disbelief on Stella Young's face. He sighed. Another thirty-something failing to take adequate precautions. Resting his elbows on the arms of his chair he linked his fingers and swivelled the chair to face her. "I can see this has come as something of a shock. I'm sure if you go home and take a couple of days to think about it, you'll come round to the idea. After all," he swivelled back and squinted at his computer screen, "you are thirty-seven now."

"Your tests are wrong," Stella announced confidently. She tutted and looked at her watch. "I don't know what's happened here, whether you have mixed up my results or something, but I am not pregnant. Was there anything else you have to tell me? I'm a busy woman, Dr Abraham, and can't waste this sort of time on erroneous results."

Her look was unforgiving, and the doctor leaned forward and peered at the screen again. He sighed as he scrolled through the results he had received. Looking up he shook his head.

"No, no, I don't think there has been any mistake." He turned back around and attempted another smile. "Perhaps you should just pop behind the screen and remove your trousers. I'll give you a quick examination. If you are five months pregnant, I'll be able to tell by examining you." He looked down at her stomach. She certainly didn't look five months pregnant, but then again it wasn't flat either. He looked back up at Stella and her stare was cold as was her tone.

"I am not pregnant. Not unless you believe in an immaculate conception, that is," her top lip curled in a half smile, "and I really don't think I have been chosen to bear the second coming."

"I understand that's what you might think, but I do assure you -" He was interrupted by Stella's snort of derision.

"Dr Abraham, please listen to me, and listen carefully." Her voice was commanding. She had swivelled on her seat and was tapping his desk with her index finger as she spoke. "I am gay, a lesbian, I bat for the other side, call it what you will. But unless I have a very, very, long gestation period, I am not pregnant. I have not had sex with a man since, ooh let me see now," she pulled back the sleeve of her jacket and looked at her watch, then raised her eyes to meet his, "about ten years." She sighed. "So I say again, I am not pregnant."

Stella Young stood and picked up the strap of her handbag, which hung from the back of the chair. "I think I should leave now. I will, however, expect you to find out the cause of this farce and get back to me before the week is out." She hoisted the strap over her shoulder.

Dr Abraham shook his head. He didn't care about her sexual orientation, but the woman was definitely pregnant. She had probably had a one night stand and now didn't know how to tell her partner. He jumped to his feet and placed a hand on her arm.

"If that's the case then I really do think I should examine you, because we know something isn't quite right, don't we?"

He pulled his hand away as she looked at him coldly.

"Are you patronising me? Do you think that perhaps I've been screwing men and I am in denial of some sort?" She spat the words at him, and he looked away guiltily. But still he held his hand towards the examination bed.

"I am not patronising you, of course not. I am happy to arrange for another doctor or a nurse to either carry out the examination, or to observe," his tone was soft, "but I think we need to resolve this. What harm can it do?"

Stella considered this. She had nothing to lose, and she would have something to use against this idiot should the need arise. She nodded curtly and he held the curtain back.

"Splendid, just step behind the curtain and remove your trousers. You can keep your pants on. Pull your top up, and cover yourself with the sheet. I'll be back in a few moments, once I've found someone to assist."

He pulled the curtain across the bed as Stella stepped forward, and it shielded her from the room. Shaking his head, he went in search of an assistant.

Fifteen minutes later, Dr Abraham stepped back from the bed and raised his eyebrows at the nurse before turning back to Stella.

"Well, you are definitely pregnant. It might not be as much as five months though, the baby doesn't feel that advanced. I think we should get you scanned as soon as possible. Get yourself dressed and the nurse here can log into the hospital and get you an appointment.

Three days later, Stella climbed into her Mercedes and turned the key in the ignition. She pushed a button to lower the roof, and whilst she listened to the hum of the electric motor she stared at the grainy image of the child she was carrying. Her pregnancy was too advanced for a termination to be considered.

Now, seven months later, aware that she must trace her child's father, Stella tapped the Grainger's business card on her desk. Sighing deeply, she picked up the phone and dialled the number.

CHAPTER ELEVEN

Patsy brushed down her coat and took a deep breath before entering the Graingers' office. She had been there several times since agreeing to join them, but today was her first day as an employee, a partner in fact. She grinned and pushed the door open.

Chris Grainger was on the telephone. The caller was obviously verbose and his pencil flew across the pad in front of him. He looked up and waved her in and then tapped his cup and nodded. Patsy raised her eyebrows; this was going to be home from home. Chris had obviously taught Meredith all he knew. She smiled at him and picked up his mug. Making her way to the kitchen, she eyed the door to her right, and grinned again. Sharon had insisted on having it sign-written and her name had been stencilled on it: "Patsy Hodge Partner".

When she returned with the drinks Chris was putting some papers in a brief case. He opened his top drawer, took out a small camera and placed it on top of the case. He then clipped it shut and put it by the side of his desk. He held out his hand for the coffee.

"Patsy, I can't tell you how pleased I am that you're here today. Sharon's got this awful stomach bug and I think she'll be off all week." He took a swig of his drink. "You're going to have to meet with Stella Young. Nasty lady, Sharon was going to do it and . . ." He slapped his forehead. "Sorry, Patsy, I quite forgot. How was Paris?" He returned Patsy's grin.

"Paris was fabulous. I will tell you all when we have time. So, who is this woman and what does she want?" She pulled out the chair in front of his desk and sat down.

"I have no idea. I met her briefly when I was looking into how your stalker was getting in. You remember, we told you she sacked the girl that left Branning alone with the keys. I gave her my card as you do, and last week out of the blue she called. She wanted Sharon to go to her, but Sharon didn't like her tone and insisted that she come here for the initial consultation." He shook his head.

"We've never done that before. Anyway, she wouldn't say what it was about. She's due in at ten so brace yourself."

He glanced up at the clock. "Right, I need to make a few calls before I leave. I doubt I'll be back today but you can get me on the phone. Why don't you go and settle yourself in to your new office?" He smiled at her. "And as the Americans would say, 'Welcome aboard'. Seriously, Patsy, it's really good to have you. Sharon's left you some notes to help you out, by the way."

He rolled his eyes as Patsy left him but not before teasing him about his awful American accent.

She closed the door behind her, and stood with her back resting on it as she surveyed her new office. The walls were white, and the carpet was a burnt red colour, which matched the main office. The dark wood, kidney-shaped coffee table matched the smart-looking desk in the corner. Behind the desk sat a large leather executive chair, which Sharon had insisted on. Patsy thought she might just disappear into it. Two small couches sat on each side of the coffee table. Patsy knew that in the tall wooden cabinet she would find an array of magazines ranging from *Hello!* to *What Car?* to ensure all customers' tastes were catered for.

She walked to her desk and her fingers skimmed the smooth wood. Switching on her computer she pulled the small file from her bag and placed it in the centre of the desk. The screen lit up and after a few seconds a diary page appeared. She noted that Stella Young's appointment had been moved to her column, and that Chris had to be in Leeds by eleven o'clock. Pulling open the top drawer, she found a file on which Sharon had written "Crucial Information" and in brackets underneath, "unless you need to change it". Patsy smiled and opened the file. It contained several lists outlining the charging structure for the various jobs they might undertake, how to explain and then charge expenses, and a small list of who to always say no to. Patsy was attempting to memorise the various charges when Chris tapped on her door.

"Right, I'm off. Penny will get in about quarter to ten and stay until around four. She takes half an hour's lunch break at midday if we can spare her. Good luck and enjoy. Oh, and don't forget you can refuse to take on whatever Stella Young wants if you're not comfortable with it."

Patsy thanked him and watched him disappear before returning her attention to the lists. Ten minutes later the telephone rang. She swallowed as she looked at the flashing button on the handset, and she realised she was nervous. She picked up the receiver and pushed the button.

"Patsy Hodge, Grainger and Co. How may I help?" She heard the sing song tone to her voice and frowned, that would have to go.

The caller was a new client, who believed one of his staff was stealing from him, but he didn't know who or how to prove it. He wasn't sure if they dealt with that type of thing. Patsy assured him that they did and suggested he come into the office for an initial consultation. She smiled as she did so, that would be twice now that Grainger and Co had insisted on an initial consultation at the office. Patsy was hoping to fit him in the next day when Chris would be around, but he insisted it was urgent and wanted to come in that afternoon. Patsy clicked into the diary and made an appointment for two thirty, thanked him, and blew her fringe up as she replaced the receiver. Today was certainly going to be a baptism of fire.

The next hour or so passed quickly as she acquainted herself with on-going cases Chris had left out for her. Before she knew it, Penny tapped on her door and announced the arrival of Ms Young.

Patsy pulled a new pad from her drawer and placed it on her desk, together with a new pencil. She then stacked the other files neatly to one side and went to greet her first client. She walked into the main office with more confidence than she felt, and held out her hand.

"Good morning, I'm Patsy Hodge, nice to meet you. Please come through."

The woman was dressed in a well-cut trouser suit under which was a silk blouse. She wore high stiletto heels, which caused her to tower head and shoulders above Patsy. Her auburn hair was cut in a neat bob, and it swayed as she shook Patsy's hand firmly. She followed Patsy into the office. Patsy held her hand out towards the seating area.

"Please take a seat. Can we get you a drink? Tea, coffee, water . . ."

"I'll have water please, and I'll sit at the desk. I'm here to do business, not have a coffee morning." Stella Young walked to Patsy's desk and sat in one of the two chairs in front of it. She placed her handbag on the other.

Patsy grimaced at Penny as she asked her to bring the water, and then went and sat opposite her first client.

"How can we help you, Ms Young?" She pulled her pad to the centre of the desk, and picked up her pencil. Patsy watched Stella Young draw in a deep breath as she mentally structured what she was going to say.

"Let's wait for the water to arrive." Stella smiled a thin-lipped smile, and looked towards the door.

Whilst she waited Stella Young took an envelope from her bag, removed the contents and read them. She made no attempt at small talk. She looked up as Penny came into the room and watched her place the tray on the end of Patsy's desk. Once Penny had closed the door, Stella leaned forward, and passed the document she had been reading to Patsy.

"I need you to read and sign this before we speak."

Patsy quickly scanned the document. It was a basic, but thorough, confidentiality agreement. Patsy was to agree that no aspects of the case would be shared with any individual outside of Grainger and Co, and only then on a need to know basis, unless express permission had been received from Stella Young. Patsy raised her eyebrows and smiled briefly. She then drew in a deep breath and placed the document on the desk and smoothing it flat, she responded to the request.

"Ms Young, without knowing what it is that you want us to do, it is impossible to sign this document. If you could provide a basic outline, it might help me to decide. I do hope you understand that." She watched Stella's impassive face form a frown.

"Why? You sign the document and I will tell you what I require. If you don't want or feel unable to do the job, I'll find someone that does. But you mention the detail of our discussion to anyone and I will sue your arse off." She had stopped frowning but held Patsy's gaze. "And I promise you that is not an idle threat. I don't waste my breath, Miss Hodge, so please don't waste my time. I fail to see what relevance the detail of the case has to you signing that agreement."

Patsy had to force a smile before responding. "You may wish us to do something which is not lawful, which in itself, depending on what that is, may not be a problem. However, I should advise you that until last week I was a serving police officer and my partner is still a police officer. Therefore, should we come across, let's say serious criminal activity, I would have no option but to report that to the police." She shrugged, "I'm sorry but that's the way it is."

"Define 'serious'." Stella's lips had almost formed a smile.

"Drugs, money laundering, serious assault," Patsy began, and then paused. "I don't know whether I am able to give a definitive answer."

"But you wouldn't mind going through someone's rubbish and looking at post you may find there? You wouldn't mind entering a building uninvited if you thought what you wanted was in it?" Stella scratched her head. "Or perhaps entering someone's garden or land to get a photograph, uninvited? You see I believe all these things fall outside of the law, but they are things your profession must do every day and worse." Stella picked up her glass and sipped the water. Then inclining her head, she looked back at Patsy. "What if I asked you to collect personal items from some people, nothing that would harm them, nothing of value, and nothing that they would even miss?"

"I would probably say yes. But I still need some form of exemption on this agreement." Patsy patted the paper beneath her hand.

Stella Young was silent for a moment considering her options. Eventually, she suggested, "Shall we agree that you add 'with the exception of any information of law breaking which may cause harm or danger to others, which may be reported to the police'? Would that satisfy you?"

Stella smiled now it was Patsy's turn to consider her position. Patsy thought that she should smile more often. Aware that with that exception inserted, a myriad of possibilities were covered, and there was very little that she couldn't make fit that description, Patsy nodded her agreement.

"That sounds most reasonable to me. Would you like me to hand write it in and we shall both sign the amendment, or do you want it typed?"

Stella thought about this for a moment. "Typed I think. Draft it out and get your girl to type it," she instructed crisply.

Patsy nodded and quickly jotted down the amendment and handed it to her client.

"Will this be acceptable?" she asked and when Stella nodded she excused herself and took it out to Penny, closing the door behind her.

"Quick, get Chris on the phone and read this to him asap. If he's all right with it, type it up, and bring in two copies please." Penny had already picked up the receiver to dial out. "You're a star Penny, thank you."

Patsy walked slowly back to her office.

"Penny is on the telephone at the moment, but shouldn't be too long. Is there anything I can get you whilst you wait?"

"No thank you. Would you say you are trustworthy, Ms Hodge?" Stella asked.

"Of course, what an odd question." Patsy was becoming irritated with her new client.

"Why did you leave the police force?" Stella continued.

"Because my boss became my partner, a recipe for disaster, and I wanted the challenge of doing something less restrictive. Is it important?" Patsy watched Stella shrug.

"Why didn't you just transfer somewhere else? Did you not want a career?"

"For many, many reasons, but is it of relevance?" Patsy was now annoyed at the inference, and was relieved when Penny came back in with the documents, which she handed to Stella. Stella read them quickly, nodded and handed them to Patsy.

"Right, let's sign this and get on. Time is money," Stella paused to smile at Patsy, "for both of us." Stella pulled a pen from a slot inside her bag and signed the agreements. She passed them across to Patsy who did the same. "Now, if you're ready I will tell you what I require."

Patsy pushed the agreement she had just signed back to Stella, and pulled the pad in front of her. She smiled at Stella who leaned back in her chair and crossed her legs. Placing one hand on top of the other she rested them on her knee. Patsy hoped that the excitement bubbling away inside of her didn't show as she waited for Stella to begin.

"I want you to find the father of my son," Stella began. Patsy began to make notes. "It won't be easy. In fact, it could prove impossible. However, I am willing to do whatever it takes to track him down. There is a six-week slot during which I will have conceived. I have a list of possibilities, and I will need you to obtain their DNA. I already have some samples, but I'll come to that. I'll need you to get their DNA tested against my son's, and if we are unsuccessful we will go back to that period and see what else comes up." She paused and Patsy finished her notes and looked up. "Is that clear?" Stella's face was impassive, and she gazed relentlessly at Patsy. "I am assuming you have facilities to hand that are able to test DNA? I would hate to have any further delays."

Patsy smiled and nodded confirmation. Stella was an attractive, well-presented woman, but unless her demeanour had changed recently, Patsy found it difficult to believe she had bedded so many men that she didn't know where to start looking for the father of her son.

"I am assuming that if you already have some samples from which DNA can be established, you are still in touch with some of your lovers? How long ago was this by the way?" Patsy asked, pencil poised to jot down the answer.

"A year ago, maybe a little longer. And, Ms Hodge," Stella leaned a little closer to the desk, and she clasped her shin with her hands, "we are not looking for a lover. We are looking for a rapist."

Patsy's head jerked upright. "I am so sorry, but I really don't understand. I am assuming the police have been unsuccessful but -" She stopped as Stella raised her hand.

"Ms Hodge, the police have not been involved, nor will they be."

"But why? If you believe you know who it might have been, why would you not report him?" Patsy was tapping her pencil lightly against her pad. She had never heard anything so ridiculous. Unless of course, the woman wanted to find the man and take her own revenge. Whilst this may be more rewarding to the victim, it wasn't something Patsy thought she could condone. Suddenly something clicked and she pointed at Stella Young with her pencil.

"You said a year, possibly more. Now that doesn't add up. I think you need to start at the beginning." Realising she was still pointing at Stella she slowly lowered her pencil.

"In July, last year, I was told I was pregnant. As I had no idea when I conceived, their best guess was between four and five months. When Sebastian was born, he was very small and this clouded the issue still further. Therefore, the best guess is that I conceived in a six-week period in March to April last year. If we are unsuccessful, we can extend the period you need to check." She nodded curtly as though that explained it.

Patsy was shaking her head. "I understand the confusion on the dates due to the birth weight, but how do you not know when you were raped?"

"One has to assume I was drugged. I remember absolutely nothing about it." Stella inclined her head a little. "You do know that that happens, don't you?"

Patsy bristled as the sarcasm was unnecessary. "Of course, but most woman know that something happened, or if they are not sure, at least when it may have. I am assuming you didn't have a lover at this time or that he has been tested and is not the father?"

"I had several lovers during that time, but none were male, and therefore that gives me a little bit of a problem. Would you not agree?" Stella sighed and glanced at her watch.

Patsy nodded absently. Her mind was racing with all sorts of questions, but she decided to hold back for the time being rather than irritate Stella any more than she appeared to be already.

"So how have you obtained the samples you have so far?"

"Most of them are my employees." Stella raised her eyebrows at the look of shock on Patsy's face. "Ms Hodge, the majority of men I meet are through my business activities. I do of course have male relatives, a male hairdresser, a male postman, do I need to go on?" She shook her head as though Patsy was dense. "I have been working on the basis of opportunity as that seemed more logical."

"Quite, and please call me Patsy. There is one other thing I need to know before we agree terms on this case." Patsy looked directly at her and held her gaze. "If we are successful what do you plan to do with the information? It would appear you are not in need of child support so I am not quite sure what you are hoping to achieve."

"I would like to watch him die a slow and painful death, but I need him alive. Sebastian has a rare liver disorder and whilst he is responding well to treatment, there may come a day when a transplant is the only viable option," she sighed deeply and closed her eyes momentarily, "but one of those nasty little quirks of nature means that a donation from me is unlikely to succeed. And I'm told on that basis the father is highly likely to be a perfect match," Stella lifted her hands in a helpless gesture, "so the irony is that I need him to be fit and healthy."

Patsy had no idea how to respond. She couldn't imagine a much worse situation for the woman, and any form of condolence would seem hollow, so she nodded curtly and smiled.

"Right, now I know how important this is, the sooner we get on with it the better." Patsy opened her bottom drawer and pulled out the Grainger and Co terms and conditions, and then from the appropriate coloured sling she took a list of charges for various services that might be undertaken. She scrolled down the list. "Ah, as I thought, there are no set fees on lab tests so we will just charge you cost for that." She looked up at Stella who nodded agreement. "I'm unsure as to whether they have a lab that they use regularly, but I have a friend who is a pathologist and he will be able to point me in the right direction. I will have to explain what I want, but not for whom. I'm assuming that's acceptable?" Again, Stella nodded, and Patsy stood and smiled at her. "Right, please have a read through these and let me know if there is anything you aren't happy with. I'll just get the card machine; you will appreciate that we do take part of our fee in advance. But for me to work that out I'll need more detail on the likely time scale. I'll leave you to read through the contract for a moment."

Patsy closed the door quietly behind her and put her thumbs up to Penny, who grinned back at her. She picked up the machine and waved it at her.

"Will I cope with this?" she asked.

"Of course. Go and take your first fee." Penny punched the air and Patsy curtseyed.

Stella was signing the contract as she walked back into the office and she tapped it with her pen.

"I've signed this and correct me if I'm wrong, but three thousand pounds in advance should more than cover half the fee." Stella pulled her purse from her bag and selected a card.

Patsy placed the card reader on the desk and pulled her pad towards her. "That depends on how long this is likely to take. How did you reach that figure?"

Patsy was playing for time as she had no idea how to make this calculation. To her mind the job would take as long as it took. She doubted it would be a full-time role and wished that Chris was here to guide her. She mentally crossed her fingers hoping Stella wouldn't realise this.

Stella sighed, hoping she wasn't going to have to negotiate. She knew she could wipe the floor with Patsy on that front, and she just wanted the job done and quickly. Her instincts told her that Patsy would deliver.

"I already have six samples ready for you. I will arrange for you to come and work with me, and come into contact with as many men that I think may be . . ." Stella paused, looking for the correct word but gave up and shrugged, "let's just say, responsible. We should be able to do that in four days, assuming none of them are on holiday or unavailable of course, and not necessarily consecutive. We may then have to arrange other situations where you can come into contact with those that are not connected with my work. Some of that may be in the evenings. Taking your daily rate and out of hours charges, and knowing that I will pay your full expenses during that period, I can see no reason why three thousand pounds should not be at least fifty per cent of your fee. Even with the laboratory charges. We aren't going to haggle, are we, Ms, I'm sorry, Patsy."

Stella smiled but it was purely a movement of her mouth. The rest of her face remained impassive. Patsy returned the smile and nodded, deciding that she would rather have a telling off from Chris than argue with Stella Young right at this moment. She passed the machine to Stella who inserted her card.

"Splendid, we both need to make some arrangements. I suggest you start work at my Clifton branch on Wednesday. But you can come and see me early tomorrow morning to pick up the samples I already have and agree a strategy. I will leave you with copies of my diary for the relevant period so you can peruse them and ask any questions you may have tomorrow."

Stella punched in her PIN and passed the machine to Patsy. It chugged out a receipt which Patsy tore off and held out to her. Stella slid it into her purse and took out a business card. She looked at Patsy and then pointed to the machine.

"You need to press enter again to get your copy."

For the first time, Patsy saw a genuine smile from the woman sat before her. She grinned. "Sorry, I'm new to being paid for what I excel at." Patsy delivered this with a confidence she didn't feel. She watched Stella smirk and then look away to scribble something on the rear of the card. Stella held it out.

"My business details on the front and my home address on the rear. I'll see you at home at seven thirty tomorrow morning. I'll leave you with this." Stella stood, lifted her bag on to the desk, and took out a large envelope which she handed to Patsy. "It's not exciting reading. I've made notes in red with my thoughts where applicable."

"Thank you. I'll get onto this straight away, and sort a lab out." Patsy held out her hand, "See you tomorrow."

Patsy showed Stella Young to the door and stood watching her for a while as she made her way to the car park. A feeling of excitement was competing with a nervousness she had not felt for a long while. She walked calmly back to her office and recovered the card machine and receipt to give to Penny. Penny smiled as Patsy approached her desk, and giggled as Patsy held her hand up for a high five.

"I am officially a private investigator," she beamed at Penny. "Now all I have to do is deliver. I feel we should have champagne, but tea will do. Can I get you one?"

An hour later, Patsy was still making notes on the copy of Stella Young's diary. The woman certainly had a busy life. Both business and social appointments filled most dates during the period in question. Her mobile rang and she was pleased to see Frankie was returning her call.

"Hi, Frankie, thanks for coming back to me so quickly. How are you?" She smiled as she spoke.

Patsy had a soft spot for Frankie Callaghan. She had worked with him on a murder enquiry which unbeknown to them had involved his family. If it hadn't been for Meredith, she may well have had a relationship with him.

"Pats. How splendid to hear from you. I have news, but first tell me what you want. You sounded so cloak and dagger. It must be this new job."

"I'm well, Frankie, thank you. Yes, it's the job. I've been thrown in head first and need you to point me in the right direction. I have to get some DNA tests done, it's for a paternity case, and for reasons which I cannot divulge there are going to be quite a few of them. Who can I use that is quick, effective and reasonable?"

"Hmm. There are several that spring to mind. How many are there likely to be and how quickly do you need the results?" Patsy noticed that Frankie's voice had taken on a professional tone.

"Upward of fifty is my best guess," Patsy heard Frankie take a sharp breath, "but I wanted to send them through in batches, because I still have to collect most of the samples."

"What type of girl is . . . no sorry, I won't ask. Actually, I will. More than fifty? How on earth is that possible? Patsy Hodge, is your client a lady of the night?"

"No, but she doesn't know who impregnated her. It could be one of many men that she works with."

"Ah, an office party gone wrong then?" Frankie paused for a response.

"Possibly, yes. Can you help Frankie? I'm picking up the first samples tomorrow morning."

"Of course. What sort of samples are they, and how are you going to collect the rest?"

Patsy didn't have the answer to that question, but Frankie was probably the best man to advise her. She smiled knowing he wanted to get involved. It was far less exciting or challenging than his normal work. She was relieved to have him working with her.

"Not sure, only met the client today. I'll know more tomorrow. What are the best samples for me to collect? And it needs to be collected covertly. The client doesn't want this publicised in any way."

"Ah well, the best would be blood or saliva swabs. Difficult if you are unable to be open about this. Is there any way she could rope in her HR department?"

"I'm sure she can. Why?" Patsy asked hesitantly, wondering where he was going with this. Frankie gave a short laugh.

"Some companies these days will have a clause in their contract with regards to random drug testing. They can't enforce it, of course. It would be something like employees will submit to random drug tests, but if she can get urine samples from all male employees, then you could test for DNA too. Not quite cricket, but I'm assuming you don't much care on that front."

"Not a lot, no," Patsy was grinning. That would make things a lot quicker and easier. "So, the name of the company?"

Patsy scribbled the details down on her pad and thanked him once more.

"Oh, what was your news, now we have the business stuff out of the way?"

"Sarah has agreed to be my wife. We are engaged to be married," Frankie announced proudly. "Probably going to have a bit of a do, but only asked her last night so it's all very new. We're buying the ring this afternoon. On that note I'd better get a move on. Give my best to Meredith. I'll call you soon just to see how you are doing."

"Oh, Frankie, that's wonderful. Congratulations! Give my love to Sarah, and let me know when the party is. Thanks for your help Frankie, I owe you a pint."

Thirty minutes later Patsy had spoken to Stella Young, who confirmed she did have such a clause in her contract, and would work out how best to implement it. Patsy had also spoken to the contact Frankie had recommended, and ordered the necessary kits from the laboratory. She had surprised herself by negotiating a reduced cost due to the volume of tests she was likely to need. She smiled contentedly as Penny stuck her head around the door.

"I'm popping out to the shops. Do you want me to grab you a sandwich? Your next client is due in an hour. Oh, and by the way Chris called in and was really chuffed with the new case. He said I was to pass on his congratulations and that he would call you tonight." She smiled as Patsy waved her in.

"I could eat a horse, but a sandwich will do. You can also buy us each the largest bun they have. We're celebrating. Lunch is on me." She pulled a note from her purse and handed it to Penny. She was about to ask if they had heard from Sharon when her telephone rang. Meredith was calling so she quickly thanked her and took the call.

"Hello, I wasn't expecting to hear from you today. How's the investigation going without me?"

"I just called to ensure you were enjoying your first day and not dying of boredom." He lowered his voice, "And, of course, to check if you had your knickers on."

Patsy could hear the amusement in his voice, but still her stomach did a little somersault. Meredith could have that effect on her, even on the telephone.

"I do, but that can be remedied before I come home, if you like. And for the record, I'm not bored, I've just taken on my first client, who I think will be a nightmare, but still, it's my first and I got three grand up front."

"Hmm. Well you can tell me all about that later, right now I'm concentrating on you walking through that door." He sighed. "Actually, I might be a little late, I'll have to let you know later when I know how things pan out."

"Are you on to something then?"

There was a slight pause before he answered, and Patsy wondered if he was considering if he should tell her or not. She didn't feel upset by that, as she had just been wondering how much she could tell him, given that she had signed the confidentiality agreement. She shook her head at the speed at which their world had changed.

"The bus driver came in today, and was presented with a different set of shots including several faces that we pulled together from those we had lying around. Guess who he came up with?" Meredith paused but not long enough for Patsy to speak. "Anna Carter. I'm awaiting her arrival now." Meredith heard Patsy gasp. "Just when you think you've hit a brick wall. Hang on a minute . . . right, got to go, she's here. I'll see you later." With that he terminated the call.

CHAPTER TWELVE

Meredith walked into the interview room and looked at Anna Carter. Her eyes darted over to him. She looked worried, as so she should. He pulled out a chair and sat next to Jo Adler, then reaching across the desk he pushed the buttons on the recorder.

"Anna, thank you for coming in again. Do you understand that you are still under caution?"

Anna nodded, and Meredith pointed to the machine and smiled.

"Yes," she said quietly, "but I don't know why."

"Would you like us to arrange a solicitor for you, Anna?" Meredith asked quietly.

"No. Why would I need one? Please tell me what's going on." Her voice was shrill and she placed her hands on the edge of the table that separated them and leaned forward. "Please tell me what it is you want? You're scaring me with all this caution stuff."

"Anna, we agreed last time we met that your ring was shown in one of the photographs taken on the number seventy-eight bus. You told us that it wasn't you on the bus, even though that ring was unique to you. We visited the jeweller as you suggested, and she has confirmed that it was a one-off design, and that she made the ring to fit the stone which had a natural shape. She remembered you; she called you Marilyn. And she confirmed that she'd not made anything similar."

Meredith leaned back in his chair and crossed his legs beneath the desk. "We have also spoken to the driver of that bus, and he thinks that you did get on the bus that day. We showed him in excess of fifty photographs and he chose you. Why would he do that if you weren't on the bus that day?" Meredith paused for her to answer.

Anna was shaking her head before she spoke. "I don't know. I wasn't there." She looked at Jo Adler. "You believe me, don't you? Why is it important anyway? It wasn't me, but what if it was? Why do you want to know?" Anna's concern was manifesting itself as anger and she issued her last question through clenched teeth.

"Because around one o'clock that day, someone walked up to a young man called Andrew Short and stabbed him. He died instantly." Meredith's face was grave. "From the eyewitness accounts, we have of that person, we have located them on CCTV. We followed them from Corn Street down to the centre, and across to the bus stop outside the Hippodrome. We then see them board the number seventy-eight bus. At the same time, the CCTV from the corner of Colston Street shows them boarding the bus, the camera inside captures their hands as they pay their fare. They were your hands. With your ring."

Anna's hands flew to her mouth and then dropped back down to the table. "No. No, they were not. They were not," she gave a strangled sob. "Why are you saying this?"

"The next day you go to work as normal and someone shoots you. Why did they do that, Anna? Was it revenge because they knew you had stabbed Andrew Short? Were you in some way involved with the drugs racket he was part of? Tell me, Anna, what was your connection to him? I can understand the pay back element, but I've yet to understand why you would want Andrew Short dead."

"I don't. I didn't. I don't even know him. I saw it on the news, but it wasn't me." Her bottom lip trembled and she swallowed. "I think I want a solicitor now. You're trying to blame me for something just because of a ring. I didn't do it and I want to go home."

Meredith sighed and exchanged glances with Jo Adler. "Interview suspended at two thirty pm. A duty solicitor will be sourced for Ms Carter." Meredith stopped the recording and looked at Anna. "DC Adler will find you a duty solicitor as quickly as possible and then we will speak again. Can we get you some coffee or water?"

Anna shook her head. "No but I want a cigarette please. Can I go and have a cigarette?"

Meredith nodded and jerked his head towards the door. "Come with me."

He strode down the corridor to the incident room, and Anna struggled to keep up with him. Meredith pushed open the door and called for Seaton to join them, and the three then made their way to the fire escape. Meredith lit a cigarette and passed it to Anna.

"Anna, Tom is here in case you say anything. A witness, okay?" Anna blinked, unseeing, out at the car park below as she smoked her cigarette. Meredith watched her closely, and she caught his gaze.

"I didn't do it, you know. I know you have to ask and all that, but it wasn't me." The first tear fell. "It wasn't me."

Meredith nodded and said quietly, "Then you need to work with me to prove it, Anna. Things are not looking good at the moment." He saw she was shivering. "Come on, let's get you a cup of tea and see how long the solicitor will be."

Meredith led the way back to the interview room. He ran his thumb and forefinger up and down his nose, pondering Anna Carter. He wasn't sure if he believed her, or if he just wanted to believe her.

Jo Adler came in as Anna took her seat at the table.

"A solicitor will be here in about an hour," she smiled at Anna. "Do you want a cup of tea and some biscuits?" Anna just wanted tea, and a uniformed officer stepped into the room with her to await the solicitor.

Meredith walked slowly back to his office. If it was Anna, then it shouldn't take long to track down who shot her. But if it wasn't, this case could run and run with so little to go on. He sighed and looked out at the incident room. There was little activity as most of the team were out trying to tie something to Anthony Wilson.

He frowned and walked to the door. "Where's Trump?" he shouted at no one in particular. Seaton looked up, clearly amused.

"In the canteen, Gov, he's with the ladies from Croatia."

"What?" Meredith demanded. Seaton merely shrugged and shook his head.

Meredith glared at him. But knowing he had some time to fill before he could speak to Anna again, he made his way to the canteen. He could do with something to eat, so he would kill two birds with one stone. He entered the canteen and looked around. It was fairly quiet and Trump and the two girls stood out like a sore thumb. Walking to the counter he ordered a pasty and a mug of tea. He took his tray and sat several tables away from Trump and the two women.

"Trump, a word."

He saw Trump's body language alter from very important person to someone caught in the act. He controlled the urge to grin. Trump dragged a chair out from under the table and sat opposite him.

"Hello, Sir. I'm sure you're wondering what I'm doing here with Natalia and Katrina. Katrina is Natalia's sister by the way and they won't be separated. To be quite honest with you, I'm asking myself the same question, but it seems I'm lumbered until the translator turns up."

"Hmm, what's the latest on that?" Meredith picked up his pasty and took a bite.

Trump glanced at the clock. "She should have been here an hour ago. These two were waiting at the front desk but they kept demanding to see me, so I was encouraged to bring them down here. It's damned hard work having a conversation in sign language, I can tell you. I'm shattered and I have a date tonight."

"Really, who's the lucky lady then? You are a fast worker. It must be your elegant sophistication, girls like a posh boy." Meredith sucked a lump of pasty from his lip. "Actually, don't tell me. How did you get on over at *Crimebusters?*" He picked up his tea and leaned back as Trump's face lit up.

"Rather well actually. I managed to get an extra minute of so out of them. Old Dawn was very helpful, she said she may even convince them to give us longer. Hopefully, we'll have a little bit more information before it goes out. I've got the outline on my desk, just didn't have time to get it to you before those two showed up again. I hope the hostel can take them again tonight, it was murder on Friday." He frowned and shook his head.

"Why, what happened on Friday?" Meredith finished his tea, and banged the mug back down on the table, preparing to move.

"I ended up with both of them on my sofa bed. They were quiet at first but once they got going, well, talking for England pales into insignificance when compared to Croatia." He rolled his eyes. "I'm so glad they found them a place for the weekend, and if I'm lucky, for tonight. It wouldn't do bringing a lady back with two young ladies traipsing around half naked." He smiled at the thought, and looked at Meredith knowingly.

Meredith shook his head.

"Are you naturally stupid or do you have to work at it?" Meredith had lowered his voice. "Those two, or Natalia at least, may become part of an investigation, and it wouldn't do if we have a member of the team shacking up with them. However innocent, and I am going to assume it was innocent."

"Of course it was. They had no room at the inn on Friday. What could I do? Send her back to Wilson? Mind you, I wasn't expecting her to bring her sister back with her when she went to get some things." Meredith's mouth twitched and Trump rolled his eyes and sighed. "Seriously, Sir, what do I do if there is nowhere for them to go tonight? I can't take them back again for many reasons, not least Dawn."

"Dawn?" Meredith spat out the name like an insult. Trump looked puzzled. He couldn't understand why Meredith was being so dense.

"Dawn Jessop, the girl from *Crimebusters*. She's a good sort and we're going for a drink tonight, and before you ask, she suggested it, not me."

Meredith ran his hands over his face and then looked at Trump. His lips pursed as he chose his words, not for subtlety, but for impact.

"I've been there and done that." He waited until the penny had dropped. "You will call her and cancel. She's bad news and as far from a good sort as it is possible to get. I won't paint you a picture, Trump. Suffice to say, this is an order and not advice or a request. That woman will eat you up and spit you out and not even notice your paths have crossed."

Meredith pinned Trump with his stare. "If you feel you should ignore my order, I will have you transferred, and I don't care who your bloody uncle is. Do we understand each other?" Meredith watched Trump nod solemnly and banged the table. "Good, well I've got an interview to get to, and you have two ladies to entertain, so I'll leave you to it."

Meredith left Trump contemplating the call he needed to make to Dawn Jessop and returned to the interview room and Anna Carter. He wondered why life was so painful sometimes, and why it was him that had been lumbered with the Super's nephew. He found Jo Adler leaning on the wall.

"Has the duty guy turned up yet?"

"Duty lady actually," Jo raised her eyebrows. "To be honest she doesn't look old enough to have left school, but she seemed efficient."

Meredith stepped forward and peered through the viewing panel. The duty solicitor sat holding Anna's hand and was nodding as Anna spoke to her. Meredith had not seen her before. He knew he wouldn't have forgotten her. She was petite and had a mop of fuzzy ginger hair that had all but managed to escape the lime green scarf intended to pull it back into a pony tail. Her black suit looked a little too big for her, and a large ladder in her tights climbed from her ankle to her knee. Anna glanced up at him causing the woman to turn towards him. She looked much the same age as Anna.

"Let's see if we can move this along then."

Meredith tapped, and then opened the door. He smiled at Anna and strode forward, his hand held out in greeting to the woman sat holding her hand. "DI John Meredith, let me know when you're ready to recommence the interview." He smiled at her.

"Jane Roscoe. We can get on now if you like, as Anna will be out of here in five minutes. Nice to meet you, DI Meredith."

Meredith detected a slight Scottish lilt to her accent. "Really?" He took a seat opposite and winked at her. "Come on then, do your worst."

Meredith smiled his most charming smile and held her gaze for a little longer than necessary. Noticing the slight flush hit her high cheekbones he looked away satisfied.

"As I understand it from Anna, you have all but accused her of stabbing one," she paused and looked at the legal pad in front of her, "Andrew Short. And all on the basis of a poor quality photograph taken of a ring. Now, I don't know how things work in your world, DI Meredith, but in mine that's not even close to circumstantial. I believe Anna has co-operated fully with the questions you have asked, and I can see no point in her staying here any longer if she can be of no help. So we'll be off as soon as you have given me a copy of the recordings of all your interviews to date with my client."

Jane Roscoe took a deep breath and nodded curtly. Meredith was surprised that she didn't hold her hand out for the recording. He nodded respectfully before leaning forward on the table, his eyes holding Roscoe's gaze once more, and they twinkled as he saw the flush reappear.

"Very succinct, Ms Roscoe," he inclined his head, "or may I call you Jane?" He smiled again. "Could you just touch on the fact that the bus driver identified Anna from over fifty photographs, chosen at random?" He remained still, his eyes not moving from her face.

She blinked several times and cleared her throat. "But of course, Anna has told me she catches a bus on that route every day to and from work. The driver will remember her as *a* passenger, and not as the person you are looking for." She tore her gaze away and looked down at her pad.

Meredith turned his attention to Anna. "I hope you feel more at ease now Jane is here to help you." He smiled as Anna nodded. Roscoe shook her head and tutted but didn't look at him. "Then I am sure Anna will not mind taking part in an identity parade. We have several witnesses including the bus driver who had a look at the person who stabbed Andrew Short. I'll get it organised then, shall I?" He smiled at Anna again.

"Yes, because it wasn't me, Mr Meredith. I know you believe that, so if this will help of course I will. When will it be?" Anna was smiling as she agreed, and Jane Roscoe met Meredith with a cold stare.

"I will want to approve those chosen to join Anna in the line-up, I'm sure you will understand that DI Meredith. I will also wish to be present, so plenty of advance warning as I'm a busy person."

Meredith smirked. "But of course, Jane, of course." He stood and looked at Anna. "It won't be today Anna I'm afraid, but we'll be in touch. Now, do you need a lift home? If so, Jo will organise that for you."

Meredith left the room closing the door behind him. Jo Adler shook her head at him.

"You did that on purpose. I wish I could make it work the other way around." She shook her head. "I take it you want me to get onto organising the line-up then?"

"Indeed, I do. Make sure they're all the same height and build, and all in jeans and grey hoodies. You might want to chuck some boys in for good measure. Anna is a pretty girl, I can't believe that those who think they saw who stabbed Andrew Short didn't mention it was a girl. And just what did I do on purpose?"

"Turned on the Meredith charm, incapacitated her momentarily. And don't say you don't know, I've seen it in action before."

Meredith raised his eyebrows. "I have absolutely no idea what you are talking about. Anna might need a lift home. Get it sorted so you can get on." He strode away. As he punched his code into the door at the end of the corridor Adler rushed to catch up with him.

"What if she wasn't wearing makeup? I've never seen her without makeup, but I know what every woman knows," Adler nodded at him. "It makes a big difference."

Meredith nodded thoughtfully. "Well I've seen her with little or no makeup on at the hospital, but you're right, go with that. Well done, Adler." He pushed open the door and went to his office.

Patsy thanked Penny for the tea and biscuits that she had just delivered and for her help that day. She asked her to leave her office door open so she could hear if anyone called for entry. She heard the main door click shut behind Penny, and pulled the notes from her previous client back to the centre of her desk. Lifting the receiver, she dialled Chris Grainger's mobile.

"Hi Chris, sorry to bother you, can you speak?"

Chris confirmed that he could. He was sitting in an airport arrivals lounge, and had twenty minutes to kill.

"Splendid. I've just seen my second new client of the day, and to be honest I got carried away when he offered a bonus of two thousand pounds if we can start next week. So I've taken two thousand as an advanced fee, but I'm not sure you'll believe that I should have. Although, I do have an idea of where to go with it."

"Tell me what he wants. I'm sure we can sort something. Penny told me it was a fraud."

"Yes, it looks that way. From the sound of it someone is ripping him off. He sells office supplies all over the south west and has sales people working on a self-employed basis dotted around his patch. They turn over big money; most of it is done online, but he still has these sales people that go out and ensure customers' needs are met. They all have access to both the ordering system and bank account, and supposedly on a restricted basis. It got a bit complicated when he explained how that worked. To be honest I think he's become so paranoid he can't see the wood for the trees, and he doesn't know who he can trust. He's been monitoring it for three months closely and -"

"Monitoring what?" Chris interrupted.

"I'm sorry, I'm not detailing this am I? He's been monitoring his bank account. He noticed about five months ago that the bank balance was down, but sales had not dropped and commission drawings by his sales chaps remained pretty much where he would expect them to be. When the balance dropped for the third month running he started matching one with the other and it doesn't make sense to him."

"Why doesn't he ask his accountant? Surely he reconciles the bank account if it's that big an enterprise?" Chris suggested. "I'm not saying we shouldn't get involved of course, a fee is a fee, but it doesn't sound like a job for us until that shows an anomaly."

"Well that's where his paranoia comes in. Tucker, that's his name, George Tucker, thinks this is a sleight of hand thing. The accountant worked with his IT consultant to set the system up. He says he asked them vague questions so as not to raise any alarms, and both said as you did, if the books balance, they balance. It could be a wild goose chase, of course."

"Hmm, whether or not there is something going on it sounds like a decent fee for us. You said you had some thoughts. What were they?" Chris stopped speaking and Patsy heard the nasal tones of a tannoy announcement. "They've just announced that the flight I'm waiting for has arrived, so if my chap shows I might have to go. Just keep talking."

"Okay, very quickly. I came into contact with this girl who is a computer wizard on a case I was working on. She works magic with spreadsheets and computer systems. She works via an agency as a rule, but I'm sure I could get her to take an interim look into this at least. Provided she's free. What do you think?"

"Sounds good to me, we would have had to bring someone in anyway . . . Listen, Patsy, I must go. They are coming through now. I'll call later."

Patsy replaced the receiver and smiled. She had only seen Linda Callow once since leaving hospital, and she thoroughly enjoyed her company. It would be good to speak to her, and even better working with her again. She dialled Linda's number.

"Copper number two! What can I do for you?" Linda answered the call on the second ring.

"Ha. Hi, Linda. Lots I hope, but for the record neither Tanya nor I are coppers anymore. How are you?"

Linda Callow had been working on an IT project for the local hospital, which became entangled in a police investigation. She had saved the two main contacts on her mobile as Copper number one and Copper number two. Tanya Jennings was now in prison and Patsy a private investigator.

"Noooo. You've left the police force? My God, did you kill someone too?" Linda had an excitable personality and screeched into the phone.

Patsy grinned and held it away from her ear.

"I didn't, but I am now a private investigator, and that's why I'm calling. I need your help, so how are you fixed at the moment?"

"OMG. I will have to think of a new name for you . . . no, no. I've got it. You are now PHPI – Patsy Hodge Private Investigator," Linda giggled. "It makes you sound like either an insurance policy or an STD. Ha! I'm sticking with it, I'm afraid. Let's start this conversation again. Hello PHPI, I'm bored stiff, but other than that well. You sound like you have an exciting life. How can I help you?"

Patsy repeated the information she had given Chris, but withheld the client's name. She knew Linda was taking notes, as she kept say "yep, yep" at the end of every sentence, but she didn't ask any questions.

When Patsy had completed the detail, she crossed the fingers on her free hand. "So what do you think? Are you free to help? He wants someone asap. I've agreed we'll start next Monday." Patsy held her breath.

"Am I free to get my deerstalker out? You're asking am I free?" Linda was clearly excited. "Actually no, but I will be. I'll give the agency a ring and get back to you in twenty minutes or so?"

"Of course, but don't do anything rash, Linda. I don't know how long this will take. We'll pay the going rate of course, but I don't want you to queer your pitch with anyone."

"Don't panic. They love me too much to let me go. Catchya later." With that she was gone.

Patsy took a deep breath and picked up her tea which was now almost cold. She grimaced but drank it anyway. Ten minutes later Linda rang back.

"PHPI, 'tis I, la Linda. I've spoken to the agency and they were of course devastated at losing me, but they can get someone here on Thursday. I can do a handover on Wednesday, so I'm all yours. Is this an hourly rate or fixed fee, by the way? Sorry, I hate doing the business stuff but one does have a mortgage and a dog to support." There was a short pause. "I suppose really I should have sorted that out first. What were you planning to pay me?"

"Oh dear. I have no idea. I assumed there was a going rate. Now you have to give me ten minutes. I'll call my partner Chris and get back to you. Don't worry, he won't try and get you to take less than the going rate. I've already explained how good you are."

"Like you'd know! It's not major. Between you and me I'd probably do it for the experience and to put it on my CV, as long as I won't starve. Call me later. Must dash for now as the boss is doing the rounds. Bye."

Patsy called Chris, but it went straight through to his answer machine. She hesitated for a moment and then called Sharon. Sharon answered immediately.

"Thank God. Civilisation. Patsy, how are you doing? Tell me all, I'm going mad here." Sharon's voice had a nasal quality. "I'm feeling very sorry for myself, although I think the tummy element of this bug is almost over."

"Oh poor you, you do sound awful. Do you want a full update or just the question I had?"

"Go for it chapter and verse. There is only so much daytime television a girl can take. I can't believe I wanted to retire. Mind you, I am abandoned at the moment." Sharon sneezed loudly. "Sorry about that, took me by surprise. Two new clients on day one I hear, most impressive, come on tell me all."

For the third time, Patsy gave details about George Tucker's case, and then the plans for Stella Young. She then came full circle and asked about remuneration for Linda.

"Well, if we know who we are using and therefore the quality of their work, we usually offer a high percentage of the overall fee. The split would be dependent on how much we had to do. But if it's a new contact like your friend Linda, we would make it a much lower split, and then give a bonus on a successful outcome. What is the fee likely to be on this one?" Sharon listened as Patsy explained the structure she had agreed. "Well there you go, that's easy. Give her forty per cent of the fee then add a grand to the bonus, and everyone should be happy. Patsy, I have to go, bye." Sharon hung up abruptly and Patsy stared at the phone and shook her head.

Patsy called George Tucker and explained that unexpectedly a case had come to a conclusion and she could get someone to him on Thursday. Tucker was not happy with that as too many people would know that something was going on. They agreed to meet at the Graingers' office again, and he assured her that he could log in remotely to demonstrate his problem, and would bring paperwork.

Patsy called Linda, and smiled at her greeting.

"PHPI so soon, I hope that means it's good news."

Patsy quickly explained the payment terms.

"PHPI, that sounds bloody marvellous, and a bonus too? Just one little detail you forgot to mention, forty per cent of what? Come on, don't tantalise." Linda laughed. Patsy smiled at her own excitement. Not only had she signed up two new clients, but she would be working with Linda too. She told her the fee agreed for the first forty hours. Linda whistled into the phone.

"That will do nicely. I'll see you Thursday then. Thanks for thinking about me." Linda had started to say goodbye when she remembered something. "Oh, don't go. I knew there was something else. When we were speaking earlier you said you had to consult your partner Chris. Now the last time I looked your partner was Meredith. Tell me you haven't dumped the hunk, Patsy," she laughed, "and if you have, could I have his number? Oh God, was that inappropriate, did he dump you?" She sounded worried and Patsy laughed out loud.

"No, I'm still with Meredith, and so the answer is no, you can't have his number," she joked. "I meant my business partner. Meredith and I are still very much together, thank you. See you Thursday."

Patsy smiled and leaned back in her chair and thought about Meredith. Their weekend away had not got off to a good start. Their late evening flight out of

Bristol had been delayed, and Meredith nearly refused to get on to what he called the toy aeroplane that was to fly them across the channel. He had not previously admitted his fear of flying. When they landed in Paris, the rain was torrential, and the taxi driver had dropped them off at the wrong end of the one-way street where their hotel was situated. They were soaked through by the time they reached it. Meredith had still been complaining when they eventually went to bed. The rest of the weekend had been wonderful, even if it was a little chilly.

They had visited all the places that they had planned to, and had eaten in some wonderful restaurants. They found a lovely bar on the corner of Avenue des Gobelins and Boulevard Saint Marcel, and Meredith had become hooked on their Mojito Royale cocktail. He had even promised the waiter they would come back later in the year. On the last morning, Meredith left her in the hotel to get ready, whilst he went in search of some cigarettes. He had been gone quite a while and she had become irritated at the waste of their weekend. Rather than sitting waiting in the hotel room, Patsy had decided to wait at the café next door to the hotel. She watched the world go by sitting wrapped up in her winter coat underneath the electric heater, and smiled as she watched him return. He was rushing up the street towards the hotel, his lips moving quickly. She knew that he was not just talking to himself, but complaining. She ordered him a coffee and grinned as he spotted her.

"Did you have trouble finding a tobacconist?" she laughed, as he plonked himself into the adjacent chair.

"None at all. It was finding one open that was the challenge. Nobody told me Paris closed on a Sunday. I had to walk miles." He accepted the tall glass of latte gratefully from the smiling waitress, and wrapped his hands around it until they could no longer bear the heat. "Right, we'll finish this and then we're off."

"Ooh, that sounds exciting, where are we going?"

"Notre Dame to start with, apparently it's walkable but we'll take the Metro just in case." He scooped some froth from the top of his drink with the spoon, and dabbed it on her nose. "I have a surprise for you." He smiled his lazy smile as her eyes widened in surprise. "Don't get too excited."

They walked around Notre Dame and agreed that it was a magnificent building. Meredith, who was in a particularly good mood, had even agreed to let other tourists take their photograph. They then walked to yet another café and Meredith smoked a cigarette and held her hand as they looked at the river.

Patsy was unable to remain patient any longer and squeezed his hand. "So what's the surprise? Here we are, and there is Notre Dame." She pointed at the cathedral, resplendent in the winter sunshine on the other side of the Seine.

Meredith's eyes twinkled and he stubbed out his cigarette. "Let me pay a visit, and we'll be off." He glanced at the bill and paid the required amount of euros, leaving quite a generous tip.

Patsy watched him disappear inside and waved at a couple waiting for an outside table to indicate that they were leaving. As she stepped onto the pavement she saw Meredith talking to a waiter who was gesticulating and speaking nineteen to the dozen. Patsy grinned knowing Meredith would not understand a word.

He rolled his eyes at her as he joined her at the pavement. "I think it's down here." He pointed along the river. "To listen to him, you would think I had asked directions to London. Come on."

They walked alongside the Seine with Meredith checking every sign that they passed until he found the right one.

"We're here," he nodded at the sign and Patsy looked up. "Pont des Arts"

"What happens now?" she smiled as she took in the collection of artists and their work trailing across the bridge over the Seine. "Can we go and look?"

"We can, but you will need this." Meredith handed her a black marker pen.

She took it frowning. "I can't draw you know. Please don't tell me you've got me here for something arty, because you can forget it. I've had the most wonderful weekend so far, and I'm not about to ruin it." Whilst she meant every word, her tone was light as she knew she would never see these people again.

Meredith laughed. "Don't be daft, come on." He pulled her up onto the bridge and pointed to one side.

Patsy squinted at the side of the bridge and noticed that hundreds of padlocks had been attached to the grill. She looked at Meredith, shrugged, and walked a little closer. She turned to him and grinned.

"Really?"

"Really," he replied and pulling his hand from his pocket he handed her a padlock. "I think you have to write on it, and then we fix it to the bridge." He kissed her forehead. "It's a symbol of our love. You then throw the key into the Seine meaning it can never be opened."

Meredith watched as Patsy's chin trembled and her eyes glistened. He pulled her to him and kissed her in a way that made a few tourists stop and applaud. Patsy flushed as he released his grip a little.

"I love you, Patsy Hodge, and I was planning on asking you to marry me, but I think that would scare you at the moment." His voice was husky and he raised his eyebrows at the elderly lady standing behind Patsy, who had stopped to watch, and indeed listen. The woman smiled and nodded at him to continue, and he grinned at her. "So here on a bridge over the Seine in Paris, freezing bloody cold, and in need of a pee, I am declaring my love for you. Write on the padlock."

The elderly lady applauded again and Meredith laughed with her. Patsy pulled the top from the pen with her teeth and wrote on the padlock. She handed it back to Meredith who read it and nodded. He walked across and locked it onto the bridge. He then handed the key back to Patsy who kissed it and hurled it into the Seine. The elderly lady applauded for the third time and leaned down to read the padlock.

"Johnny and Patsy Feb 2012– Eternity. Now that's nice," she said in an American accent. Walking forward she poked Meredith in the chest. "I've lived here in this city of love for almost thirty-five years, and that's probably the best proposal I never heard, if you know what I mean. Now go get a room." She winked at him and then walked away to speak to an artist. Patsy grabbed Meredith's hand and called to the lady. She led Meredith over to her. Patsy held the camera towards the artist.

"S'il vous plaît." He nodded and spent several minutes positioning them with the American. He took several different shots of the three of them posing. The one on which the American had hugged Meredith around the waist was Patsy's favourite photograph of the weekend.

Patsy's mobile rang, and brought her back to the present. She cleared her throat and answered it. Chris had noticed a missed call and was checking that everything was ok. Patsy quickly brought him up to date and he was delighted with the day's events. They agreed to catch up the next morning following Patsy's visit to Stella Young. Patsy hung up and looked at her watch and she decided to call it a day. She had had a wonderful first day in her new job, and now she wanted a wonderful evening. She was pretty sure that Meredith wouldn't let her down.

CHAPTER THIRTEEN

Michael Brent turned up the heating in the car and opened the window slightly. He took a cigar from the packet and lit it. Puffing the blue smoke into the car, he opened the window a little further. Holding the cigar between his teeth he watched Councillor Richard Hancock turn the corner and walk down the hill towards The Council House. He took another puff and flicked the ash out through the open window. Hancock was now walking up to the entrance of The Council House. Brent glanced at the clock, as always Hancock was bang on time. It was seven forty and by eight o'clock Hancock would be sitting at his desk, with a coffee and a Danish pastry, reading his emails.

Hancock placed his foot on the first step leading to the entrance when a woman called to him. He turned and smiled at her, and then waited for her to reach him. She grinned at him, tapped him on the arm, and then nodded and walked away. Hancock shook his head, bemused, there were some odd people about, and more of them seemed to be coming out of the woodwork since he had announced he would be running for Mayor of Bristol, later in the year. At least this one was pleased to see him. He continued the journey to his office with a grin on his face.

Brent pushed the cigar out through the gap in the window and onto the pavement, and before indicating to join the traffic he pushed the call button on his steering wheel. A grunt from Tony Wilson echoed in the car and he turned the volume down a little.

"I need you to arrange a meeting with Derek," he instructed, "and it has to be today. Hopefully, I'm off to get a little sun on my back for a couple of days."

"Nice. Where are you going?" Wilson was blinking rapidly in an attempt to wake himself up. He'd only been in bed three hours.

"Marbella if I can get the flights. Only three days, but long enough to keep the wife happy. I'll meet him this afternoon. About three o'clock at . . ." Brent slammed on his brakes and held his hand on the horn for far longer than necessary.

"Bastard taxi drivers, they don't look, and they don't indicate. I could have had my boy in the car." He shouted at the back of the taxi whilst gesturing with his free hand. He drew in a deep breath. "Are you still there?"

"Yes, boss." Wilson was now standing in his bathroom peeing into the toilet bowl. He was wondering why he had been woken at this ungodly hour if Derek was not required until three. Natalia hadn't turned up for work again last night, and he had visited other clubs well into the early hours of the morning hoping to track her down. He'd ended up banging on the door of her flat at four thirty in the morning, and that resulted in a row with a neighbour. After giving him a slap, he'd come home, and now he just needed some sleep.

"Three o'clock at the suspension bridge. Just make sure he gets there, and Tone, don't be seen with him." Brent hung up.

Irritated, Wilson stared at the phone for a second before pulling the flush and leaving the bathroom. As he stepped onto the landing he bumped into his son.

"What are you doing up?" he growled.

"I got to get ready for school, Dad." The boy grinned at him and Wilson ruffled his hair.

"No, go back to bed. Let's have a lie in. You're still poorly, you are." Wilson pushed him towards his bedroom.

Wendy Straker walked onto the landing wearing only a baggy tee shirt to join them.

"He can't have another day off. They'll be sending social services round here. He's already behind on his reading and stuff. He likes school, don't you?" She smiled at the boy who nodded. Wilson snarled and barged past her causing her to stumble against the door frame.

"Do what you want. God forbid I should be right. Just leave me in peace, keep the noise down, and make sure I'm up by half ten." He slammed the bedroom door behind him.

Wendy Straker wondered what she was supposed to wear to take the boy to school if she couldn't get in the bedroom. She put her fingers to her lips and took his hand, deciding that they would have some breakfast. She would try and sneak into the bedroom once they had eaten, and then if she couldn't get any clothes he would have to be sick again. She sighed and wished she could escape Wilson, but knew she wouldn't try, not again. Wendy Straker now lived a waiting game. Wilson would tire of her eventually, and she'd heard that he was having a thing with one of the girls at the club. She had to live with the hope that he would go and shack up with her.

Trump tapped on the door frame of Meredith's office and stepped in through the open door. Meredith glanced up at him.

"Ah, Trump, an update if you please."

"Yes, Sir, as I mentioned earlier, I think we may have something to work on. It turns out Natalia was quite helpful in the end. All we needed was an interpreter." He pointed to a chair, "May I?"

"Of course, get on with it, what have you found out?"

"First, we established that Tony is *probably* the father. Although that is not an absolute certainty, and he doesn't want her to have the baby unless it's his, so he asked her to go for a termination with the other chap, Toby Samson. I don't think it was any more than a lift though."

"And the threats to kill her?" Meredith asked and Trump sighed.

"I don't think it was any more than an idle threat. You know, 'If that baby isn't mine, I'll kill ya!' that sort of thing." Trump had affected an accent, but stopped at the look of sheer disbelief on Meredith's face.

"What was that, Trump? This isn't an episode of *Eastenders*. Get a grip man. You'll be calling them all slags next." Meredith shook his head. "What else?"

"Quite. Sorry. It would seem that Wilson then arranged for her to have an abortion, but at the last minute he couldn't take her for some reason. That's when Toby Samson appeared. But she refused to go and ran away from him. Samson tracked her down at home and she thinks he told her the boss would sack her if she was pregnant. Later, she somehow managed to convey to Wilson that if the boss was angry then she would tell him it was his fault. Wilson saw red and had her pinned up against a wall by her throat and made similar threats about killing her. He got one of the other girls who understands English a little better to tell her to get rid of the baby or else."

"And all this helps us how?" Meredith supported his head with his hands and leaned back in the chair. "Because whilst I'm happy we have rescued Natalia from these men, if indeed that's what we have done, I don't see how it helps us."

"Well, here's the thing." Trump saw Meredith raise his eyebrows, and hurried to reassure him, "I'll keep it brief." Meredith nodded and Trump continued.

"Via the interpreter, I asked various questions, about who the boss was, what did he do, what else went on in the club? Et cetera, et cetera. And in summary this is what she said. The boss, as she knows him, is a man called Brent. He doesn't go in very often, and when he does the girls are not allowed to approach him unless chosen. He spends much of his time in an office above the club, which she has never seen. Although some of the other girls that were chosen have. Not that that's a help as she had no further information on that score. Anyway, she likes Brent, even though she has never had anything to do with him," he paused for effect, "because Tony is frightened of him." He paused for effect again and Meredith sighed.

"Trump, please get on with it, you're starting to irritate now. I'm glad the bully Wilson has someone to be afraid of, but how are we helped by this?"

"Because she was standing outside the incident room, waiting for me to give her a lift to the hostel, and when I came out she looked over my shoulder at the board," Trump pointed through the glazed walls of Meredith's office at the incident boards. "She pointed at it and said, 'She was with him'." Meredith threw his hands up in irritation. "Well she didn't, not in those words, so I got a photo of the two victims and took her back to the interview room with the interpreter."

He glanced at Meredith whose body language was still showing signs of irritation, so he cut to the chase. "It transpires that Anna Carter made a very brief visit to the club with Brent on one occasion that Natalia knows about, and that Andrew Short had been in several times. He had a crush on one of the girls apparently."

Meredith flipped himself forward and slapped his hands on the desk. Several of the people working in the incident room looked round to see what had happened.

"Trump, you got there in the end! It was just a matter of patience. Why you couldn't have walked in here and said, 'Guess what, Gov, both of our victims were in Sensations recently, is beyond me. But well done, none the less." Meredith grinned at him. "We have the ID parade later this afternoon. We'll get that out of the way first, and then question Anna Carter again. See if you can get hold of an up to date photograph of Brent before then. At last, something to get our teeth into. Find out where he lives, as depending on what Anna has to say about it, we may need to pull him in." Meredith rubbed his hands together. "What have you done with Natalia now? If this goes anywhere she may be needed for a further interview, or even to give evidence in the long term."

"She and her sister have been taken to a hostel. It's run by a charity set up to help girls, with no home, get on their feet. Gives them an address and support in finding a job, teaches them English if necessary. They are expected to -"

"Shut up, Trump. Are they safe there?" Meredith interrupted with a sigh.

"Should be, Sir, yes, but I will make sure that Gemma, that's the interpreter, knows that they shouldn't go into town." Trump stood up, now ready to escape the confines of Meredith's office. "Right, I'll get onto the photograph."

Trump left the office and Meredith smiled. If things went well they would be able to beef up the slot on *Crimebusters*. A thought occurred to him and he bellowed at Trump. "Trump, back here." Trump walked quickly back into Meredith's office.

"Sir?"

"Jessop. Did you sort that out?" His eyes narrowed as he waited for an answer.

Trump nodded. "I did. She's one scary lady. I didn't get to make the call until quite late on because of the interpreter and one thing and another, and she was not best pleased. I think I blushed at some of the language she used." Trump shook his head. "If it's all the same to you, I'd like to give *Crimebusters* a wide berth."

"I'll think about it." Meredith bit back the smile. "Find Adler and tell her I'd like a word."

Patsy got out of her car and looked around. Stella Young's home was magnificent. The huge mock-Tudor detached house, set in large grounds, looked down on her as her feet crunched on the gravel leading to the front door. As she stepped up onto the porch she could hear the baby crying. She pushed the bell and its chime echoed around the hall beyond and the baby stopped. A woman of a similar age to Patsy dressed in jeans and a pale blue polo-necked sweater opened the door and smiled.

"You must be Patsy, come on in, we're in the kitchen. I'm Tessa." She stepped back so that Patsy could enter the oak-panelled hall. Patsy looked around as she followed the woman towards the back of the house. A substantial staircase wound its way around the side of the hall, up to a galleried landing. Peering up Patsy could see that solid oak doors were set into recessed arches in the walls beyond the banister.

Tessa opened a door in the centre of the wall at the back of the hall. "Stella and Sebastian are in here."

Patsy stepped into a warm and cosy kitchen. Steam came from the spout of a shiny stainless steel kettle, sitting on the hob of a blood red cooking range. A large bay window with a cushioned window seat overlooked the rear garden, and in the rocking chair standing in the bay sat Stella feeding her son a bottle of milk. Patsy smiled at her.

"Good morning, Stella, I hope I haven't arrived at a bad time." Patsy leaned forward and looked at the tiny face sucking frantically on the teat of the bottle. "He's gorgeous." She stroked the tiny hand clasping Stella's finger.

"No, of course not. He'll be finished in a moment and we can get down to business. In the meantime, can we get you anything? Have you eaten?" Stella smiled at her. Gone was the officious business woman of the day before; Patsy was looking at Stella, the mother, apparently a whole different person. She agreed to some coffee and a croissant and sat at the farmhouse table, in the centre of the kitchen whilst Stella finished feeding and winding Sebastian. When she had changed his babygro, she held him out to Tessa. "Here, you can take him now, he's ready to be put down." Tessa took the baby and cradled him in her arms making cooing noises. Stella kissed her on the forehead. "Come and join us once he's settled." Stella watched them leave the kitchen and then joined Patsy at the table.

"I've obviously been giving this matter a lot of thought since our conversation yesterday, and I have some proposals. That is, unless you have anything you wish to say having now looked at my diary." Stella picked up a large teapot and poured some into her mug. Patsy shook her head.

"I have a few queries, but please fire away," Patsy smiled. She liked the relaxed version of Stella.

"Splendid. Well I think we should take advantage of using a drugs test as a smoke screen. My concern is having anyone disappear on us if we do it branch by branch. I have twenty branches now, and whilst I appreciate we could track them down I am concerned by the delays that might cause." Stella stood and went to fetch a note pad from the dresser. "Each year we have a conference followed by an evening of awards. Traditionally we hold that at the end of March, but I see no reason, other than getting a venue sorted, why we can't bring that forward. Then during the day, we can separate the boys from the girls, and set up some form of testing centre. As it's an all-expenses paid function, all the staff should attend with a few exceptions and I am perfectly willing to close the offices for a day to get this sorted." Stella raised her eyebrows. "I'm thinking Friday week if I can find a venue." She flipped a page of the note book. "In the meantime, we can work on bringing you into contact with those others that may be responsible. How does that sound?"

"Perfect. The only day I'm not available this week is Thursday, but that will probably only be for the morning." Patsy leaned towards the pad. "What did you have in mind?"

For the next two hours Patsy and Stella produced a plan of action. Eventually they had just one last appointment to arrange. Patsy was to attend the gym where Stella's former personal trainer worked.

"I don't go to the gym at present," she rubbed her back. "I pulled something trying to lose the baby fat. But I'm sure Tessa would be more than happy to go with you as long as you are happy with that."

"Of course, why wouldn't I be? Do I look that unfit?" Patsy asked pulling in her tummy and Stella burst out laughing.

"Far from it, Patsy." Her eyes quickly appraised Patsy, and Patsy cursed inwardly as she felt the heat hit her cheeks. Stella had the good grace to ignore it.

"What I meant was that some people are uncomfortable with our lifestyle and those that don't approve think that there may be an attempted seduction at any moment. Ridiculous, but true. I have never seduced anyone that didn't want me to." She raised one eyebrow and her eyes twinkled.

"Oh, I see, you must have met my partner then." Patsy giggled. "It's not that he disapproves, you understand, I think he just feels under threat when confronted by a gay man." She shook her head. "Anyway, let me know when it's convenient and I'll pop it in the diary." Patsy closed her note book. "Well if that's the lot, I'll leave you to your day."

Stella stood and held her hand out. "Thank you, Patsy. Tessa will give you a call later. Come, let me show you out." As Stella led Patsy back into the hall, Tessa appeared carrying Sebastian.

"He's awake but not hungry. I think he just wanted a cuddle." She smiled.

Stella took the baby from her. "Then I will oblige. Tessa, I need you to take Patsy to the gym. It's going to have to be one evening if we want to do it sooner rather than later. When would suit you?"

"What about tonight? Is that too soon?" Tessa asked Patsy.

"No problem at all. What time is best for you? I'll come and pick you up."

"Oh not before eight, it's too crowded. It's open until ten thirty, so shall we say I'll be ready for eight fifteen?" she suggested.

Patsy walked back to her car thoughtfully. She was looking forward to getting back to the office and populating her diary with the meetings she had just agreed, and getting the first samples off to the lab. But she hadn't been to the gym for over a year and she hoped she wouldn't let herself down.

Meredith met Jane Roscoe in the viewing room, pleased that he had decided against a video line-up. He nodded at the line of people in the room beyond the one-way mirror.

"You're happy with Anna in position four then?" he asked.

Jane Roscoe walked along the gallery. Before her she saw eight very similar young girls and two boys. All were dressed in trainers, straight blue jeans and a grey hoody. The hoods were worn up with the edge of the hood positioned just in front of their ears. All were devoid of makeup. She looked at Anna Carter who was very pale and staring at the floor. She sighed and nodded at Meredith.

"Good. Do you any preference as to who we bring in first? The bus driver, the bank clerk, the shop assistant or the bin man? You choose the order."

Meredith walked forward and tapped the glass in the door and beckoned Jo Adler to join them. Jo opened the door and stepped in.

Jane Roscoe shrugged. "Let's have the shop assistant. We'll save the bus driver until last," Roscoe decided, and Jo Adler left the room. She returned seconds later with Glenys Matthews. She asked her to stand at one end of the long window.

"Okay, Mrs Matthews, I want you to think back to the thirty-first of January, when you were walking down past the Grand Hotel. You saw a person walking quickly in the direction of Corn Street and later happened across the scene of Andrew Short's death. Look very carefully at the people in the room opposite, take your time, and when and if you are sure you see that person in the room just call out the number on the wall above their head."

Glenys Matthews walked slowly along the line. "Can they step forward please? I'm a little short sighted."

Jane Roscoe snorted and Meredith sighed. He nodded at Jo Adler, and she pressed a button on the wall and asked the line to step forward. They did so and Mrs Matthews scrutinised them again. "It could be three or four, but they all look so similar I don't know which one of them it is."

Meredith thanked her and she was shown out.

Jo Adler returned with Terence White, the bin man. He had been sweeping the pavements as Andrew Short's murderer walked quickly away from the scene. They repeated the process. When White had walked the line three times he turned to them.

"I've been thinking about this all night, trying to come up with a vision in my mind. If I'm right, it's number four or number seven. He placed his hands on his chest. They have the right shaped boobs, but I need to see them smile. That will confirm which one." Meredith nodded at Jo Adler and she asked the line to smile. For the best part, it was a pitiful attempt but Terence was only looking at two of them. "Number four," Terence announced confidently. "I remember the teeth."

Meredith thanked him and Jo Adler brought in the bank clerk. She appeared to be more nervous than some of those in the line-up, and despite walking the line four or five times she was unable to identify anyone. She shook her head tearfully. Jo Adler led her out and collected the bus driver, David Evans. He took his role very seriously and stopped in front of each person and stared at them intently. Then he strolled along the line with pursed lips. Several of those in the line-up had begun to fidget. Meredith was watching Anna closely. He was concerned she was about to faint when Evans announced, "Number four."

Jane Roscoe's head fell and she bit her lip as Jo Adler took him out. She looked at Meredith who was himself a little shocked.

"It won't stand up, you know. The first woman admitted to having bad eyesight and chose two of them, the bin man was more interested in their chest, and as I've said before the bus driver will have seen her on the route on many occasions. Can we get her out of there please, oh . . . right." As she spoke Jo Adler had opened the door and allowed the line-up to file out. She took hold of Anna's arm and led her back to the interview room.

Meredith shook his head at Jane Roscoe. "I'm afraid that's not right. He only started working this side of Bristol on the thirtieth. So Anna Carter was not a regular fare of his." He patted her shoulder. "Let's get this sorted then." He walked briskly to the interview room and Jane Roscoe called him back as he reached the door.

"I would like to see my client alone first," she informed him.

Meredith nodded. "I'll be in my office, give me a shout when you're ready." Meredith shoved his hands in his pockets and ambled back to his office. He hadn't expected that result, and he was not looking forward to applying the necessary pressure to get Anna to admit to the murder of Andrew Short. He sighed heavily as he pushed open the door into the incident room. Seaton walked across to him waving some photographs.

"Shots of Michael Brent, Gov. We were lucky and caught him leaving the house early this afternoon. He walked into Clifton Village, had a coffee then walked across the suspension bridge and back. We've also got these. Brent was featured as a partial solution to the housing shortage. He locked horns with the council over planning and the paper took his side." Seaton handed the photographs to Meredith and followed him into his office. "I take it the line-up was no good then? Not judging by the look on your face anyway."

Meredith sat and spread the photographs out on his desk. He shook his head.

"The line-up was a great success, two definite IDs, and another that won't stand up. But enough for us to really push her now. This stinks, Tom, but I don't know why. But I reckon this chap might help us." He tapped a photograph of Brent leaving the café.

An hour later he had yet to begin interviewing Anna Carter. She had gone to pieces at the news that she had been positively identified, and it had taken quite a while to calm her. He glanced at his watch and knew it would be a long day. It was almost five and his stomach rumbled as he wondered where the day had gone. He walked along the corridor and knocked on the door to the interview room. He stepped in and asked Anna and Jane Roscoe if they wanted anything from the canteen and then set off at a brisk pace to collect their order. Standing in the queue at the counter he pulled out his mobile and texted Patsy.

Sorry, going to be late positive ID on Anna.

A few minutes later a response came in.

Oh no. I'm out tonight leaving 7.45 be back 10ish to soothe you.

He smiled, slid the phone back into his pocket, and as he placed his order he wondered idly where she was going. Balancing his purchases on a tray he carried it carefully back to the interview room. He kicked the door, and watched as Jane Roscoe prised her hand out of Anna's and came to open it. He walked in and placed the tray on the table.

"I think Anna wants to speak to you now." Jane Roscoe tore open a couple of sugar sachets and stirred them into a mug of tea which she placed in front of Anna. Meredith nodded and stepped back outside and sent someone to collect Jo Adler.

When Jo had settled herself, Meredith pushed the record buttons and announced those present. For good measure, he also reminded Anna of her rights. Once he had completed this task he leaned back in his chair and smiled at Anna. She stared at him blankly so he sighed and began the interview.

"Anna, I have no doubt Jane has told you the results of the identity parade. Is there any comment you would like to make as to why three out of four people positively identified you as being around on the day that Andrew Short was stabbed?"

"It was two," Jane Roscoe cut in.

Meredith's glare was harsh. "Sorry, Anna, is there any reason that two people would identify you?"

Anna shook her head. Meredith told the tape she had done so.

"Do you think they were lying?"

Again, Anna shook her head. Meredith advised the recording.

"Then how do you account for it?"

Anna shrugged and shook her head. Meredith sighed and described her actions.

"Are you frightened of anyone, Anna?"

Anna frowned and shrugged, then shook her head hesitantly. Meredith flipped open his file and put the photograph of Michael Brent on the desk. Anna blinked rapidly.

"Are you frightened of this man?"

Anna shook her head and sniffed loudly. She then looked at her hands grasped tightly in her lap.

"Who is he, Anna? I need you to answer because, apart from anything else, I'm getting tired of describing your movements." He winked to let her know he was joking. He detected a slight twitch at the corner of her mouth.

"His name is Michael Brent," she said quietly.

"How do you know him?"

"My mum used to work at one of his offices, and I babysat for Mrs Brent sometimes."

"Did you have a relationship with him?" Meredith asked, and watched Anna frown and her nose wrinkle.

"No." There was disgust in her tone.

"Did he ever take you out?"

"No." Her voice maintained the same level of distaste.

Meredith inclined his head and stared into her eyes. "Why does the thought disgust you? He's a good-looking man, and from what I hear he is also wealthy and successful."

"What's that got to do with it? Do you think I'm cheap?"

Her face had clouded and Meredith smiled to reassure her. He didn't release her from his gaze, and he gave his head a slight shake. "I don't think that at all. I don't know the man, but I know you do, and I would like you to tell me about him." He nodded slightly as though giving her permission to open up.

Anna drew in a jagged breath and blinked several times before searching for Meredith's eyes again.

"He is a horrible man. He is a bully, a liar and a cheat. I would be happy to know that I never have to see him again. But . . . anyway, looks and money count for nothing."

"But what, Anna?"

Anna shook her head firmly, her jaw had set. "Nothing," she snapped and then added, "I don't like the man, why can't we just leave it at that?"

"What did he do to you, Anna?" Meredith chewed his lip as she shook her head. "If you dislike him so much why did you go to the Sensations night club with him?" Meredith watched her eyes widen before she blinked again, and raising her hand quickly she caught the escaping tear before it reached her cheek.

"How do you know that? It was once and he tricked me. I didn't stay long." Anna closed her eyes and lowered her head as unwelcome memories fought for attention in her mind.

Meredith left her for a while. Leaning forward he picked up a twin bar of chocolate and removed one of the bars. He held the packet out towards Anna. "Eat something, you must be starving." She didn't move so he placed it on the table in front of her, and bit into the bar he had taken. He nodded at Jo and Jane Roscoe. "Help yourselves, I think we are in for a long night."

He smiled as Anna looked up at him with a concerned expression on her face.

"How long? My mum thinks I'm here to look at photographs and she'll worry." A look of anger came upon her face and slapping the photograph of Michael Brent with the flat of her hand she swept it off the table. "And I don't want to look at him."

"Then talk to me, Anna. Let me help you." Meredith turned his attention to Jane Roscoe. "I think we can both see that Anna is scared of something, something that may have some part in the reason she is here today. I think you need to convince her that speaking to us is the right thing to do. Make her eat something too."

He reached over, his fingers poised on the controls, and spoke to the recorder, "Interview suspended at six fifteen." He stood and stretched. "I'm in need of a comfort break, let's all be back here in twenty minutes." He reached across and squeezed Anna's hand. "I do want to help you, Anna." He inclined his head and looked at her for a while, and then turned and left the room taking another bar of chocolate with him.

He walked next door where Seaton had been watching the interview. Opening the second bar he took a bite and slumped down in the chair.

"You're nearly there, Gov. I think you broke that off too soon."

"No I didn't. Now she's got to worry about her mum and whatever Brent did," he shook his head, "and we're nowhere near the stabbing yet."

"She'll tell you. She's bought into your charm, don't worry." Seaton pushed him with his elbow. "Just keep looking at her and she will cave. You old dog."

Meredith turned slowly to look at him. "I'm not playing her. I am, believe it or not, genuinely concerned. If she stabbed Andrew Short, there was a damn good reason for it. But it wasn't for money or revenge, and, somehow, I don't think it was a romantic interest, so we have to find out why. If she's charged, we need to get as much out of her as we can to help her." He shook his head. "I can't believe you thought I was playing her."

It was Seaton's turn to shake his head. "You don't even know you're doing it, do you?" He jerked his thumb behind him. "That girl is hanging on your every word. She actually looked worried when you suspended the interview. My advice is get back in there and play on that."

"I'm going for a fag and a think. I'd also better ring Patsy and let her know the score." Meredith watched Seaton stifle a grin. "What? What have I done now?" he demanded.

Seaton wagged his finger at him. "How long have I known you, fifteen, sixteen years? I've never seen you check in mid-interview before. That's something new for me to get my head around."

"Sod off Seaton." Meredith left the room grinning. Once out on the fire escape he called Patsy.

"Hello, handsome, I couldn't believe it when I read your text," Patsy answered. "How's it going?"

"About as well as you would expect. Where are you off to tonight? I'm going to need a lot of soothing," he smiled into the phone before lighting his cigarette.

"I might need some myself. I'm off to the gym. One of my client's contacts works there so I'm going with her partner to get some evidence." Patsy could hear the disapproval in Meredith's silence, but she ignored it and carried on talking. "I am now hunting through my boxes trying to find my trainers, although I have a little while. Tessa isn't picking me up until eight fifteen. I was going to cook something that was easy to reheat. Is there anything you fancy?"

"I thought your client was a woman?"

"She is," Patsy grinned, knowing it would be mirroring Meredith's reaction. "Behave yourself, so is there anything you fancy?"

"Can't answer that on the grounds of self-incrimination." Meredith laughed out loud. "Oh, Patsy, what would I do without you?"

"Get off the phone. Let me throw some clothes into a bag, and try not to be too hard on that poor girl. I'm going now, I'll see you later. Love you. Bye."

Meredith walked back to the interview room, smiling, and replaying the conversation. He suddenly had a thought and quickened his pace. Jo Adler was standing outside the room chatting to Seaton.

"When you searched for the trainers did you find anything else?" he asked.

"Anything else like what? Something crucial to the case that we kept secret from you? What do you mean, Gov?"

Meredith shook his head at the sarcasm. "I'm not sure, but I'm working on it. Are we good to go?" He nodded towards the interview room, and Jo confirmed that they were. "Good then, get in there with Seaton."

His two officers gasped in amazement, demanding to know if he'd lost the plot.

"I know exactly what I'm doing. I didn't, but I do now. Seaton you're the bad cop, Jo you're the silent one, and when she needs protecting from you she'll ask for me." He held his hands up in mock defence. "Don't look at me like that. It was you that gave me the idea. Now get on with it."

Seaton opened the door and took the seat Meredith had vacated. He confirmed that they were ready to proceed and pushed the buttons on the recorder. He announced who was present in the room. Before he had asked his first question Anna held her hand up.

"Where's Mr . . . I mean DI Meredith?"

"He's become involved with another matter," Seaton smiled at her. "Don't worry I'm up to speed with the previous interview. I have no idea why DI Meredith was so interested in Brent though, I'm more interested in why you stabbed Andrew Short." He raised his eyebrows and turned to a clean sheet on the large pad in front of him. "So let's start there Anna. Was Andrew Short an ex-boyfriend, or perhaps someone that tried it on and went too far? Did he perhaps rip you off on some drug deal?" Seaton banged the table with the flat of his hand. "Come on, Anna, tell me!" His voice was loud, his tone angry and Anna flinched.

"I won't have my client harassed in this way. Please moderate your tone," Jane Roscoe demanded and Seaton nodded at her curtly.

He looked at Anna, his face angry. "I'm sorry Anna, but this is just wasting time. It will all come out in the end, so let's get it over with. Please answer my question."

"I didn't, he wasn't." Anna blinked furiously trying to hold back tears of fear and anger. "You ask DI Meredith, I know he believes me."

Meredith sat in the observation room and watched as Seaton slowly increased the pressure on Anna Carter. He asked the same three questions in different ways for the next thirty minutes. His tone was aggressive and his expression hard. After twenty minutes, Anna had started crying. Silent tears fell as she repeated the same denial. Meredith looked at his watch and decided to step in. He walked to the interview room and opened the door. Seaton announced his arrival for the purposes of the tape.

"Sergeant Seaton, there's a matter you need to attend to in the custody suite, I'll take over now." Seaton scraped the chair back and nodded curtly at Anna before leaving the room. Meredith told the tape Seaton had left and announced his own arrival. He smiled at Anna.

"How's it going, Anna?" He smiled his charming smile, and leaned forward resting his forearms on the table. He watched Anna gasp in a rally of breaths, her shoulders rising with each effort. Eventually she gave a shuddering sigh and wiped her face dry with the flat of her hands.

Jane Roscoe tapped the table with her index finger. "DI Meredith, your sergeant is a bully. He barely maintained control. I don't want him anywhere near my client again. If you are thinking of repeating such tactics I will suggest that you charge my client or release her."

Meredith's face fell. "A bully? I'm sorry, that's not like him at all. I think it must be this case, you know, waste of a young life and all that. Anna, are you okay?" Meredith looked genuinely concerned and Anna managed a small smile.

"I am now he's gone. I can't tell him what he wants because it wasn't me. How do I make this stop?" Anna put her elbows on the desk and buried her face in her hands. "I just want to go home. I want this to stop."

"I know, Anna, but you must see how difficult it is for us, what with the ring and the ID parade results. Oh dear." Meredith gave a baffled sigh and shook his head. "I'll tell you what Anna, let's leave the Andrew Short thing and go back to Brent. Because I know you're lying to me about that."

Anna opened her hands so her face peeped through the frame they had created and she nodded.

"Okay but you're not to say anything to him. I don't want to have to speak to him or anything." She groaned into her hands. "What do you want to know?"

"Anything. Everything you know. Why don't you just start at the beginning?" Meredith remained leaning on his forearms, and nodded for her to start.

"My mum used to work for him. She worked in the office at his factory doing admin, and I did some temporary work there during the holidays. We didn't see much of him really, then one day he came in and was working in his office, when suddenly he started shouting. He was on the phone and banged it down. The manager went to see what was wrong, and, apparently, a babysitter had let them down and he had an important do to go to that night. My mum said I'd do it, and I didn't mind," she paused and her expression hardened, "but I didn't know them really. That was about two years ago. Anyway, for the next year I babysat once a month or so. Good pay, and they paid for a taxi home."

Anna paused and screwed her face up as she tried to put things in chronological order. She inclined her head and looked at Meredith. "Do you know, I've only just realised when he started. He closed his factory down and mum lost her job, he gave her a good pay off though. But it was the next time I babysat, he . . . well he tried it on." She shook her head. "I'm so stupid not to have worked that out before." She stared at the wall behind Meredith lost in her own thoughts.

"What happened, Anna?" Meredith prompted. He watched as her shoulders drooped; she couldn't look at him, and stared into her lap.

"Nothing really. They got back just after midnight and they were both drunk, but Liz was really bad. She flew into the house, straight into the loo, and threw up. He was quite rough with her, but he managed to get her up the stairs and he put her to bed. I heard him go and check on Jimmy and when he came down he just stood there staring at me. I asked him if he was all right, and he did this long speech about being lonely, and marrying the wrong woman. He came over to me and ran his hand down my face and told me he should have married a nice girl like me."

She shuddered at the thought. "I was quite flattered. I didn't fancy him or anything, it's just he was Michael Brent, and he obviously thought I was a nice girl." Anna looked up at Meredith and this time she held his gaze. "Not everyone realises that. For some reason, I attract men that think I'm . . . I'm a slapper, I suppose. I'm not." Anna stared at Meredith daring him to contradict her.

He nodded solemnly. "What happened then?"

"Not much. I sympathised and said it was just because she was drunk. I told him he wouldn't be so sad in the morning. He told me he was always sad, that their marriage was a sham, and how it would be good to have someone to talk to. Then he just started talking. Telling me about Jimmy and the plans he had for him, the holidays he wanted to take him on and that sort of stuff. Suddenly he pulled me up against him and told me he wished he could make plans with me. I told him not to be stupid and he turned. He got hold of my chin," she put her hand up to cup her chin, "and pushed me up against the wall. He said that no one told him he was stupid, and he did this weird laugh then tried to kiss me. We struggled briefly, and then the doorbell went because I'd ordered the taxi when they had got home. He just let me go, gave me my money, and said goodnight like nothing had happened.

"The next day he turned up at work with this huge bunch of flowers and apologised. He said that it had been the drink and I had to forgive him, so I did." She shrugged. "They were both drunk I thought it was a one-off," she sighed. "Then I did something really stupid, I let him take me out to lunch a couple of times, and we went to the theatre to see a matinée performance of *Grease*. It wasn't regular, just every now and again," Anna gave a cruel laugh, "and because I'm a stupid naïve cow, I thought he only wanted some company that didn't nag. When all he wanted was to control me. He told me he loved me and that he would divorce his wife, and I told him, I'm not your girlfriend, just your friend, and I'm not going to sleep with you. He accepted that. He told me it was refreshing and that he wanted to stay friends."

She shook her head and dragged in a deep breath. Sad eyes stared into Meredith's. "Then I started seeing this really nice lad. He'd come down to work in Bristol on a six-month project with an insurance company. He was lovely and we had such a laugh. Then one day he didn't show up. I called him for over an hour, and eventually he answered and told me someone in his family was poorly, and that he had to go home and he wouldn't be able to see me again. Ten minutes later, Brent turns up, just driving by."

She raised her eyebrows and shook her head. "He took me for a drink and I cried on his shoulder," Anna threw her hands up in disbelief. "I actually cried on his shoulder. Anyway, a couple of days later he turns up and asks me to babysit. I thought what harm can it do? They got home quite early, Liz was smashed but he was sober. He said he hadn't been drinking because he had a headache. Then he offered to drive me home. He told Liz he would drop me off and call in at the club . . ."

Anna groaned and leaned forward burying her face in her hands. Meredith allowed her time to collect her thoughts, and exchanged glances with Jo Adler.

Jo leaned forward and patted her arm. "Would you like a drink or a break, Anna?" she asked softly and Anna shook her head. She let her hands fall away from her face.

"No, let's get this finished so I can go home." She swallowed and cleared her throat. "I couldn't exactly demand he pay for a taxi, and I didn't have enough money so I accepted a lift. We had hardly got to the end of the road when he said he thought he had better go to the club first. When we got there, I said I'd sit outside, but he insisted I went in as it wasn't safe." Her nose wrinkled in disgust. "It was horrible. It stank, and all these lecherous blokes were sat there watching these two girls on poles. One of them was actually, you know," she nodded at Meredith, "playing with himself under his coat, it was so obvious." Anna tutted. "I felt so sorry for those girls having to smile at them and pretend they liked them. Brent asked me if I wanted a drink, and I said no, I wanted to go. He told me to relax, he wouldn't be ten minutes and he disappeared. I was quite scared as all these blokes at the bar kept talking to me and I didn't want them to think I was a dancer or on the game or anything. Then this bloke said Brent asked me to go to his office and took me upstairs. He had a second room off his office, a bedroom. He'd left the door open so I could see it. I don't think I've ever been so frightened."

She paused as a wave of shuddering breaths took hold. "He told me he loved me, that he couldn't bear not having me. That tonight was the night, or words to that effect. He poured me a drink and sort of made me drink it, most of it went over my top because I was telling him no. Then he assaulted me, okay."

Anna licked away the tear that had reached her lip. A silence followed. Meredith nodded very slightly.

"Did he rape you, Anna?" Jo Adler asked, her voice soft with concern.

Anna jerked her head towards Jo. "No. Because then you would really have to arrest me for murder. He did his best though. He fought with me and ripped my blouse and my knickers." Anna rubbed her hands over her thighs. "I had bruises on my legs for weeks, but I elbowed him in the throat somehow. It wasn't intentional, but it sort of incapacitated him and I ran out. One of his blokes was on the door and grabbed my arm, I told him I'd stabbed Brent so he ran one way and I ran the other.

"When I got outside this bloke was getting into a taxi and I jumped in with him. He could see I was scared and he just nodded and let me sit there. We didn't speak until I asked him if I could get out at the end of our street and he let me. I think he thought I had been raped, because when I got out instead of saying goodbye he said 'I'm sorry', like he had done something wrong. That was when I started crying. I'd been so strong up to then."

She rubbed the flat of her hands up her cheeks towards her eyes and coughed. Then she looked back at Meredith, who locked her gaze. "He didn't rape me, I will never say anything officially and it's over. I don't babysit and I haven't seen him since. It was him that warned that lad off I was seeing though. He roughed him up apparently and told him how bad it would be if he didn't go home. He called a few weeks later and made me promise not to tell in case Brent went looking for him. I actually think that in his own twisted mind, Brent did care for me, but he didn't like it because he couldn't have me." She held her head upright and nodded. "So there, it's done."

"Did you know that man in the taxi?" Jo Adler asked, and from the corner of her eye she saw Meredith grasp his pen tighter and blink permission to Anna. For the first time a gentle smile flickered, and Anna looked at peace.

"You know I did. Well I didn't, I had no idea who he was until you showed me his photo in my bedroom. It was Andrew Short. So you tell me why I would stab someone that saved me from Brent?" Her challenge was defiant.

Meredith sighed. At last something that tied it all together. He knew it had been there. Now he had to work out why she was denying it, and more importantly, why she had done it. Then, of course, there was the little issue of who had shot her. He looked at his watch, it was past eight and everyone needed a break, if not a good night's sleep to consider what had been said.

"Anna Carter, I am arresting you for the murder of Andrew Short. You will be held here tonight and appear before Bristol Magistrates Court, sometime tomorrow. Do you have anything to say?" Meredith's voice was low, and for the first time in his career he felt the need to apologise to a murder suspect. He shook his head to clear his thoughts. "Would you like to ring your parents or would you rather Ms Roscoe did that for you?"

Anna was stunned and she sat staring at the wall behind Meredith.

"Anna, did you understand what I just said to you?"

Jane Roscoe reached out and touched Anna's shoulder. "Anna, would you . . ."

Anna looked at her for a split second before she passed out.

A pleasing aroma filled Meredith's nostrils as he stepped into the hall. He breathed in deeply and, eyes shut, he rolled his head around allowing some of the tension to fall away. He opened his eyes and called to Patsy.

"I'm home. Where are you?" Shrugging off his coat, he hung it over the newel post and pulled his already loosened tie off. Patsy's head appeared over the banister on the landing.

"I'm about to get into the shower. Dinner's in the oven, come on up and talk to me." She laughed as he took the stairs two at a time and pulled her into his embrace. "I take it you need a hug." She stood on tiptoes and kissed the end of his nose.

"I don't want to talk about it," he smiled at her, "not yet anyway. Let's eat first. How did you get away so early anyway?" He released her and then followed her into the bathroom. He sat on the edge of the bath as she reached into the shower cubicle and switched on the shower.

"Partly because I was lucky, but mostly because I am lazy." She turned to grin at him as she allowed her towel to slip to the floor before stepping into the shower. "The trainer tripped over an abandoned kit bag, and I caught him and got his DNA under my nails, and all in the first ten minutes. I played at training for the next twenty minutes, but I was absolutely knackered. Tessa, bless her, agreed that as the job was done we'd call it a day."

She paused to lather the shampoo into her hair. "I didn't realise I was so unfit, I really will have to start going to the gym again." She yelped as Meredith pulled back the curtain and stepped into the shower with her. "I wasn't expecting that." She turned to face him and reached for the body wash. "Here let me help you, you still smell of cigarettes." She wrinkled her nose and squeezed the soapy liquid into her hands and began rubbing it into his chest.

Meredith smiled at her. "Several things. First, I have a great workout to keep you fit," he raised his eyebrows, "second, I promise to try and give up, and finally I like you helping." He looked down briefly and she followed his gaze. "Now come here."

Patsy raised herself on her elbow and looked down at him. A few more lines seemed to be etched into his temple, and although he lay with his eyes closed, the smile he always wore following lovemaking was playing around his lips. She detected the slight frown creasing his forehead just at the end of his eyebrows. She leaned down and kissed him.

"Tough day for you today, but at least you have something to work with now." She sat up and swung her legs off the bed. "That Moussaka will be burned to a crisp if I don't rescue it." She turned back as Meredith gave a deep troubled sigh. "What is it, Johnny?" She used the name in an attempt to make him smile.

He opened one eye and peeped at her shaking his head. "I'll ignore that." He rolled onto his side to look at her. "I think I'm losing my touch." He shook his head. "Everything says she did it, but I can't get there. I don't think she did, and the worst thing is there's this voice in my head," he tapped his finger on his temple, "and it's telling me to prove she didn't, rather than find out who did, and I don't think that's one and the same thing with this case." He raised one eyebrow.

"I won't, I'll get on with the job by the book, and just hope it doesn't come back and bite me."

CHAPTER FOURTEEN

Patsy walked up behind Meredith, who was sitting at the kitchen table, and leaning down she wrapped her arms around his neck and kissed the top of his head.

"I hope you have a better day today. Just do what you do, you'll get there." She stepped back a little allowing Meredith to turn round, and sat on his lap.

"The trouble is, Patsy, what will happen to her in the meantime? Anna Carter is teetering on the brink, and I don't want to be responsible for pushing her over." He kissed the base of her throat. "You smell nice. And what are you up to today?" Placing his hands on her shoulders he eased her back a little. "You look good too. Quite the business woman." He noticed Patsy's smile was forced. "What have I said? You've got that 'just agree with him smile', and it doesn't work on me anymore." He dropped his hands allowing her to stand.

"I'm doing no such thing. I have no idea whether you're right or not. I think you should question why you think she is innocent. She's a good-looking girl and a sweetie to boot. That doesn't mean that something didn't push her over the edge and drive her to do it. You never know if her denial is not an act, she may have blocked it out."

Patsy inclined her head. "Look, I liked the girl, but if I was working this case I would be trying to find out why she stabbed him. Not why she couldn't possibly have done it, and trying to find the clothes. I just think you might be thinking with the wrong part of your anatomy." She raised her eyebrows and then looked at her watch. "I have to go, my first meeting is in half an hour."

"I don't believe you said that. I have always been able to rely on my gut instinct, and to be quite honest, I'm offended that you think otherwise." He pushed his chair back noisily as he stood. "Very offended in fact."

Patsy stepped forward and tilted her head to kiss him. "Well don't be. Think it through again . . ." she paused, "you are a wonderful, handsome, and considerate lover." She grinned at him. "You are also an efficient, fair, and effective copper." She pulled him closer by tugging on his shirt and stared into his eyes. "I'm not sure if you know this, but you're not perfect you know." She pushed him away after kissing the tip of his nose. "Now I really have to go or I'll be late." Grabbing her coat as she made her way to the front door she called back, "Don't nurse that pride, get back on the horse, and get on with it."

Meredith stood looking at his feet for a while as he considered what she had said. Was she judging him on his past errors with women, or simply pointing him in the right direction? Was she right? He raised his hands above his head and stretched. There was only one way to find out. He wondered what time Jane Roscoe started work. He needed to interview Anna Carter again, and the sooner the better.

Patsy tapped on the locked door of Stella Young's Clifton branch. Inside a tall, dark-haired man walked towards the door smiling. He opened the door and held out his hand.

"You must be Patsy Hodge, come on in. We're up in the board room. I'm Bruce by the way." He locked the door behind them, turned and led Patsy through the office. Her heels clicked on the wooden floor as she followed him. Reaching the bottom of the stairs, he stepped to one side. "After you, the board room is right at the top, just keep going."

As Patsy reached the top of the stairs, she could see Stella Young sitting at a highly polished table through the open door to the board room. She walked forward confidently and held her hand out. She had agreed with Stella that she would be introduced as a new business manager, and not knowing who else would be present, or what they would know she knew, she had to act the part.

Stella greeted her warmly. "Hi, Patsy, nice to see you again. Grab a coffee over there and come and join us."

Stella nodded to a low cabinet where a coffee pot sat percolating next to a basket of muffins. Patsy poured herself a coffee and grabbed a muffin hoping she would get the opportunity to eat it. She sat at the table opposite Stella.

"This is Samantha, my PA and life saver." Stella smiled at a smartly dressed woman, sitting behind a laptop, at the far end of the table. Samantha raised her hand and smiled at Patsy. Despite her immaculate clothes, hair, and makeup,

Patsy guessed she was in her early sixties. "Oh and don't call her Sammy. Only Bruce here gets away with that." Stella nodded at the man who had let Patsy in. "This is Bruce Williams, my marketing director. They both know why you're here. I have no secrets from either of them."

Patsy greeted them both as she pulled her note pad from her bag and placed it on the table in front of her. Flipping open the cover she noted that Bruce's DNA had been sent off in the first batch of samples already collected by Stella. She wondered how that conversation had gone down.

"Right, let's get straight down to it, they will be here for a nine thirty meeting. The purpose of the meeting will be to discuss the Cherry Tree development in Patchway. Patsy, you should take notes because they will expect you to have at least a basic handle on this, even though you are the new girl."

Stella paused and sipped her coffee before nodding at Samantha. Samantha picked up a remote control and pointed it at a projector suspended from the ceiling above the table. A large white square appeared on the wall at the end of the room, which slowly warmed to a picture of Samantha's desktop screen. She clicked some buttons and a large sign announcing the opening of the Cherry Tree development appeared. Stella picked up the commentary.

"You are going to hear this again when they get here, but in a different format. Take notes of the key players and the mix of units. You never know, they might want to get into conversation." Stella nodded and the picture changed. "Cherry Tree development was built on reclaimed brownfield land on the outskirts of Patchway, formerly home to warehousing and a petrol station. There was fierce competition for the land, and eventually a syndicate was formed with the approval of the council. Syndicate members were Stella Young Property Services, Greene and Sons Construction, and Coopergate Developments. Coopergate were late to join the syndicate after the buyout of the original member Blaze Solutions."

Stella paused as Bruce snorted, "Expulsion more like, band of cowboys." Bruce grimaced as Stella turned to look at him. "Sorry. It still makes me bloody angry. All that time wasted." He raised his hand towards the screen for Stella to continue.

"As I was saying, this syndicate was approved by the council to buy and develop the site for housing. There was a little scuffle over planning and volume, but eventually Cherry Tree was built, it's almost complete, and we have the following units." Samantha changed the slide as Stella progressed through the commentary. "Ten four-bedroom detached houses, thirty-five three-bedroom houses, and eighteen two-bedroom apartments will be sold. Proceeds will go to the syndicate and Stella Young Property Services will sell them for a reduced fee." Patsy saw Bruce nodding from the corner of her eye. "A further thirty units dotted around the development will be rented on a co-ownership scheme, and it is envisaged they will be let and eventually sold to working families who score enough points on our assessment criteria. Finally, forty units will be rented for a minimum of thirty years to provide more private rented accommodation in the area. Stella Young Property Services will deal with the management of these units, profits going to the syndicate, and we will not be allowed to discriminate against housing benefit recipients if they are able to provide a guarantor."

Stella paused to finish her coffee, skimming her notes as she did so.

"Pictured here from left to right are the following people," Stella pointed towards the screen as she spoke. "Andy Jenkins of MD Coopergate, Jeremy Green, senior partner at Green and Sons, me of course, then we have Richard Hancock former council leader, currently head of housing at the council, and I hope soon to be Mayor of Bristol." Stella nodded to confirm her words. "Next to him is his wife Geraldine Hancock. The cocky looking chap is our all-time favourite Michael Brent, of Blaze Solutions, Sandra Copperfield from Copperfield and Jones, and finally Sean Connolly of Connolly, Bates and Standing."

She looked away from the screen and towards Patsy. "All of the men will be here with the exception of Brent and Connolly. As mentioned earlier, Brent is no longer part of this project, and Sean Connolly couldn't raise enough capital. Hopefully, you will get to meet them at the function on Friday. I was meeting with all these men throughout the period in question, as it was the tail end of the bid process, and the winning syndicate Cherry Tree Homes Ltd, was awarded the contract on the day I had my first scan."

Stella raised her chin. "You already have my opinion of who it won't be of course, but that shouldn't cloud your judgement, and until they come back clean, we have to keep an open mind." Stella tidied the papers in front of her into a neat pile. "Right, I think we need fresh coffee and a quick comfort break before they get here. Is there anything you wanted to clear up first?"

"Only to confirm that Frankie Callaghan can supervise the testing, as you know, a medical professional is required by your contract of employment. Whilst he is mainly employed by the Home Office, he does apparently do private work. This is usually only when someone wants to pay for a second opinion on a post mortem, but he will make an exception in this case," Patsy informed her as Stella nodded and stood up.

"Good news." She smiled briefly. "Now if you will excuse me for a moment, Samantha will you do the honours please." Stella left the room and Samantha busied herself with the preparation for the next meeting. Bruce Williams had opened a note book and was reading through his notes. Patsy went to look out of the window whilst she considered how she was going to achieve her task. She reorganised a stationery tidy whilst she pondered this. By the time Stella had returned to the room everything was neat and tidy, and Patsy had an idea on how to obtain at least one of the men's samples for DNA testing.

"They're on their way up," Stella announced and Patsy returned to her seat.

Patsy sat through the first hour and a half of the meeting, carefully observing the men in question and half listening to the matters being discussed. At one point Richard Hancock had pulled her into the debate.

"What about you, Patsy? What do you think about the criteria for the co-ownership housing? Have you had time to study that yet?" he asked.

Patsy shook her head. "I'm afraid not, but I hope it is weighted in favour of those in useful, giving services. Nurses, firemen, paramedics, that sort of person. They give an awful lot to the community for a very low salary, so they struggle to get on the housing ladder. But it's only my first week so this is all still a bundle of facts and figures at the moment." She had answered hurriedly, but it obviously pleased Richard Hancock, who said with a smile, "I like this girl, she thinks like me."

Patsy returned his smile thinking that she very much doubted that. By the time they broke for coffee, Patsy had noticed that Jeremy Green suffered from severe dandruff. He had hung his jacket over the back of the chair, so therefore collecting that sample should be simple. Andrew Jenkins had combed his hair as he entered the room and she saw the comb being placed in his coat pocket which now hung on the coat rack just outside the boardroom. That was her first planned point of call, but as yet she had no idea what she was going to do about Richard Hancock.

Stella announced that the meeting would recommence in twenty minutes, and Patsy, who was closest to the door, stood quickly and walked outside. She hovered around the coat rack pretending to be on a call as the men filed passed her and downstairs to the toilets. She took her opportunity and removed the comb quickly, taking it back into the board room and then dropping it into an evidence bag. She stood and walked to the stationery tidy and selected the sticky tape. Winding it sticky side up around her hand she walked to Green's jacket and quickly patted it firmly several times with the tape. Then, and with a little difficulty, she placed the tape in a second evidence bag. Now there was only Hancock to deal with. He was the first to re-enter the room. He smiled at her.

"So, Patsy, what did you do before you came to join the incomparable Ms Young here?" He smiled across to Stella who smiled back at him. Patsy could see no reason not to tell the truth.

"I used to be a police officer. Things got a little too jaded, obstructed by red tape, the usual." She raised her eyebrows. "And, of course, Stella has offered me a very good job." Patsy fiddled with the tape as she spoke. "I hope I don't let her down." She wound it round her hand again as Richard Hancock walked towards her.

"That would explain your thoughts on the co-ownership stock. I can't say I disagree, we'll have to think about that." He nodded towards Stella. "I've only known Ms Young since this project was announced and I have to say you could have a worse teacher. Stella's taught me a thing or two about this business, and I'm sure you won't let her down." He had reached Patsy's side and looked at her hands. "What are you up to there?"

Patsy held her hand up. "This is my home made de-fluffer, look," Patsy picked up his hand so that his palm was laid across the back of her own. She pressed firmly down on the top of them with her taped hand, and then lifted it off with a flourish and presented it to him. "Just about anything sticks to it, oops sorry I got some hair there." She pulled the tape off her hand and rolled it into a ball before dropping it in the bin. "Sorry about that I don't know what came over me." She caught Stella Young's nod of approval, as Hancock laughed.

"Don't worry about it. My wife Geraldine keeps attacking me with something that looks like a little rolling pin full of tape. This was gentle in comparison." He looked up as the other two men returned to the room. "We'd better take our seats and get this lot sorted. I have another meeting at two o'clock."

Patsy sat through the rest of the meeting trying to concentrate on what was being discussed in case she should be brought into the conversation, but her mind kept wandering to her next meeting and, inevitably, Meredith. She was relieved when the meeting was called to an end. She waited until Stella had left to show them out then quickly recovered the tape from the bin.

"That was a damn good hand job if you don't mind me saying," Bruce commented and raised his eyebrows. Patsy stared at him.

"Don't worry about him, he thinks he's Sid James or Benny Hill," Samantha advised, shaking her head. "You have no idea who I'm talking about do you, you're far too young. Let's just say our Bruce here fancies himself as a comedian, the type that largely became extinct in the late seventies." She laughed, "Just be grateful you missed them." She began to clear the table. "It's like working with a child some days."

"Come on, Sammy, you love it," Bruce grinned at her. "I'm what puts that twinkle in your eye, and the spring in your step. Without me your life would be all forms, spreadsheets and tenancy agreements." He ducked as Samantha took a swing at his head playfully. He picked up his papers and stood to leave. Leaning across the table he thanked Patsy. "Thanks for this," he inclined his head towards the door. "Her bark is worse than her bite you know. As for me, well none intended, and all that." He winked at her and left the room as Stella returned.

Stella walked to where she had been sitting and studied her notes for a while leaning against the table. She remembered Patsy was still there, and looked up and smiled at her.

"Well done, Patsy, nice work. Three down, and two more this afternoon. I think you might want to keep that roll of tape in your bag, you know." Stella glanced up at the clock. "I'm going home for lunch, you can either join me or I'll meet you back here at two. Which would you prefer?"

"I'm going to get down to the post office and get these off to the lab. Then I'll go home too if you don't mind. I need to catch up on some emails. I'll see you back here at two."

Patsy left the two women in the boardroom and made her way back to her car. She dialled Meredith as she walked. Her call went straight through to voice mail and she left him a brief message. Having sent the latest samples off to the lab via special delivery she drove towards home determined to create something nice for dinner; she was fed up with ready meals, so she decided to shop on the way. She was standing in the queue at the supermarket when Meredith returned her call.

"Sorry I missed you, I was interviewing Anna. So you're leading the life of Reilly now you have left the force. I don't even know what a lunch break is . . . sorry Patsy I have to go, Seaton is back."

He hung up and Patsy smiled at his assumption she would know how crucial it was that Tom had returned to the station.

Meredith placed his phone on his desk and watched as Seaton and Rawlings hurried towards his office. They obviously had some sort of news.

Seaton started speaking before he was in the office. "We managed to speak to five of his mates. All individually, so hopefully we've not been given a crock. It appears that Andrew Short did indeed upset Brent." He placed the bag of doughnuts he'd been carrying on the desk and opened them. As he rummaged in the bag, he added, "Not about the girl though, it was about him dealing in the club." Seaton pulled out a doughnut and bit into it, the jam dripped onto his chin. He nodded at the bag. "Help yourself." He then attempted to collect the jam with his tongue, but unsuccessful he rubbed his fingers across his chin and sucked the jam off them noisily.

Meredith took one from the bag and bit into it. "Go on then, get on with it," Meredith said with his mouth full, and nodded towards Rawlings, who rolled his eyes and opened his note book.

"We interviewed Jones, Sperring, Allcock, Brown, and McIntyre. All knew that Short had been going to the club. He'd pulled one of the dancers on her night off but she wasn't that keen. He was trying to bribe her with, and I quote, 'a few Es and some puff', they're a classy outfit. She played with him for a while, and he took the opportunity to make some sales while he was there. Then he got a call from someone unknown. We know that was our friend Wilson. They all said he was bricking it after he met with this unknown in a car park in town. He wasn't touched but whatever was said put the fear of God into him. He didn't go to the club again and gave up his true love," Rawlings made inverted commas with his index fingers as he said 'love', "for the sake of his health. So we have a definite tie into the club. What we have to figure out now is why Anna would stab him."

Meredith rubbed his hands together to remove the remnants of sugar from his fingers, and ran his tongue around his lips. "Did he mention a ride in the taxi with her?"

"Sarge?" Rawlings nodded at Seaton as he took a doughnut, and Meredith smiled at the now familiar name for Seaton.

"Well, two of them did. We didn't mention her name of course, we just asked if he'd mentioned a ride with a distressed girl," Seaton confirmed. "McIntyre said Short had mentioned something but he'd been smoking and couldn't remember the detail. But Allcock had seen him the morning after, and said he was quite worried about it. Short had seen the girl come in and hang around for a while, and was considering chatting her up when she'd been taken upstairs. His girl wasn't working and he'd nothing to sell so he called it a day a little while later. As he got into the taxi the girl came rushing out in a right state and jumped in. He could see she was messed up. He told Allcock she was shaking, and again I quote, 'her tits were hanging out'. He didn't know how to respond so he gave the taxi driver his address and halfway there she asked to get out. According to Allcock, Short waited at the end of the road until he saw her go into a house. He told him she was a looker and he hoped he'd bump into her again in different circumstances." Seaton shook his head. "Little did the poor bastard know, aye?"

Meredith sighed. "Well, the file has gone across to CPS so we should hear back on that quite quickly. They'll want her up in front of the magistrates sooner rather than later. Her mother is camped out in reception refusing to leave. I'm not her favourite person. We have nothing on the knife. No prints, no fibres, no anything. We have nothing on the gun either." He leaned back supporting his head with his hands. "And we have no clothes . . ." He leaned forward suddenly. "Where's Trump?"

As the men had only just returned to the station they both shrugged. Meredith bellowed for Trump even though he could see he wasn't in the incident room. A few moments later Trump appeared carrying a tray of drinks.

"Did you call? I saw they came back bearing gifts so made some coffee." Trump placed the tray on Meredith's desk. "May I?" he asked and took a doughnut before they answered. Holding it between his thumb and forefinger and poised to bite into it, he looked at Meredith. "How may I help?" He bit into the doughnut.

"Have you spoken to the Super?" Meredith asked, and watched as Trump's shoulders slumped. Trump nodded still chewing, he swallowed.

"I have and I know," he sighed, and Seaton and Rawlings exchanged glances unaware of what news he had received. "Mind you, I'm pleased for him, I just wish this wasn't his parting gift." He paused as all three men looked at him. His eyes widened. "Oh bugger, have I just put my foot in it?"

"Quite possibly, Trump, would you like to share?" Meredith prompted. Trump sat it the third chair more gracefully than a man should be able to and Meredith frowned. "I'd like to say in your own time, but as I have got to see him in half an hour, forewarned and all that."

Trump glanced guiltily over his shoulder before leaning forward and saying in a low voice. "I suppose everyone will know by the close of play. He's been promoted. He's been given the Chief Super post in Devon. He'll be gone within the month." He sighed and leaned back as the three men digested this information.

"Do we know who we're getting?" Meredith asked. He didn't always see eye to eye with his boss, but he would rather the devil you know every time. Trump shook his head and finished his doughnut.

Seaton leaned forward to look at him, a puzzled expression on his face. "So why so glum, Louie, surely it's better for you in the long run if your important uncle doesn't work in the same station?"

It was Rawlings' turn to look at Trump.

"Uncle?" he spluttered. "No one tells me anything in this place." He looked at Seaton accusingly as Trump sighed again.

"His parting gift to me was to tell me I had to do the *Crimebusters* thing on Monday. I tried to get out of it, but he was having none of it. Now I have to face that mad woman again, and to be quite honest, I'm a tad nervous."

"And so you should be," Meredith warned, his face serious. "Steer well clear, stick to business and keep it at that. Tell her you have something nasty you don't want to pass on." He rubbed the bridge of his nose. "Work with Adler and see Andrea downstairs too, but I want a 'have you seen these clothes' thing included. No mention of Anna's possible involvement. I understand we've been extended by five minutes so we can cover the shooting too. Those bloody clothes have to be somewhere. Adler went in with a search warrant and there's nothing even remotely similar. Right, get a rough outline to me by close of play, and then tomorrow we'll send Adler with you to meet with Ms Jessop and keep you out of trouble. You two start digging the crap on Brent, and I mean deep."

With that they were dismissed, so they took their drinks and Seaton snatched the bag of doughnuts as Meredith made to take another one.

"Sorry, Gov, my need is greater. You know the old saying; little pickers wear bigger knickers." He grinned and left the room.

Meredith glanced at his watch. He would be a little early if he went now, but he could congratulate the Superintendent and then get on with some work. There wasn't time to get to the canteen first so the sooner it was over and done with the better. He walked briskly to the Superintendent's office, tapped sharply on the door and went in.

"You wanted to see me, Sir?"

"Ah yes, take a seat, Meredith. I have news." The Superintendent glanced at his watch. "Sorry about this. I'd like to make more of a song and dance about it but there isn't time I'm afraid. I have to be in Exeter by six, and I've a stack of stuff to get through." He tutted and Meredith nodded his head signalling his understanding. "To cut a long story short, today several chaps have been suspended. I say several, what I mean is ten." He shook his head and looked disappointed. Meredith simply raised his eyebrows. "Anyway, there is no likelihood of them coming back, none at all. There's been a shakeup and as a result as from tomorrow morning I will be Chief Superintendent." He paused and nodded towards Meredith. "And you will be Detective Chief Inspector. Congratulations, old man." He stood and held out his hand to a surprised Meredith.

Meredith shook his hand and also his own head at the same time. "Are you serious, Sir? I thought I was about tenth in line for the next job."

"Ah well, they have no one to replace me immediately, and wanted someone capable and senior based here, what with the cases we have on at the moment. I could think of no one more suited than you, so I nudged them in the right direction."

"Thank you, Sir." Meredith nodded but was still too shocked to smile. "I'm delighted of course, but more than a little surprised."

"Well you shouldn't be. They'll bring in a new man," he raised his eyebrows, "or woman, of course, to replace you as soon as possible, but from whatever time you arrive tomorrow morning you'll have the reins on these cases until they find a replacement for me. Now, on that note," he sat and slid a file from the pile on his desk and opened the cover, "Anna Carter, it's a no-go I'm afraid." The Superintendent shrugged at Meredith in a 'what can you do' manner.

Meredith frowned. "What's a no-go?" He leaned forward, trying to read the file upside down. The Superintendent flipped it shut and handed it to him.

"Taking this charge any further. Not at the moment, anyway. Too much of a hot potato for the CPS with so little evidence," he scratched his head. "They correctly point out that the eye witnesses will probably fold under questioning from a hostile QC and then what do you have? Nothing," he answered his own question. "Added to which she was a victim of a serious crime herself. They say retain her passport, give her a warning about disappearing and build a case. You are not," he peered at Meredith over his glasses, "I repeat not, to question her again unless some significant new evidence comes in. You can see their point, 'shooting victim wrongly arrested for murder, whilst her own attacker roams free'." The Superintendent pulled his hand across the space between them as he spoke.

Meredith nodded. "Yeah I understand. I'd better get my finger out then." He tapped the file on his knee before standing.

"I couldn't have put it better myself. Congratulations once more, I'd like to join the celebrations but Devon calls. I should be back sometime the day after tomorrow all being well." He stood and shook Meredith's hand then walked him to the door and opened it. "Control that Maverick side and you'll be sitting in this office in a couple of years."

Meredith walked back to his office pondering this sudden change in fortune. He had applied for promotion the previous year, but was told that he was in the middle of what was claimed to be an illustrious queue. Instead of going back to the incident room, he made his way to the fire escape where he lit a cigarette and called Patsy.

"I've just been promoted," he announced abruptly as she answered the phone.

Patsy was walking back to Stella Young's office. She stopped dead and squealed into the phone. "Really? Brilliant. Congratulations. I am so happy for you, so proud of you. I wish I was there to give you a hug."

Meredith smiled into the phone. "A hug wouldn't be top of the list, but it would do until I got you somewhere quiet." He dragged in nicotine from the cigarette. "Seriously though, Patsy, I now know the meaning of the phrase, gobsmacked." He laughed. "Do you know I'm so shocked I'm almost too embarrassed to tell the team."

"What?" Patsy demanded, laughing at him.

"I said almost," Meredith clarified. "Now get off the phone, I'm a very important person and I have work to do." He grinned as he listened to Patsy laugh again. "I love you, Ms Hodge, see you later."

"And I you, Detective Chief Inspector. Now go and show off, and let me know if I should meet you at the pub tonight."

Meredith stubbed out his cigarette and chewed his lip. He would go and release Anna Carter before he started celebrating.

Brent sat at the oversized desk in his study and listened to his wife moaning to the cleaner about their cancelled trip. He picked up the card again and tapped it thoughtfully against his chin and wondered why he had been invited. There had to be a catch, there always was. He placed the card back in the centre of his desk and brushed it lightly with his fingers, as he pondered whether or not he should just ask, ignore it or simply turn up. His curiosity got the better of him and he picked up his phone. He scrolled through his contacts until he found the number and then leaned back in his chair as he listened to the ringing tone. Stella Young answered on the fourth ring.

"Michael how nice to hear from you. I assume you got the invitation," Stella smiled into the phone. "To be honest, I wasn't at all sure that you would call."

"Now why would that be? You know I have the utmost respect for you, Stella. What I don't understand is why you have invited me. Surely this is purely for your staff. I can't understand where I fit in."

"It is primarily. But you know how it goes, Michael. Showing how successful you are is always useful. I always invite a handful of local bigwigs as it impresses the staff, and hopefully the guests. I know you are not one to hold a grudge and that you're aware I was not involved in the decision about Blaze Solutions," she paused wanting to give the impression she was considering something. "I feel I should tell you that Richard will be there though, so I will understand if you don't wish to attend. I wouldn't want you to feel embarrassed or awkward. I know there is no love lost there."

Stella grinned at Patsy knowing she had just secured Michael Brent's attendance. Patsy nodded her approval. Stella certainly knew how to play the game.

The smile that had been false anyway fell from Brent's face, and he scowled as he spoke although his voice remained level. "Don't be silly, Stella. That's all in the past, I'd be delighted to come, in fact I'm brushing off my dinner jacket as we speak. Nice venue by the way. I'll see you next week."

Brent hung up and called Wilson. "I want a meeting with Derek tomorrow morning. Tell him to go to the food court in the galleries and sit in the corner by the window. I'll be there by nine thirty." He hung up without Wilson uttering a word, and nodded at the invitation. He would show them what happens when you tried to mess with Michael Brent.

Rebecca stopped at the entrance to the sitting room as Derek slid the phone back into his pocket. Her face screwed into a sneer as he glanced up guiltily and looked away.

"Who was that?" she demanded. "Please tell me it's another woman and you will be running off with her. I have to know there is a light at the end of this tunnel." She watched as her husband buried his face in his hands and sighed heavily, the outward breath being forced noisily around his hands. "Just tell me, Derek. Even by your usual standards you have been acting strangely of late."

Derek slowly pulled his hands away from his face and looking at her through weary eyes, he gave a slight shrug. "I'm sorry I disappoint you. It's just business that's all. I am struggling with some issues, and, to be quite frank, I have no idea how to resolve them." His voice was low and there was desperation in his tone.

Rebecca snorted. "Struggling? Really? How can that be, you hardly even work part time these days. All those people that you . . ." she banged clenched fists against her thighs in frustration. "You make me feel sick. Look at you, sitting there feeling sorry for yourself, when you should be out there looking after the business to keep your family. What happened to the man I thought I was marrying? Where has that proud soldier gone? I remember how much the men used to like you and come to you for help. What would they think of you now?" she snorted. "I can see now that Major Henderson was right. All that ridiculous nonsense about a career in show business. Ludicrous! Where did that get you? Nowhere, that's where. Our savings were demolished and you ruined the opportunity to build something worthwhile. Now you seem to just do enough to keep afloat. I bumped into Teresa Brown who told me you weren't there again yesterday afternoon."

She walked into the room and stood looking down at him in the armchair and gave a little laugh. "What you didn't understand is that show business is filled with handsome men, or at least men with charm and a talent to entertain." She shook her head slowly. "So here we are fifteen years on and you still haven't managed to achieve any form of success. Unless gambling and running up debts can be classed as success, that is." A low groan came from her throat. "You are useless, you hear me use -"

She didn't have the opportunity to complete her sentence as Derek flew up out of the chair with surprising agility. He grabbed her by the shoulders and pushed her backwards until he had her pinned against the wall. He leaned forward until their noses touched and he applied pressure, squashing Rebecca's nose back against her face.

"I am at the end of my tether, woman. I need your support, not more nagging you stupid, stupid bitch. Useless am I? You have no idea what I am capable of, so just remember that." He growled through gritted teeth and saliva gathered at the corners of his mouth. He tilted his head so that his forehead pressed against hers. "You treat me with a little more respect, and if you can't manage that common courtesy will suffice. I give you fair warning, I can't cope with much more, now get out of my sight."

He leaned back and twisted his wife's body roughly, then gave her a shove which propelled her towards the door. She made a noise that sounded as though it had come from a wounded animal, and ran from the room. Derek placed his hands against the wall and bowed his head as he listened to her running up the stairs. He heard a door slam and stood upright. His shoulders back, he took a deep breath causing his chest to rise, which he held whilst he thought about the options in dealing with his wife. It was possible, but dangerous; he would have to get this business with Brent out of the way first. He exhaled noisily as he thought about Brent, and his shoulders sagged back to their customary slump.

Patsy snuggled into Meredith and stroked his chest lightly. He looked down at her just able to see her silhouette in the darkness and reached out to pull up the duvet.

"Thank you," she whispered and her lips brushed his skin.

"What for covering you up, or showing you just how well a Detective Chief Inspector can perform after imbibing far too much alcohol?"

"Both," Patsy laughed and slapped him, and then she pushed herself up on her elbow. "The team were so pleased for you. Even Trump seemed genuinely happy, despite meeting with Dawn Jessop this afternoon. Well done, handsome." She leaned down and kissed him. "We're in a good place you and I, let's hope it continues. I am thoroughly enjoying my job, and it's giving me my first opportunity to see how you scrub up. Although I am going to have to buy a new dress. Do you have an evening suit?"

"I do, and if I do say so myself I look rather dapper in it." Meredith yawned and pulled her back down against him. "I'm quite looking forward to seeing you in a posh frock. Are you sure Chris won't want to escort you?"

"No, he's taking Sharon away for the weekend." She gave a little laugh. "I can't wait for them to meet Linda tomorrow. I think Sharon is only coming in because she wants to check her out."

"Ah yes, loopy Linda. I hope she works out for you. Not that I'm complaining, but why do you have to be there for the evening do? Aren't you doing the wicked deed during the daytime proceedings?"

"I have to attend the evening do because there are two men attending that I need samples from that aren't staff so they won't be there during the day. Stella wasn't sure how to get me into their company. Some bloke called Brent and another whose name has completely escaped me."

"Michael Brent?" Meredith asked, suddenly fully awake and interested in the conversation.

"Yes, I think so. Do you know him?"

"Only by name, small world isn't it. Can we go to sleep now, please? You've used me and abused me, and now is not the time to start a conversation. Good night, Patsy Hodge PI." He manoeuvred her body so that she faced away from him and then pulled her back against him. He smiled at such a golden opportunity to meet the man that seemed to be tangled within his two cases. He decided not to mention it to Patsy in case she withdrew the invitation.

"Good night, DCI Meredith." Patsy smiled as she lay in his arms and listened to his rhythmic breathing believing him to be sleeping. She drifted off to sleep as she thought about how much their lives had changed in a few short months. Meredith remained awake a while longer. Staring into the darkness, he hoped he would be given the opportunity to speak to Brent.

CHAPTER FIFTEEN

Meredith clapped his hands. "Right you lot, let's make this short. First, Trump will give us a brief and sober update on the *Crimebusters* show next week." There were a few sniggers as the team turned their gaze to Trump who was looking decidedly worse for wear. "Then Seaton can update us on what he's dug up on Brent so far, and we can assign tasks for the day." He nodded at Trump who straightened up a little. "Over to you, Sergeant Trump."

"DCI Meredith," Trump nodded back. "I met with Dawn Jessop and one of the camera crew, and it has been agreed that we will have a full ten minute slot on *Crimebusters*. It's planned that we will split this into two sections, and the first will concentrate on Andrew Short. We'll take the walk he took with the camera, and then film the route we think the assailant took. We'll end his section by showing the clothes we believe his attacker was wearing, and then move to Anna Carter's shooting. That is unless anything new comes up on Short in the meantime."

He took a deep breath and swallowed and felt decidedly nauseous. "Is there any chance we might have another coffee whilst we do this?" he asked, wishing for the umpteenth time that morning that he had the sense not to drink so much.

"Get on with it, Trump," snapped Meredith.

"Yes, DCI Meredith. Anna Carter. Well, we haven't got much here. No ballistic evidence from the gun, and not even a reasonable description of the chap that pulled the trigger. However, given the close proximity of the locations, we will do a segment along the street to Joey's Diner, and then off the other way towards town. We will labour the fact that Anna is a good, clean-living and sensible girl. Still at home with her parents, and so we'll go for the 'has anyone you know been acting strangely angle'. That is unless, as with the Short stabbing, we come up with anything else before we go live."

Having completed his update Trump slumped back in the chair, and Seaton swivelled his to face his audience.

"If I may, DCI Meredith," Seaton grinned and Meredith pursed his lips and nodded. The lines developing around his eyes betrayed his amusement. "Michael Brent, handsome, successful and fingers in many murky pies," he pointed up at the board. "On the face of it, he is simply an entrepreneurial businessman trying to make a fortune. Member of the Bristol Business League, the Round Table, sits on various local charity boards, a regular pillar of the community to all outsiders looking in. But as we know nothing is for nothing, and Brent's various businesses all benefit to one degree or another by his associations.

"The only time he let himself down publicly was a little more than a year ago, over the Cherry Tree syndicate that was disbanded and reformed. Whilst no stones were openly cast in his direction, when the syndicate reformed he was no longer a member. A couple of reporters got hold of this and he gave a vitriolic interview which all but suggested that Councillor Richard Hancock was bent. Hancock, ever the politician, responded by suggesting the reporters had misunderstood Mr Brent, and that he had nothing but the utmost respect for the sterling charity work that he did." Seaton shook his head. "We know from Anna Carter that he rules his little empire by fear, and will take what is not given willingly. Three of the syndicates and or companies to which he is connected have other similar characters as partners or directors. I've got a meeting with the fraud team later this morning to see what they have on him and or his various cohorts." He nodded at Meredith. "That's it from me, DCI Meredith."

Meredith narrowed his eyes, his amusement waning. "Thank you, Sergeant Seaton." He looked around the rest of the team. "Any more for any more?"

The briefing lasted another ten minutes with various updates that didn't amount to much.

"Right, get on with your allotted tasks and keep me informed of any developments." Meredith made to move away and then hesitated and turned back to them. "For the record, we haven't got time for job titles, so let's cut the crap." He smiled and made his way back to his office. As he reached the door he turned. "Trump, make the coffee you're so desperate for, then get in here, you too, Seaton."

"What is it, Gov?" Seaton asked as Trump closed the door.

"Just want your opinion on something. You've seen how vulnerable Anna Carter is, and you know how bad Michael Brent can be, and this is between us you understand." He looked at them and both nodded. "I have the opportunity to socialise with Mr Brent next Friday night and as *Crimebusters* goes out the night before, what do you reckon, should we shake the box a little?"

"How do you mean Sir?" Trump's head had started thumping at his temples.

"What if we just add to the content for *Crimebusters*? Get the crew to film the outside of Sensations and the last message will be, despite not knowing each other, both victims were seen at this club shortly before they were attacked, so police are looking for information which may explain this coincidence. You know the sort of thing. I know it will rattle his cage, but my question is will we be putting Anna at risk?"

There was silence for a few minutes while his two sergeants considered this.

Seaton was the first to respond. "I doubt it, although she won't like us mentioning she's been there, given the nature of her visit. Perhaps we should mention that it was totally out of character. He won't do anything, but you're right it will give him a jolt if he is involved."

"Oh, he's involved. What do you think, Trump?" Meredith watched as Trump grimaced.

"I think it means I have to go back to *Crimebusters*, and if I didn't know you better I might suggest you had orchestrated this just to make me suffer." He smiled briefly. "Seriously though I concur with Tom, should it have any effect it will be good for us. We just need to keep a close watch on those involved. Once we have lit the blue touch paper we shouldn't stand back." He cleared his throat. "May I be excused now? I must get some painkillers before my head explodes." He rubbed his temples with the middle finger of each hand.

"Go on, get on with it, then get your arse down to *Crimebusters*." Meredith jerked his head towards the door and both men left.

All he had to do now was be patient. It was a week until the show and he hoped something else would arise in the meantime.

Patsy arrived at work early. She wanted to write up reports for the file that she knew Chris, and more particularly, Sharon would want to see. She pulled the calculator from her drawer and totted up how much the work she had done so far had cost Stella Young. She whistled as she saw that three days' work was the equivalent to almost a third of her previous monthly salary, and she entered it into their accounts system. Sharon and Chris arrived as she completed the task and she went out to greet them.

"How are you feeling?" she asked Sharon and hugged her.

"I'm fine now, a bit croaky that's all. More to the point, young lady, is how you are getting along? How do you find working with Stella Young?" Sharon walked to Penny's desk and switched on the computer.

"She's okay actually. She calls a spade a shovel but that makes life easier really. Where are you to off to next week? I can recommend Paris," she smiled as Chris groaned.

"Don't go giving her any more ideas. We're off to the sunshine or at least I hope so, a long weekend in Tenerife will do us nicely. The hotel has a spa so her ladyship is more than happy," Chris announced sitting at his own desk. "What time is Linda due in?"

"Before nine she said, so any minute now. I haven't told you the news. have I? Did you hear about Meredith's promotion?"

Chris clapped his hands together. "And about time too! Well, that calls for a celebration. What do you think Sharon?"

"Sounds good to me, then you . . ." She paused as there was a knock at the door. It opened slowly and Linda stepped in.

"Only me." Her smile was hesitant. Patsy stepped forward to greet her and was surprised that Linda appeared to be a little nervous.

"It's so good to see you," she held her hand towards Sharon. "This is Sharon and this is Chris," she then nodded towards Linda, "and this is Linda, computer woman extraordinaire."

Chris stood to shake her hand, and Linda shoved what she was holding under her opposite arm and shook his hand, and then turned to Sharon.

"Nice to meet you. I have to say I'm just a tad excited. I've never worked for a private investigator before." She raised her eyebrows and shrugged happily.

Patsy held her hand out. "Here let me take your coat." She watched as Linda looked around for somewhere to put her things. "Give me whatever that is, and we'll set you up in my office."

Linda stepped forward and handed Patsy the bundle from under her arm, and then allowed her bag to slide down her arm to the floor before she removed her coat. Patsy examined the bundle and grinned. "You really are loopy, do you know that, Linda?" She laughed and held up the two items so Chris and Sharon could see them. "A deerstalker and a magnifying glass! What were you going to do with these?"

Linda was hanging her coat on the rack in the corner and she grinned.

"I was going to come in wearing the hat and peering through the glass, but I thought that was a bit much, even for me." She frowned as she took back the items. "Who said I was loopy anyway?" she demanded.

"Meredith, but I don't think he meant it," Patsy assured her.

Linda's frown fell away. "Ah that's okay, he was probably messing," Linda smiled and Sharon snorted and shook her head, knowing she was looking at another young woman caught under Meredith's spell, however innocent that might be.

Linda followed Patsy into her office, and she drew a line with her finger under the name stencilled on the door. "PHPI, how swish. I wondered what the attraction was, and now I know. Right, where do you want me?" she asked walking towards the desk. "I really, really like this."

Patsy smiled at her as she ran her hand along the desk. "I was going to ask you for advice on that actually. Whatever it is you're going to be looking at, you both need to look at the same screen. I thought I would turn the screen around and you could both sit on this side of the desk. What do you think?"

"Yep, that'll work. What time is he due in?" Linda asked as she placed the deerstalker and magnifying glass on the coffee table.

"Nine thirty," Patsy walked to the other side of the desk and swivelled the monitor. "Is there anything else you might need?" she enquired as Linda arranged the keyboard and chairs to suit her purpose.

"Just a writing pad, if you have one. I've got mine but it's a bit tatty for this outfit." Linda took the pad Patsy had extracted from the cabinet and placed it to the right of the keyboard. "Okay, I'm ready to go, come on down Mr Tucker." She looked expectantly towards the door and shrugged when no one appeared. "I suppose that was a big ask. Right, lead me to the kitchen instead, let's get some coffee on the go."

Patsy showed her to the kitchen, taking orders from Chris and Sharon as they went. As they returned to the reception area George Tucker struggled in through the door with several large box files and a battered brown leather brief case. Chris jumped up to assist him, and took them through to Patsy's office.

"Nice to see you again, Mr Tucker." Patsy introduced him to the others. "I'll go and get you a coffee, and while I'm doing that, why don't you recap briefly to ensure I explained your problems to the others correctly."

Patsy took Tucker's coat and he sat heavily on one of the two sofas. He took the files from Chris and laid two next to each other on the table, having pushed the deerstalker and magnifying glass to one side. Sharon rolled her eyes as he did so. He then balanced the third file on top of the other two and opened it.

"This is where I first noticed it." He turned a few pages and pointed to a bank statement which had balances highlighted with a lime green marker. "You see here, these are the sales coming in from A, E and F divisions and these from B, C and D. He pointed to figures highlighted in blue and yellow. "You will note the references begin with the appropriate letter, then these . . ." he slid one of the bottom files out and flipped it open.

"If you'll excuse me, Mr Tucker, I'll leave you with the ladies, they're the experts in this type of thing." Chris shook his hand and walked out of the office. He went to see Patsy in the kitchen. "I know these jobs pay well Patsy, but one sentence in and I was nearly asleep. I'll leave you girls to it. I have some calls to make so I'll hold the fort until Penny arrives."

"No problem, I'm not sure that I will understand it myself. I'll probably leave Linda and Sharon to it once the initial bit is out of the way." Patsy slid some biscuits out of a packet and onto a plate, and then placed it on the tray next to Tucker's coffee. "Wish me luck," she smiled as she made her way back to her office.

It didn't take George Tucker long to explain how he had picked up the differences. As he had been monitoring the situation for so long he was able to demonstrate his concern, but had begun labouring the point.

Linda was itching to get on with it. "Right, George. You don't mind if I call you George, do you?" Linda smiled as he confirmed that was fine. "I can see your point with this lot," she waved her hand over files, "but as you rightly say, it doesn't explain the outcome on the general bank account. Without looking at the system it's difficult to be certain, but the way your commissions and discounts are worked out in the background is too complicated. There are too many movements before one becomes the other. Do you see?" Linda looked at Tucker expectantly, but he gave a half shrug and shook his head. "Okay, let's get logged in to your live system and I'll buy some stationery or something and show you. Come on." Linda stood and walked to Patsy's desk.

"Oh right, I'll warn you that I'm no good on computers. I can do the click through thing well enough, but I don't know how it works behind the screen."

He looked anxious as he stood to follow her. "Will you need my laptop? I can log in with that too."

"Ah good, that will make it easier for me to show you." Linda slapped the desk. "Put it on here then, let's get this show on the road." She leaned forward and assisted in removing the laptop from the briefcase. "Why do you use that old thing?" she asked nodding at the briefcase. "You should get one of the modern ones. You do sell them, and they weigh nothing."

"I... I'm not sure, habit I suppose." Tucker glanced at Patsy for support and she smiled and nodded agreement. She was hoping Linda's quirkiness wasn't going to get in the way, as it was clear she was on to something. She glanced at Sharon who had remained sitting on the sofa and was watching proceedings carefully. Her face was impassive and Patsy had no idea what she was thinking.

Linda set the laptop up and arranged the two screens so they could both be seen easily. She nodded at the chair next to her. "Sit there, George, and tell me how your log in works for the back end. I'll just log in as a customer."

Her hands flew speedily over the keyboard and in a few seconds Tucker's online ordering service was displayed on Patsy's monitor. Linda clenched her fists and pursed her lips as she watched the painful process of Tucker logging into his own system. Her eyes darted between the keyboard and the prompts on the screen. When he had finished, she sighed before smiling.

"Can I say, George, that when we've discovered where the missing money is, you really need to look at this lot." Linda jerked her finger towards the screen. "Too many clicks and not enough information on the screen at one time. Your customers must die of impatience before they get to buy anything. I can help you with that, but let's find where the money is going first. Then you'll have enough to pay us for the extra work." Linda smiled at him and then leaned back a little and winked at Sharon who merely raised her eyebrows in response. Linda went back to the ordering system.

"I am going to buy four boxes of paper. Why am I buying four I hear you ask yourself? Because with four, two things happen, watch this. First, I get a multi buy discount for the three, see ten per cent of the total comes here, then the fourth is half price, and the discount is shown here." She pointed to a column of figures on the right-hand side of her screen, and turned to face George. "Now I am going to buy some pens, so I type that in search. Here we go, I chose the ones I want and this is the bit I'm talking about." She jabbed a finger at the screen, "It tells me these are on offer with multi buys so I have to click to go to the offers page, then I check the offer and chose the quantity," she turned to him and tutted. "Now unless I see that, to add this to my other order, I have to click here, which for the purpose of this demonstration I will." She sighed as she waited for the system to catch up. "Now I have to click here." She did so with a flourish then looked at her watch.

"It does seem to be taking a time, doesn't it? I've never been through the whole process before."

Linda nodded in agreement and tapped her watch. "Over seven minutes to buy two items and still here," she pointed back at the column of figures. "Instead of showing me overall discounts I'm building up a tidy little tree killing exercise should I want to print it. And," she shook her finger at George, "that's if I noticed the need to click back earlier. If I hadn't, the paper order would have been lost." Linda waved her hand dismissively. "Anyway, I digress, what I now want to see is how these," she ran her finger down the column of figures, "work in there." She pointed at Tucker's laptop and reached for his mouse. "May I?"

Tucker nodded and watched in sheer admiration as Linda clicked away with the mouse, opening and closing different elements of the accounts package. She stopped occasionally to write something on the note pad, and opened a document onto which she copied and pasted either sections of the screen or formulae she had revealed.

Sharon had come to join Patsy and they watched her. Linda mumbled to herself as she worked, and finally, after ten minutes, she typed an instruction into the screen and a list of names appeared on the left hand of the window, whilst a complicated looking formula appeared on the right. She tapped the screen.

"You, right?" she queried and Tucker leaned forward squinting at the screen before concurring. Linda leaned back in her chair, her hands on her hips. "As I thought." She drummed her fingers on the desk for a second, before clicking away again. "And this is?"

Again, Tucker squinted at the screen, but this time he shook his head. "I don't know."

Linda changed the screen. "And this?"

Again, she watched Tucker shake his head. This procedure carried on for thirty minutes or so. Occasionally Tucker looked triumphant when he was able to answer her questions. Eventually, she pushed the mouse away.

She turned to Tucker and shook her head gravely. "George, you have three major problems. The first is your system is crap," she smiled, "but that can be fixed. The second is that whilst it appears to be so basic as to be prehistoric, I think someone is playing a smoke and mirrors game. Because here," she clicked on the document where she had copied and pasted screen shots, "the balance is correct according to the order and the discounts, and here the balance is also correct but different." Linda turned the screen to face him, "And finally here, a different balance again but that is because the commission for the sales rep has been taken off and appears to be correct because it tallies with this and this," she scrolled down the document and tapped the screen again.

"But how . . ." George stopped speaking as Linda wafted away his question and continued her commentary.

"However, and I just tested this three times, even allowing for discount et cetera you appear to lose three per cent on each of these transactions and," she scrolled down further, "five per cent on these. But," she waved her finger at him, "not always, and without starting from . . . look, I can see your eyes have glazed over now." She smiled at him and Sharon and Patsy exchanged glances. "The good news is, you're not going mad. The better news is I can track this back, and the even better news is that by the time I've finished you'll have a system to be proud of." She winked at him again. "And I can start straight away." She held out her hand. George Tucker nodded, then looked at Patsy and Sharon, and then nodded again.

He shook her hand. "How long do you think it will take?" he asked.

"The basic stuff not long, should get there by tomorrow. Do you know how many sales you make over the weekend?" she asked and Tucker shrugged.

"Not many, negligible really, Tuesday is our biggest day. Why do you ask?"

"Because once I've done the first thing I need to do and worked out how to put right whatever's wrong, I'm going to need to pull the plug. Putting it all back again may take me a while, maybe as long as two days, but it's your shout. I can do some, possibly even most, whilst you're still live, but that would take much longer and be more painful," she tilted her head to one side, "for me because I'm impatient and you because it will cost more. So over to you, George."

Linda patted him on the shoulder and resisted the urge to take a bow.

"Right, let's get some more coffee and leave Mr Tucker to have a think about that," Sharon said warmly. "More coffee, Mr Tucker?" she nodded as he confirmed he would like some and jerked her head towards the door. The two women followed her out into the reception area where Chris was speaking quietly to a young man who was obviously upset. Chris ushered him away to a meeting room.

Sharon led them into the kitchen. Once there she grasped Linda's face between her two hands and planted a noisy kiss in the middle of her forehead. "You little star. Where have you been all my life?" She looked over her shoulder at Patsy. "A bloody gem she is. That would have taken us at least a day with the chaps we use just to understand what they were saying. The drinks are on me, I'll make these."

Linda grinned happily at Patsy as Sharon filled the kettle. They gave George Tucker ten minutes alone before returning to Patsy's office.

He stood up as they entered. "Let's do it, but I want to get on with it now. I reckon I'm around thirty to forty grand down, so the sooner the better. What do you want from me?"

Linda explained what she wanted. It was agreed that she would work the rest of the day remotely from Patsy's office, and then the next day go to Tucker's where the main server was based. Within twenty minutes his laptop had been repacked and Patsy was carrying his folders to the car. When she returned to her office Linda was already busy at work. She looked up as Patsy returned followed by Sharon.

"Thanks for this job. The work needed is pretty standard really. There is one part I might do with my fingers crossed, but it's the whodunit part that gets me excited. One thing I wondered though, is what do I do when I know who did it?" Linda looked from one to the other.

"That's up to the client," Sharon informed her. "You tell them the result and they decide how they want to move forward. Some don't want customers to know their business was compromised so they just let people go, others call in the police. When you are certain, and I mean one hundred and ten per cent certain who has been doing what, we tell Mr Tucker, or George as you are allowed to call him, and he decides. He's the one that reports it to the police and you give a witness statement and provide the evidence you have." She held her hands out. "It's as simple as that."

"Okay, I understand." Linda looked away and back to her screen. Within seconds she was oblivious to their presence.

Sharon and Patsy left her to it and returned to the reception area.

"I need to ring the lab and see if there are any results in yet." Patsy looked at Penny's empty desk. "I'll sit here. Where's Penny by the way?"

"T'up North." Chris attempted an accent. "Her mother lives just outside Leeds and has been involved in a car crash. Penny got the call early this morning, so she'll be off for a few days. Luckily Sharon hasn't got to go out much."

Patsy sat at Penny's desk. "That's a shame. I hope it's not too serious." She lifted the handset and called the laboratory for the results. A few minutes later she hung up. "Nothing doing on those that have gone in so far. I'll update Stella Young."

She dialled out again. Stella picked up the call on the first ring.

"Patsy, what's new?" she snapped, clearly agitated, and Patsy wished she had better news for her.

"Not much, only that we have eliminated all those tested so far. Fingers crossed for tomorrow."

"Yes indeed. We might have to change those plans. My damned physio has let me down again, the idiot. It's the second time this month; he'd better sort his act out or he'll lose my custom." She sighed. "Sorry, Patsy, shooting the messenger and all that, but I'm struggling to pick up the baby at the moment, and I haven't got time to waste messing about chasing him. I'm told he should be in tomorrow so hopefully I'll catch him early, and we can still head down to Taunton."

There was a pause and Patsy heard a door slam.

"Right, I'm back at the office now. I'll call you later to confirm our diary for tomorrow. Oh and we do have several that can't make the conference so we'll have to get to them scheduled in too."

Patsy hung up and insisted that Chris take Sharon out for lunch and then shop for their son's birthday present, whilst she held the fort and worked with Linda. Sharon was delighted.

"An afternoon off with your gorgeous wife, what more could you ask?" Sharon teased Chris as he reluctantly pulled on his coat. He had updated Patsy on the case in the Midlands and knew that she could make all the necessary arrangements without him, but it felt odd handing over the file. He knew that it was something he would have to get used to if Sharon had her way. He sighed as he opened the door for his wife, and wondered if he could ever come to terms with it.

Patsy made short work of arranging flights and booking the hotels that Chris would need the next week and she immersed herself in the detail of the case. She smiled as she saw the shortcuts that Chris had taken to obtain information. Shortcuts that were unavailable to the police, if they wanted the evidence to stand up in court. She knew she would enjoy not having her hands tied with red tape.

A little before four o'clock Linda suddenly appeared at the doorway brandishing her note pad.

"I think I know how they're doing it. I can't be sure until I get onto the server tomorrow, and I need his other staff's login details, but I'm almost there. You will have to think of an appropriate name for me now that I am an official sleuth." She grinned. "I need more coffee and then I'll write up some notes for you."

"A name? You mean Loopy Linda isn't going to stick?" Patsy teased, and Linda narrowed her eyes.

"I am many things, such as eccentric, extrovert, dazzling," she waved her finger at Patsy, "but never, ever loopy. Actually, I was thinking of something far more obvious. Leave it with me, I'll work on it."

An hour later she had not only written up the notes of her work to date, but had updated the Grainger software to make invoicing easier. She linked her arm in Patsy's as they left the office.

"Do you know, I think I might alter the course of my career. I might look into how I can promote myself for work like this. This is so much better than writing programs, not that that isn't interesting, of course, but there are no personalities involved. Except mine." She laughed. "Are we going for a drink then? I think we should celebrate me joining the detective fraternity."

Patsy considered this for a moment and then decided to take Linda to the Dirty Duck.

A few minutes after six o'clock the two women were sitting in front of the fire. Patsy had spoken to Meredith who had agreed to join them as soon as he could. Frankie had called and was popping in to finalise the arrangements for collecting the samples at Stella Young Property Service's conference.

Louie Trump pushed open the door to the bar and glanced around. There was no one he knew in the bar, and he took a seat on a bar stool and ordered an orange juice and lemonade. Patsy returning from the toilets noticed him reading the back page of a discarded newspaper, which was soaking up a spillage on the bar. She tapped him on the shoulder.

"Not drinking tonight then, Louie?" she asked looking at his glass.

Louie turned and beamed at her. "Oh at last, a friendly face." He slid off the bar stool and embraced her. "Hello, Patsy, how are you? I hope your day has been better than mine. Are you meeting the boss?"

Patsy pushed him away. "Blimey, you must have had a bad one. That was an

enthusiastic greeting. Yes, Meredith will be over in a while, come and join us."
She nodded towards Linda who was sitting up straight in her chair and smiling at
them. "I'm with my . . ." Patsy paused briefly, "my friend and colleague Linda."

Trump flashed a smile at Linda and picked up his drink. He followed Patsy
back to the table and she introduced him formally. Trump sat next to Linda.

"So Linda, a work colleague of Patsy? Are you a private eye too then? I have to
say I never expected the world of the private detective to be littered with so many
beautiful women."

Patsy groaned and he slapped a hand against his chest and turned to her.

"I speak the truth! Why the groan? Surely to goodness, even in these days
of women's equality, a genuine compliment cannot be out of place." He sighed
dramatically and shook his head in bewilderment.

Linda leaned towards him and nudged him with her shoulder. "Don't worry
about her. You can dish out all the compliments you wish, and I will receive them
gracefully. I'm not a women's libber. I will take whatever you care to hand out,
because *I know*. I appreciate what we need to do." She winked at him and sipped
her drink.

"Know what?" Trump looked at Patsy for an answer but she shrugged. He
turned back to Linda. "You will have to enlighten me."

"Only if you promise not to tell the others, or it could cause untold damage
to the delicate balance of peace on earth. Well almost." She paused awaiting his
response, and when none was forthcoming she added, "You will have to promise
or my lips are sealed."

Trump looked at her solemnly and drew a cross on his chest, then pretended to
zip shut his mouth. He leaned towards her. "My lips are sealed, please open yours."

Patsy groaned again and the other two looked over and hushed her.

Linda rolled her eyes at Trump. "Louie, you have to understand, that not all of
us know. I'll enlighten Patsy too, although I suspect that she knows really."

She waved Patsy forward and Patsy obliged. The three huddled over the table
as though part of some great conspiracy.

Linda took hold of Trump's hand and patted it. "It's quite simple. Women
are superior to men." She held a hand up to halt any denial. "I know it's tough
to accept, after all the brainwashing you have been through. This secret is only
discussed behind closed doors. Picture this. An open fire burns in the hearth, and
men sit on overstuffed leather furniture smoking cigars. They speak in hushed

tones, plotting. And their plot is to ensure that *we*," she waved her finger back and forth between herself and Patsy, "never find that out. What shock horror there would be if the women of the world found out that they were really in the driving seat? What would happen then? Women politicians, business leaders, and God forbid, prime ministers. But women prevail and the secret spreads. Little by little, those women in the know sort things out."

Ignoring Patsy's grin, Linda paused for a moment as though wondering whether to share more insights, and giving a little nod she leaned closer still.

"Think about this, Louie, the next time you feel superior to a woman. What sex were this country's greatest monarchs?" A satisfied sigh escaped her lips, and she leaned back in her chair. "That's right. Elizabeth I, Victoria, and now our own dear Elizabeth II. They all lasted far longer than their male counterparts for a reason." She tapped the side of her forehead, "Mental capacity."

Trump snorted and started to laugh, his shoulders bouncing up and down.

Linda slapped his hand. "It's not funny, Louie." She shook her head, a serious expression on her face. "But you are like most men when they find out and are still in denial." She pointed heavenward. "Why do you think HE chose women to bear the children?" She nodded sagely. "That's right, because men would not be capable." Linda took a large swig of her drink and grinned at him as she slapped his shoulder. "But look on the bright side. He tried to ensure you were stronger, in a physical sense of course, certainly not mentally. He had to make you think you were better so we could manipulate you. See, simple!"

Trump leaned back in his chair and studied Linda. He gazed at her, a smile almost breaking free.

Linda raised her eyebrows. "And now you feel the need to compliment me once more." She waved her finger in a circular motion. "Go on, it's safe. Only those of us who haven't worked it out yet can't accept a compliment." She dropped her hand to her lap, "In fact, I am actually expecting one now."

"Well then, dear lady, I shall not disappoint. I have had a pig of a day and you have relaxed my troubled soul. Now I am no longer in turmoil, but content with my being. Knowing, as I now do, that I am in your capable hands, my troubles are dissolved, my heart is light. The very least I can do is buy you a drink. What can I get you?"

Grinning, Louie stood and looked down on Linda. Patsy wondered if she had disappeared.

Linda closed her eyes in a slow blink of consent and looked back at Trump. "A white wine spritzer would be lovely, thank you, kind sir."

Patsy shook her head as Trump went to the bar. "Do you use that often?" she asked, grinning at her friend, who was still watching Trump.

Without looking at her, Linda replied, "Only when I want to catch one. Red hair or not, he's quite something."

"What? Louie, really?" Patsy shook her head in amazement, and Linda spun to face her.

"Of course. I suppose you can't see it because you're all loved up with Meredith, but it's there. I think I have just released his better side." She nodded towards the door. "Talk of the devil, here's your bloke."

Patsy turned and watched Meredith approach Trump at the bar. He looked over and her grin grew. He shrugged at her asking an unspoken question, and she shook her head in response, refusing to tell him the secret.

Linda giggled. "Nicely done, PHPI. It wouldn't do to let too many in on the secret. It simply upsets the balance."

Meredith carried the drinks back to the table. He leaned down and kissed Patsy. "I hope your day was better than mine. I'm guessing it was as you look very relaxed." He straightened up and looked at Linda. "Hello, Loopy, I hope you're not leading my chaps astray." He nodded at Trump.

"Give me a chance, I've only known him five minutes." Linda looked at Trump and patted the seat next to her. "Sit down, Louie. I have some leading to do."

They spent the next twenty minutes bantering, comfortable in each other's company. So much so that Meredith jumped to his feet when Frankie Callaghan arrived with his new fiancée, Sarah.

He slapped Frankie on the shoulder. "Sherlock, mate. Good to see you, and I understand congratulations are in order. So, congratulations." He lifted Sarah's hand and kissed it. "Congratulations, Mrs Sherlock."

Linda nudged Trump. "You see. Although he doesn't know it, he has just shown he is subservient to her. You lot think that opening doors and the like is simply being chivalrous. It is, to a degree of course, but it is really your subconscious acknowledging the superior being."

Trump roared with laughter and Meredith turned to him.

"What's the joke?"

"I couldn't possibly tell you. This earth's fragile balance and the well-being of future generations may depend on it." Trump looked to Linda for approval, which she delivered by blowing him a kiss.

Meredith shook his head and took orders for drinks. Frankie and Sarah settled themselves at the table. When Meredith returned the newly engaged couple were toasted, and they told the others of their wedding plans.

"A smallish affair, given that neither of us has much family, and you are all welcome to join us of course." Frankie smiled at Linda. "That extends to you and Louie. We would be delighted to have you there. Wouldn't we?" He turned to Sarah for confirmation which she gave.

Trump's lips twitched as he accepted the kind offer. He and Linda had been taken for a couple, and Frankie had asked Sarah for permission to invite them. Perhaps Linda was on to something. Neither Linda nor Louie had attempted to correct Frankie in his assumption.

Meredith leaned towards her to say something but was interrupted by his phone ringing. He pulled it out of his pocket and frowned at the screen.

"Excuse me, I must just take this." He stood and walked out of the bar. A few seconds later they could see him pacing up and down in the car park. It was clear he was less than happy with the information he was receiving.

"So, Pats, what's the plan of attack for next week? If we could just touch base now it would be great. Sarah and I are away for the weekend and I'm off to Cardiff for a conference on Monday for three days." Frankie looked at the others. "Sorry to talk shop, but needs must I'm afraid."

His concerns were dismissed by the others and he and Patsy went to sit at an empty table in the bay window. Patsy pulled her note book from her bag, and talked Frankie through the plan for the Stella Young Property Services conference. She was winding up the conversation when Meredith returned looking far less relaxed than when he had left. He slumped into a chair.

"Is everything all right, Sir?" Trump enquired. "Is there anything I need to know or do?"

Meredith stared at him and shook his head, a look of distaste on his face, as though Trump had asked an inappropriate question. "Nope."

"Oh okay, it's just, I thought . . ." Trump shut up when he caught Meredith's withering gaze, and returned his attention to Linda and Sarah who were discussing flowers.

Meredith watched Patsy's interaction with Frankie. As she closed her pad, their conversation complete, Frankie winked at her and she patted his knee. Meredith bristled. He was only too aware of how close Patsy had come to having a relationship with Sherlock, and this familiarity didn't sit well. He stood abruptly, his chair scraping the floor. The others looked up at him.

"Time to go. Got some stuff to do, I'm afraid. Enjoy the rest of your evening." He took hold of Patsy by the elbow as she reached the table. "Is it okay with you if we go now?" It was a statement rather than a question. "I have things I need to sort out."

It had been agreed earlier that Meredith would only have one drink to enable him to drive home. He, like Trump, had had more than enough the night before. Patsy's brow creased as she wondered what news had been delivered when he took the call. She could see he was irritated and decided it would be best if she agreed with him. It had been a lovely evening so far and she didn't want one of Meredith's moods to ruin it. She lifted her coat off the back of the chair and pulled it on, looking at Linda.

"Are you going to be okay to get home? We can give you a lift and I'll pick you up tomorrow to collect your car." She smiled at Linda's look of disgust.

"I'm having fun, it's far too early to be going home," Linda looked pointedly at Meredith who ignored her. "Louie has agreed to give me a lift so I'll be fine." She winked at Patsy and Trump grinned, hoping his run of bad luck with women had just changed.

"Great, we'll be off then. Bye all." Meredith turned and walked away. Patsy shrugged at the others and rolled her eyes. They nodded an unspoken agreement as she waved goodbye.

Meredith had already started the car when she reached the car park. She climbed in and pulled the seat belt across her.

"Was it bad news?"

"What?"

"The call, of course. When you left the bar, you were Mr Happy and when you returned you were back to Meredith proper." Patsy knew that her sarcasm would not be missed and she didn't care. He had irritated her with his superior manner. As this thought crossed her mind she smiled and remembered Linda's words.

Meredith had turned to look at her and caught the smile. "Are you laughing at me? Are you deliberately trying to wind me up?"

"No. Of course not, why would you say that?" Patsy turned to face him.

"What's wrong? Tell me and let's have done with it."

"Nothing's wrong with me. You're the one making sarcastic comments and grinning like a school girl." Without warning he hit the centre of his steering wheel with the flat of his hand and blasted the horn. The cyclist he was overtaking wobbled in alarm and shook his fist as Meredith sped past.

"Bastard cyclists, they should be banned."

"What did he do?" Patsy demanded. She had decided that if Meredith wanted a fight he could have one.

Meredith half turned his face towards her, and shook his head before looking back at the road in front. "He was there, wasn't he?" came his irrational response.

Patsy closed her eyes and sighed. Perhaps it wasn't worth a row. She would bide her time. He would tell her once he had calmed down, she knew that.

Once home, they spent an uncomfortable and silent hour in front of the television. Meredith flipped from one channel to the next, before he announced he was going for a shower and disappeared upstairs. Patsy listened to him banging around and when all became quiet she realised that he had gone to bed. Her anger simmered to the surface again and she stomped upstairs. She went into the dark bedroom and turned on the light. Meredith groaned and pulled the duvet over his head.

"Sorry, I didn't realise you had gone to bed," she snapped, "I'm going to have a bath."

She didn't switch the light off when she left the room. Forty minutes later when she returned the light was still on, and Meredith was feigning sleep. Patsy applied some moisturiser to her face and climbed into bed. She was careful to lie as far away from Meredith as possible. She stared at the ceiling wondering what had set him off. After five minutes, he reached out and pulled her to him. She didn't resist but snuggled into his embrace.

"Sorry," he murmured into her hair.

"Forgiven. But take heed Meredith, one day sorry won't be enough. You have to speak to me when something winds you up like this. Don't worry, you don't have to tell me what it is now, it's far too late and I'm tired, but think on."

"I will." Meredith kissed the top of her head and squeezed her. He lay staring into the darkness as she drifted off to sleep, and wondered why he made his life so complicated. He should have just told her.

CHAPTER SIXTEEN

The next morning Patsy met with Linda at the office. Meredith had gone with Trump to see David Stone, the lad Brent had warned off Anna Carter. They had arranged to meet at lunchtime.

"Morning, PHPI, I made a breakthrough yesterday. I reckon I'll only need to have George's system down for half a day to sort this out." Linda began to explain her theory and Patsy held her hand up.

"Gobbledy gook, Linda," she laughed. "You know I have no idea what you're talking about. How long until you're ready to go?"

Linda glanced up at the clock. "Twenty minutes should do it. I want to get this right first." She pointed at the screen of her laptop. "There's plenty of time for a coffee."

Patsy left her to it and made the coffee. As Linda was working in her office she went to reception and picked up the post. She shuffled through until she found the envelope she was looking for. It was the written confirmation from the laboratory that the samples provided so far had been negative with regards to the paternity test. Patsy had already received an email to that effect, but she had yet to share that information with Stella Young. By the time she had called Stella, updated her, and made arrangements for the next week, Linda was ready to leave.

"So how did you get home last night?" Patsy asked as she pulled onto the main road. "And more importantly, how did you get in this morning? Your car wasn't in the car park."

"Louie gave me a lift home. He is the perfect gentleman you know. I got a taxi in this morning. I'm picking my car up when we've finished at Tucker's."

"Oh, I wasn't planning on staying with you. I'll be no use at all. Give me a ring when you've finished." Patsy sighed inwardly. She had planned to spend the rest of the day with Meredith in the hope she could find out what had set him off the night before. She was pleased with Linda's response.

"No need, PHPI. Louie is picking me up, then we're going to pick up my car and I'm going to cook him dinner."

Patsy shot a glance at Linda before returning her attention to the road. "Cook him dinner? Already! You don't let the grass grow, do you?"

"Why would I? He's a really nice bloke. We hit it off and life is short. Why would anyone put off the inevitable? Unless of course it's a bad thing in which case . . ."

Patsy told her she got the message, and attempted to tease her as they completed their journey. Linda didn't bite. She was looking forward to her first date with Louie Trump. Patsy pulled into the car park of a non-descript warehouse with a "Tucker's Office Supplies" logo displayed along one side. To the left of the warehouse was a small red-brick building with a smaller logo above the door. Before she had turned off the engine George appeared in the doorway and waved at them.

"Blimey, he's keen," Patsy observed. "I think he's taken a shine to you too." She released her seatbelt and retrieved her handbag from the rear footwell.

"Oh course he has. PHPI, I am a magnet to men who need to be guided." Linda tutted. "I thought you'd worked that out at least. Whilst this is a normal state for men that come into contact with me, this one is after my IT skills rather than my body. He wants me first for my brain, and second for the rest." She smiled across the roof of the car. "Unfortunately for him, he only gets the first and he has to pay for that."

Within half an hour Linda was set up on Tucker's main server, and was clicking away with the mouse, occasionally glancing at her notes. The screen in front of her flickered as page after page of code scrolled by.

Patsy smiled at George Tucker. "It means absolutely nothing to me. I have to read a manual twice just to install software."

"Me too, although I'm hoping Linda here will teach me a trick or two. Once we get to the bottom of this. I had thought about doing a course, but it takes too long. I just want to know what I need to know for the business."

"I'm sure that can be arranged, George," Linda piped up without looking away from the screen. "Right, I'll let this lot run. It should take ten to twenty minutes and then we're taking this bad boy down. Did someone say they were making coffee?"

"Yes, of course. I'll get Gemma on to it. How do you take it?" George Tucker was already at the door. As Linda placed her order Patsy made her excuses to leave.

"Linda will do her thing now, and I'll keep in touch by phone. There's no point in you paying two of us. If she discovers anything today, I'll come back in."

Tucker showed Patsy out. "I'll be sticking around," he advised with a shrug. "You never know, I might even learn something."

Patsy drove back into town wondering how to spend the rest of the morning. Meredith was unlikely to be back before midday. Remembering she had to buy a dress for the awards evening she headed for Clifton village. She had heard a new boutique had opened there, and that was as good a place to start as any.

The shop assistant held open the door as Patsy struggled out with an assortment of carrier bags. Not only had she managed to find the perfect dress, but she had bought Meredith a shirt and completed a grocery shop. Feeling pleased with herself she headed back to her car. Having packed her purchases into the boot, she crossed the road and bought herself a takeaway latte. She placed the cup on the roof of her car as she rummaged in her handbag for her keys. As she looked up, she saw Meredith emerge from Appleton's restaurant a little further down the road. Before she could call to him, he turned his back and strode off in the opposite direction. Patsy pressed the fob to unlock the car as a woman stepped out of the restaurant. She also turned her back to Patsy and called to Meredith. Patsy watched as he came to a halt and turned to face the woman. He was quite some distance away now, and she couldn't see his facial expression, but she heard him roar "NO" at the top of his voice before turning away. The woman stood looking after him for a few moments before going back into the restaurant.

Patsy chewed her lip as she considered her options. She chose the one she considered to be the least confrontational. Leaving the coffee sitting on top of her car she hurried towards the restaurant.

The waitress smiled warmly and showed Patsy to a table in the window. Patsy's eyes darted around the room as she followed her. The woman was sitting at a table set against the far wall. Patsy sat facing her. Waving away the proffered menu, she ordered a coffee and toasted bagel, and pulled her phone from her bag. Placing her elbows on the table she held her phone between her hands as though she were reading a message. Her eyes scanned the woman. Patsy guessed she was in her late thirties. She wore jeans tucked into black leather boots and a heavy knitted sweater. Her blonde hair had been scooped up and was held in haphazard fashion by a large plastic clip. Her roots needed touching up. The woman pulled a handbag towards her, causing the cups on the table to clash.

Patsy noted Meredith must have eaten with her as there were two plates and two cups on the table. She guessed that the empty plate was Meredith's. The woman pulled out a compact and applied fresh lipstick before summoning the waitress. Meredith hadn't paid before his departure, and the waitress returned with the bill. As the woman stood to leave Patsy dropped her gaze and concentrated on the screen. When she was in shot, Patsy took a photograph. Dropping her phone back into her bag she called to the waitress.

"Sorry, something's come up. May I have my order to go please?"

Back at the car Patsy removed the coffee from the roof and dropped it into a nearby bin. She then sat in the car sipping the coffee from the restaurant, and studying the photograph of the woman. She looked vaguely familiar but Patsy was unable to place her. Whoever she was, she had clearly annoyed Meredith, and his reaction demonstrated it was not business. She jumped as the phone beeped at her. The message was from Meredith enquiring when she would be home. She told him she was on her way.

Meredith opened the door as she unloaded the bags from the boot of the car. He stepped out and took them from her.

"And there was me thinking you were working," he grinned at her. "I hope there's a pressie for me in here."

"That depends on whether you have been a good boy or not." Patsy forced herself to remain open minded. "I did go to work first. I had to make sure Linda was set up at the client's place. I thought you might get tied up with Anna's ex so I thought a little retail therapy would do me good."

"Well, I have been a good boy, so I'll take my just desserts. The kid was useful in as much as we know who put the frighteners on him. It was Wilson. He would only speak off the record until we can confirm we have something concrete against them. He is terrified of repercussions. They did a good job on him." Placing the bags on the kitchen table he pretended to peep in them. "I left him with Trump as I would rather be here with you."

Meredith turned and pulled her into his arms. Patsy stiffened at the blatant lie.

Kissing her on the forehead he muttered, "So what have you been buying then?"

Patsy pulled away, willing herself not to challenge him. "Mainly groceries, but this," she held up one of the bags and leaned across the table selecting a second, "and this, are for later. I'll pop them upstairs whilst you start unpacking the groceries." She hurried from the room.

Hanging up the dress she told herself she was being paranoid, and that, if prompted, Meredith would explain what he had been doing. She laid the shirt she had bought him on the bed and returned to the kitchen. Pulling the plain paper bag containing the bagel from her handbag she waved it at Meredith.

"I wasn't expecting you this soon so I bought myself a snack. Have you eaten?"

"No, I thought I would save myself so we could have lunch together." He turned away and put a box of cereal in the cupboard. "What's in the bag anyway?"

"Just a toasted bagel, I went into Appleton's restaurant and treated myself. A reward for all my hard work." She watched him closely but he didn't flinch. Stepping forward she looked at her watch and patted his stomach. "I'm very impressed with you, if you have waited this long to eat. It's a whole five hours since you ate breakfast. Unless of course you have been snacking on something." Smiling up at him she searched for any sign of guilt; there was none.

He pursed his lips and looked injured. "I cannot believe you have just accused me of snacking. Not a thing has crossed my lips since I left this house." He wrapped his arms around her. "Now that I'm back however, there are lots of things my lips could be doing."

Patsy forced a grin. "But not before I've fed you I suppose. Lay the table, I'll do you a mini fry up as you didn't have a cooked breakfast."

"Are you all right?"

"Of course, why do you ask?"

"Nothing, you seem a little tense that's all. I did apologise about yesterday, didn't I?"

Meredith was watching her carefully, and Patsy cursed silently, wishing she could hide her emotions as well as Meredith obviously could. She raised her eyebrows and grinned. "You did, and I'm fine. Now lay the table."

Meredith turned away and opened the cutlery drawer. He knew she had something on her mind, but given his own performance the night before he decided not to press the point. He even tried small talk whilst they prepared and then ate their lunch. This only provided Patsy with confirmation that he was up to something, and she knew she had to confront him. She decided to do it gently.

"Go and find a rubbishy film on the TV. I'll bring some tea through and we can snuggle on the sofa," she instructed.

"I thought we could go upstairs for a siesta."

Meredith had that look in his eyes and her stomach muscles clenched. She was very tempted.

"Later. Let my lunch settle first."

Meredith turned away and mumbled to himself as he scuffed down the hall. He dropped onto the sofa and switched on the television. By the time Patsy had arrived with the tea, he was engrossed in a game of rugby. He looked up as she put the tray on the table.

"Good shout, Hodge. I didn't realise that there was an international on. Come on, sit down, this promises to be a good match."

Patsy snuggled into him and half watched the game on the television. At half time, she flipped onto her back, her head in his lap, and looked up at him.

"You would tell me if there was ever anything wrong, wouldn't you?" She watched as his brow furrowed and he allowed his head to fall forward to look down on her.

"Because . . ."

"No reason. You were in an unexpected strop last night, and something seems not quite right today. All I'm asking is that if there is something going on in there," she reached up and tapped his temple, "you'll tell me. I don't ever want to find out about something important via someone else."

"Like who?" Meredith jerked his head up and looked irritated.

Patsy sighed. "Like no one. I'm saying that if there is ever anything I should know, I want to hear it from you."

Meredith dropped his head back against the sofa and stared at the ceiling contemplating her request.

"Spit it out. Who's said what?" He let his head fall forward and stared at her. His gaze was intense. "I have nothing to tell you that you need to know. Someone has obviously said something so let's have it out on the table so we can deal with it. I don't want whatever this is about to fester."

He sighed as Patsy shook her head.

"Haven't we just established that you will always tell me if there is something I need to know?" Meredith nodded at her. "Good, then there is nothing. It's your turn to make the tea. If you hurry, you'll get back before this kicks off again." She jerked her thumb at the television.

Lifting her head up with one hand, Meredith lowered his head until his lips brushed hers. "I'll make the tea if we get a siesta when the game's over," he whispered and kissed her as she nodded agreement.

Patsy was listening to Meredith bang about in the kitchen, and just as she decided to mention what she had seen, the doorbell rang. She called to Meredith telling him she would get it, and opened the door. Standing on the doorstep was the woman from the restaurant. Patsy forced a smile and the woman did the same.

"Is John in?" the woman asked as Meredith came out of the kitchen carrying the tea tray. She looked away from Patsy and raised her eyebrows, giving Meredith a little shrug. "I'm sorry, I didn't realise you had company."

Patsy bristled at the inference that she was a temporary fixture. Her expression hardened and before Meredith could speak she held out her hand.

"Patsy Hodge. Do come in, and you are?"

As the woman took her hand Patsy gently pulled her forward causing her to step over the threshold.

"Julia," she replied, pulling off her gloves and shoving them into the pockets of her coat. "Julia Meredith."

Patsy's mind swam as the woman began to unbutton her coat. Was this an ex-wife? Patsy watched the woman hang her coat on the newel post before walking to Meredith and kissing him on the cheek.

"You'll need another cup, John," she pointed to the tray in Meredith's hand.

Patsy looked from the tray and up to Meredith expectantly.

He smiled a nervous smile. "Patsy, meet my sister, Julia. Julia, meet my . . ." unsure what to call Patsy and with an uncertain grin he settled for, "meet my padlock, Patsy."

"Your what?" Julia shot a look at Patsy, who was smiling.

"Hi, Julia. It's great to finally meet you. Meredith didn't mention you were visiting."

"It's a surprise." Julia studied Patsy for a while. "Padlock as in ball and chain? I didn't think there was a woman born that could chain John down."

"There isn't. It's the not trying that catches him." Patsy pushed open the door to the sitting room. "Please come in and sit down. Meredith tells me you have twin boys, but you've not brought them with you I see." Patsy hoped her irritation at Julia's comments didn't show. Meredith had a reputation, and Julia would know that she knew that, but somehow her remarks still seemed a little inappropriate.

"Ah, so you're the one playing hard to get," Julia smiled kindly at Patsy, "good luck with that."

Patsy was just about to ask her what she meant when Meredith returned with the tray so she let it pass. The two women allowed Meredith to be mother, and the three made small talk for a few minutes. It was clear that neither Meredith nor Julia were interested in the conversation. Patsy knew they had probably covered most of it off at their meeting earlier in the day.

"Are you in Bristol just for the day? How long does it take to get here from Swansea? It's a shame we didn't know you were coming, we could have made arrangements to go out somewhere."

"It's a flying visit, I'm afraid, but I need to see John on some family business. I'm glad I caught him in."

Patsy sensed rather than saw Meredith stiffen, but she certainly saw the look which told Julia to proceed at her peril. Julia's features hardened and Patsy realised how like Meredith she was. It was why she had looked so familiar earlier. No one spoke and tension began to build. Patsy was relieved when her phone started to ring. Standing, she snatched it up from the arm of the settee and glanced at the screen, already heading for the door.

"Its work, I'm afraid. I'll take it in the kitchen so as not to disturb you." Patsy rolled her eyes as she answered the call, "Hi Linda, how's it going?"

Pulling out a chair she sat at the table as Linda began her update. Patsy could hear that Meredith and Julia were now in a heated conversation, but they kept their voices low, and with Linda gabbling away in one ear she was unable to pick up on anything other than the odd word.

"Are you listening to me?" Linda demanded and Patsy smiled knowing that her free hand would be resting on her hip.

"Yes, of course. Sorry, I got distracted for a moment. I'll summarise for you. It is a little more complicated that you at first thought, but the IT guy is in the clear, you think, because he's been helping you. The accountant turned up to collect some bits for the VAT return and you don't like him. George has gone off to meet with a client and . . . Sorry Linda, repeat the last bit again."

"George has gone to the golf club to meet a client but promised he wouldn't play. Not that it makes any difference to me. But I'm sure he wasn't expecting the accountant, and the accountant clearly wasn't planning on hanging around until he realised I was here. Whilst I am a man magnet I don't like that. Now there are only three of us here, and the receptionist, Gemma, is going in a moment. I asked if you could come and join me. There are some bits you can do for me to speed this up, and I don't want to be stuck here on my own with him, he's a tad creepy. He could be Wilde by name and Wilde by nature. So can you tear yourself away from Meredith or not?"

"Give me twenty minutes. Meredith has some family stuff to sort out anyway." Patsy frowned. It wasn't like Linda to get spooked, and she wondered what the man had done to cause Linda to call in backup. She pulled her coat on and walked back down the hall to collect her bag from the sitting room. She slowed her pace as she heard Meredith shout out a sharp "No". He then lowered his voice and his words were muffled, but she caught the end of the sentence as she pushed open the door.

". . . if you want to. I really don't know how to say this any other way, but I'm not getting involved. Not again."

"But, John you must. If you . . . Oh hello, Patsy." Julia looked Patsy up and down. "Are you going somewhere?"

Julia looked worn out; lines of concern had appeared at the corners of her eyes and Patsy marvelled at just how like her brother she looked.

"Work calls," Patsy smiled at her before turning her attention to Meredith. "Linda has an issue with the accountant or something. I'm going to rescue her but I shouldn't be long, a couple of hours, tops." Patsy leaned over the back of the sofa and planted a kiss on the top of his head. She turned back to Julia. "I hope you'll still be here when I get back, it would be nice to get to know you." She picked up her bag and slung the straps over her shoulder.

"Sorry, Patsy. Another time maybe, I have to get going in a moment." Julia sighed and looked at Meredith.

He smiled at Patsy and told her to keep in touch. The siblings sat and looked at Patsy, waiting to resume their conversation once she had left the room. Patsy departed quickly, leaving them to it. She sat in her car for a while wondering what Julia wanted Meredith to do. She hoped he would tell her later, as the look of irritation on Julia's face when she arrived had now been replaced with a sad acceptance. Patsy also hoped that whatever it was, Meredith had made the right decision. Sighing she released her handbrake and pulled away.

Linda looked up and smiled at Patsy as she entered the room.

"Hi, Linda, so what's up? I couldn't quite get the gist of what . . ."

With an almost imperceptible movement of her head and some frantic eye movement, Linda let Patsy know they were not alone. Patsy stopped speaking and looked to the left. A man in his mid-forties flashed her a smile that replaced the smirk that had gone before.

He stood and held out his hand. "Paul Wilde. A pleasure to meet you. I always thought that computer experts were nerdy geeks, who wore glasses and ill-fitting clothes. Oh yes and they have limp handshakes and can't meet your eye during conversations. I now stand corrected." His eyes darted from Patsy to Linda and back again. "I'll put money on the fact that whoever recruits in your company is a chap."

The smirk returned and Patsy pulled her hand away. Her eyebrows rose a little and she hoped the distaste she felt hadn't registered on her face.

"Then you would have lost your money, Mr Wilde. Now I don't wish to be rude, but Linda and I need to get on. I understand George will be back shortly and I doubt there's anything we are able to help you with." Patsy forced a smile.

"Oh I wouldn't say that . . . Sorry, what did you say your name was?"

"Hodge. Patsy Hodge."

"Well, Patsy, you could help me do a lot of things, but I'm actually here as I thought I could help you. In fact, I know I can." His lips twitched and his eyes travelled down to her boots and back up again.

Patsy's face remained impassive. "Many men have thought that, unfortunately, though most proved to be disappointingly wrong." Patsy shrugged and gave a dejected sigh. Linda's eyes twinkled with barely concealed amusement. Patsy walked to the door that stood open behind her. She stepped behind it and pulled it back further still. "Nice to meet you, Mr Wilde," Patsy dismissed him, "I'm sure George won't be long."

Despite his smile as he passed, his eyes told her she had just made an enemy, or lost a potential friend at least. She closed the door behind him and waited until she heard his footsteps recede along the corridor before she spoke.

"What's the panic? What's he said or done to spook you?"

"Well, apart from being a W," Linda moved her cupped hand back and forth, "he got quite shirty when I wouldn't tell him what I was doing. Then he tried to chat me up, which was fine, almost obligatory, but the pleasantries didn't last long. He kept coming to stand behind me. It means I haven't got much further with finding out who all this leads to." Patsy had pulled a chair from another desk and sat down beside her. Linda nudged her. "Nice dispatching, PHPI. Impressed."

Patsy winked an acknowledgement. "So how much longer will it take you?"

"An hour or so. Maybe a little longer, I'll know more once I get back in." Linda's fingers flew over the keyboard. "Which is now."

She hit the enter button with a flourish. The two women watched a stream of digits scroll across the screen until a prompt for a password appeared. Linda tapped it in quickly and then watched as numerous overlapping boxes appeared in front of her. "I've set you up on the system as a rep and I've written out some orders I need you to place so I can . . . Bear with me I just need to . . ."

She became engrossed in her work so Patsy went to make coffee. The receptionist came into the kitchen.

"Hello, you must be Patsy," Gemma smiled as she opened the fridge for Patsy to replace the milk. "George should be about another thirty minutes. He says I can go, but I was to check and make sure you would still be here when he returned. If not I was to give your colleague the alarm code and show her how to set it. Will you be much longer?"

Patsy explained that they would be an hour at least, so they would definitely be around when George returned. She then took the opportunity to question her about Wilde.

"It's unusual to see an accountant at work on a Saturday. Are you particularly busy at the moment?"

"No. I thought that was odd too. He only comes in once or twice during the quarter, and even then he has a young clerk with him who does most of the work. Apparently, George forgot he was coming in to meet with him today, and he's going to wait. Is he getting on your nerves?" Gemma leaned forward and said in a whisper. "I can't stand him. Joanne left because of him."

A movement outside the door made her jump and she flushed. Patsy opened the door and looked up and down the corridor. George Tucker was entering the room where Linda was working. Patsy smiled at the girl.

"Don't panic, it was George, he's back early." Patsy left Gemma making George tea and hurried down the corridor with the two mugs she had prepared.

"Hi, George, I've ordered one for you." Patsy held up the mugs. "You're a busy man and no mistake. We've just met Paul Wilde. Apparently, you forgot an appointment with him. How was the golf?"

"I didn't have anything booked with him," George Tucker's brow furrowed and he shook his head, "and I didn't play, I just tied up a deal with an estate agent. I wonder what Paul wants? I hope this isn't more bad news. Ladies, excuse me please, I'll be back in a moment."

George left the room and Patsy handed one of the mugs to Linda.

"Hmm, that's interesting. Wilde told thingy on reception that they had an appointment. We must find out more when he comes back." Patsy looked at Linda and could see she wasn't listening. "Linda, helloooo."

Linda glanced up at her briefly and then back at the screen. "Someone is playing with me," Linda tapped the screen in front of her. "I changed this a moment ago, and now it's back to how it was. Let's try again."

Patsy watched as Linda highlighted a string of digits and deleted them before replacing them with what appeared to Patsy to be random characters. Linda scribbled something on a pad and glanced at her watch. She sighed.

"Right, we'll have to wait a while and see what happens."

"Do you think it's Wilde?" Patsy asked as Linda continued to work on the program. "What did the IT guy have to say?"

"Could be Wilde, he's so smarmy, I would love to catch him with his hand in the till, but nothing points to anyone yet. I don't think it's the IT guy though, he was really helpful. Gave me a couple of shortcuts . . ." she paused as Patsy gasped. "What's wrong?"

"You haven't told him what you're doing, have you?"

"Do I look stupid?" Linda tutted. "I told him I was working on the ordering, which I was, and trying to make it more efficient, which I did. He will of course know that that gives me access to all things financial, and that to achieve what I told him I was after I would have to change the program. He was totally cool and, as I said, he even told me how to get where I wanted to go quickly." She frowned and shook her head. "Which begs the question, why the system was so cumbersome on the front end. But for the moment at least, my money's on smarmy pants out there. He showed up about an hour after I stopped the drip feed."

"And how did you come to be speaking to the IT guy?"

"He was working some glitch with the barcode reader in the warehouse, apparently, and could see that George was logged in and sent me, or rather George, a message. We got chatting."

"He called you?"

"No. On Unix you can use the write command to send a dialogue . . . Oh it's not worth it, Patsy, you've glazed over again. Just pretend I texted him." Linda clicked a few more buttons. "I'll tell you what would be useful - could you find out from George how much access Wilde has to the system?" She rolled her eyes. "That is, of course, if he knows. I'm sure he told me it was just accounts for VAT and reconciliations, so he shouldn't be able to get to this, there's no need." Linda slapped her hand on the desk. "There you go, it's changed back again. Go and find out what Wilde is doing right now. In fact, now would be a good time to get him back in here as then we would know if it's him or not."

Patsy left Linda to it and made her way to George Tucker's office. She tapped on the door and George called her in. Paul Wilde was leaning back on a chair in front of George's desk. His hands supported his head and he pulled himself forward as she entered.

"Sorry to interrupt, George, I know this must be important, but when you have five minutes could we borrow you for a little extra background info." Patsy turned and smiled at Wilde. "You too if you have time Mr Wilde, we may be able to get this sorted today which would be good news all round. The new ordering system would then be ready for Tuesday."

"Why, what happens on Tuesday?" Wilde shot a glance at George Tucker who shook his head at him.

"It's our busiest day on orders, Paul, I thought you would've realised that." George pushed his chair back and stood up. "We're not busy, Patsy, Paul here only popped in for a chat so let's go and see what Linda wants. The sooner things get sorted the better. Paul." His tone left little doubt that Wilde was expected to join them.

Wilde stood and smiled at him. "Of course, anything that makes life easier."

An hour later, Linda had the information she required from George Tucker and had tested the amendment twice whilst Wilde was still in the room. Whoever it was reversing her amendment, it was not Wilde.

"Thank you for your help gentlemen, we'll get on now and hopefully get this tied up. Linda, how long do you think you'll need?" Patsy looked towards Linda as she stood to open the door. Linda was frowning and her fingers were hitting the keyboard a little harder than usual. Patsy grinned at the two men. "She gets like this."

"I might be concentrating but I'm not deaf," Linda spun round on her chair. "Another hour today, but I may need to come in tomorrow, George. How long are you here for now?" Linda glanced at her watch. "I'm conscious that I'm eating into your weekend."

"I'll be here until five at the earliest. I've got to sort out some paperwork for the contract I signed earlier. Give me a shout when you're done. Paul, I'll let you out."

Linda waited until the door was closed.

"Well, it's not him. Three times I tested it whilst he was here, and to be quite honest, unless he's a very good actor, his grasp on this system is about as good as yours. So plan B, I need to meet with Toby the IT guy. But not today as I'm being picked up in an hour by Louie." She grinned at Patsy. "You can go now if you like. We did the bit I wanted you for, apart from putting Wilde in his place of course. Thanks, Patsy."

Patsy collected her things, said her goodbyes, and drove straight home to Meredith. The house was quiet as she entered the hall. Shrugging off her coat she called out, but there was no response. She pushed open the door to the sitting room and found Meredith asleep on the sofa. Closing the door quietly she went to the kitchen and poured herself a glass a wine, which she sipped as she prepared a casserole. Sliding the casserole into the oven she decided to wake Meredith, and made some coffee. He stirred as she placed the mugs on the table.

"Good day at the office?" he asked, rubbing the sleep from his eyes.

"Not bad, not finished though, unfortunately." She smiled at him. "Linda has a date with Louie tonight."

Meredith snorted out a laugh. "Ha. I don't know which one to feel most sorry for." He held up his hand to her and pulled her onto the sofa with him. "What do you fancy doing tonight? Shall we go out to eat?"

"I've just put a casserole in the oven. I thought we could have a quiet night in. Although we could go for a drink after, if you want. Is it likely Julia will still be around?"

"Nope. She's gone home, she sends her regards though. So, you want a night in, do you? I hope you have something planned to fill the time," He kissed her. "In fact, no time like the present. How long will the casserole take?"

Patsy returned his kiss. "Long enough."

Meredith carried the two glasses and the open bottle of wine into the sitting room. He smiled at Patsy as he nudged her with his knee to move further along the sofa.

"That was an almost perfect evening." He glanced at his watch as she took the bottle from him. "All that, and it's still only eight o'clock." Dropping onto the sofa he pulled her to him and kissed her forehead. "Thank you."

Patsy tilted her head up and frowned at him. "What do you mean 'almost'? What was missing?"

"Pudding," he laughed as she elbowed him in the ribs. "There's an Al Pacino movie on in a while, would you like to watch it?" He hit the remote and the television came to life.

"What's it about? Mind you, with Al Pacino does it matter . . . that will do nicely." She grinned as Meredith shook his head in mock disbelief and began to flip through the channels.

"Were you expecting Julia? She looked very worried about something. I'm sorry I had to dash out."

"Not really, she said she would be in Bristol but not that she would come round. And work is work, you have to do what you have to do. Talking of which . . ." he nodded at the screen as a trailer for *Crimebusters* was playing.

"*. . .and on Monday's show we will be featuring the shooting of Anna Carter.*"

A picture of Anna appeared on the screen that changed seconds later to a photograph of Andrew Short. This time the screen was split and the second half showed a grey hoodie, blue jeans and a pair of trainers.

"*The fatal stabbing of Andrew Short, and the clothes police are anxious to trace. We also have a reconstruction of the bungled warehouse robbery in Avonmouth that left a security guard hospitalised.*"

"Fingers crossed that will bring something in." Meredith sipped his wine.

"I hope so." Patsy patted his chest. "Something will click I'm sure of it. What did Julia want?" she asked as casually as she was able.

"Not much. Just family crap that I don't want to be involved in."

Meredith's response was clipped but Patsy pressed on regardless. "Oh dear," Patsy sighed, "you obviously don't want to talk about it, but can I just say something?"

"Why ask? You will anyway." There was no amusement in his tone.

"She looked like she needed your help. It was obvious I was in the way, so whatever it was I think she needed you. You might want to reconsider for her sake if nothing else." Patsy nodded her head against his shoulder. "There, I've said it."

"Good." He gave her a little squeeze and tuned the volume up a little on the television. "Here we go." The opening bars of the musical score for the film filtered into the room.

"You'll consider helping her, with whatever it was then?"

"I will."

"Is it likely you might think of her needs rather than your own with whatever this is? Sorry to keep on, but she looked so sad." Patsy felt Meredith stiffen.

"I said I would reconsider. I made no other promises, Patsy. Now if you're looking for a row we can keep this going, if not give me a cuddle and drop it."

CHAPTER SEVENTEEN

Meredith kept his head perfectly still but his eyes followed Dawn Jessop around the room. She was looking good, and they had exchanged a brief but courteous greeting. She also looked calm and appeared to be oblivious to his presence. That was fine with him, but he knew how quickly she could change tack. He glanced at his watch. *Crimebusters* was currently running a commercial break and the whole of the first half of the show had been dedicated to Andrew Short and Anna Carter. As yet, the team had not taken a single call. Meredith shrugged at Seaton who caught his gaze and shook his head.

Louie wandered over to him. "This is a tad disappointing, is it not? I thought Dawn did us proud with what we had to work with, but not a sausage." He paused as the phone rang.

Travers picked it up. "*Crimebusters*, DC Travers speaking, how may I help?"

Louie and Meredith listened to a one-sided conversation with Seaton typing as quickly as he was able to update them. There were four officers taking calls and their systems were set to update Meredith as details were logged in.

Louie tapped the screen. "I spoke too soon. That looks good. Do you want me to go, or are you going to send a uniform?"

"I'll go." Meredith was grateful for an excuse to leave and escape the close proximity to Dawn Jessop. "I need a fag anyway. Give me a shout if anything else occurs," He pulled on his coat. "Oh yes and keep your distance." He nodded curtly at Dawn Jessop and left the room.

On the other side of Bristol, Michael Brent's wife called her husband into the sitting room.

"Mike, your club is on the telly. Quick, quick, come and look."

Brent strode into the room and stared at the screen.

"*...both victims were known to have visited this club here in the recent past.*" The reporter held his arm up and the camera shot changed to the facia above the club entrance. "*Sensations is a lap dancing club, and friends and family of Anna Carter say it would have been totally out of character for her to be here. So why was she seen here by several witnesses? Did perhaps you see her here? I would remind you that all calls to the incident room will be treated in confidence, and you may, if you chose, remain anonymous. Andrew Short had a brief relationship with one of the dancers that worked here, and police have yet to speak to her. If you are watching, please come forward. I would stress that you are not in any trouble.*"

As the reporter walked towards the camera the club remained in background.

"*So, two young people, attacked within twenty-four hours of each other, and unfortunately one of them died at the scene. Both crimes committed within a short distance of each other, both victims seen here in the months before they were attacked: coincidence or not?*" Again, he swung round to point at the club. "*If you have any information please, please call now. Now a reminder of the clothes worn by the killer of Andrew Short, a typical wardrobe for most youngsters, but do you remember seeing anyone wearing this outfit on that day?*"

The screen shot changed from the club to the clothing.

Liz Brent looked up at her husband. "Did Anna go to the club? She wasn't a dancer surely . . ." Her nose wrinkled as she said 'dancer', her expression one of suspicion. "She didn't seem the type to me. Did you know she went there?"

"What's the fucking acid face for? You don't mind taking the money it brings in, so don't get high and mighty with me. Just remember where you were dragged from." Brent snarled at his wife, his fists clenched by his side.

Liz Brent jumped off the sofa. "Dragged? Dragged? I wasn't dragged from anywhere. I lived around the corner from you, remember? So don't you go telling me to remember where I came from, because you bloody well know!" She lifted her hand and jabbed her finger towards him. "I asked you if you knew she went to the club. What would be of interest to her -"

Her question was cut short as the back of her husband's hand met the side of her face, and she stumbled backward. Shocked, she ran her tongue along her bottom lip and could feel the wound caused by her teeth. Brent had hit her in the past but only when he was drunk. He was stone cold sober now, so she had obviously touched a nerve. She wondered which one as he leaned forward and grabbed her face with his hand. His fingers on one side and his thumb on the other, he squeezed hard and her cheeks compressed, forcing her lips into an ugly pout. She whimpered in fear at the sheer hatred in his eyes.

"You ever point at me again and I will break your finger off. I don't live at the club, and I have no control over who goes there." He sucked the saliva at the corners of his lips into his mouth. "Even if I did it's no fucking business of yours. Now get out of my sight." With a violent thrust from his shoulder he released his grip, and with the flat of his hand on her chin he pushed her away from him. She tripped on the rug and fell to the floor. "Get yourself sorted out before Jimmy comes down," Brent snarled at her before he turned to leave, "he's not had his milk and biscuit yet."

Liz Brent rolled over and onto all fours, her arms were shaking and her fear was replaced with bravado at the mention of her son. She had seen the way Brent had looked at her, and that caused her to worry about her future. She knew he played away from home and it hurt, but it was better to accept that than face a life without him, and his money of course. Sometimes the only reason they spoke to each other was because of James. She blinked and drew in a deep breath; she couldn't retaliate physically but she knew how she could hurt him. She swallowed and ran her tongue around the inside of her mouth to lubricate it. She knew what would frighten him all right.

Pushing herself up onto her knees, she said quietly, "I didn't deserve that. If you ever hit me again I will take James and I will leave you. I promise you that."

Her eyes widened with fear as her husband turned, sprang over the sofa, and knocked her to the ground with his knee. Instinctively, she raised her arms to cover her face but he pulled them away. With one hand, he pinned her arms to the floor above her head as he knelt and straddled her. His face was contorted with anger as he placed the flat of his free hand on her throat and leaned his weight onto it. The pain was excruciating and she closed her eyes believing she was about to die.

"You stupid fucking bitch. One thing you will never, ever do is take Jimmy away from me. If you want to end up like them," he jerked his head towards the television, "you just keep talking shit like that. I think it would give me great -"

"Dad! What you doing? Can I play? I'm not tired honest."

Brent forced a smile as he looked at his son in the doorway.

"Hello son. We're not playing. Mum's not very well and she fell over, I'm just helping her up. You go and get your milk and I'll be with you in a minute." He winked at his son who raised his hands and slapped them on the side of his legs.

"Not again, she fell down yesterday as well." He turned and walked away. "Silly Mummy."

Brent listened to his son dragging the bar stool out at the breakfast bar. He leaned down so that his mouth was next to his wife's ear.

"Silly Mummy," he hissed, "new rules now Liz. You've overstepped the mark and then some. You don't drink, you don't go out without my permission, and you don't question me again. Are you clear on that?"

Liz Brent managed a nod, and a ragged sob escaped as Brent released the pressure on her throat.

"Sorry, Mike," she croaked.

"Too late for sorry," Brent stood looking down at her, "don't forget." He pointed at the television screen which now had an advert for a supermarket running, but Liz understood the message and nodded. "Go to bed." Brent grabbed her sweater and pulled her to her feet. "You look a mess. I'll take Jimmy to school tomorrow."

Meredith parked his car across the drive and squinted to make sure he had the right house. He switched off the engine and flicked his cigarette through the window before closing it. He hurried down the path, pushed the bell, and stepped back. As he did so he caught the twitch of the curtain. The light came on in the hall and through the opaque glass panel at the side of the door he saw a figure shuffle to the door. The door opened four inches or so before the security chain halted its progress. A short woman with grey, frizzy hair peered through the gap. Meredith pulled his warrant card from his inside pocket and flipped it open.

Holding it towards the woman's face he stepped forward. "Mrs Henderson? I'm DCI Meredith. You called *Crimebusters*." He smiled at her as her eyes darted from his hand to his face and back again. "Can I come in? It's a bit parky out here."

The woman closed the door and released the chain before opening it wide enough for him to squeeze through.

"Come in quickly then. I'm so glad you didn't come in a proper police car. I don't want to be a . . . what do you call it? A target," she nodded to herself, "and I didn't know, did I? I just thought it was . . . well, rubbish. Although common sense tells you it wouldn't have been, doesn't it?" She looked briefly at Meredith as she walked to a door halfway up the hall. Meredith followed her and she waved towards a chair in the corner of the room. "Have a seat." She picked up a remote control from the arm of the opposite chair and switched off the television. "Will I get into trouble over this? Because I didn't know, how could I? Can I remain anonymous like they promise?"

Meredith watched as the woman perched on the edge of the chair and tapped her knees with the flat of her hands. She was clearly agitated as she had been during the call to the helpline, but he had yet to find out exactly what she knew.

"Mrs Henderson, no one need know that I came here. Depending on what it is you have to tell me, we may not even need to speak to you again." He smiled at her. "I understand you know something about the clothes that the person who stabbed Andrew Short was wearing. Was it someone local?"

Muriel Henderson shrugged and shook her head. Meredith tried not to look irritated.

"But you have seen someone wearing an outfit similar to that shown on the telly." He looked towards the television. Muriel Henderson shook her head. Meredith raised his eyebrows and sucked in a breath. "But you called and said you had seen -"

"I did not. I did not say I saw someone wearing them." Indignantly Muriel pulled her shoulders back and looked Meredith in the eye. "Don't you go making stuff up about me. I don't know anything about the killer. I knew I shouldn't have called." She raised her hands in a helpless gesture, cupping her face and shaking her head.

Meredith saw the tremble and reached across and patted her knee. "Nothing is going to happen to you, Mrs Henderson, but I am confused. Let's start again and you tell me exactly why you called *Crimebusters*."

Meredith sighed inwardly believing he was on a wild goose chase. If this woman had seen someone wearing the outfit, she had obviously changed her mind about sharing that information through some fear of retaliation.

"It was the same day as it happened. Although I didn't know that then, did I? It wasn't until the next day I read about it, but I swear I didn't know about the clothes until just now." She pointed at the television. "In fact, I don't usually watch that *Crimebusters*. I nodded off and when I woke up it was on. As soon as I saw them I knew." Muriel nodded at Meredith.

"What did you know, Mrs Henderson?" Again the forced smile.

"That it was the clothes. My heart nearly stopped." Muriel rubbed her hand across her chest.

"Have you seen the clothes?" Meredith was utterly confused.

"Of course. Why else would you be here?" Muriel tutted in frustration and Meredith nodded solemnly.

"Where?" He decided to keep the questions simple and let her do the talking.

"In the bin, well sort of on top of it."

"When was this?" Meredith smiled.

"Like I said, on the day he was stabbed."

"And you're positive it was that day?" Meredith's heart sank; that was almost three weeks ago, so if this woman had seen the clothes in a bin they would be long gone now.

"Of course, I won didn't I?" she grinned at him. "Full house on the last game, I won the jackpot."

"Bingo?"

"Yes," Muriel frowned at Meredith, wondering if he were a little slow.

"Where do you play bingo then? Was the bin nearby?" Meredith was trying to remember if he knew of any bingo halls in the vicinity.

"The one on Baldwin Street. I meet my sister there. But the bin wasn't there," Muriel shook her head, "it was the one by the bus stop, you know by the shops on the Longcross."

Meredith pursed his lips. He knew the bus stop she was talking about, and if she had a big win at bingo it was unlikely she had the date wrong. Things were not looking good with regards to recovering them. He sighed, hoping that she may have seen someone leaving them there. He jotted down what she had told him and, rubbing the bridge of his nose, he asked, "So did you see who put them there?" He pulled his hand away from his face, and inclined his head. "If they were in the bin, how do you know they are the clothes we're looking for?"

He mirrored Muriel's expression as her eyebrows rose in amazement.

"I didn't see who it was. I was getting off the bus you see, and I saw them put the clothes in there, but it was dark and I didn't take any notice of them. Of course, I didn't think of anything of it then. It was cold so I put my hands in my pockets and had the sweet wrappers in there," she looked at Meredith and he nodded in agreement although he had no idea where this was going, "so I walked to the bin and got rid of the wrappers. Then I saw the shoe sticking out of the bag."

"Bag?" Meredith pinched the bridge of his nose and reminded himself to be patient.

"Yes, the bag the clothes were in." She tutted, exasperated, and leaned over the arm of the chair. Grunting she lifted up a Marks and Spencer carrier bag. "This bag."

She held it up towards Meredith before resting it in her lap. Meredith looked at the bag. He could see that a pair of trainers were sitting on a grey garment, probably a hoodie. Slowly he grinned and pointed at the bag.

"And you had a peep and thought you would take it? I'm right, aren't I?" Still grinning he winked at her. "You brought them home and have had them here ever since?" He leaned forward and squinted into the bag.

Muriel became defensive. "But I didn't know, did I? How could I know?" she huffed. "It's our Charlie, he gets through trainers like they're going out of fashion, and our Jean, that's my daughter, can't keep up. I had a look at the size and they were a size five which is our Charlie's size. Whoever put them there didn't want them so I didn't think it would do any harm and they looked like they'd hardly been worn. Of course, when I got them home I realised they were brand new, still got the labels in and everything." Muriel shook her head. "I'm sorry, I didn't know."

Meredith beamed his smile at her. "Mrs Henderson, you did right. If you hadn't taken them then they would be mushed up on some dump now. You might just have helped solve a murder." He nodded towards the bag. "You haven't washed them or anything?"

"No because Charlie was supposed to be coming over last weekend but he's got the flu. The whole family have it, and they didn't want to give it to me, not with my chest." Muriel put her hand on her chest to prove the point. "This has been sat on the kitchen chair until tonight. I bought them in here to make sure that I wasn't going mad when I saw them on the telly."

"So only you have touched them?"

"Yes, I'm on my own now."

"Mrs Henderson, I could kiss you, you wonderful woman." Meredith stood and looked down on her.

"Well I never did, you cheeky bugger." Muriel flushed and grinned at Meredith. She held up the bag. "You'll want to take this now then."

Meredith went to take the bag, but changing his mind he pulled back his hand. "I do indeed. But I don't want to touch it. As we know, only you and the killer have touched it. Have you got a bin liner or something bigger we can put it in?"

Muriel pulled her hands away from the bag as though it were contaminated, and nodded at him. She leaned to one side causing the bag to slide onto the chair and pushed herself up, shivering.

"You've given me the eeby jeebies now. Just think, a killer wore that stuff and I was going to give it to our Charlie. I'll get you a bag. I don't want that in here any longer than necessary." She shook her shoulders and grimaced. "I won't be a minute." She left Meredith staring at the bag, and returned a few minutes later with a large black bin liner. "Here you go."

Meredith took the bag and opened it. "If you could just drop it in." He smiled at her but she shook her head.

"I can't, I can't touch it. Not now that I know."

Meredith resisted the urge to roll his eyes, and gave her the opened bin liner. "I understand, just hold that open then." Meredith slid his pen through one of the handles of the carrier bag and lifted it from the chair. He tilted the pen until the bag of clothes slid into the liner. He then took the liner from Muriel and tied it in a knot. "I'll need your fingerprints, Mrs Henderson, just to identify them from the others on the bag." He looked at his watch. "You can either come with me now, or I can get someone to pick you up in the morning. Which would you prefer?"

"Oh my goodness, I've never been to a police station before. What do you think I should do? Shall I call our Jean?"

"You can do. In fact, yes, you call your Jean. I'll pop these into the car and call the station and then you can decide what you want to do." Meredith left Muriel dialling her daughter's number and went to the car. He put the bin liner in the boot and lit a cigarette before dialling Travers.

"Have they done the update yet?" Meredith asked abruptly as Travers answered.

"Not yet, Gov, not sure there will even be an update yet, we've got nothing much come in on anything."

"I've got the clothes."

"What? Actually got them, are you sure?"

"Well, no, not one hundred per cent, but near as damn it. My gut tells me I do."

"I know, and your gut is rarely wrong. I'll let them know. I take it you're going back to the station then?"

"Depends, I want to get these to forensics soonest. I'll give Sherlock a call first to see who's on." Meredith saw that Muriel was in the doorway waving to him. "I've got to go now, I'll catch up with you later." He hung up, flicked his cigarette away and walked back down to Muriel who told him she would come to the station the next day with her daughter.

He dialled Frankie Callaghan as he made his way back to the car. "Sherlock, nice to speak to you. Any of your lot on duty tonight?" he asked as he turned the key in the ignition.

"Good evening, Meredith. You sound happier than the last time I spoke to you. When you say 'my lot' I take it you mean the forensic team." Frankie shook his head. Meredith's total disregard of previous encounters never ceased to amaze him. The last time they had seen each other in the Dirty Duck, Meredith had been in a foul mood and almost frogmarched Patsy from the premises, without so much as a by your leave. Apparently today Frankie was considered worthy of attention.

Meredith's hands-free had kicked in and he dropped the phone onto the passenger seat.

"Of course I mean forensics. I have the clothes." Meredith announced which gained Frankie's immediate interest.

"Actually, I have no idea. But I'm free," Frankie glanced at his watch. "I can meet you at the lab in thirty minutes if you like."

"I like very much, Sherlock. I'm on my way so get your skates on."

Meredith scrolled to Patsy's number and pushed the call button on his steering wheel. He explained what was happening and told her he wasn't sure when he'd be home, and then called Trump to do the same thing. He got Trump's answering service and left a curt message. Twenty minutes later he pulled the bin liner from the boot of his car and made his way to Frankie's office. Frankie appeared five minutes later.

Meredith stood and picked up the bag from Frankie's desk. "Here you go Sherlock, let's get on with it." He shoved the bag towards Frankie.

Frankie rolled his eyes and took the bag.

Meredith pulled on a pair of gloves as Frankie spread a large white sheet of paper across an examination table, before placing the bag on it. Frankie untied the bag and lifted out the carrier. Having disposed of the bin liner, he carefully removed the items from the carrier bag and spread them along the paper. He flipped a switch on the overhead light and the illumination intensified.

He peered at the items closely and drew in a deep breath.

"Well, these certainly match the description of the clothes on *Crimebusters*, and at first glance most of this is brand new. Look here," Frankie turned one of the trainers over, "this still has the shop label on, and whilst that in itself is not uncommon there is very little damage to it, which means it hasn't been worn that much."

He placed the shoe back on the table and pulled the sides apart. "It also still has the price on the inside which shows these were reduced. The ink from the pen making the reduction has been smudged, possibly by a sweaty foot." Replacing the trainer, he pulled down a magnifying glass on an extendable arm from the light fitting above, and manoeuvred it over the hooded sweatshirt. "Hmmm. Interesting." Frankie walked to a trolley at the side of the room and picked up a small aerosol. He shook it as he made his way back to the table.

"Speak to me, Sherlock," Meredith commanded.

"Sorry. There are minute dots on the front of this hoodie. Look here." Frankie beckoned Meredith forward and repositioned the glass.

Meredith squinted at the dots. "Blood?" he questioned, and moved the glass to the right-hand cuff of the hoodie before grinning at Frankie. "And on the sleeve too it would appear."

"We'll soon find out; if it's blood it will glow once I've applied a little luminol." Frankie switched off the overhead light before spraying in the cuff. The tiny dots glowed a bright blue colour and Frankie nodded at Meredith. "Blood. I'll get some swabs and a sample."

Frankie swabbed the sleeve before cutting out a small square section from the front of the hoodie and setting it to one side. He then took a large roll of clear tape and stuck a length on the sleeve of the hoodie and pulled it off and examined it. He shook his head and repeated this process all over the garment both inside and out. "And we have three strands of hair and some fibres which could be from anywhere but not this." He tapped the hoodie before folding it and placing it in a large paper bag. He checked the pockets of the jeans and recovered a bus ticket. Meredith grinned as Frankie photographed it. It was a ticket issued at the right time and on the right journey. Frankie then repeated the process with the tape on the jeans and then the trainers before turning his attention to the carrier bag.

"Did your witness say if she put them in the bag or were they already in it when she found them?" he enquired as he prepared to dust for prints. "What do we have here?" He unfolded a till receipt. "This may be of use. They used a card to purchase socks and pillow cases." Frankie photographed the receipt before bagging it.

"They were in the bag. But she did find it in a bin, albeit on top. She can't even be sure if the person she saw at the bin put it there. However, it was the same day so hopefully not too much contamination. As soon as we're done here email the photos across to me." Meredith fell silent as Frankie worked the bag.

"Right, that's all we can do for tonight. The samples have to go for testing, but I reckon you have five different sets of prints on this. One will be your old lady, and fingers crossed another will be your killer. Some of them had some sort of substance on them which may help. If you go and get the coffee, I'll run them now."

"That's the boy. I knew you were the man for the job, Sherlock." Meredith grinned and Frankie threw him a sardonic look and picked up the camera.

"White with one, Meredith, you know where everything is."

Meredith found Seaton in the corridor and updated him as helped make the coffee. They carried the steaming chipped mugs back to Frankie. Frankie looked up and shook his head.

"What's wrong? Don't tell me you can't find a match." Meredith strode forward and placed Frankie's coffee on the table next to him and leaned forward peering at the computer screen.

"Quite the contrary actually. The first set came up trumps." Frankie sighed. "They belong to Anna Carter."

"Shit. I'd better warn the Super. Travers get hold of bloody Trump, he's not answering his phone. Then get Adler and go and pick her up . . ." He paused frowning and looked back at Frankie. "You said some of the fingerprints had a substance on. Any idea what?"

"Nope, but we can test tomorrow. Why, what do you think it might be? It would speed things up if we know where to start looking."

Meredith looked at Seaton. "Tell him," he instructed, "tell Frankie what the substance will be."

Travers shook his head and held out his arms. "How would I know that?" He rolled his eyes at Frankie. "I think sometimes he thinks I'm psychic . I tell you . . . Oh bloody hell, you think it's ink, or toner or something like that." Seaton replayed Anna Carter's father rubbing his hands on his shirt as he hurried down the hospital corridor.

Meredith nodded. "See, you get there in the end. Bring the father in too." He sighed deeply. "Thanks, Sherlock, get the photos across for us. Tell your lot to process that substance first thing. The father works with photocopiers and printers. Then get the hair sorted. I'm sure Anna will give us a sample without too much bother. Seaton, when you've sorted Adler, get on to Ms Roscoe and tell her we'll be questioning her client tonight." He pulled his phone from his pocket. "I'll call the Super and meet you back at the station."

Liz Brent could hear her husband's voice and she winced as she climbed off the bed and crept to the bedroom door. She held her breath as she opened it just enough to put her ear to the gap. Her husband continued to speak and she relaxed a little.

"I know what I said. But that was then, this is now, things have changed. Don't make me spell this out. I'm not in the mood."

Liz missed the next part of the conversation and realised her husband was pacing up the hall, into the kitchen and back out again. Tentatively, she stepped onto the landing and leaned against the bannister.

"Just do it," came his voice. "I don't care how you do it. Shit, Tone, you are really starting to piss me off." There was a pause and then Liz's blood ran cold as she listened to her husband's next words. "Because she's a fucking liability now, that's why. I want rid of her. Yes, that's exactly what I mean, and the sooner the better. Now stop pissing about and meet me at the club in half an hour."

Liz listened to the phone clatter onto the table in the hall, and realised that Brent would be coming up to get changed. She dashed back into the bedroom and pulled the duvet over her shaking body. Seconds later Brent entered the room. He walked to the bed and stared at her; she opened eyes that betrayed her fear and returned his gaze.

"I'm going out. You stay here, you stay off the booze, and you start acting like a proper mother to that boy."

Brent walked to the wardrobe and retrieved a clean shirt from a hanger. He pulled his tee shirt over his head and picked up a can of deodorant from the dressing table, which he then sprayed liberally over his body and under his arms. As he buttoned up the fresh shirt he walked back to her.

"I don't know how long I'll be, but whatever time I get back I'll be coming to smell your breath."

He turned and left the room. Liz heard the front door slam and the engine of the car roar into life. Her body was shaking and her mind was in overdrive. She needed to calm down and to think this through carefully. She needed a plan and she needed to escape. What she needed most was a drink, but she didn't dare, not until she knew what she was going to do. She closed her eyes and groaned as she realised she had wet herself. Sobbing, she threw back the duvet and tore off her clothes. Naked and shivering she stripped the bed and remade it.

She went into the bathroom, turned on the taps, and poured in some bubble bath. Hurrying downstairs, she shoved the dirty linen into the washing machine and pushed the start button. As the machine began its cycle she eyed the bottle of vodka in the glass cabinet longingly. Turning away quickly she snatched up her cigarettes and returned to the bathroom. She lay in the hot soapy water, chain smoking as she considered her predicament. As she stubbed out her fourth cigarette the door to the bathroom opened. Defensively, she wrapped her arms around her naked body and looked up expecting to see Brent. Closing her eyes, she breathed a sigh of relief as her son strode to the toilet and sat on it before noticing her.

"Hello, Mummy, you're having a bath." He swung his legs to-and-fro as he perched on the toilet.

Liz blinked and tears of relief escaped as she attempted a smile. The wound in her lip opened and she tasted the blood in her mouth.

"I am, but I won't be long. You're such a good boy." She sniffed back a tear. "You go and jump back into bed and Mummy will come and read you a story." She watched as he slid back to the floor, pulled up his trousers and pulled the flush. Instead of leaving the room, he walked towards her and leaned over the bath. Very gently his little finger traced the bruising on her face.

"You got a bruise when you fell, Mummy, you are silly. It's not as big as mine, look." He sat on the floor and rolled his trouser leg up to display a large green bruise on his knee. "Mine doesn't hurt though, and I didn't cry." James Brent pulled himself up by holding onto the side of the bath, and he ran his finger along her eye socket. "There, I've taken your tears away. Don't cry, Mummy, I'll look after you."

Liz sat up quickly and splashed water onto her face to hide the tears that now flowed freely. It should be her looking after him, not the other way around. She had to find a way to get him as far away from her husband as possible.

Through her sobs, she instructed her son to go back to bed. "I'll be two minutes, I have to clean my teeth. You chose a book and I'll be there in no time."

"I know which one I want. I'll surprise you," he called as he ran from the room.

Twenty minutes later Liz switched off his bedside lamp and quietly placed the book on his dresser before leaving the room. She went to her bedroom and tapped the screen on her telephone and found the symbol for the internet. She was not very good at this on the telephone, but she daren't risk using Brent's computer, as she didn't know how to hide what she was looking for. Eventually she found what she was seeking and walked to the bedroom window. Switching off the light and opening the curtain just enough to keep sight of the drive, she dialled the number. If her husband was to return she could terminate the call and get into bed. She was going to do this, but she had to box clever if she was to succeed.

~ ~ ~

Meredith looked up wearily as Louie Trump entered his office. "Where have you been?" he asked, noticing Trump had changed since he last saw him. He looked very dapper. "Nice shirt, did we interrupt something?"

"I had a date. *Crimebusters* had finished, and I didn't see the harm. When I left we had nothing much, so I clocked off. The restaurant was quite up market and so I silenced my -"

"With?"

"I beg your pardon?"

"With whom? Who were you with?" Meredith hoped that he wouldn't get the answer he was expecting.

"Ah, I see. Linda, I took the lovely Linda to -"

"Fine. Right, that's enough of your love life. I'll bring you up to speed. Not that there's much to be done now." Meredith leaned back in his chair and rested his head in his hands. "The programme worked, we have the clothes. We're still awaiting some results but it seems Anna Carter is our killer. Fingerprints on the bag, and I'm sure the test results will provide DNA evidence to link her to the murder. Second set of prints on the bag do belong to her father, although I think that's circumstantial. She simply used a bag that was lying around in the house. True to form she fainted and then lost it, and is now with the doctor. We won't get to speak to her again tonight." He yawned and stretched his legs out in front of him.

Trump watched Meredith's feet appear on the other side of the desk.

"Tomorrow we have to work on the why. Without the why it will be difficult to pin it on her even with the evidence. I had a brief word with what's-his-name from the CPS."

"Well, at least that's almost one down, leaving us with just one to go. Perhaps we'd be better off working out who shot her. It was obviously revenge for Short's murder. If we work it backwards so to speak, all may well be revealed." Trump stopped speaking as the door was pushed open and Jo Adler appeared.

"Sorry to interrupt, Gov, but I've got a woman on the phone for you. Won't give her name but she says it's about the two cases on *Crimebusters* and she sounds scared. I think you should take it." Adler nodded at the phone on Meredith's desk. "Line three."

Meredith allowed himself to fall forward, and bringing his hands down in a flourish he snatched up the receiver. "DCI Meredith, how may I help?"

Jo Adler walked into the room and took the seat next to Trump. They listened to one side of the conversation as Meredith jotted down notes, and looked at them with a surprised expression on his face. Having agreed to meet, he replaced the receiver carefully. He looked at his two officers, his eyes wide, and a smile twitching at the corners of his mouth.

"That was Michael Brent's wife. She thinks Brent is responsible for both Andrew Short and Anna Carter." Meredith shook his head. "She's scared, very scared, so with the exception of Seaton and Travers not a word of this leaves this office. She'll meet with me tomorrow, probably in the morning but can't agree anything until she knows where her husband will be." Meredith rubbed his hands over his face. "Nothing for bloody weeks, and then it all comes rolling in at once." He sat upright and slapped his hands on the desk. "Right, it's going to be a long one tomorrow, so let's get home. I want you bright-eyed and bushy tailed in the morning." As Trump and Adler made to leave, he added, "And don't forget, not a word about Brent's wife. I think she's right to be scared of him and I don't want anything we do to cause her trouble."

CHAPTER EIGHTEEN

Meredith stepped up behind Patsy as she loaded the dishwasher and wrapped his arms around her waist. "Sorry I missed you last night. You were dead to the world when I got in." He kissed her neck as she straightened up and turned around in his arms.

"Me too." She stood on tiptoe and kissed his nose. "How was Anna?" She watched the sadness appear in his eyes.

"Pretty much as you would expect. She's a total wreck, I had to leave her with the doctor last night. Her father confirms that the bag came from their house and that it was his wife who had purchased the stuff listed on the receipt, hence his fingerprints. But he too is in total denial that Anna had anything to do with stabbing Short." Meredith shook his head. "She is involved somehow, but try as I might I can't put the knife in her hand."

"Do you think perhaps she's covering up for someone else? That she knew them, perhaps agreed to dump the clothes for them?"

Meredith shrugged. "I have no idea. Sherlock has them working on the hair and other samples from the clothes this morning. We'll have more of an idea by lunchtime hopefully." He raised his hand above her head and looked at his watch. "I'd better finish my tea, I need to make a move in a minute. What have you got on today?"

As he walked to the table to collect his tea his phone rang. He turned it to face him with his finger and let it ring out.

"Someone you didn't want to speak to?" Patsy nodded at the phone.

"Withheld number, and I never answer them. If someone wants to speak to me they'll leave a message and then they have to give me their number." His phone bleeped indicating a message had been received. "You see, it works." He picked up the phone and called his answer service and listened whilst the message was played. He closed his eyes momentarily and sighed deeply, then terminated the call and dropped the phone back on to the table. "Nothing important." Picking up his mug he drank the remaining tea, and handed the mug to Patsy. "Right, I need to get a tie, then I'm off."

Patsy watched him leave. His response to the call had told her it was important. She heard the bathroom door close behind him and walked to the table. Her fingers drummed against her leg for a few seconds before she snatched up the phone and hit the recall button. Her chin fell to her chest as she too listened to the tearful message.

It's me, Amanda. I thought you might want to know it's over, so you needn't worry about coming. That is if you were going to come. It's all over.

Patsy heard the sob as the message ended. She hung up and replaced the phone; her heart was pounding in her chest and there was a slight tremor in her hand. She needed some space to think about this before she spoke to Meredith. Grabbing her bag from the work surface, and pulling her coat from the newel post as she walked through the hall, she called up to Meredith.

"Something's come up. I'll call you later. Bye." She slammed the door and hurried to her car.

Meredith pulled the flush and washed his hands. Walking across the landing to the bedroom to collect his tie he called down to her.

"What did you say, sorry I didn't hear you." He pulled the tie from over the mirror. "Patsy, did you hear me?" He lifted his collar and put the tie around his neck as he trotted down the stairs. He stopped at the mirror in the hall and knotted the tie before walking to the kitchen. "Patsy I said . . ."

It was evident that Patsy wasn't there. He walked through to the lounge and looked out the window, and saw that her car had gone. He frowned as he returned to the kitchen and picked up his phone. He called her as he pulled his jacket from the back of the chair. Jamming the phone between his ear and his shoulder he shrugged the jacket on. The call went straight to her answer phone. He didn't leave a message, and, miffed, he too slammed the door as he left the house.

Patsy had parked in a cul-de-sac around the corner, knowing Meredith would pass on his way to the station. She waited a few minutes after seeing his car pass the end of the street, and then returned home. Was Amanda a current or former lover? If she was, it was she who had ended it and not Meredith. Although she had said 'that is if you were going to come', which indicated there was a question on that. Patsy clamped her teeth together hoping that would stop the thoughts whirring round in her mind. It didn't, and as she pulled her car back onto the drive she resolved to have it out with Meredith when he got home that evening. In the meantime, she needed to keep her brain occupied. She filled the kettle and called Linda. They arranged to meet in an hour at Tucker's for an update.

Meredith looked at his phone as he sat at his desk and bellowed for coffee. His team exchanged knowing glances and assumed he had a hangover. His phone was working but she hadn't called. He dialled her number again and told himself to be rational. Something urgent had obviously come up, but what was so urgent that she couldn't even come and say goodbye properly? How long would that have taken? His call went through to the answer service again and he dropped it on the desk. Trump tapped and popped his head around the door.

"Brent's wife on line two for you." His eyes glinted with excitement. "I wasn't convinced she'd call back. Good news, what?"

Meredith lifted his hand and rested it on the receiver. "Where's the coffee?" Trump gave an apologetic shrug and left Meredith to take the call. Meredith drew in a deep breath and slowly blew it out before hitting the button for line two.

"Meredith. Good morning, Mrs Brent, thank you for calling back." He put his finger in his other ear as Liz Brent whispered into the phone.

"He's still here but he's taking James to school at half eight, then . . ." Meredith didn't catch the next part as she had moved the phone, "so can you meet me in the carpet shop at the mall. I need to be doing something he would expect."

"I can, what time?"

"I'll be there by nine o'clock unless something happens in the meantime. I have to -" she terminated the call and Meredith looked at his watch; he had enough time for a coffee. He bellowed for Jo Adler, and she came to his office and stood in the doorway arms akimbo.

"I take it you have a hangover. Well, your coffee is on the way so you can stop shouting . . . Sir." She smiled at him and he rolled his eyes. "So what did you want me for?"

"You're coming with me to meet Brent's missus. Got to be at the mall for nine, you can drive."

Trump appeared behind Adler and she stepped to one side to allow him to enter. He placed the steaming mug of coffee on the desk before Meredith.

"There you go. I hope that does the trick, I have some paracetamol if you need them." He smiled at Meredith. "How did you get on with Mrs Brent?"

"I'm meeting her at nine with Adler. I don't have a hangover, and I don't need to be spoken to like a child. Now both of you piss off for a minute and let me drink this in peace."

Patsy took a deep breath of the cold fresh air as she walked across Tucker's car park. She had missed a call from Stella Young assuming it was Meredith. She would see what was happening with Linda then call Stella. She had also received a text from Chris Grainger and was meeting him later back at the office, so all in all she had enough on her plate to keep her thoughts from Meredith. It wasn't working though. Tucking her hair behind her ears she pushed open the door and smiled at the receptionist.

"George and Linda are waiting for you in the same meeting room as yesterday. Would you like a tea or coffee?" The receptionist smiled and Patsy ordered a strong coffee and made her way down the corridor.

"Patsy, I know what was going on the other day. I phoned a friend last night and explained what was happening, although not why of course," Linda paused to smile assurance at George Tucker, "and it was so simple it was positively genius. I have, however, thwarted the plan."

"Can you explain what you're talking about in words that I will understand? Or shall I just take you at your word." Patsy forced a smile and George Tucker laughed a loud raucous laugh. Patsy turned to him; despite his laughter his pallor was ghost like and small beads of sweat were forming on his forehead. "Hello, George, I'm glad someone's in a good mood."

"Humph," George grunted, "I don't know about that, but we've been awaiting your arrival so Linda can explain it to us at the same time. I asked exactly the same question." George pulled a large handkerchief from his pocket and mopped his brow. "All this cloak and dagger stuff will be the death of me. I had Toby on last night asking why I didn't just ask him to sort out whatever it was I wanted. He knew I was lying, mainly because I'm not technical enough to lie well. I gave him some rubbish about a fresh pair of eyes and what have you, but he didn't believe me."

"Right, can we get on with this as I still have some way to go now I can stop it happening." Linda was impatient and didn't mince her words. "You two can go and have a nice chat once I've explained as I'll need to concentrate then."

Patsy winked at George Tucker who nodded at Linda.

"You carry on, my dear. The sooner the better."

"Okay, if you are sitting comfortably." Linda cleared her throat and walked to a white board on the wall behind her and drew a box in red pen. "This is Tucker's mother system. It's where all the data and orders for everything are processed," she drew a blue circle within the box, "and within the mother system is an accounts package that calculates salaries, commissions, and discounts." She drew several lines leading away from the box and put circles at the end of them. "These are the various sales people who earn that commission, and these are the customers connected to the sales people, who earn discounts on their orders." She drew three little triangles and connected them to the circles. "When an order is made the information travels from here to here, and into this area where the various and necessary amounts are calculated and deducted or added, depending on whether it's a discount or commission. They then travel back out to the correct person, be that customer or salesman. Are you with me so far?"

Patsy and George nodded.

George smiled at her. "So far so good, Linda, keep going."

"Good. So what I did at the weekend was to sever these links, one by one. I only wanted to do it for a limited amount of time, just till an order came in and I could see how the commission or discount was distributed." She rubbed out the lines that joined the sales people to the main system. "I didn't get far as within ten minutes or so of me doing it, the severed links had been amended. That's not difficult, anyone could do it, even you two if you'd been shown how, because you simply go to the . . . Oh forget that bit, you're glazing over again. Anyway, what I couldn't work out was who was doing it."

"That's right, you thought it might be Paul Wilde but it happened when he was in here with us. Was it the IT guy?" Patsy was pleased she had managed to follow Linda's explanation. She grimaced as Linda shook her head and shrugged.

"No idea. Because here," she drew a small X on each line leading from the mother system, "is a self-repairing program. It's probably the best thing about this whole system." Linda nodded approval at George. "As I was saying, here is a little gem. It allows any numbers to flow this way," she drew arrows towards the mother system, "but anything coming back out must have a formula attached and if it doesn't it goes right back to where it originated from and looks for the formula. If none is there it defaults to the last setting. You see, self-repairing like this, money will never be processed unless it's been processed." Linda watched as Patsy and George exchanged glances and shook her head. "What bit of that didn't you understand?" she demanded. "School children could understand that. I should have found it immediately, my trouble was I was blinkered, I was looking at the end here instead of the overall picture." Irritated she tapped her pen sharply on the board.

Patsy and George assured her they were following, and she narrowed her eyes revealing her disbelief as she concluded her lesson.

"I'll just accept that then. So now I can simply delete this element of each pathway one by one and see what happens. Given that Tuesday is your busiest day it should only take a couple of hours. Once I know that I can check everything, so class dismissed." She went back to her seat and remembering something pointed at George. "Oh yes, and I've disabled the link to the bank. It won't affect any money coming in, that will just sit there, but it will stop money going out until we know what's what. Okay?" She smiled at George who shrugged acceptance.

"What can I do then? You could have told me that on the phone." Patsy inclined her head. "I do have other meetings today, I'm afraid."

"I need you to process some orders. I've set up several bogus customer accounts, via two new sales people, also bogus. Once I've tested what happens to them using the system as is, I can use them as guinea pigs before getting to work on genuine accounts. I should only take an hour, and we need to crack on. You see?"

"Of course. What do you want me to do then?" Patsy raised her eyebrows and smiled at George as he made his excuses and left them to it.

Jo Adler pulled into the car park of Carpet City and parked halfway down the rank of spaces. It was still early and there were only a handful of cars there.

"Do we know what she looks like?"

"Nope, but I told her I'm tall and handsome so she'll find us." Meredith winked as Adler snorted at his reply. The lights came on in the shop and an overweight man in an ill-fitting suit unlocked the door. "We'll sit tight until she shows. Assuming she does. She's very jumpy."

As he finished speaking a black Alpha Romeo pulled into the space nearest the door. It was driven by a lone female. They watched as the woman pulled up the large collar on her coat and wrapped a pashmina around her shoulders. She climbed out of the car and looked around before hurrying towards the shop.

"That's our girl, I'll put money on it. Come on."

Meredith climbed out of the car and strode purposefully towards the door. Jo Adler had to trot to catch up with him. They entered the shop to find the woman stood side on to the door. She was flipping through carpet samples on a stand, but her eyes were on the door. Meredith smiled and walked towards her. He saw her brow crease and her eyes narrow with fear. He walked past her.

"I'm Meredith. If it's me you want, you'll find me by the offcuts." The woman allowed Jo Adler to pass before she turned and followed slowly.

Meredith was rubbing his hand along the pile of carpet that had been reduced by seventy per cent according to the large paper sign pinned to it. Adler stood several feet away. Liz Brent stopped several rolls away and did the same.

"Mrs Brent?" Meredith watched the woman nod. "Follow me over to the rolls they cut while you wait. Walk past the aisle I'm in and go down the next, I'll meet you halfway down." Meredith turned and picked up Adler's hand. "You come with me and when we're in position you go and shield Mrs Brent from prying eyes." He walked away dragging Adler by the hand. Once Liz Brent was in position he instructed Adler to go and stand several feet in front of her, and once there pretend it was she that was speaking to him.

Meredith bent his knees and peered at Liz Brent through two rolls of cheap nylon twist carpet.

"You talk, I'll listen and when you've finished I may have some questions. Does that work for you?" He watched her nod her head in agreement as her eyes darted down the aisle.

"I don't know why or even if he did it himself, but my husband sorted those two kids. He as good as told me last night."

Liz lisped slightly as she spoke and Meredith saw the wound in her swollen lip. He also noticed her hand go to her throat and he saw her wince as she began to speak. Brent had obviously given her a hiding, hence her fear, and he hoped that this wasn't some sort of elaborate pay back.

"When you say as good as, what does that mean?"

"I called him in last night when his club came up on the telly. He was proper mad about it. When I questioned him, mainly about Anna Carter, he got nasty.

We had words," she gestured towards her face, "and he told me if I didn't behave myself I'd end up like those two."

"I appreciate the courage it took you to come here and talk to me, but that doesn't really mean anything, does it? It could be taken as an idle threat. You know, along the lines of if you're not careful I'll bloody kill you. That type of thing. Telling you you'll end up like them does not add up to he did it. Much as that would please me."

"Oh, he did it. He was so mad seeing the club on there. Mike has this thing that no publicity is bad publicity; he says it's all free publicity. He wouldn't have cared if that poor boy had been stabbed on the club doorstep if it brought a few more punters in." Liz ran her tongue along her swollen lip. "It was also the way he said it, but I know I can't prove that. I'm telling you, Mr Meredith. His problem was that you pushed on the right button."

Meredith exchanged a glance with Jo Adler. This was going to be a total waste of time. Even if Brent was involved, his wife knew nothing that would tie him to the crimes in question.

"You know Anna Carter, don't you? Tell me about that."

"She used to babysit. She was scared of him, you could see it a mile off. Which just made him more interested, thrives on power he does."

"Why did she stop babysitting?" Meredith watched Liz Brent frown and shrug.

"She got a boyfriend I think. Anna was spending time with him when he was free. Her mother told me he was studying here or something. Does it matter that she's not babysitting?"

It was Meredith's turn to shrug. "I'm just looking for a motive, that's all. I take it that other than this one reference you hadn't previously thought him involved?" He watched as defeat took over her being. Her chin dropped, her shoulders slumped, and she sighed as she covered her face with her hands. Her fat lip trembled as she responded.

"So you can't do anything? I've got to go back to that bastard and explain my every move, whilst trying not to speak to him for fear I'll wind him up." Sad eyes gazed deep into Meredith's. "He's going to kill me, you know." She brushed away a single tear.

"I'm sure that's not true, although he's a lout and a bully. In my opinion, for what it's worth you'd -" Meredith didn't complete his advice.

"I heard him tell someone last night." Her tone was flat, and she caught the next tear with her thumb before it reached her cheek.

Meredith gritted his teeth. He really wanted to sort Brent out, irrespective of whether he was involved with the Short and Carter case. The man was a bully.

"What did he say?"

"Something like, she's become an effing liability, I want her gone." She sniffed. "Then someone must have asked him did he mean dead, and he said that's exactly what he meant." She pointed at her face. "That was five minutes after he did this, which was because I told him if he ever touched me again I would take James away. That's when he hit me the second time and did this." She pulled the scarf away from her throat to reveal extensive bruising across her neck. "So, don't tell me it's not true and it was an idle threat. It wasn't."

"Mrs Brent, I'm sorry but without evidence I can't touch him. I can help you get away from him though, you and your child. There are places -"

Liz Brent threw her head back and laughed. It didn't last long as she winced at the pain caused by the exertion. She held her hand to her mouth and shook her head.

"There are two ways I'll get away from him, Mr Meredith. The first is if one of us is dead, and the second is if he's in prison. My preference is the first option, him of course, but in the absence of that, you banging him up would do."

She leaned forward and rested her forearm on the carpet so that her face was as near to the gap between the rolls as possible. "He thinks I'm thick you know, and I do admit to playing on that. I'm not it just helps if he thinks that way. It gives him power over me." Liz waved her hands at the side of her face before leaning forward again. "For instance, I know it would be stupid of me to tell you I will kill him if he touches me again," she held Meredith's gaze and knew he understood, "so I won't. I will try and find out what's been going on though, so you give me a number I can get you on at all times." She stood up and rummaged in her handbag.

Meredith looked at Jo Adler and shook his head sadly. They both knew the risk she would be taking.

Liz tapped at the screen of her phone before passing it through the gap to Meredith. "Put your number in there."

Meredith looked at the screen. Liz Brent had added a new contact, Carpet City. He needed to enter his number, which he did, before pushing the phone back through the gap.

"Thanks," she dropped the phone back into her bag. "You leave first. I need to buy something or he'll wonder why I came." She watched Meredith nod acceptance and turn to walk away. "Work on this at your end, Mr Meredith, as I don't want you to have to take a call that tells you it's too late. You seem like a nice man, I hope I can trust you." Liz turned and walked away.

"Bloody hell, Gov, this is going to be tough. My money says he's involved, but she's taking a hell of a risk spying on him. Did you see the state of her? We'll have to tread carefully on this one."

"You think I don't know that?" Meredith snapped. "Not a word to anyone. Need to know basis and I'll decide who needs to know. Now, let's get back to the station and start digging."

Patsy closed her notebook and smiled at Stella Young.

"I think we have everything covered now. I'm sorry that we've not found who we're looking for yet, I was hoping we would find out before your conference. That way you could just relax and enjoy it."

Stella pulled her head back and looked at Patsy as though she were speaking a foreign language.

"Enjoy? Don't be silly Patsy, one doesn't enjoy these things. They're simply business." She shrugged, "Every time I think I have your measure you say something that surprises me." Stella looked at Patsy's frown and smiled. "Not always in a bad way, you understand. Simply surprising, that's all."

"But surely you enjoy your work? How can you put in so many hours and not enjoy it? It can't be only about the money."

"It's not. The day job is enjoyable, well for the best part it is. But watching your staff get drunk and make fools of themselves is never enjoyable." Stella drummed the table with her manicured nails. "How can I explain this? I'm unable to choose my family," she rolled her eyes, "unfortunately. But I can choose my friends carefully, so I do. When I employ staff I do so with even more consideration."

She waved her finger at Patsy, "But I choose them on their ability to the job. I don't care whether I like them, and more often than not I don't. Therefore, I would never in any other circumstances choose to socialise with the majority of them. You wait until ten o'clock on Friday evening, if you last that long, and you'll see exactly what I mean. I've found over the years that ten o'clock is the hour at which even the most level headed and studious member of staff begins to lose what good sense they were born with."

Stella stood and turned away from the table and poured herself another coffee. "I take it I shouldn't bother offering you one; you'll be off soon if your meeting starts at three."

Patsy grinned at her back knowing she had been dismissed. "No thanks, I'll be off now." She stood and collected her things. "Unless you think of anything else, I'll see you on Thursday at the venue to ensure we're ready to go on Friday. Have a think about the drugs thing, it's an extra twenty pounds a test if you want to go the whole hog."

Patsy hurried to her car. There was a bite in the wind that stung her face. Once in the car she knew she should call Meredith if the silence was not to spiral into a major confrontation. She dialled his number. It rang several times before it was answered by Louie Trump.

"Hi, Patsy, sorry DCI Meredith is in the little boys' room. How are you?"

"Hi, Louie, you do make me laugh. You can call him just Meredith when he's not there, you know. I'm well, but in a hurry. Tell him I called and I'll catch up later. Take care. Bye." Patsy hung up relieved she didn't have to pretend everything was all right.

Back at her own office her phone rang as she locked the car and she ignored it. An hour later she had updated Sharon and Chris Grainger on both cases. Sharon was still suffering and blew her nose noisily.

"I'm sorry, I should be tucked up in bed, but with Penny stuck with her mother there's no chance of that." She walked in the direction of the kitchen. "I can, however, spoil myself with some coffee and posh biscuits. I take it you two want one?" She didn't wait for an answer but disappeared into the kitchen.

Patsy smiled at Chris. "Congrats on the new job, Chris, it sounds very exciting. I almost wish I were free, I could quite fancy flying off to Europe on a job."

"It's not as sexy as it sounds, Patsy. Hours of your life sitting in airports, aeroplanes and taxis. And only the occasional excitement in what is for the best part a boring existence. Still it pays the bills, and madam here gets what she thinks is cheaper duty free perfume. It's no cheaper than the shops on the whole, but she won't have it." He laughed before stifling a yawn. "I'm sorry, didn't get much sleep last night," he jerked his head towards the kitchen, "she was very restless. I think it's the spare bedroom for me tonight. Meredith is okay about Friday, is he?"

"Yes, why shouldn't he be?" Patsy responded a little too quickly, and realised she sounded defensive.

Chris tipped his head back and looked down his nose at her. "What's up?"

"Nothing, why would you ask that?" Patsy attempted a smile.

"I didn't get to where I am today without knowing when something was up, madam." Chris attempted humour.

Patsy's cheeks could only manage a twitch.

"Chris, I am fine, Meredith is fine, we are fine. I promise nothing is up." She looked up as Sharon struggled through the kitchen door and lowered her voice. "Now shut up or I'll have Sharon on my back."

"Now I know I'm right," Chris whispered as he stood. "Can I help you with that, my little petal?" He shook his head at Patsy as he hurried to help his wife. As he returned with the tray there was a sharp rapping on the door. He tutted. "Why don't they read the sign and push the button."

Sharon went to investigate. Seconds later Linda bounded into the room.

"My God, she's like an excited spaniel," Sharon exclaimed as she followed Linda in a more sedate manner. "Linda, calm down, my nerves can't take it."

"Sorry, sorry. But I've done it. I know what they're doing and how they're doing it. I know how long they've been doing it and how much money has gone so far." She paused for breath and looked from one to the other. "Go on then, ask me how much."

"How much, Linda?" Chris grinned at her; her enthusiasm was infectious.

"Thirty-seven thousand, five hundred and sixty-two quid. So bloody clever. But I've explained it to George and he told me to stop it going on. So I have." She grinned triumphantly.

"Sit down, sit down," Chris waved his hand up and down. He summarised as Linda sat and unbuttoned her coat, allowing it to fall over the back of the chair. "You know what, how and how long. You know how much and you've stopped more going. What you have yet to enlighten us with, is who. Who is doing the dastardly deed?"

"That's why I'm here. I have deciphered the coding, with a little help, but I don't know the name of the account. Well I do, but it's numbers not names. What I don't know is whose account it is." She paused again and looked at the tray. "What lush looking biccies, may I help myself? Thanks." She leaned forward and took a biscuit, which she immediately bit into.

"What we have to find out is who the signatory is," mused Sharon.

"Yes," Linda held up her hand as a request that they wait whilst she finished her mouthful. "That's why I'm here. I explained all that to George, bless him he is a tad slow, and I explained now was the time to decide whether or not to go to the police." She looked from one to the other expectantly. "That's right, isn't it?"

Patsy nodded, but Sharon raised her eyebrows and Chris shrugged.

Patsy's eyes widened in amazement. Grinning, she turned to Chris. "Are you suggesting breaching client confidentiality, the Data Protection Act and several more laws I know you will be more than aware of? I'm sure -"

"And that's why I came here rather than phone you." Linda shook her head at Patsy and sighed. "I know you'd go all holier than thou, what with just coming out of the force and being all loved up with Meredith. George wants to know who it is before he decides what to do." Linda ignored Patsy's grunt of indignation and looked to Chris. "We can do that, can't we? I thought that you might know someone, but if you don't, well, let's just say I have my sources."

Sharon looked at Patsy and tutted. "Should we have this conversation without you in the room? It's a teeny tiny thing," Sharon held up her thumb and forefinger to demonstrate how small.

Patsy was momentarily bemused. "How small? I'd like to make a career of this. I don't want to be locked up before I get the chance."

"Stop being so prissy, this is the very least you'll have to do." Sharon laughed and then added quickly, "Don't mind me, it's the cold effecting my judgement."

"Come on then. What are we going to do?" Patsy ignored the snigger from Linda.

"I know a man that can. Leave it with me for an hour." Chris looked at Linda. "Come on my little detective, what bank, what account number et cetera?"

Linda threw an 'I told you so' glance at Patsy and followed Chris into Patsy's office. Patsy pulled a face at her, and picked up a biscuit.

Sharon looked at her and shook her head. "Is there something wrong, Patsy? You don't seem yourself today. Everything you have said, well until now, has been positive, but your demeanour would suggest otherwise." Sharon wagged her finger as Patsy opened her mouth to respond. "No, don't get defensive, you need to get whatever it is that's bothering you off your chest or sorted out. I know that it's not to do with us needing to bend the rules a little. You always knew that would arise, so one has to assume it's Meredith. Now I'm not going to pry but I'm here if you need a chat . . ." Sharon sneezed into a tissue. "Sorry about that. As I say, I'm here if needed."

Patsy stood and walked away from Sharon, collecting the used cups as she did so. "There's nothing wrong Sharon, well not that I know of yet, anyway. I'll make some more coffee, but thanks for the offer, it's appreciated." Patsy forced a smile. "I'll check and see if those two want something." She walked to her office door, and the mugs in her hands clinked together. Chris and Linda were deep in conversation. Chris looked up as she entered.

"I've drawn a blank at the moment," he shrugged, "my chap isn't answering so we'll leave it for an hour or so to see if he comes back to me." Chris tapped the mobile on the desk. "If he doesn't, Linda thinks she knows a friend of a friend that will oblige. I don't like using unknowns as a rule, but we'll see." He stopped speaking as Linda's phone rang. She pulled it from her pocket and standing she walked to the window that overlooked the car park.

"Hi, Toby, what can I do for you?" Linda turned to Patsy and Chris and mouthed something neither of them understood. "Oh dear, I've obviously done something wrong then. I can't get back to it until tomorrow." As she listened to the response she used her fingers to imitate a gun and placed them on her temple. "Oh I don't know about that," she told the caller, "I've spent an age sorting it out, I'd need to speak to George first. Well, there's no need for that. Of course I'm not. I have other jobs on. George is the boss. I'll check with him when he's available and get back to you."

"The IT chap I take it?" Patsy asked.

Linda nodded and walked back to her seat. "It was. Bugger! I was hoping we'd have the answer before I took that call." She looked at the mugs in Patsy's hand. "You making coffee or what? I need something stronger but caffeine will do for the moment. He's realised that I've locked him out of the system and thinks I'm after his job. I can't let him back in until we know who controls that bank account." Linda looked at Chris. "Can you give your bloke another call?"

Her face fell as Chris shook his head.

"Nope, the deal is you call him and he comes back to you. If he doesn't answer it's because he can't. Don't get all wound up by some jumped up IT guy. If he's innocent he'll understand, and if he's not, there's no harm done."

Before she could respond her phone rang again. It was George Tucker. She put the call on speaker and placed it on the desk.

"Hi, George, I'm assuming you're calling about Toby."

"I am, five times in twenty minutes he's called me. I'm ignoring his calls, but in the last one he said he wanted to come round and see me. He sounded too angry, if you know what I mean. I think it could be him. Have you got anywhere yet?"

"No, not as yet, George, these things take time. Look why don't you take yourself off out for a couple of hours, that way if he comes round you won't be there. Or you could just blame me and pretend you can't get hold of me. I'll ignore calls from both of you."

"I suppose so. Can't you speed it up a bit?"

Linda looked at Chris Grainger and shrugged. "We'll try, George. I promise I'll get back to you as soon as we have news."

She terminated the call and looked up at Patsy who had walked forward and was standing behind her chair.

"Sounds like it's Toby, doesn't it?" she tutted and Chris answered the question.

"Actually, I don't think so. If it was him he would be stupid to show his hand by getting agitated. I think it's just wounded pride that George brought someone else in to do the job."

Patsy wasn't convinced. "I hope you're right, but if not we need to get this sorted sharpish. George sounded genuinely concerned. Let's give your chap another fifteen minutes and then try Linda's contact." She rolled her eyes at Linda. "Yes, I'm making the coffee now," she grinned and left the room.

When she returned, Chris was pacing up and down impatiently and Sharon was pulling her coat on. Both looked shocked.

"What's happened? Where are you going?"

"We've just had a call. It's Jack, he's been in an accident and they've taken him to the General." Chris explained as he took hold of Sharon's elbow. "We need to get over there. I'll leave you to deal with the necessary."

He picked up the mobile phone and held it out to Patsy. She placed the mugs on the desk and took it from him.

"Of course. Do you know how serious it is?" she asked, and Sharon gave a sob.

Chris grimaced and shook his head. "They said he was still unconscious when he arrived. They've taken him for a scan."

"Well, get yourselves down there pronto. We'll sort out this end. Give me a ring when you know what's happening."

Chris had opened the door and was ushering Sharon through it.

"Will do," he paused briefly and nodded at the phone, "and be careful. He's not the easiest of blokes." He turned to his wife. "Come on love, it's going to be fine." The door closed behind them.

Patsy picked up a mug of coffee and walked towards her office. She beckoned Linda with a jerk of her head.

"Well, if this is going to be a waiting game we may as well sit comfortably." Patsy led the way to the two sofas and placed her coffee and the mobile on the table that separated them. She dropped onto the seat with a sigh, and lifting her legs she unzipped her boots and removed them. She rested her feet on the edge of the table and smiled at Linda who was doing the same on the opposite side. "Now we're alone you can let me know what's what with you and Louie."

For the first time that day her smile was genuine.

Meredith strode into the incident room and walked to the board. He picked up a pen and next to a photograph of the clothing they had recovered he wrote: Hair – Anna Carter; Blood – Andrew Short; Skin – Anna Carter. He turned to the team who were watching him.

"Conclusive. Not only was the hair hers, but particles of skin found in the cuffs of the hoodie and the right knee of the inside of the jeans were hers too." He glanced up at the clock, it was almost four fifteen. "Trump, give her brief and the CPS a ring. Adler, get her into an interview room, we need to see how she reacts to this."

Jo Adler and Bob Travers questioned Anna Carter for almost two hours. Apart from shaking her head and crying almost continually, she only spoke to repeat that she hadn't done it. Meredith watched from the next room. At six thirty he tapped on the door and called them out.

"This is going nowhere, so I'm toying with the idea of throwing Brent back into the mix. What do you think?"

"Gov, are you sure? It was only yesterday you said we had to keep that under lock and key. Can you trust Roscoe?" Adler shook her head as Meredith shrugged.

"Let's find out." He pushed open the door and smiled at Anna Carter before turning to Jane Roscoe. "Ms Roscoe, may I have a word?" He pushed the door open a little further and as she left the interview room, he took her by the elbow and walked her further up the corridor. "Can we have an off-the-record conversation? Can I trust you?" His gaze locked her eyes on to his. "You see, whilst all the evidence tells us your client is guilty, I have my doubts. I want to try something but it can't leave that room, because if it does someone will get hurt. Seriously hurt. Personally, I don't want that on my conscience, how about you?"

Flustered, Jane Roscoe pulled her eyes away from him and looked down at her lapels as she brushed imaginary fluff away. She set her face in what she hoped was a look of genuine indifference and allowed her eyes to meet his once more.

"That girl is on the brink of a nervous breakdown. It should be clear to any idiot that she will not admit to this as she didn't do it. I will give you another thirty minutes during which time you will change tack. Should you fail to be constructive I will summon the doctor and make a complaint about you personally."

Meredith's smile appeared in his eyes first, and Jane Roscoe cursed silently as she felt the colour rise in her cheeks.

"But any names or inferences made will not leave that room? Am I able to trust you, Ms Roscoe?" The smile had reached his lips.

Jane Roscoe cleared her throat and a dimple appeared on her right cheek. She quashed the smile.

"Of course, DCI Meredith, now let's get on with this. Your clock is ticking." She tucked an errant strand of hair back behind her ear and walked away. She smiled at Anna as she re-entered the interview room. "Stay strong, Anna," she looked at her watch, "another twenty-five minutes and we'll have you out of here."

Meredith took Bob Travers' place and waited whilst Jo Adler turned to a fresh page in her note book. Having announced the time and who was present in the room he turned his attention to Anna. She attempted a smile. Meredith looked away momentarily as he saw the lines of worry that now scarred her beautiful face.

"Anna, you are aware that all the evidence we have relating to Andrew Short's murder indicates that you killed him. This includes the eye witnesses from the identity parade." He paused as Anna nodded. "Despite being unable to provide an alibi, or explain how your DNA and Andrew Short's blood were found on the clothing worn by the killer in a bin not too far from your home, and in a bag covered in your fingerprints, you continue to deny your guilt." Meredith watched Anna nod. "On that basis, we need to look at other possibilities. To consider if it is possible that someone would have set you up. Do you understand what I'm suggesting?"

Anna's frown turned to a small smile and she nodded enthusiastically.

"You need to speak, Anna," Meredith smiled and nodded at the recorder, "it saves me a lot of talking."

"Yes, I understand."

"Is there anyone you can think of that would have done this? Anyone at all that would have the ability to do this?" Meredith folded his arms and leaned on the table that separated them, and by so doing he put his face closer to hers. Anna shook her head. "Speak please, Anna," he encouraged softly.

"No."

"Did you tell anyone about your taxi ride with Andrew Short?"

Anna began to shake her head and said quickly, "No, no one."

"Did you see Michael Brent after that night?"

"No."

"Would you be surprised if I told you that someone close to Michael Brent has suggested that he was responsible for both killing Andrew Short and shooting you?"

Anna's face contorted as she attempted to process that information. She raised her hands from her lap before allowing them to drop back again. Closing her eyes, she drew in a deep breath. When she opened them, she looked at Meredith for what seemed like an age, before she uttered the last thing she would say that day.

"People think I'm thick because I'm pretty, but I'm not. I'm not a mastermind either, but I have already worked out that someone is making it look like I killed that lad. I don't know who, I don't know why, and I certainly don't know how. What is it you think I've been thinking about since you first suggested that I did it? But I'm telling you, Mr Meredith or DI Meredith, or whatever I'm supposed to call you, I did not do it." She enunciated the words slowly and clearly.

This time it was she that held Meredith's gaze. "I trust you, I know you will help me if you can, but I can't help you with this. I simply don't know how to. I have to leave it to you to help me, and I know you will if you can." Anna shook her head, and without taking her gaze from Meredith, she said to her solicitor, "I want to go now please, Jane. I can't do this anymore. If Mr Meredith can't help me then he'll just have to send me to prison." She closed her eyes, dismissing Meredith.

For the first time in a long while Meredith felt nervous. It didn't show as he announced the end of the interview, or as he promised to do his best as Anna was taken back to the cells. But he was. Anna had gift-wrapped the responsibility that was already his, and placed her future firmly in his hands. It was not a burden he wanted. He looked at Jo Adler who patted him on the shoulder.

"You had your table turned, Gov. That girl just gave you a taste of what it's like to sit opposite you. The question is, what now?" Adler nudged Meredith and gave a cheeky wink. "What did it feel like to be Meredithed?" She saw the twitch of a smile.

"Shit," he responded before rubbing his hands over his face, "now we have to hope that Liz Brent can come up with something more concrete than a threat."

Anthony Wilson watched the glass sail through the air before hitting the door that led to the gents' toilet. Rather than shatter as he expected it too, it bounced off the door and cracked in two as it hit the ground.

Brent turned to face him. "So you *think* she's been arrested then?" Brent sneered as Wilson shrugged and shook his head.

"As far as I can work out, she was arrested then released without charge, then picked up again after the *Crimebusters* programme. He reckons she 'was helping with enquiries'," Wilson effected a squeaky voice before adding, "but she hasn't been charged yet, she's still at the local nick."

"And your contact is who? How reliable is he?" Brent demanded.

Wilson sighed. This was the part where he had to admit there were too many links in the chain.

"He's the husband of a clerk that works at the solicitors," Wilson picked up his pint to avoid making eye contact with Brent.

He flinched as Brent roared, "The husband of a fucking *clerk*? How reliable is that?" Brent paced a step closer to Wilson and looked over his shoulder at the barmaid trying to busy herself as far away as possible. "Oi. You. Bring me a bottle and a fresh glass." As the girl reached for a bottle of brandy, Brent loomed closer to Wilson. "My office, now. You can explain to me how that's the best we can do."

Wilson walked towards the stairs leading to Brent's office. Brent snatched the bottle from the barmaid. "Clean this place up," he snarled looking at the glass he had thrown. "The doors open soon."

Wilson stood swapping his weight from one foot to the other as he waited for Brent to join him. Brent was in over his head. Wilson was convinced it was only a matter of time before it all came tumbling down around his ears. The thing he had to work out was how to distance himself from Brent. He'd told him he was pushing his luck, and it would appear that despite the current predicament he still wanted to go ahead on Friday. Lost in his thoughts he started as Brent snapped.

"Sit down and tell me about this clerk. Who is she?"

"Her husband is a regular here. He picked up a dose from one of the girls and had a quiet word. You remember Tabitha? The one with the fish lips that we got rid of?"

"And this is relevant because?" Brent was tapping his glass against the side of the bottle and Wilson pulled the chair a little further away from the desk as he took a seat.

"He gave us a load of crap about how his missus worked for a solicitor and he would sue us. We quietened him down by letting him see the doc that sorts the girls for us, and now he has freebies every now and again." Wilson snorted. "He won't forget to use a condom again in a hurry. He was one of the surveyors used by Hancock on the housing development. I figured it might be useful to have something on him, so we have a selection of photographs. As it turned out it was." Wilson grinned at Brent who had stopped tapping his glass. "Then when you asked me to sort Anna Carter I remembered his missus worked for the solicitors representing her. So he asks the questions and then gives me the answers." Wilson finished his pint.

"Biggest problem is there is a time delay. He can only ask her at night and then let me know the next day. He called me just now to let me know there was no more news because his wife had left work before the brief got back."

"So the soonest we'll know something is tomorrow night? You've got to be kidding me. Don't we know anyone at the station?" Brent poured a healthy measure of brandy into his glass and knocked it back. He smacked his lips together. "Tell him to take her to lunch tomorrow. I can't wait until tomorrow night."

"I always thought this might be dodgy, but no one will trace this back to you. Has something happened?" Wilson was not convinced by his own words, and Brent panicking was totally out of character. He needed to assess whether he should go and see his cousin in Glasgow for a while.

Brent refreshed his glass and stared at Wilson as the amber liquid gurgled into the glass

"What? You mean anything more than them knowing that they both came here and showing the club on a crime programme?" Brent's top lip curled into a snarl.

"I know that, but like I say they can look but they won't find, will they? We sorted the Franklyn bloke." Wilson looked away from Brent as he continued. "I'm probably speaking out of turn. But is there something you're not telling me? You seem quite . . . quite . . . well, fact is, you seem quite jumpy to me. It makes me worry."

Wilson looked at the floor awaiting the explosion he thought would come. Brent remained silent. Eventually Wilson had to give in and look at him.

Brent stared at him. "Piss off Tone. I don't want to do something I might regret. We'll catch up tomorrow."

Wilson blew out a sigh of relief and hurried towards the door.

Brent called to him. "Send the barmaid up. Now!"

Wilson smiled apologetically as he instructed the barmaid to join Brent. He wouldn't want be in her shoes at that moment. Not for a million quid.

Patsy jumped as Chris's mobile rang. They had first spoken to his contact over an hour ago when he had simply taken the details from Linda and told her to leave it with him. He also instructed them to answer first time as he would only call back once.

Linda looked at Patsy. "You speak to him this time. I think I let him bully me." She made a sad face and Patsy picked up the phone.

"Hello, do you have news?" Patsy flapped her hand at Linda who giggled.

"Who is this?"

"I'm a work colleague of Chris. He's still at the hospital."

"What happened to the other girl?"

"She's here with me. Would you rather speak to her?" This time it was Linda's turn to flap her hand; she was more than happy for Patsy to deal with it.

"No, but I'm not happy about this."

"Well I'm sorry about that, let's cut to the chase, shall we? Do you have the information we require?"

"No."

Patsy rolled her eyes at Linda. "I'm sorry? Is there a problem?"

"Yes, but it's too long to explain. Call me back in twenty minutes." He hung up.

"Well we'd better put the kettle on. I have to call back in twenty minutes." Patsy looked at her watch and groaned. "It's half eight now, it will be midnight before we get home at this rate."

"Will Meredith be missing you? Come to think of it, you haven't called him since I got here. Is that why you're out of sorts today?" Linda picked the mugs up from the table.

"I am not out of sorts. Why does everyone keep saying that?"

"You just answered your own question really. Give him a call then."

"What? I'm not sixteen, Linda." Patsy stretched and yawned before standing and following Linda to the kitchen.

"Then call him. It will solve the problem, or break the ice, whichever is needed."

"What? You talk absolute crap sometimes, do you know that?"

"And now you're snapping at me, and it's not because you're tired. You've sat here for over an hour listening to me tell you about Trump and my other conquests. Not a mention of Meredith, and that's odd because usually you can barely manage a sentence without some reference."

"Rubbish! Shit, I snapped again didn't I? Linda, I'm a little miffed with him at the moment, it's nothing serious." Patsy mentally crossed her fingers. "But if it makes you happy I'll call him."

"That's a good girl." Linda disappeared into the kitchen.

Patsy walked back into her office and called Meredith. He answered on the first ring.

"I'm sorry I haven't called, just got out of an interview with Anna Carter. Forensics weren't kind to her. Have I ruined dinner?"

"No, no it's fine. I've been tied up too, still not finished either. I'm awaiting a call from one of Chris's contacts." Patsy drew in a sharp breath. "You don't know, do you? Jack has been in an accident. He was unconscious when he arrived at the hospital, which was best part of four hours ago and neither Chris nor Sharon has called with news." She listened whilst Meredith agreed how awful the situation was. "Anyway, with any luck I'll be home by ten. What about you?"

"Pretty much the same, see you there." Meredith sighed. "I missed you today. Got to go, bye."

She smiled into the phone as Linda returned carrying the freshly made coffee.

"There you go, a smile. That was worth it, wasn't it? Right, come on then, that's almost twenty minutes. Call that bloke and let's get home."

Patsy nodded and picked up the mobile. He answered on the third ring and Patsy hit the speaker button. His tone was still clipped and dictatorial.

"It's me."

"Still at the hospital, is he?"

"Yes, still no word. Do you know his son?" Patsy attempted to personalise the call.

"That's not relevant."

"What news then? You obviously don't want to chat, so let's get on with it." Patsy smiled as Linda gave her the thumbs up.

"As I said before, none." Seemingly exasperated the man sighed.

"Then why am I calling back?"

"I need to be sure you're kosher and not some copper or smart arse trying to catch me out."

"I'm not, so get on with it." Patsy put her finger to her lips as Linda let out a laugh.

"The holder of the account you gave me is fictitious. He doesn't exist. Money goes into the account and each time the balance hits more than two hundred pounds it's transferred out again to another account held by Jason Simons. He died some ten years ago. It's an online account and I'm assuming the address is false. The money is withdrawn from various cash points across the West Country, but there are three in Bristol used on an irregular but regular basis, if you get my drift."

"Sort of. Where are they?"

"How do I get paid, with himself not being available?"

"How do you normally get paid?"

"You should know that."

"Oh for God's sake, this isn't the CIA, you know. Just give me the information."

"Hmm, you interest me, young lady, I think we should meet. You bring the cash I'll bring the information."

"Where?"

"The usual place he will know."

Patsy sighed. "When?"

"Tomorrow morning. Ten thirty, don't be late." The call was terminated, and Patsy tossed the phone onto the coffee table."

"Idiot. Anyone would think he was a member of some major crime ring. Not a jumped up little computer hacker. All this bloody cloak and dagger stuff. I'm surprised that Chris does business with him."

"How do you know he's not?" Linda shook her head at Patsy as though disappointed.

"Not what? Don't you start. I suppose I'd better keep hold of this. If Chris doesn't answer his phone this time I think I'll get down to the hospital and try and find out what's going on."

"How do you know he's not part of a major crime ring? Chris will have lots of dodgy contacts, given his previous career, and needs must and all that. If you're going to the hospital do you want me to come with you?" Linda followed Patsy out of the office and switched off the light and closed the door. She pulled on her coat as Patsy put the dirty mugs in the kitchen.

"No, it's fine you get off home. Meet me here first thing. I'm not sure what we'll do with you whilst we're waiting for an answer. I'll leave you to update George Tucker." Buttoning her coat Patsy set the alarm and locked the office.

It was ten thirty when Patsy finally pulled onto the drive. Meredith was already at home. She had decided to let the phone call drop. He would either tell her about it or not. If he didn't it didn't mean he had anything to hide; she had to trust him if their relationship was to work. After all, she had thought that he had a liaison with a woman the other day, and that turned out to be his sister. She gave a little sigh as she put her key in the lock. That didn't mean she wouldn't be watching him though.

CHAPTER NINETEEN

Patsy woke to the sound of Meredith slapping the bedside cabinet looking for his ringing phone. It stopped ringing before he found it and he turned on the light. Patsy lifted her head and squinted at the red numbers on the clock. It was five thirty. She flopped back down putting her forearm across her eyes. The house phone began to ring.

"That doesn't sound promising." She peeped out from under her arm as a naked Meredith left the bedroom. "Put the kettle on, I'll make some tea," she called and he grunted in response.

She listened as he ran down the stairs and smiled at the image in her mind as the ringing stopped. Whoever it was the conversation was brief as only seconds later Meredith returned to the bedroom.

She rolled onto her stomach and pushed herself up onto her elbows. "Did you put the kettle on?"

"No time." Meredith pulled boxer shorts from a drawer and put them on. He picked up a pair of socks and sat on the edge of the bed. "Looks like I've got another murder on my hands." Socks on, he walked to the wardrobe and pulled a shirt from a hanger, which he threw onto the bed. "Better splash a bit of water on first." He sniffed his armpits and wrinkled his nose.

"Was it Frankie?" she asked as he walked out to the bathroom.

"No, he's at some bloody conference or other, it's his underling. Some girl of about ten," Meredith called back.

Patsy didn't understand the rest of what he said as he had started to brush his teeth. She lay there listening to him splash about, which was followed by the usual sound of the deodorant can being half emptied. He came back into the bedroom and his still wet hair dripped onto the shirt as he buttoned it. He studied her as he pulled his trousers on.

"What?" she asked, her brow furrowing.

"I haven't got time to tell you. I'll show you later though." He leaned across the bed, slapped her backside, and planted a kiss on her upturned forehead. "I'll call you when I can."

Patsy switched off the light and dozed off. Two hours later she was awoken for the second time by Meredith's phone. She scrambled to his side of the bed and answered it without thinking.

"Did I wake you? Please tell me you're still in bed naked. I could do with something to cheer me up."

"I am. You forgot your phone."

"That's your fault for distracting me. I'm at the morgue, they're going to do the PM now, so I'll hang around for a while. Where will you be later or will it be easier if I pick it up from home?"

Patsy blinked and thought about her itinerary for the day. She had to meet Linda and then go to Blaise Castle to meet the chap with the information on the bank account. She hadn't mentioned it to Meredith the night before as updating him on Jack's condition took precedent.

"Office first thing and then a couple of meetings. It's probably best I leave it here for you. Unless you want me to drop it into the station later when I have a minute?"

"No, leave it in the kitchen and I'll swing by later. Oh God, here comes the ten-year-old dressed up like a doctor, I'd better go. Catch you later, bye."

Patsy climbed out of bed, showered and dressed. She took the phone to the kitchen and placed it on the centre of the table. Pulling her own phone from her bag she called the Graingers' home number for an update on Jack. She popped in two slices of toast and filled the kettle as she listened to the ringing tone. She was about to hang up when Chris answered. He confirmed that Jack was comfortable after a night in ITU, and that it was unlikely he or Sharon would make it into the office until later that day. Patsy agreed that Linda would man the office for them.

She placed her phone next to Meredith's and sat down with her breakfast. As she bit into the toast she eyed Meredith's phone, and the fingers of her free hand drummed the table. Wiping her fingers on a piece of kitchen towel she pulled the phone forward and opened contacts. Amanda was the fifth contact. Patsy pursed her lips and clicked on messages. She stopped chewing as she read the message from the previous afternoon.

I got your message, pick me up in Broadmead. I'll be outside McDonalds at two o'clock on Thursday.

It was a response to a question posed by Meredith. He had deleted the question. Why would he do that and leave the answer? She saw it had come in at six thirty the evening before. Meredith would have been questioning Anna Carter at that time, and he had probably forgotten about it. She sighed and returned the phone to the home screen. Her appetite lost, she threw the toast into the bin and wished she had a cigarette. She checked Meredith's man drawer and found a crumpled packet containing one cigarette. Lighting it on the gas ring of the cooker, she opened the kitchen door and stood on the threshold blowing the smoke into the murky morning air.

Her previous resolve to wait for Meredith to share with her had gone. Now she had to decide whether to confront him, which would reveal she had been checking up on him, or go to the meeting to see what happened. That would be spying on him. She wondered which was worse. Both options made her feel sick to her stomach. Taking a long drag on the cigarette she decided that she might possibly discuss the situation with Linda. Sharon would have been her first choice but she had enough on her plate.

Walking back into the kitchen she extinguished the cigarette under the tap and dropped the butt into the bin. Meredith's phone vibrated indicating a message had come in. Using all her will power she picked up her handbag, collected her coat from the hall, and left the house.

Halfway to the office, she stopped at a newsagent and bought a packet of cigarettes. When she arrived, Linda was already there, pacing up and down, awaiting her arrival.

"Come on, PHPI, we have to prepare for our meeting with the guy from the CIA."

Patsy forced a smile. "I know, but it's not until ten thirty, calm down there's plenty of time."

"What did Chris say? Is he a big-time baddie or just up himself?" The excited Linda persisted as Patsy unlocked the office and switched off the alarm.

"From what I gather a bit of both. Chris arrested him way back when computer hacking was new; they couldn't pin anything on him but he didn't know that. He testified against some bad boys and now enjoys living a life believing there are assailants around every corner." Patsy tapped the side of her head and rolled her eyes. "He still dabbles in electronic tracking and the like, but Chris thinks only for a select few."

Patsy dropped her bag onto the coffee table and turned to Linda, taking the post she had collected from the door mat. "You put the coffee on, I'll open this, and then we can plan the day. It's unlikely we will see Chris or Sharon today. Jack is out of danger but still has a long way to go."

Meredith strode into the incident room and was pleased to note that, as instructed, a new board had been placed on the wall to the side of his office, and opposite the two existing cases. He walked to it and picked up a pen.

"Right you lot, listen up." Underneath the name and photograph of Joseph Franklyn he listed the injuries. "Cause of death – strangulation with his own tie. But not before he had put up a struggle. He took quite a severe kicking, and has multiple bruises over his body caused prior to death." Meredith nodded at Trump. "Check your email, I told them to send the photos to you."

Trump clicked into his inbox and nodded. "They're here. I'll print them off."

A few moments later the printer in the corner chugged into life.

Meredith resumed his update. "There was something under the fingernails, but apparently not skin. The results will be sent through as soon as confirmed, but fake leather was the initial thought. Best guess is our man was wearing cheap gloves."

"We know it's a man, or assuming?" Tom Seaton asked as he walked to the printer to collect the photographs.

Meredith held out his hand for them as he returned. Meredith shuffled through the prints and chose two, which he fixed to the board. He pointed to the chest of the dead man.

"This is a line of bruising caused by contact with a hard edge. Given where and how he was found, probably made by the kerb." Meredith tapped the next print which showed an iron shaped bruise on the man's back. "They reckon this is the mark made by the boot which forced him down onto the edge of the kerb, and held him there whilst they grabbed his tie, twisted it round, and then pulled until he died." He tapped the ruler which had been placed under the bruising. "This bruise is 150 millimetres wide, or the best part of six inches for those still working in English. Wide enough to indicate it was unlikely to be a woman. The force used was considerable, and they have a partial print from his jacket. The x-ray shows that two ribs and several vertebrae were broken." Meredith turned to face them. "There are some other bits and pieces too which you can pick up from the full report when it arrives. I left them to it. Now, what do we have on our victim?"

Meredith perched on the edge of the table as Tom Seaton stepped forward.

"Joseph William Franklyn, aged fifty-three. He ran his own surveying business. His wife reported him missing yesterday afternoon. Duty sergeant took the detail and it came up when we put him into the system. Basic missing person's report on my desk." Seaton paused and looked at Meredith. "What was the time of death?"

"Best they can do is early hours of Tuesday morning. Somewhere between two and six. His wife was right to be worried about him. Strange she didn't report it until the afternoon though. Any known associates?"

"Interestingly he got his name in the newspaper several times. Originally, he was one of the surveyors employed to work on the new Cherry Tree development. The council were keen to prove that they had used local businesses and contractors to work on the project. There had been some demonstrations about building on the land. He was contracted by Blaze Solutions, but they were later dropped when some problem was found. Haven't got to the bottom of what problem yet, but I will."

Seaton paused and grinned at Meredith. "What?"

"Guess who else is connected to Blaze Solutions?"

Meredith raised his eyebrows and a smile appeared. "Don't tell me. It's Brent." He clapped his hands as Seaton nodded confirmation. "Splendid. Right, let's do a little more digging and I reckon we can consider paying Mr Brent a little visit." He stood and jerked his head backward towards the board. "Get that updated, and Adler and Trump get across to see Franklyn's wife. The son identified him so she knows. The rest of you, keep digging."

Patsy smiled as Linda told her about an appointment she had booked for Chris the following week.

"I know it's a missing person, but it sounds like a bit more than that, doesn't it?" She tutted as Patsy shrugged. "Well, if he doesn't want to do it, I will." She paused as Patsy laughed out loud. "What, you don't think I'm capable?"

"Of course I do, but you wouldn't know where to start." Patsy glanced at her watch. "I'd better get going soon." She closed her note book and slid it into her bag. "Now don't make any more appointments, just take the detail and I'll call . . . hang on a minute."

She picked up her phone and answered the call.

"Hi, Stella, how are you? What can I do for you?"

Linda watched a frown appear on Patsy's face as she listened to Stella. Patsy uttered a few "buts" but little else as Stella commanded the conversation.

"What time is it?" Patsy eventually managed, and looked at her watch again as she received the answer. "I have another appointment at ten thirty, and I can't guarantee being there by eleven fifteen although it may be fine. Can't you change it until this afternoon?" Patsy shook her head at Linda. "Okay, leave it with me, I'll try to rearrange." She hung up and sighed. "I know she's paying us good money, but to expect me to be able to drop everything on her order does grate."

"What does she want?"

"She's going to see her physiotherapist and wants me to join her. She had initially discounted him, but now she thinks it would be prudent to check him out." Patsy realised that Linda didn't have a clue what she was investigating and, remembering the confidentiality agreement, she waved her hand dismissively. "Don't worry, it's a long story. I need to phone and try and get the other meeting put back."

"Is that wise? I could go instead." Linda's eyes glinted and she rubbed her hands together.

"No, Linda, you couldn't. We need someone to man the office." Patsy pulled Chris's pay-as-you-go phone from her bag and called the number. This time it was answered almost immediately.

"What do you want?" he snapped.

"We have a little problem and I was wondering if we could meet this afternoon?"

"No." There was a hesitation, "What problem?"

"Another client has a problem, and with Chris being stuck at the hospital I wondered if -"

"I don't like problems, they worry me."

"As it's not your problem, it shouldn't." Patsy knew her sarcasm would wind him up, but she wasn't in any mood to soothe a male ego today.

"It is if you mess me about," he snapped. "Look, forget it. It's clear Chris shouldn't leave women in charge. He should have known that would never work."

Patsy heard the challenge, and should have ignored it, but she didn't. "Fine, as you are obviously so busy we'll stick to ten thirty. If we have any similar issues arise

I'll use one of my own chaps. They're far easier to work with," She looked away as Linda threw her hands into the air in amazement. "My colleague Linda will meet you outside the entrance to the museum as agreed. How will she recognise you?"

"I'll find her. Describe her."

Patsy described Linda's outfit as Linda danced from one foot to the other.

"Yeeha. Leave it to me, PHPI. I'll get it sorted. Give me your notes then."

Five minutes later, Patsy watched the excited Linda pull out of the car park, and she called Chris and left a message explaining what was happening. She then pulled on her own coat and set the alarm. Now she was alone again she had time to think about Meredith and his meeting the next day. She pulled out the packet of cigarettes and smoked one leaning against the car before setting off to meet Stella Young.

Stella took her arm as they walked from the car park to a large Victorian house. The property housed several different practices that shared a reception. The brass plaques to the side of the door gave the names of the dentist, physiotherapist, chiropodist and optician. The receptionist recognised Stella immediately.

"Good morning, Ms Young. He is expecting you. I'll let him know you're here. Please take a seat."

"I'll stand. My appointment is in less than two minutes, and he'd better not keep me waiting this time."

Patsy was impressed; the receptionist didn't even flinch as she picked up the phone and announced their arrival. She was clearly used to dealing with demanding customers. A few seconds later she heard heavy footsteps approaching them. A man entered and held out his hand to Stella.

"Stella, welcome. You look wonderful as always. Sorry I had to cancel our last appointment. Family issues I'm afraid, but enough of that. Let's get you sorted."

Patsy assessed the man as he greeted Stella. He was around fifty years of age and wore a tweed suit which had seen better days, but his shoes had been polished to a high sheen. He was overweight and small beads of perspiration glistened around his hairline. His fingernails were so badly bitten they were all but non-existent. He seemed pleasant enough but deep lines spreading out from the corners of his eyes and down from his mouth gave him a haggard appearance.

Stella took her hand back and held it out towards Patsy. "This is my colleague and friend, Patsy Hodge. It is she you will be treating, not me. Her need is greater than mine. Unfortunately, she pulled something in her back or shoulder at the gym."

As Stella introduced her, Patsy saw the brief widening of the man's eyes as he tried to assess whether she was a genuine friend or a sexual partner. She bit back a smile as she wondered whether Stella's sexual partners often needed to visit a physiotherapist. She stepped forward and held out her hand, smiling as she did so. He took her hand and smiled kindly at her.

"A pleasure, Patsy. Christie, Derek Christie at your service. Follow me ladies, let's find out what's causing the trouble then." He turned and led the way down the corridor to the right of an ornate staircase. He opened the door and sat them in two chairs in front of a large leather-topped desk. He started questioning Patsy as he swapped the tweed jacket for a more professional short, starched white overall. "How long have you had the pain, when did it first start, and is it worse now than when you first experienced it?"

Patsy fabricated her answer, and from the corner of her eye she saw Stella give a slight nod of approval. Derek Christie asked her several more questions and jotted down her answers. When he was content he had sufficient detail, he stood and pointed behind her.

"If you would, step behind the screen and remove your clothing from the waist up. Pop your shoes off and lay face down on the bed," he paused. "I'm assuming you are comfortable with Stella remaining in the room? Some clients are a little shy, you see."

Patsy confirmed that was fine. Silently, she cursed Stella as she undressed. She raised her eyebrows as soft classical music filled the air. As she lay down on bed and placed her face in the hole she was surprised to find that the bed was heated in some way. She heard running water and assumed Christie was washing his hands. He was, and they were warm to her skin as he placed them flat on the small of her back.

"Now just relax for me, Patsy. I'm going to work my way up and we'll soon find out where the issue is." His voice was low and reassuring.

Patsy wondered if he would pretend to find something wrong in an attempt to entice her back. She didn't know how much he charged, but she knew it would be more than she would ever have considered paying. Despite his manipulations, and his discovery of muscles she didn't know existed, Patsy found the treatment both painful and relieving at the same time. The man clearly knew what he was doing. Patsy had to keep reminding herself that she was here to work.

When he had finished, he tapped her lightly between the shoulder blades.

"There you go, you should find that easier. There's no damage, but your muscles were totally knotted across the top of your shoulders and particularly bad at the base of your neck. Get up slowly when you are ready and pop your things back on." Patsy heard him move away as he continued to speak. "I doubt it was anything sustained at the gym. More likely hunched shoulders in front of a lap top and stress. What line of work are you in?"

"She works for me," Stella answered and laughed. "Therefore, of course, hunched in front of a laptop and stressed."

Patsy dressed quickly and wondered how she was going to obtain a sample. She considered faking a trip and grabbing him. She looked around the treatment area but there was nothing obvious there. Flexing her shoulders and moving her head from side to side, she decided that even if she failed to get a sample the visit had not been a complete waste of time. She stepped from behind the screen to find Stella waiting, hand on the door.

"I'll sort the account as usual, Derek, thank you for your time. I'll make an appointment with the receptionist." Stella opened the door and inclined her head indicating Patsy should leave. Patsy gave a little shrug and thanked Derek Christie before leading the way back to reception.

As they entered the room the receptionist punched a number on her phone.

"Hello, Mr Christie, Mr Wayne and his patient are ready when you are." Replacing the receiver, she smiled at Stella. "Ms Young, an appointment for you? When would be convenient?"

Patsy followed Stella out, pulling the door shut behind them, and she scanned the brass plaques for Mr Wayne and shrugged as she found it.

"Stella, I'm sorry but there was no opportunity for me to get a sample. The treatment was great though."

"I have it in my handbag," Stella replied. "I have often seen his comb sticking out from his breast pocket. I simply needed him to be otherwise engaged." She tapped her handbag and smiled at Patsy. "I have it bagged too." They entered the car park and Stella handed the sample to Patsy. "I must dash now, we have IT issues at one of the new branches. But it was lovely seeing you Patsy," Stella smirked. "Until tomorrow."

As Stella walked away Patsy flushed and shook her head at the inference. Turning to walk in the direction of her car Patsy checked her phone to see if Linda had been in touch.

~ ~ ~

Linda pulled into the car park of the Blaise Castle Estate and was please to find they had improved it since the last time she had visited. Most of the potholes had disappeared. She pulled the collar of her coat up and shoved her hands into her pockets. It was a damp and miserable February morning and she was grateful that at least it wasn't raining. As she followed the path between the hedges that shielded the car park, she was surprised to note that, despite the weather, two groups of lads were playing football on either side of the path that led to the house. Pulling her hand from her pocket she checked her watch. She had fifteen minutes to kill and not even the slowest walk along the path to the house could be stretched that long.

Entering the café she ordered herself a takeaway coffee, and watched a red-nosed father catching a toddler as he shot off the end of the slide in the children's playground situated next to the café. She smiled as the toddler waddled back to the ladder to repeat the process. As she left the café she was almost bowled over by a Labrador chasing a ball.

"Sorry about that," his breathless owner called as he too trotted past. "She's been in the stream and knows that eventually that means a shower. She doesn't want to go home." He stopped running and bellowed at the dog. "Bessie come!" The dog stopped, knowing that her master was no longer playing and, tail between her legs, she came to sit before him. He ruffled her head. "Good girl."

"She knew you meant business then. Why didn't you just do that the first time?" Linda grinned at the man, who now stared at her his head to one side.

"Because then she wouldn't have had the fun of running away." He continued to look at Linda, a puzzled look on his face.

Linda decided she needed to move on. The man was clearly interested in her, but she had a mission to complete. She waved goodbye to the dog.

"Bye, Bessie, be a good girl and enjoy your bath."

She nodded at the man and followed the path in front of her, at the end of which stood Blaise House. It was now used as a museum depicting life at the time at which it had been built. She reached the entrance and looked around, there was no one about. She wandered around the perimeter and back again, but still no one there. Walking to the wall in front of the entrance she took a seat and sipped her coffee. She waited for thirty minutes with no joy, and at five to eleven she wished she had brought Chris's phone with her. Her nose and her backside were freezing, and her feet were numb. She texted Patsy and waited a further ten minutes. When Patsy didn't reply, she decided to call it a day and made her way back to the car park.

As she approached her car, an old Mercedes estate pulled alongside her and the window opened. A voice called to her.

"Linda, is that you?"

She bent to peer through the window.

"Get in, I'm being followed. I have the information that you want, I'll give it to you as we drive and then drop you back here."

Without thinking Linda opened the door and got in. She turned to the man. It was Bessie's master.

"You? Why didn't you say?"

"Because I had to make sure it was you and that you were alone." The man indicated and pulled out onto the road. "And while I was doing that I realised there was a possibility that the bloke in the BMW was following me."

"What bloke?"

"Tut. Didn't you notice him? I couldn't make out if it was you or me he was after. We'll find out now." The man repeatedly looked up to his rear-view mirror. "Are you all right if we go on the motorway?" he asked as he indicated to turn onto Station Road.

It was then that Linda realised she had climbed into a car with a total stranger. A stranger whom Patsy thought was a little mental. She swallowed.

"Why? Why do you want to go on the motorway?"

"Easiest way to lose someone, or at least it is for me." He appraised her for a moment. "Why do you look so worried?"

"I'm not worried. Well, only if someone is following us," Linda lied as she swivelled in her chair to look out of the rear window. Bessie obscured the view a little but there were no cars were behind them. "I think you're all right, there's nothing there."

She heard him sigh and turned back.

"They wouldn't let you see them, would they? We'll know once we're on the motorway."

Linda wondered if she should open the window and scream at the people in the garage as he pulled onto Cribbs Causeway. She couldn't open the door and jump as the car was travelling too fast, and apart from anything else she had her new coat on. She slid her hand in her pocket and found her phone. She decided to press buttons in the hope that someone would realise she was in danger. If indeed she was in danger. Realising she needed to keep the man on side, she started talking.

"So what did you find out? You may as well tell me now that we're almost sitting comfortably." She took her hand from her pocket hoping that she had achieved something and pulled a note book from her bag. She found a pen and rested it against the note book and slid her left hand back into her pocket and tapped at the phone screen.

"Alex Watson and John Simmons. The first is fictitious, the second is dead."

Linda attempted to write. It was difficult to move the pen without the pad slipping off her leg. She drew her hand from her pocket slowly and allowed her phone to slide to the side of her leg away from the driver. She wrote down the names and slid her left hand back and without moving her head she looked left and opened a message to Patsy.

"What do we do with them? How can we trace people that don't exist?"

"You're kidding, right? Why would Chris employ someone so dense?" the man asked and added, "No offence, but you're not very bright are you?"

They had reached the main roundabout and he indicated left to take the M5 southbound. Linda turned and looked behind them again. Now there were six or seven cars behind them, none of which were BMWs.

"I have a string of qualifications, if you don't mind. But I stick to all things IT and rarely if ever break the law. Not knowingly anyway. And for your information there is no BMW behind us. Your imagination is working overtime, pal. What's your name anyway?" She looked left again and tapped in "with man" and hit the send button before opening another message.

"What qualifications? You work in IT, don't you?" The man sounded genuinely interested. "What do you do then? Trevor, by the way." He raised one hand from the steering wheel and bent his fingers in a wave.

Linda mirrored the gesture. "Nice to meet you, Trevor. Now, where to start about me."

Linda started with the college course she had attended when leaving school. By the time she got to how she had been employed by the Graingers, Trevor was indicating to leave the motorway at Weston Super Mare. Instead of turning back in the direction of Bristol, he drove towards the town. Linda's heart skipped a beat.

"Where are we going?" she demanded. "My car is miles back that way." She jerked her thumb behind them.

"Don't panic, I think I've lost them." Trevor turned to look at her. "Do you fancy a walk along the prom at Weston? I'm starving so I could do with something to eat. You could tell me how you cracked this case you're working on."

Linda was duly flattered and smiled at him. She really should go back to the office, but what harm could taking a lunch break do? Patsy was due to go back there anyway.

"Sounds good to me. Nothing better than eating fish and chips in the sea air."

Trevor smiled and accelerated a little. It was a long time since he'd lunched with a woman. Linda was good looking and interested in the same things he was. Perhaps his luck was changing.

Meredith looked up as Adler came into his office.

"I hope you come bearing gifts. Something has obviously pleased you."

Still smiling, Adler took a seat. "You're going to love this. Franklyn used to frequent a lap dancing club. He confided in his son when he got a dose from one of the girls," Adler grinned as Meredith leaned forward. "He told us before his mother came down. And when she did come down, bingo! She hadn't called to report him as missing earlier as he had previously gone through a spate of," Adler raised her eyebrows, "what she called 'late night adventures'. She initially assumed he was having an affair so one night she followed him. He went to a tacky club, her expression not mine, and hours later came out and went straight home. She pretended her sister had been ill to explain why she had arrived home after him." Adler stopped speaking as Meredith began to drum his fingers on the desk. "What?"

"You can fill the others in on the niceties. Get to the point." He held both hands up and bent his fingers back and forth as though calling her forward.

"I was. There are two bits to this. But I won't explain why then." Adler sighed and shook her head as if he were an errant child.

"You can put the detail in your report, just get on with it."

"Right so, between the eyes. The club she followed him to was . . ." She held up an open palm for Meredith to complete the sentence.

"Sensations," he obliged.

"And the reason she was particularly worried was because she had found *what* when searching for evidence of an affair a couple of weeks ago?" Again, she held up an open hand.

Meredith shook his head and his eyes narrowed.

"Because she had found a bag of clothes totally out of character, and for which he had no explanation. Louie has taken them straight to the lab." She looked knowingly at Meredith who shook his head.

"More detail needed please." He ignored the smug grin that appeared.

"One pair of black trousers, the type a workman might use. One black round neck jumper, one non-descript blue jacket with a pair of leather gloves shoved into the pocket, and last, but certainly not least, a black woollen beanie. Please remember this is a professional middle-aged man. He wears a suit and tie to work, and chinos, shirt and tie with jacket when he socialises. His wardrobe did reveal he had an old pair of cords for working in the garden though." Adler watched as the penny dropped.

"You think he was our shooter?"

Meredith closed his eyes and without opening his eyes, he summarised. "You're thinking that he shot Anna, who the day before stabbed Short, and now he has been put out of his misery. So, we have three totally different people, with no known connections, except one." He opened his eyes slowly. "Sensations, aka Brent."

Taking his hand from his face, he rested it on the edge of his desk and slid down low in his chair. He rested his head on the back and stared at the ceiling. "I like your thinking, Adler, I like the tie to Brent, and I like the fact that we have new evidence. This must be a blackmail thing. Unlikely we are going to get Anna to give up why she stabbed Short, and Franklyn is in the morgue." Meredith drummed his fingers on the desk. "What we need to find out is what Brent had on them. We need a search warrant for both club and home address." He sat up slowly. "Go and start the paperwork, I'll give the Super a ring. It's at moments like this, I wish he wasn't in Devon."

Adler nodded and was almost out of the door when Meredith cursed.

"Bollocks." He looked at Adler. "If we're right about this, Anna could be in danger. We don't know how well connected Brent is. If he's taking out those who do his dirty work, then Franklyn failed with Anna. He should have killed her. Is she at Eastwood Park yet?"

"Nope, still at the magistrates' court, but she will be remanded in custody there. What do you want me to do?"

"Nothing. I'll give Jane Roscoe a call and explain why she shouldn't apply for bail, which I know would be a long shot anyway. I'll also try and explain why she should insist on segregation." He looked at his desk for a moment. "I'm not sure how Anna will cope with that, but it's better than the possible alternative." He pinched the bridge of his nose before looking back at Jo Adler. "Go on then, get on with it, I've got calls to make."

Patsy sat at her desk and replayed Linda's voice mail on speaker phone. It was no clearer. Linda said something that sounded like 'comfortably', and then she heard a male voice, but couldn't make out what he was saying. Patsy pursed her lips. The call had probably been made by mistake, either from Linda's handbag or pocket, and the male voice was more than likely the car radio. But if that was the case, then where was she? She glanced up at the clock. Linda had texted her at eleven o'clock advising that Chris's contact had not turned up but she would give it another fifteen minutes. At half eleven she had received the voice mail, and at twenty to twelve the text which simply said "with man". It was now three o'clock, and she hadn't responded to Patsy's texts, and her calls were going straight through to the answer service. She terminated the current call and her phone rang almost immediately. She didn't check the caller ID.

"Is that you, Linda?"

"No, it's Chris. Sorry, Patsy, but things are not too good here -"

"Oh, Chris, I'm so sorry. What's happening? How's Sharon? Is there anything I can do?" Patsy listened to the sigh and then a brief silence as Chris composed himself.

"Well the good news, the very good news, is that he's come round and early indications are that there is unlikely to have been any permanent brain damage. He's responding to most stimuli as required and has managed a basic conversation. Still dosed up on painkillers of course, so that's a good thing, in as much as that element can only get better." Again, he sighed. "The less than good news is he's not responding to any tests on his legs." Chris choked out the last word and Patsy's heart went out to him.

"Poor, Jack, I'm sure it will come back, Chris. It is early days after all."

"That's what the doctors are saying, so I'll go with that. But I can't see us getting in over the next few days. How is everything?"

"Don't you worry about that. Everything here is . . ." Patsy hesitated, she was concerned about Linda and Chris may be able to point her in the right direction. It was better she asked now than try and track him down later. "There is just one thing. Linda had to meet with your contact today. He was late and then she said she was with him, but it's been hours. How well do you know him? I'm a little concerned as she's not answering her calls."

"He's harmless, Patsy. A little odd granted, but not weird. I'm sure she's fine. Have you called him?"

"Not as yet. Do we have an address for him?"

"Not current. That's not the way it works, Patsy, but I have to say I think you're over-reacting. Linda probably hasn't charged her phone." Patsy heard voices in the background. "Patsy, I've got to go, I'll call later to check all is well."

"Of course, go and do what you need to do. And don't worry about calling. You're right, I'm just over-reacting. Give my love to Sharon."

Patsy stood and paced up and down her office wondering if she was worrying too much. She knew on the face of it she was, but something told her Linda would have found a way to contact her. She picked up the pay-as-you-go mobile and called Trevor. The answer phone kicked in.

"Hi, it's Patsy. I wondered if Linda is still with you, she's a little late getting back to the office. Please call me."

After several minutes more pacing, she decided that some form of action was needed. Linda was probably sat in the café that overlooked the park, talking rubbish about all things IT. It wouldn't hurt to go and check. Patsy picked up her car keys, put on her coat and set the office answer phone.

Twenty minutes later she pulled into the car park at Blaise Castle. It was starting to get dark and there were only a handful of cars there. She spotted Linda's car immediately and pulled into the space next to it.

All was secure with Linda's car, so Patsy walked through to the café. The waitress was putting chairs up on a table, and a man in blue overalls was mopping the floor behind her. She looked up at Patsy as the door opened.

"Sorry, we're closed." She smiled and turned away to pick up the next chair.

"It's okay. I don't want anything, I'm looking for someone. When did your last customer leave?"

"About twenty minutes ago. Who have you lost then?" Hearing the concern in Patsy's voice the girl put the chair in her hands on the table and walked over.

The man stopped mopping and leaned on the handle of his mop to listen.

"She's in her late twenties, about five feet four with reddish-brown collar length hair. She had a long navy woollen coat on. She was driving that little red hatchback." Patsy turned and pointed through the door towards Linda's car.

"She came in for a coffee hours ago, I think." The girl looked at the floor, a frown of concentration wrinkling her brow. She looked at Patsy. "I'm sure she came in around ten o'clock, it may have been a little later, but there or thereabouts. I was filling the cake stand and she commented on it."

"That sounds like Linda," Patsy nodded, "and you haven't seen her since?" Her heart sank as the girl shook her head. Patsy turned to the man with the mop. "I don't suppose you remember her?"

"Don't think so. I went to empty the bins in the car park around half eleven."

"Have a crafty fag more like," the girl laughed and the man nodded.

"Yes, I take a coffee and have a ciggy break around half eleven and check the car park bins at the same time. You wouldn't believe what people dump out there." He shook his head.

Patsy wished he'd get to the point, and a little too sharply asked, "But my friend, you saw her?"

Patsy kept her face impassive as the man shrugged before shaking his head.

"Possibly, there was this short bird, I only noticed her as she was talking to herself. She came in the car park and was walking that way," he pointed towards Linda's car, "and this car pulls up. Had a dog in the back and she got in. So it could have been her." He shrugged again.

Instinctively, Patsy knew it had been Linda.

"Is there CCTV in the car park?"

Again, the man shrugged. "Yes, but it's rubbish. There's a camera on the side of here," he pointed towards the ceiling, "but it will only cover the entrance. They wouldn't spend the money for more."

"At least that's a start. Can you show me please? Where are the recordings kept? Are they here?" Patsy watched as he returned the mop to its bucket and then followed him to the door. He held it open for her and then led the way to the side of the building.

"See, the camera is up there, and as I understand it, it films here . . ." The man walked back along the side of the building and through the gap in the hedge to the car park. He stopped and pointed at the entrance. "There. When they did it up, someone questioned it, but what with vandals and costs they thought this would be sufficient."

"Have you got access to the recorder?"

"No," the man snorted out a laugh, "I'm far too lowly for that. You want Greg Harris." He checked his watch. "He might still be around. He'll be locking up the house, if you're lucky."

"How do I get hold of him?"

Thirty minutes later, Greg Harris pulled out a chair for Patsy, and switched on a monitor in a small room at the rear of his office.

"This shouldn't take long. I've only had to do this twice before." He smiled at Patsy kindly. "I shouldn't be doing it at all for you," a look of worry flashed across his face, "but Detective Sergeant Trump confirmed he would be here shortly, so I suppose the sooner we get on with it."

Harris flashed a look at the man from the café as though to confirm this was a one-off breach. He leaned forward and pushed the play button and then fast forwarded to 10.15am. They watched the few cars that had entered the car park at that time drive in. Patsy asked him to stop it when she spotted Linda's car. The still was grainy, and although you could see there was an occupant at the wheel, identification was impossible. She shook her head and Harris restarted the tape. Five minutes after Linda's car had entered a BMW estate pulled in.

The man from the café stepped forward. "That's the car. That's the car that she got in. If it was her, of course."

"Well done, Bob," Harris commented, as he froze the frame.

As before identification of the driver was impossible, but the passenger seat was empty. Patsy pointed this out.

"We can't see who he is, but he didn't have anyone with him. So whoever he picked up got here by other means. Right, can you take it back frame by frame, and let's see if we can get the number plate?"

"I know part of it," Bob announced. Patsy swung round to him, a look of disbelief on her face. He smiled. "Only because it's my missus's initials and age. The first part is KB50. Kathy Burns and she's fifty next birthday. I thought she'd like that plate on her old banger." He laughed as Patsy wondered why he hadn't thought that might be important before.

After several frames they had the whole registration and Patsy called Louie Trump. He sounded worried and told her he was only five minutes away.

"I'll get a check done on it. I should have the information by the time I get to you. And Patsy, not a word to DCI Meredith. I'm supposed to be waiting at the station for a search warrant."

Greg Harris walked Patsy back to the car park.

"I hope your friend is safe. I'm sorry we couldn't be more help." He stopped walking and allowed Patsy to walk through the gap in the hedges first. "Is this your man?" He pointed at Louie Trump as he swung into the car park.

Patsy thanked him for his time and hurried to Louie's car. Pulling open the passenger door she jumped in.

"Thanks, Louie, I owe you one. Anything yet?"

"I have an address in Lawrence Weston, less than a minute away. But what were you thinking, Patsy? What was she doing? She's an IT geek, for goodness sake. What on earth possessed you to think she should do something like this?" Louie banged his hand on his steering wheel to show his frustration. "Now, are you coming with me or shall we take separate cars?"

"I'll follow you. I feel bad enough already, Louie, but you're right. Let's just find her for now, and then you can kick me. But for the record, it was one computer geek meeting another. She was only collecting information."

"That says it all really. We know what these nerds are like, don't we?" Louie looked at his lap. "I'm sorry, Patsy, you're right of course. Let's get going."

Patsy went to her car and as she followed Louie out of the car park she pulled the cigarettes from her bag and lit her fifth one of the day. The address to which the car was registered was less than a mile away. Patsy parked on double yellows and jumped out of her car, scanning the road for the BMW.

"It's not here. Not that I can see anyway," she observed, as she followed Louie up the path of a tatty looking local authority house.

A child's pram was rotting upside down on the middle of the lawn, the curtains gaped at the top of the front window where their fixings had come loose, and a sign on the door warned that dangerous dogs lived there. Louie hammered on the door with his fist. It flew open, and a well-built, barefoot man wearing only a pair of shorts stood before them.

"What's the fucking panic?" he snarled and his eyes opened in amazement as Louie stepped forward quickly, and using the momentum placed his forearm across the man's chest and propelled him backwards until he had him pinned against the hall wall. The man grimaced as the light switch dug into the flesh on his back.

Louie fished in his pocket and held his warrant card inches from the man's face. "Trevor Baines? I'm DS Trump and I would like you to tell me the whereabouts of Linda Callow." Louie pushed a little harder on the man's chest as Patsy stepped into the hall.

She was impressed; she had always thought Louie would be a softly, softly, copper.

The man grinned. "You had me worried for a minute there, mate. I'm not Trev. The tenancy is in his name but he's moved out about eighteen months ago."

"Can you prove that?" Patsy asked, as Louie slipped his warrant card back into his pocket.

"I can if your mate would get off of me." Louie released his hold and the man flexed his shoulders. "What's he done then?" he asked, as he walked to the end of the hall, Trump on his heel. He pushed open the kitchen door and picked up a wallet from the table. Pulling out his driving licence he handed it to Louie, and asked again, "So what's Trev done?"

The driving licence confirmed the man to be Fredrick Hall. Louie chewed his lip as he handed it back. Patsy noticed his shoulders sag a little. Ignoring Hall's question Louie continued in a pleasant tone.

"I'm sorry about that, but we are investigating a serious crime. Can you tell me where Baines is living now?"

Louie and Patsy watched the change in stance as Hall lied.

"No idea, mate, not seen him for eighteen months, as I said." His nose wrinkled and he pulled his considerable shoulders back. "Now I'm in the middle of me training, so I'll see you out."

"Where does he live? It's really important. Please help us, my friend might be in danger." Patsy blinked rapidly at him, and held her hands to her face. "Please," she croaked. She watched as the man's chest deflated a little.

"What do you mean, danger?"

Patsy stepped forward and placed a hand on his bicep. "I'm not with the police. My friend went missing earlier today and was last seen getting into Baines'

car. DC Trump here is investigating, not me. I just want to find my friend."
Patsy's voice broke and she looked away, allowing her hand to fall to her side.

"Sorry, love, I don't know where he is." Hall shook his head.

"Yes, you do. I told you he was weird. What are you protecting him for, you wanker?"

A woman whose body had seen considerable enhancement stepped into the kitchen. Her bleached white hair, black at the roots, was held on the top of her head by a large clip. Overly large lips pouted at the man, and her breasts strained to be released from the skimpy vest top she wore above equally skimpy shorts.

She looked at Patsy. "He is such a wanker. He's got no loyalty to Baines, hardly knows him, it's 'cos he's a copper." She jerked her head towards Louie who smiled before looking her up and down for the third time. The woman turned her attention to Hall. "Get his address. Now."

It was clear who wore the trousers in their relationship. Hall smiled at her adoringly and nodded before walking into the dining room. She followed him.

"Thank you. Much appreciated," Patsy acknowledged.

Trump turned to stare at her. All traces of emotion had vanished, and he realised she had been acting to play on Hall's better nature.

"You're welcome. He's a weirdo. I never liked him, glad I only met him a few times. He talks crap, and he's got this look. Just stares at you. I knew he was up to something though. Everything has to be a secret. He only gave Fred his address because they're related in some way. Just weird." She nodded and her breasts jostled for position in the vest top.

"Here you go." Hall returned, and held out a piece of paper to Louie. "That was a while ago, but I think he should still be there."

Louie thanked him and started towards the front door. "Come on, Patsy, let's get down there."

Patsy turned to follow him and then looked back at Hall. "She's right, you know. You are a wanker."

She slammed the front door as she left, and then hurried down the path to join Louie.

"I'm going to have to call this one in now." Louie shook his head and held the piece of paper up. "This is a good twenty minutes away and we don't know what we'll find when we get there. I can't simply disappear, and quite apart from anything else this is not looking good. I'll call Tom Seaton rather than DCI Meredith."

Patsy looked at the concern on Louie's face as he called Tom, and she drew in a deep breath. She wouldn't want to be the one passing that message to Meredith.

CHAPTER TWENTY

Linda looked at her watch and cursed. "Shit. Look at the time, I've only recently started work for the Graingers and I've probably just got myself the sack. Shit, shit, shit!"

Trevor leaned across and patted her hand. "Nah, you'll be fine. After all, when you go back you'll have all the answers now."

"Yes, but that took you about half an hour to explain. I've been gone all day! Patsy will be so pissed off with me. We've spent most of the day just talking about what you do. Not that that wasn't interesting, and I'd love to meet with you again so you can actually show me, but . . ." Linda gave a big sigh and shrugged at him. "I was really enjoying working for them."

"Don't worry, me and Chris go way back. I'll have a word for you, if you like." Trevor beamed. She wanted to see him again!

"I should have tried to phone Patsy though."

"I've got a charger in the car so you can call on the way back. Come on, I need to let Bessie have a pee before we get going."

Linda nodded. When she told Patsy what Trevor had been able to teach her, perhaps she wouldn't be too cross.

"He's where? With Patsy? Am I hearing this right or going around the bend?" Meredith demanded when, on the third time of asking for Trump, Seaton had finally admitted he was on his way to Somerset. "Why wasn't I told?" He waved the sheet of paper in his hand at Tom Seaton. "We need all hands on deck and he's off dicking around with Patsy. What was Loopy Linda doing with this bloke?" He pinched the bridge of his nose as Seaton held his hands up.

"Don't shoot the messenger. He might even be on his way back here as we speak. All he said was Linda had got herself into a scrape, and he was going to sort it out with Patsy."

"What does that mean? A fucking scrape? Does the man not speak English? What time was this?"

Seaton looked at his watch. "About half an hour ago." He winced as Meredith snorted derisively.

"Half an hour ago," his tone was deliberately sarcastic, and Meredith shook his head in disappointment, "and you reckon he's been to Somerset which, by the way is a big place, rescued Loopy from her *scrape* and is on his way back. Get him on the phone now! The club opens at seven and we're going in at eight. I want to brief the team starting no later than six thirty, so tell them all to get something to eat now. It's going to be a long night and I haven't got time to mess about with his bits of fluff getting into a scrape." He jerked his thumb. "Go on then. Get on with it."

As soon as Seaton had gone, Meredith snatched up his phone and punched in Patsy's number.

Patsy had just lit her seventh cigarette of the day and didn't care. She had followed Trump down the motorway which they had exited at Weston. They had now driven up and down the same road several times. She followed him into a layby and agreed he should call someone for help in navigating. The maps systems on their phones kept taking them to a bus stop that was miles from anywhere.

Trump had asked that she didn't smoke in his car so she had returned to her own. She blew smoke through the open window as she considered whether or not to answer Meredith. She decided sooner would probably be better than later. She turned the key in the ignition and the hands-free cut in. She pushed the answer button as the ringing echoed louder in her car. Meredith didn't allow her to speak first.

"Are you with Trump?"

"Not technically, no, but I can see him."

"Not technically? What sort of answer is that? Don't play, Patsy, not today."

"I'm not playing. But I'm very well, thank you for asking. I take it you're not having a good day. Trump is in his car in front of me. Would you like to speak to him?"

"Not yet. I want you to tell me what's going on. Why is one of my officers is traipsing around the countryside with you and not sitting with me preparing to serve a search warrant on a premises connected to not one, but two murders. Oh yes, and let's not forget a shooting."

"I asked him to help because Linda got into a car with some bloke. I had the registration and needed the address, he offered to help. The address turned out to be inaccurate but we managed to get another in Somerset. It's my fault, not his, I shouldn't have dragged him into it. If you're going to bollock someone you may as well make it me."

"Oh, we'll get there, don't worry. Are you on your way back?"

"No, we haven't found her yet."

"What? Why not? I need him back here and sharpish. And just for the record, why didn't you call me?"

"You? What, so you could tell me to call back later when you're not so busy, or remind me of my lowly status is life now I'm not on the force? You've got to be joking." All the frustration that she had been trying to lay to rest came surging to the surface, and she knew she was being unfair.

"What? Patsy, is something wrong? I have to warn you, I'm getting cheesed off with this."

"What's more wrong than Linda being carted off in a strange bloke's car. More wrong than no one's heard from her since eleven this morning? More wrong than you are more interested in getting one more bloke on your team to shout at than the safety of my friend? Who for some reason best known to herself really rates you." Patsy paused to take a deep drag on the cigarette.

"And you're smoking. Apologies for my lack of concern, but she's probably in a cake shop somewhere gassing away to someone. I'm sorry okay, but Trump should have cleared it with me first." Meredith listened as Patsy took another puff on the cigarette. "Patsy, talk to me."

"It's my fault. I shouldn't have let her go. I shouldn't have called Louie, and I shouldn't have messed up your day." Patsy flicked the cigarette out of the window and noticed Trump was jogging towards her car. "I've got to go. I'll get Louie to call you." She hung up and climbed out of the car.

"Any luck?"

"Yes, I know where we went wrong." He nodded towards the open window of the car. "Meredith?"

"Yes. He'd like a call when you're free, but let's go find Linda first." She attempted a smile.

"But of course, follow me." Louie gave a sharp nod and jogged back to his car.

As Patsy climbed back into her car she resisted the urge to light yet another cigarette. They hadn't been driving for more than a minute when Trump's car indicated left, and he pulled up on a grass verge. Patsy pulled up behind him and hurried towards his car. He was on the phone, so she went to the passenger door and climbed in.

Trump sounded exasperated. "So you're safe? Linda, did you not think to call? Patsy and I are out looking for you, and Meredith will be gunning for me." He listened for a while. "No of course you didn't know. Yes, perhaps I was being a little presumptive." He paused to listen again. "I'm sorry, Linda, I'll call you later then." He now sounded very sheepish. "Bye, Linda, and sorry." He hung up and rested his forehead on the steering wheel.

"I take it she's all right then," Patsy observed and patted him on the back. "What did she say that made you apologise?"

"She was calling to say she may be a little late for our date, which of course I have to cancel. I told her off, I'm afraid, for disappearing without a word. Apparently, I overstepped the mark. As she pointed out, and rightly so, why would she be checking in with me? I suppose she's right . . ."

"Well, she might not have had to check in with you, but she bloody well should have checked in with me!" Patsy interrupted him.

"Her phone's dead apparently and she didn't have a charger with her."

"Where is she? Where has she been?"

"She's on her way back to her car, but I didn't have the courage to ask where she'd been. I'll leave that to you."

Linda pulled the charger from her phone and dropped it into her bag.

"Cheeky bugger, how dare he question me!"

"That your boyfriend then?" Trevor's smile had dropped away as he listened to the one-sided conversation.

"No. Just some bloke I was going to have dinner with. Where do you blokes get off, thinking that one date means they have some say in what you do?"

"Hey, don't tarnish us all with the same brush. I'm not like that. He's history then, is he?"

Linda turned to him and smiled. "Sorry, Trev, I'm sure you're not like that. And yes, I think he might be."

Trevor's smile was back as he pulled into the car park. Linda promised to call him and let him know the outcome of the case as she left the car. He watched her drive off before slowly pulling out of the car park, and stayed at a safe distance as he followed her home.

"Well, Bessie, I think our luck has changed old girl. I'll see where she lives so I can send flowers perhaps."

Bessie gave a whine of agreement.

Meredith banged the receiver back into the cradle and drew in a deep breath. He knew he was the cause of Patsy's foul mood, and not the missing Linda, but he had no idea why. This irritated rather than concerned him. Today was no day for Patsy to start playing games. He called Bob Seaton into his office.

"Have you spoken to Trump?"

"Yep, he's not sorted it yet, but I've put them on the right track so fingers crossed. I know we have enough to worry about for the moment, but it doesn't sound good for that girl Linda, Gov."

"No, I know, I've spoken to Patsy. I was less than sympathetic and now she has the hump with me."

Seaton gave him a look that registered no surprise at this statement, just a stoic resignation to the way things were with Meredith.

"Don't look at me like it's my fault. Where are they anyway?"

"They were lost on the A371 on the way to Weston, looking for some old farm cottage. He knows where it is now so he shouldn't be long about it. Assuming all is well." Bob Seaton shrugged and sighed.

"How serious does Trump think it is?"

Meredith was beginning to feel bad for not being more sympathetic with Patsy. If she had sent Linda off into trouble, or worse, she would never forgive herself. Meredith shuddered as he realised it could have been Patsy that had gone missing and he wouldn't have known. What was Chris Grainger thinking, letting them go off like that, without so much as a call-in plan? He immediately felt guilty for that thought, knowing as he did what Chris and Sharon were going through. He was fed up with feeling guilty; he needed to do something. He held his hand up.

"Don't answer that. I think I can live without knowing what Trump thinks a scrape is. They'll call in when they know what's what. Right, let's get this show on the road without the talented DS Trump, but first food. Let's go down to the canteen before that lot clear the troughs. Come on, you can treat me."

Patsy arrived at Linda's house a few moments after Linda herself. She joined her on the doorstep as Linda hunted in her bag for her key. Linda looked up at Patsy, her guilt evident.

"I know, I know. For what it's worth I couldn't feel worse. The time sort of ran away with me."

"Ran away with you? For God's sake, Linda, anything could have happened to you. As it was, only Louie and I were put out, but you could have caused a whole lot more trouble than that. Louie was so worried and you had the cheek to give him a telling off. What on earth were you doing?"

Linda pushed the door open and dropped her bag on the floor. She walked towards the kitchen as she responded.

"I know. Louie is calling me later. I'll thank him and then apologise. Trevor is weird but he's so interesting. He knows a lot of cool stuff that could really help us."

"Help us how? I thought you would have known who did it by now."

"I do, by chance, and believe it or not by accessing the internet from Trevor's phone. I'll come back to that." She ignored Patsy's snort. "I'm talking about in the future. The stuff he can do and has access to would really help the business. We wouldn't need to sub so much stuff out. He said he'll show me."

Patsy held her hand up. "Stop right there for a moment. You have been totally irresponsible. You know that, don't you?" She waited until Linda nodded and jutted out her bottom lip like an errant school girl. "Whatever your motives, you can't work in an industry like this and simply disappear."

"But if you'd let me explain what I can do for the business if I can get hold of the packages Trev was telling me about."

Patsy held her hand up. "Enough, Linda, for tonight. I've spent the best part of the day worrying about you, and I think we need to deal with one issue at a time. I haven't got the energy today. Tell me what you found out on the Tucker case."

Linda quickly explained how a bogus bank account had been set up using a false identity. The identity of a dead cousin of none other than Paul Wilde. Cash was withdrawn by using various cash machines across the region. Trevor had rightly pointed out that it couldn't be down to the accountant on his own. He had had to have had someone who knew how the system worked to start the drip feed into the account in the first place.

Patsy sighed. "So, the IT guy then."

"Looks like it, they were obviously working together. Poor old George, I don't know how he'll take it. Look, Patsy, I know you don't want to talk about it now, but I think I can add value to the services the Graingers offer, and help clients like George get back on track."

Patsy chose her words very carefully, she was still fuming that Linda had been so irresponsible. "Okay, I hear what you say. Leave it with me and I'll speak to Chris once things have settled down with Jack." She pointed at Linda. "But you have a think about it carefully, because to be honest I'm not convinced you have thought this through properly." Patsy stood up and lifted her bag wearily. "I'm going to go and call George and see what he wants to do about this. Then I'm having an early night. I suggest you think of a suitable apology for Louie."

Meredith concluded his briefing.

"It's a pain in the arse we couldn't get a warrant for Brent's home address so let's make sure we don't miss anything at the club. We're going in at eight as most of the girls will be there then. Perhaps we can get something from them. Remember, if they play up threaten to bring them in for questioning. I'm sure Brent will show even if he's not there when we arrive. If he does I'll deal with him." He clapped his hands. "Any questions?" He looked around the group. "Good, then get yourselves downstairs and be ready to go in the next fifteen minutes."

The team had started to disperse as Louie Trump rushed through the door. Meredith stared at him for a moment. "My office."

Louie nodded and changed direction.

"I'm not going to bollock you now, I haven't got time."

"Look, Sir, I know it was out of line of me -"

"Save it for when it's necessary. Are they all right?"

"Yes," Trump nodded rapidly. "I have no idea what Linda's been up to but I'm seeing her tonight so I'll get to the bottom of it, don't worry."

"I'm not worried, Trump. Tonight, you say? You'll be lucky, early hours of the morning possibly." Meredith sniffed and tidied the papers on his desk. "How was Hodge?"

"Patsy, you mean?"

"Of course Patsy. Old habits and all that."

"She was fine. Initially she was very worried about Linda of course, but other than that fine. Why, did you think she was in danger?"

"No, it was simply a question, don't read too much into it. We're off in ten minutes so shut up and I'll bring you up to speed." Meredith explained the plan of attack, and then stood and pulled his jacket from the back of the chair. "No snogging scantily clad ladies in the toilets, don't pick up any waifs and strays, and if Brent is there or turns up, he's mine. Come on then, let's get going."

Trump stood and walked to the door. He was a little confused as to why Meredith hadn't given him both barrels, and was relieved to still be part of the raid.

He turned and gave a curt nod. "Thank you, Sir, I deserved worse I know that . . . and about Patsy."

"What about her?"

"She was smoking rather a lot, I didn't think she did." Trump turned and left the office.

Meredith slid his phone into his pocket. That wasn't a good thing, not a good thing at all.

Brent took the stairs to his office two at a time. Meredith was sitting at his desk. He looked up as Brent approached. Standing he held out his hand.

"Mr Brent, I presume. Nice to meet you, I'm DCI Meredith. We shouldn't be long now."

"What the fuck is going on? Why was I not contacted about this?" Brent ignored Meredith's outstretched hand, and shot a glance into the bedroom as the mattress was flipped over and onto the floor.

"It's nice that you wanted to play host, but we've managed." Meredith nodded towards the bedroom as Travers ripped open the mattress. "We've found the camera but no recordings yet. Where would they be?"

"I don't keep them. They're private and used at the time, if you know what I mean," Brent waved his hand dismissively. "I rarely use the camera anyway."

"Very wise, Mr Brent. Best not to leave too much evidence lying around, you never know who might come to call."

Meredith watched as Brent's eyes narrowed and he strained to keep his face impassive. He watched as the vein in Brent's temple throbbed, and then looked at the expensive suit and caught the smell of Brent's aftershave. He thought about what Brent had done to Anna Carter and doubtless many other victims and he wanted to punch him. Instead he pulled out a drawer he had already searched and tipped it upside down on the desk. The contents spewed out, some falling to the floor.

"I've met Selina." He watched lines appear on Brent's forehead as he tried to place the name. Meredith let out a burst of hollow laughter. "You really are a piece of work. Shall I remind you?"

Brent shrugged and stooped to pick up some of the things from his drawer which had fallen on the floor. Meredith walked around to the other side of the desk and hindered his progress. When Brent straightened, Meredith stood less than six inches from him. Meredith was taller by a good five inches and looked down at him.

"Selina is an employee of yours. Barmaid come waitress. She met with you up here I understand, and is now unable to walk, let alone pull a pint. One of my chaps is on his way to see her." Meredith was impressed when Brent didn't flinch.

"I have no idea what you are talking about. Of course, I know Selina. I didn't understand the reference, that's all." Brent looked down for a moment. "Who's been misleading you? You shouldn't listen to gossip."

"I quite agree, and I never do. But when more than one person passes on a message you start wondering if there's smoke but no fire. Lots of people like talking about you, Mr Brent."

Meredith concentrated on the vein on Brent's temple. The beat had increased. He also caught the flexing of the hands to stop them forming fists.

"So why are you here? This is a clean club. I pay my taxes, I pay minimum wage or above and I don't let drugs in here. What do you think you might find?"

"Well, that's where you have me." Meredith took a step closer and the gap between their chests was now barely an inch. Brent braced his body, refusing to step backward. "Two people connected to this club are now dead. I don't know why but I will find out." He paused to nod at Travers who was signalling that he had not found anything. "But what I do know, Mr Brent, is that without a doubt it will all come back to you."

It was Meredith's turn to control his impulses as Brent looked up and laughed in his face. There was no mirth involved.

"Ha, ha, ha! DS whoever you are." Brent deliberately demoted Meredith. "I didn't know the police had a sense of humour. I have no idea what you're talking about, or even whom." Brent cocked his head to one side. "Is it whom or who? I don't suppose it matters, but if I can help you I will."

"You've already given me your help, Brent, it's just a case of finding it. I've met several of the ladies in your life, and I assure you the truth will out." Meredith leaned forward until their chests were touching and Brent could feel the heat of his breath on his forehead.

"Ladies? I don't know any ladies." Again, Brent forced a laugh.

"No?" Meredith lifted a shoulder in acceptance. "Not once they've met you anyway. I've heard you drag people down to your level," Meredith sneered, his look of disgust inches away from Brent's face.

For some reason, unknown to Meredith, this was the thing that touched the nerve he had been looking for. Brent snarled as he placed his hands on Meredith's chest and pushed him backward. Meredith lost his footing, stumbled, and ended up sitting on the floor. He nodded at Travers who rushed forward as Brent leaned forward, his arm drawn back. Knocking him off balance, Travers placed Brent in an arm lock. He read him his rights and arrested him for assaulting a police officer.

"You're coming with me, Sir." Travers held his head back as Brent attempted to head butt him. "Settle down now, you don't want to make things any worse, do you?" He winked at Meredith as he led Brent towards the door.

"Wait until I get there," Meredith ordered. "I'd like the pleasure of interviewing Mr Brent myself."

It was only nine thirty when Patsy climbed into bed. Meredith wouldn't be home for hours, there was nothing on the television, and she was mentally exhausted from updating Chris Grainger, and before that discussing the fraud case with George Tucker.

Switching off the bedside light she stared into the darkness. It seemed that today was a day for dithering when the correct course of action was obvious. George Tucker wanted to take a day or two to think about what he was going to do, despite having all the information he needed to bring charges, and perhaps even recover his money. And then there was Meredith. Odd phone calls, suspicious texts, and a rendezvous arranged for the next day. Should she confront him and see what happened, and perhaps give him the opportunity to lie? Or should she go and see for herself? She sighed, knowing exactly what she would do. It was lucky tomorrow's diary wasn't too heavy.

Meredith arrived home after midnight. Patsy listened as he washed and brushed his teeth, and when he climbed into bed she feigned sleep. Meredith lay still for a few moments before he spoke and made her jump.

"I know you're awake. Any reason you're not speaking to me?"

"Because I'm exhausted and I thought you would be too. I thought conversations would be best left until tomorrow."

"Hmmm."

"What does that mean?"

"It means you're lying and we both know it. You've had the hump with me all day. I don't know what I've done, but would it help if I just apologised? I could do with a cuddle."

Despite herself Patsy smiled into the darkness and turned onto her side to face him.

"I haven't got the hump. What is it you think you might have done? Have you done anything I might get the hump with?"

"Nope." Meredith inched his body closer and their noses met.

"In that case, all is well," She could smell the mint from the toothpaste.

"Glad to hear it, now come here." With a sudden movement, he grabbed her and rolled over so she lay on top of him. "PJs," he observed, "and you say you haven't got the hump?"

"I was cold," she lied as she wiggled free of the trousers. "I'm not now." As she returned his kiss, she decided that tomorrow would reveal all, and this might be the last time she shared his bed.

Patsy's stomach lurched as Meredith entered the kitchen. He was wearing his best suit, and despite her suspicions she appreciated the view. She turned to fill the kettle to ensure he wouldn't see the fear in her eyes.

"You look very dapper. What's special about today?" She poured the excess water from the kettle and watched it run away. "Do you have a date or something?" She flinched as he slid his arms around her waist.

"Blimey, do I frighten you?" He kissed the back of her neck causing her to shudder. "What's special about today? Hmm, let me see now. I have to interview the owner of Sensations again. He's a thug and a bully in a posh suit and I like seeing him squirm. I think one of the girls will testify against him. I reckon we're several steps closer to piecing this lot together. I had sex with a rather attractive and fascinating woman last night. Need I go on?"

Patsy turned and looked into his eyes. "So nothing special then?" Her voice remained neutral. "You're just saying mine's as big as yours to some seedy night club owner."

Meredith roared with laughter and kissed her lightly. "Something like that, yes."

Lifting the kettle from the drainer he made to turn away, but Patsy held on to him.

"You would tell me, wouldn't you?"

"Tell you what?" Meredith frowned as she shrugged.

"I don't know, anything that I should know I suppose. Anything that I would want to know, but you may not want to tell."

"What's this about? If you have something you want to know just ask. I haven't got time for games, not today." He sighed, turned away, and switched on the kettle. He heard Patsy draw in a deep breath.

"Well that's all right then. Do you want toast or cereal?"

"Just coffee for me. So nothing's wrong?" he persisted.

She raised her eyebrows and forced a smile as she lifted the mugs down from the cupboard. "Not if you say there isn't."

At eleven thirty that morning, Meredith scowled as Trump showed Brent out of the police station. The search had been fruitless, Selina, the girl he had assaulted and probably raped, refused to bring charges, and Brent's solicitor had pull somewhere as he had been instructed to charge Brent or let him go.

Brent had been very cocky, but Meredith had seen the resentment and anger in his eyes, which were never as relaxed as the rest of his face. Meredith knew that Brent was good at his game, which only served to strengthen Meredith's resolve to find out how he was linked to the three victims. Meredith pinched the bridge of his nose as he awaited Trump's return to the incident room. His team were exhausted and irritable. They wanted something to give them a breakthrough as badly as he did. Trump returned and took his seat and the room fell quiet, all eyes on Meredith.

"He's a clever bastard, I'll give him that. But Brent's in this up to his neck. It's your job to find out how. So, we go back to the beginning, and let's be more thorough." He banged his fist on the desk. "I want to know who they went to school with, where they bought their knickers, what their favourite colour was. EVERYTHING. Because somewhere there is another link, other than the club, and when we find it, we'll have him." He looked around the tired faces. "Any questions or suggestions?" he paused, and when no one responded he nodded. "Good, then get on with it. I'll make the coffee." He allowed himself a smile at the murmurings of shock. "Don't look like that, I forgot at Christmas." As he walked away the smile fell from his face.

At one forty-five, Meredith's alarm sounded on his phone. Pulling his jacket from the back of his chair, he went and stood in the doorway to his office and looked out at his team. He then stepped out and looked up at the board, newly erected, and next to the one containing what information they had on Joseph Franklyn. It had a simple heading "Links", underneath which were written two words, "Sensations" and "Vicinity". He blew out a dejected breath, there was nothing new.

He caught Bob Seaton's eye. "I've got something to do. Don't know how long I'll be, probably no more than a couple of hours. I'm local so bell me if anything breaks."

Running his fingers through his hair and smoothing his lapels he left the office.

Patsy walked out of the large two-storey MacDonald's, and for the third time in ten minutes checked her watch. She had not realised that there were two of the fast food outlets in such close proximity in town. Having checked both, she crossed her fingers and opted for the larger of the two. There was still ten minutes to go. She walked into the clothes shop opposite, and pretended to browse the racks that overlooked the street.

Patsy had had a busy morning. The meeting with Stella had gone well. Linda seemed perfectly normal despite the previous day's ordeal, and had taken on the tasks set with gusto. With the Graingers otherwise engaged, Linda was manning the phones, writing up a report for George Tucker, and updating the accounts.

Chris and Sharon were still sitting with Jack in the hospital, so Chris had asked Patsy to attend a meeting for him in Leeds. She had booked a return flight, and arranged the meeting for five o'clock at an airport hotel. She had to be at Bristol Airport no later than three, so whatever it was she hoped to see had better happen quickly. She drew in a deep breath and rolled her shoulders. Whatever good Derek Christie had done, she had already managed to undo it, and she wondered if the other shoppers could hear the clicking as she manipulated her body.

At five minutes to two, Meredith appeared. She bit her lip. How unlike Meredith to be punctual. Watching him glance up and down the road she felt cheap, and wondered when she had become so sad as to feel the need to spy on someone she loved. At a minute past two Meredith glanced at his watch before scanning the faces in the road again. He ran his fingers through his hair, straightened his tie, and glanced at the bus approaching. She watched him observe the bus pull into a stop a little further along the road. Then she saw him smile, and her heart seemed to miss a beat. She stepped a little closer to the window. Meredith was striding forward purposefully. A few more strides and he would have his back to her.

She froze as he stopped and held his arms out, and she watched a woman run into them. Patsy stopped functioning as Meredith swung the woman up and around and then hugged her to him, kissing the top of her head. By the time she had regained any sort of control, they were walking away from her, Meredith's arm around the woman's shoulders. He was obviously smitten, he looked at only her as they walked. It was the woman that guided them through the busy shoppers.

"Are you all right, love?"

Patsy turned to look at the shop assistant, who smiled warily at her. She sniffed, wiped her cheeks with the flat of her hands, and then looked at her watch.

"I'm fine, thank you. I must dash, I have a plane to catch."

Sitting in the departure lounge she replayed the scene over and over again. She hadn't seen the woman's face, and could barely remember what she was wearing. All her training had gone out the window the minute Meredith had held out his arms. She had blonde hair. Patsy remembered that from when he had kissed her head. And trousers. There had been no billowing skirt. Not trousers, jeans. Meredith had obviously thought the meeting more important than she did. He'd not taken his eyes off her.

A nasal voice announced the departure of her flight. She pulled her phone from her pocket to switch it off as she approached Gate Two. She had a text from Meredith. That had been quick, then she realised he might still be with her and a coldness flooded through her body. Clutching her boarding pass in one hand she opened the message as she joined the short queue.

Hello you. I've had a bitch of a morning. Hope you are having a good day. Mine's looking much better now. Promise not to be late.

She typed a brief response.

Glad someone is having fun. I'm about to board a plane. Don't know when I'll be back.

She switched off the phone, slid it into her pocket, and handed the flight attendant her boarding pass.

CHAPTER TWENTY-ONE

Meredith was already in the kitchen when Patsy came down. He held out a mug of coffee. "There you go. You're ready early, what time's kick-off?"

"I have to be there by eight to meet Frankie." She accepted the mug and sipped the scalding hot coffee.

Meredith studied her for a moment. "Should I ask?"

"What?"

"Why you didn't sleep in our bed last night?" He watched her shrug and wondered why she didn't meet his eye.

"After a very intense meeting, which I had to rush to get back to the airport, the flight was delayed. I sat in the airport for three and a half hours. By the time I got back it was late. I could hear you snoring," she glanced at him quickly, "and decided not to disturb you. You'd had such a late one the night before." She sipped at the coffee again before placing it on the kitchen table. "I have to dash, there's so much to do. I'll put my things into the car."

Meredith nodded and watched as she left the kitchen. He didn't offer to help as he wanted a moment to work out just what the hell he had done. He drew in a breath. Perhaps it was something she had done that was causing the tension between them. He heard her slam the boot of her car, and walked into the hall.

"What's going on?"

"What do you mean?"

"Patsy, we're not kids. Let's not play games. Something is going on, so let's have it out, shall we? Clear the air, move on."

"Meredith, I haven't got time for this," she climbed the first three stairs. "I have a day and a half ahead of me, I need to get moving."

"What time are we leaving tonight?" Still she hadn't met his gaze.

"Well, I'll already be there of course. I've taken my things, I'll get changed there, Stella has booked a room." Patsy climbed another two stairs and looked down at him. "Dinner is at seven thirty. Look, I doubt it'll be your type of thing, I don't mind if you don't want to come." She completed her journey quickly.

Meredith looked at his feet. In days gone by, he would have taken that as a slap in the face and not bothered going. He'd have found a bar, and probably a barmaid. That wasn't an option any longer. Patsy was right, it wouldn't be his thing as a rule, but he wanted to support her. He sighed as he realised that he also wanted to put a little more pressure on Brent. Was that what was holding him back from reverting to form?

Placing his hand on the banister he shouted up the stairs. "You never know, I might enjoy it. Unless we have another body turn up I'll be there."

He heard a mumbled "Okay" and he bristled. It was probably best she was leaving early as her attitude was really winding him up now. He thumped the bannister and walked into the kitchen. Leaning on the sink and staring out into the back garden, he listened to her moving around upstairs. A full-on row was not a good idea as she might tell him not to come tonight. He screwed up his eyes and blew out a breath, wondering how healthy it was for their relationship that he was avoiding an argument simply to ensure he came into contact with a suspect. He hadn't even told her about Brent yet, and more to the point he supposed, she hadn't asked about the case.

Frankie Callaghan strode across the foyer of the Grand Hotel. He smiled broadly as Patsy looked up and spotted him. She waved and excused herself and went to greet him.

"Hi, Frankie, you look smart. I've not seen you in a suit before," she smiled as she approached him. Frankie bent to kiss her cheek and she clung on to him for a few seconds too long.

"That, my dearest, Pats, is because I'm usually scrabbling around waste ground, or seedy flats somewhere avoiding getting covered in bodily fluids." Placing his hands on her shoulders he held her back and peered at her. "Is everything Okay, Pats?" He had nothing on which to base his concern except the way her fingers had dug into his arms for a few seconds, but now he was looking at her, he could see the tension in her face.

Patsy slapped his arm. "Everything is fine. I'm just so busy at the moment. Come over here, I'll introduce you to Stella and Bruce."

Introductions over, Patsy and Frankie left the growing group of employees of Stella Young and made their way to the conference room.

"Very swish I must say." Frankie glanced around the room. A dozen or so circular tables were covered in crisp white linen. They had been laid with pads, pens, and bottles of water. Sparkling tumblers had been arranged around a tall stainless steel tulip which held a numbered card. Frankie counted and each table held ten people. At the front of the room, set up below the stage, was a long oblong table set for five people. A flat white sheet hung on the stage and a projector suspended from the ceiling shone down on it, and various images of branches of Stella Young Property Services appeared for a few seconds before being replaced by the next.

"We're over here." Patsy took his arm and led him to a door at the left of the stage. She pushed it open and Frankie nodded. He was impressed. The small anteroom had been arranged so that sample pots stood in trays along one wall, and boxes to receive them along the other. The door at the end of the room said "Toilets".

Patsy walked towards it. "Come and see your station. The hotel might be swish but you'll be in here most of the afternoon."

Frankie peered over her shoulder as she opened the door. There were four toilet cubicles on the left, and opposite them two wash basins and a table with a high-backed chair. On the table were evidence bags, the labels on which had already been completed.

"For obvious reasons, she intends to call the men first, and will do that table by table. Once they enter the anteroom, Bruce will explain what's happening and they will come in here. You as a medical person will ensure that the samples are produced appropriately and not tampered with. Then pop them into the bag." She pointed to the table. "Their name badges will also have a photograph on. Just to ensure they don't try any funny business," she raised her eyebrows at him, "Bruce will do a double check to ensure they are who they should be before they come in here."

"Fabulous. What more can a chap ask? The lunch had better be good. I think I'm in for a boring day." He grinned as Patsy laughed.

"Think about the fee, Frankie, think about the fee. That should go a long way towards your wedding plans." She turned and walked away quickly.

Frankie frowned. "Pats, is everything okay with you and Meredith? You seem a little . . . not sure really, but certainly not your usual self."

Patsy turned and shrugged. "I'm not sure. Nothing serious . . . Sorry Frankie, can we get on. I need to focus on work, not him."

Frankie walked up behind her and squeezed her shoulder. "Now I'm worried. I'm always here for you, you know that."

"Of course, and thanks." Patsy nodded and continued her update. "The conference proper kicks off at nine thirty, a coffee break at eleven, and then the men should be concluded by lunchtime. We then have to do the women after lunch." She raised her eyebrows. "It will be interesting to see how they react. I wonder if any of them will do a runner. Come on then, I'll get you a coffee.

As they left the anteroom, Stella's staff were filing into the conference hall. Stella had taken the centre seat at the table in front of the stage.

Patsy walked over smiling. "We're all set, just going to grab a coffee before you start."

"Are there no facilities out there? I'll have them set something up." Stella stood and waved over a waiter. She issued her instructions curtly before turning back to them. "We've only had two call in sick, and one of those was female. So hopefully this will all be over by Monday." A frown creased her brow and she looked at Frankie. "They will get the samples processed over the weekend, won't they?"

"They should do, and they will certainly get the men done. I wouldn't . . ." Frankie paused as a man approached. He waited until Stella had spoken to him. "As I was saying, I wouldn't have recommended them if they couldn't deliver."

"Good. Now if you'll excuse me, I think we're almost ready. You're most welcome to join us before the testing starts if you wish."

Frankie thanked her and told her he might do that, although in truth he could think of anything worse than listening to a bunch of estate agents talking. Stella pointed to the anteroom where two waiters were carrying a coffee machine through the door, and a waitress pushed a trolley laden with cakes, cups and plates.

"There you go, you should be more comfortable in there now." She drew in a deep breath, adjusted her shirt collar, and pulled the lapels of her jacket forward to ensure it sat smartly. "Right, let's get this show on the road." She turned towards the room, and switched on the microphone on her lapel. "As quickly as you can ladies and gentlemen. We're ready to start."

Her voice filled the room and the hustle and bustle from her staff taking their seats abated. Patsy and Frankie walked to the anteroom. Patsy paused before entering and whispered, "Let's just listen to the first bit. The coffee won't be ready yet." Frankie followed her and they stood with their backs to the wall next to the door.

"Good morning and welcome. Thank you for arriving promptly. Before we begin I will run through the agenda for this morning." The screen behind her changed and the title "Agenda" appeared. "We need no introductions, so first let's cover off the house keeping." The first bullet point appeared. "Fire exits are located along the rear wall. Should the fire alarm sound please leave the room in an orderly manner and congregate on the green outside. Should you need to use the toilet during the proceedings, they are located over there." She pointed to two doors on the opposite wall from the anteroom. "We will take a coffee break at around eleven, and break for lunch at one."

Stella pushed the button on the remote in her hand and the next item appeared on the agenda. "Our first topic this morning is conversion rates. We will examine averages by branch, and by discipline. Our top performers will tell you why they are successful, and the rest of you will come up with a three-point plan on how you will improve your own performance."

She pressed the button again. "Then we will move on to profit ratios and examine expenditure. This will be broken down into three main cost areas: staff, advertising and promotion, and branch controlled overheads. We will then break for coffee." The screen changed. "Coffee break of no more than twenty minutes please, we do have a lot to get through. When we reconvene, we will turn our attention to productivity."

"Can we escape now? I think the excitement will kill me," Frankie whispered and placed a hand at his throat.

Patsy grinned, nodded, and held up her finger. "Let her just finish the agenda, and we'll slide off before they start on," she glanced up at the screen, "conversions." She shrugged as Frankie rolled his eyes.

Two hours later they stood to attention by the anteroom door as Stella called the room to order following the coffee break.

"We are going to work in groups now. Your subject is in the red envelope at the centre of your table. I want you to discuss this in your groups, come up with a plan, and put a presentation together. You have until lunchtime to complete your presentation, and your nominated presenter will share your thoughts with us after lunch. Whilst you're working on this there are a few other things we need to take care of. Would the gentlemen on table number one please stand and make their way over here."

Stella gestured towards Frankie and Patsy who had returned. "If you would like to go with Patsy, Bruce will explain all." The five men stood and left the table. There were a few murmurings around the room, and Stella clapped her hands. "Right, the rest of you get to work, I'll be coming round and giving you a few pointers."

Patsy smiled at the first of the men to reach her. Frankie opened the door and showed them into the waiting room. Once inside they were greeted by Bruce Williams. Stella's PA, Samantha, sat at one end of the room, with her laptop open, next to the boxes awaiting specimens, and a copy of the terms and conditions of employment resting on her lap. She was there to point out the relevant clauses should anyone question their authority.

"Morning, gentlemen, this won't take long." Bruce smiled at them. "As you are aware, there is a clause in your contract of employment which advises you may on occasion be required to take a drugs test."

The five men exchanged puzzled glances.

One of them opened his mouth to speak, but Bruce Williams held his hand up to silence him. "Let me finish, then we'll deal with any questions. This is Doctor Callaghan. He is going to supervise the production of the samples. They will be tested over the weekend, and any adverse results will be discussed, if necessary, during the course of next week." Again, he lifted his hand as one of the men stepped forward. "Samantha has a copy of the terms and conditions should you wish to read them, and also a scanned version of individually signed contracts should you wish to see those."

Bruce drew in a breath and held his shoulders back. "This testing will be carried out on all staff during the day. You may refuse should you so wish, but it goes without saying that would be considered an odd response." He smiled at the men. "Now, any questions?"

"What's brought this on then? I've worked for Stella for nine years and never even known one person being tested for drugs." The short, dapper man held his hands out awaiting the answer.

"Let's just say we have received some comments about the practices of some of the staff. I can't go into the origin, of course, but with the Cherry Tree project about to roll we need to be seen to be whiter than white. If there is to be a problem we will expose it ourselves, and be seen to be dealing head on with . . ."

Bruce wrinkled his nose, "any unsavoury issues we may have."

"But that's going to be competitors stirring it, surely, it's not like Stella to over-react. Exactly what was said?" A second man voiced his concerns.

"Not going into detail, Simon, I've explained that. Now, are all of you happy to proceed?" The five men nodded. "Good, then let's get on with it. Oh and one last thing, you mustn't say anything to anyone until the whole room has been tested. That will be sometime this afternoon, and I don't want rumours to start spreading. Am I understood?" The men nodded again and Bruce handed them over to Frankie.

Frankie stepped forward and after a quick glance at their badges handed them a small pot with their names on. He held his hand towards the toilet door.

"This way, gentlemen, I'm sure you've all done this before." Pushing open the door he stepped back to allow the men to file through. "Two at a time, and leave the doors open please." The first two men stepped forward and entered adjacent cubicles. Frankie stationed himself behind them and observed the proceedings. When they left the cubicles, he held out the appropriate labelled bag and the men deposited their samples. He waited until they had washed their hands and called another two forward and repeated the process. When all five had provided their sample, they returned to Bruce in the anteroom.

"Back to your table as quickly and quietly as possible, and don't forget," Bruce placed his fingers on his lips, "not a word."

As the men made their way back Stella pressed her microphone. "Would the gentlemen on table two now make their way across to where Patsy is waiting."

Four men stood and did as requested and the process was repeated. By lunchtime all but one table of five men had provided samples. Only two had asked to see their contracts, and none had refused.

Patsy closed the door behind Frankie and locked it, slipping the key into her jacket pocket.

"Better safe than sorry," she announced as she took his arm. "I wonder what's for lunch?"

Meredith took the mug offered by Tom Seaton and nodded to the board. "What's the latest then?"

"Not much, as you can see. Short went to the same school as Anna's sister for a year or so. Franklyn's office is around the corner from the café, so the theory is he could have been a customer, but Anna didn't recognise the bloke that shot her. Although as we now have confirmation that there was gunpowder residue on his gloves, at least we've got even more reason to think it was him." Seaton sighed. "Franklyn was involved with Brent on the Cherry Tree development, so we know Brent was lying when he said he had scant knowledge of him."

"That doesn't help, does it? We already know he's lying. What else?"

Meredith watched Seaton shrug helplessly.

"Not much. Tenuous links at best and then only to two of them."

"Okay, keep going, it's there, I know it is." Meredith turned away and walked into his office. Once there he sat at his desk and checked his mobile. Three thirty and not a word from her; he chose to ignore the fact that he hadn't attempted contact either. He lifted the copy of Joseph Franklyn's phone log and read the notes jotted by each number. There was nothing obvious. He called to Travers who was walking past the door. "Have we got a log of the calls made from his office yet?" He waved the papers.

"Not sure, I'll check and chase it if we haven't."

"Good man." Meredith picked up Anna's call log and read it for the fourth time. He frowned at an entry three days before Short was murdered. Picking up the list he walked out into the incident room and dropped it on Jo Adler's desk. "What's this? Why the question marks?"

Adler picked up the list and peered at the entry. "No idea," she shrugged.

"Well, find out. Bloody question marks, what sort of police work is that? I'll be in my office."

An hour and a half later, he heard an excited shout from Adler. He hurried out to her desk.

"Gov, I've got one. You were right, it linked all three."

"What does?" Adler's grin was infectious and he smiled at her. "Come on then, share!" he commanded as Trump and Seaton joined him at her desk.

"First off, this number is for . . ." she clicked her mouse and an imposing building appeared on the screen, "a one-stop medical place. There are five practices here; dentist, physiotherapist, optician et cetera. They share the same telephone number, but all three of our victims called or received a call from this number in the last month. Look at this, I've gone back two months." Jo Adler opened a basic spreadsheet. It had three columns representing the three victims. Below each name the date and length of each call was shown, either in blue if incoming or red if outgoing.

Meredith nodded approval. "Right, find out why they were in contact," he winked at her. "Good work, Adler."

Smiling he made his way back to his office. He could feel the energy levels rising in the incident room. He touched the wood on the door jamb as he entered and mentally crossed his fingers. They could do with a break.

His optimism was dented somewhat when Adler put her head round his door. "You're not going to like this."

His eyes narrowed. "Why?"

"The practice closes in five minutes. The receptionist said it was Friday and they had all gone home, she herself was just locking up. She spouted data protection at me when I pressed for information on our victims." Adler rolled her eyes and shrugged. "Couldn't get anything from her. However, she did agree to call the practice manager and get him to call us. So it's a waiting game now."

"Why don't we call him?"

"Because she would only tell me his surname, and there are a lot of Mr Cooks out there."

Meredith thumped his hands on the desk. "For God's sake, that's just what we need. A bloody doctor's receptionist throwing a spanner in the works." He pinched the bridge of his nose. "Right, whilst we await a call from Mr Cook, track down those that practice there. We must be able to do that surely."

Meredith was now walking into the incident room, and his sarcasm was not lost on the team who had been listening to the exchange. He surveyed the room. "Trump, Travers, Seaton, help her out. When we do get hold of one of them, get them to give us Cook's number. He *will* let you in and we *will* look at those records."

The three men nodded.

An hour later Meredith's alarm sounded on his phone so he stood up and put his jacket on.

"What's the latest?" he shouted to Trump who was standing by the printer.

"We have landlines for three of them, and have the dentist's mobile number from his wife. We're now playing telephone hide and seek. We've had no luck as yet though," he waved his finger at Meredith, "but we will." Noticing Meredith had his jacket on, he asked, "Are you going somewhere?"

"A do at the Grand with Patsy." Meredith saw the glance exchanged between Travers and Adler, who knew they had a long night ahead of them. "Brent will be there," he added, and took satisfaction from the accepting nods that followed. "I may have my phone on silent for the dinner, but contact me as soon as you have anything concrete, other than that just text me updates. I'll be in touch."

Patsy was oblivious to the number of heads that turned as she walked into the bar, and her eyes skimmed the room for Meredith. He had texted her ten minutes earlier to announce his arrival. It was the second time in two days he had been on time. Meredith was leaning on the end of the bar as he watched the other men's reaction to Patsy and a smile twitched the corners of his mouth. Their eyes met and he stood upright to greet her.

"You look so gorgeous," he whispered as he pressed his lips to her cheek, "are you sure we haven't got any time to enjoy the hotel room?" He wasn't sure, but he thought she tensed a little. "Every man in this room wishes he was me at this moment," he added as she pulled away from him.

"I doubt that very much. I have to concede that you too are looking very good." For the first time in days she gazed into his eyes, searching for a clue as to why being with him was such a challenge. He held her gaze and leaned in a little.

"If you look at me like that for a moment longer, I swear you'll miss dinner." Meredith reached out his hand and placed it on the small of her back. He allowed it to travel down to the edge of her low cut dress and two of his fingers slipped inside the dress and pulled at the top of her underwear. "Knickers, Hodge? You do surprise me. I have to confess to being a little disappointed."

For just a second, she forgot the day before and her eyes sparkled. She leaned forward and their bodies met.

"I thought it was only proper. I am working after all."

Meredith grinned as the man closest to them smirked and nodded his approval. Patsy stepped back. "What are you grinning at?"

"You seem to have attracted an audience," he said, "but then you always do."

Patsy stepped back still further and looked around. She saw Stella and Tessa enter the bar and nodded an acknowledgement. Stella made towards them, and Meredith watched as both she and Tessa appraised Patsy as they approached. He looked at Patsy and shook his head slightly, she was totally unaware of the effect she was having.

"So, this is Meredith." Stella held out her hand. "I've heard a lot about you." She inclined her head. "Do you mind if I call you Meredith? I have no idea what your first name is, and it suits you." She nodded and didn't await his response. "I'm Stella and this is Tessa, pleased to meet you."

Meredith greeted the two women and acknowledged his usual prejudice. If he hadn't known, he would never have picked them as a couple. As though she could read his mind and wanted to change the subject, Patsy interrupted his train of thought.

"The room looks lovely, Stella. I haven't seen the seating plan yet, where is it?"

"Don't worry, I've put you on table two at the front." Stella leaned closer to Meredith. "I'm assuming you know why Patsy is here, and won't be too put out that you will be sitting opposite her rather than next to her. I need to give her every opportunity with this one. Brent is an odd character," she glanced around to ensure she wasn't overheard, "I don't like him, and therefore I don't want to arrange a further meeting unless it's absolutely necessary."

"No problem, Stella, how could I object to looking at this all evening?" He held out his hand towards Patsy and she slapped it down.

"I quite agree," Stella nodded. Meredith grinned, realising he was outnumbered, and offered them a drink. Stella was about to respond when Brent entered the room. She drew Meredith to one side. "Would you mind if I didn't introduce you as Patsy's partner. Might work better if he thinks she's single. He's not brought his wife with him."

Meredith looked at Patsy. That plan suited him fine, but he didn't want to offend her.

"Fine by me," Patsy agreed as a voice boomed out.

"Ladies and Gentlemen, please take your seats. Dinner will be served in five minutes."

"Just enough time to introduce you to him." Stella put her hand on the small of Patsy's back and propelled her towards Brent.

Tessa took hold of Meredith's arm. "You get the short straw, I'm afraid. I'm sitting next to you." She turned and led Meredith to the table.

Meredith assessed her as he held her seat out for her. A few months earlier Tessa wouldn't have been a short straw. He pulled his eyes away from her cleavage and looked up. Stella was approaching the table. Brent and Patsy were following her. She raised her eyebrows at him before giving a slight shake of her head.

"Introductions where necessary then," Stella smiled and quickly introduced one to another leaving Brent until last. She reached Meredith. "Michael this is Meredith."

Meredith stepped forward and held out his hand. Patsy frowned as she noticed the amusement dancing at the corner of his eyes.

Meredith bit back the grin. "We've met I believe. How are you, Mr Brent?" Meredith was impressed with the cool response.

"Just dandy, DS Meredith, never been better," Brent smiled, and Meredith nodded acknowledging that once more Brent had demoted him.

Stella smiled and clapped her hands together. "Splendid, let's sit."

The starter was served minutes later. Patsy shot a glance at Meredith and wondered how he knew Brent. Meredith was engrossed in conversation with Tessa and Patsy hoped he wouldn't be inappropriate. As the dishes were cleared she turned to Brent and asked him what type of business he was in.

He leaned back on his chair and linked his hands, resting his elbows on the arms as he did so.

"What do I do?" He looked her up and down slowly. "That could take some time. Let's just say I'm an entrepreneur. I have financial interests in many different businesses." He smiled. "And what do you do, Patsy? Other than look edible, of course." He feigned embarrassment by putting a hand on his forehead. "I can't believe that I said that out loud." Sitting up he leaned towards her, "It's true of course, but apologies if I offended."

Patsy put her hand on his arm and leaned forward, their heads almost touching. "No offence. just embarrassment," she laughed, "but you're forgiven."

She leaned back as a waiter arrived with the main course. She caught Meredith's eye and he shook his head slightly. She frowned at him and turned back to Brent.

"I work for Stella. Only for a week or so as it happens, but I've known her a while," Patsy smiled at Stella who turned towards them having heard her name. "What's it been, Stella, a couple of years we've known each other now?"

"Must be darling," Stella leaned towards Brent. "She's captivating isn't she, and such fun."

Tessa nudged Meredith and leaned close to him. "You're staring, and you look angry. She's only playing him, so relax and speak to me."

Meredith turned to face her. "Apologies, I don't like Brent but I shouldn't neglect you. You can be my partner for the evening and ensure I don't get myself into trouble." He gave her a Meredith smile.

"I'd be delighted Meredith. But you know I'm taken," Tessa slapped his hand playfully, "and I won't be turned." Leaning in closer still, she added, "Not even by you."

Their eyes locked for a moment and Meredith grinned at her.

"I too am spoken for, but being an honest chap, I would admit that if I wasn't, I would probably try. I hope that doesn't offend."

Tessa threw her head back and laughed. The exchange had been observed but not heard by Brent, Patsy and Stella on the other side of the table. Brent sneered as Stella announced, "Well I never. I do believe Tessa is flirting with Meredith. I'll have to have words."

She let out a hearty laugh and Meredith looked over and gave a little wave. He caught Patsy's eye and raised an eyebrow. She shook her head at him, and looked down to concentrate on her dinner. Glancing back up she saw Meredith slide his phone from his pocket, and although he held it in his lap she could tell by the concentration on his face that he was sending a message. It was the second since they had arrived at the table.

"If I didn't know better, I would suggest that Mr Meredith is attempting to flirt with every woman at the table, including you," Brent commented and watched her closely to observe her response.

Patsy's nose wrinkled and she turned to look at him. "He's that type, isn't he. Thinks he's God's gift and out to prove it. I don't go in for that sort myself."

Brent lifted his hand and traced her bare shoulder with his fingers. "What type would you be interested in, pray tell." Again, he flashed his perfect smile.

Patsy was saved from answering as Meredith yelped loudly.

Tessa had kicked him under the table but was now busy rearranging her napkin on her lap. Meredith looked up.

"Sorry, touch of cramp," he explained. He held Patsy's gaze and again she caught the barely perceivable shake of his head.

When the waiter arrived to clear the dinner plates, Patsy placed her napkin on the table and stood up. She asked Brent to excuse her while she powdered her nose. He nodded courteously, his eyes trained on her breasts which were alluringly close. Tessa nudged Meredith who attempted to look away. Patsy stepped out from her chair and jolted sideways as she went over on her ankle. She grabbed at Brent's chair and found his neck first. With a short gasp of pain, he arched his back away from her, before standing to assist her.

"I'm so sorry, it was these heels." Patsy held up her foot and her dress separated, exposing her thigh. Brent's eyes flared in appreciation. "Not the wine." Patsy straightened her dress and didn't notice that Meredith was already on his way out.

She hurried into the ladies' cloakroom and locked the door. Sitting on the toilet she removed a small clear pot from her bag, and using a nail file carefully removed Brent's cells from under her nails. Securing the pot in her bag she left the cubicle, washed her hands, and left to return to the table.

Pulling open the door she stepped into the small foyer and walked straight into Meredith.

"A warning, Patsy, you're playing with fire there. I know you're working him, and I'm assuming it's job done now. But back down a little. He plays hard ball."

Patsy tutted and pulled open the door into the main room. "I can look after myself. As you say, job done. Now I think we should return for the dessert, don't you?"

"Indeed, but please stop flirting with him." Meredith paused and pointed. "Is that Sherlock?" Patsy followed the direction of his finger. Frankie spotted them and waved. Meredith nodded acknowledgement.

"Take your hand off my backside," Patsy hissed, "we're not supposed to know each other. Go and warn Frankie, or he may drop us in it." Meredith gave her a little squeeze before he removed his hand and made his way through the tables to Frankie.

Dessert had already arrived, and Brent rose as she reached the table. He pulled out her chair.

"Was that oaf giving you any bother?" He nodded in Meredith's direction.

Patsy assured him that she could handle the likes of Meredith, and made a fuss of the damage she had caused his neck. He brushed her concerns aside, and told her the sweet was delicious. She picked up her spoon and took a mouthful, aware he was watching her closely.

Patsy breathed a sigh of relief as Stella, who had taken to the stage, announced there would be a fifteen-minute comfort break before the awards ceremony began. Meredith held up his cigarettes.

"Excuse me," he smiled at Tessa, and Patsy stood and faced him.

"Would you mind if I joined you, Meredith?" Patsy smiled down at Brent, who was rubbing his hand across his face. "Sorry, it's a weakness."

Brent frowned. "What is?"

Patsy explained she was going for a cigarette and he waved her away.

"Feel free, knock yourself out." He was talking to Patsy but his eyes scanned the room searching for someone. Meredith took her arm and led her to a smoking area that had been set up below a canopy on the other side of the fire exit.

"I think he's lost interest," he murmured as she shielded the lighter with her hands to accept a light.

Patsy sighed. "Well, all's well that ends well then." Patsy took a deep drag on the cigarette.

Meredith nodded towards her now hard nipples. "Are you cold or pleased to see me? And on a serious note, would you like my jacket?"

"Bloody freezing." Patsy dropped the cigarette into the tub of sand and shivered. "I'm going back in. I'm just not this desperate."

By the time they were seated back at the table, Stella was standing on the stage with several men. A large table holding various trophies had been unveiled. Stella tapped the microphone and called for silence.

"Ladies and gentlemen, to present our awards this evening I have great pleasure in introducing the man I hope will be our future Mayor, Mr Richard Hancock." Hancock stepped forward, kissed Stella on the cheek and a ripple of applause went around the room.

Patsy watched Brent clap enthusiastically, letting it die away as Hancock began speaking.

"For those of you that have met me before, you will know the passion I have for this great and wonderful city of Bristol, and I believe it can be even better. Made better, I must say, by businesses contributing to its success in the way that Stella Young Property Services has. Not only does Stella Young Property Services provide employment across the city, but also has an ever-increasing training programme for our young people. The business is a regular fund raiser for local charities, and now, in tandem with the local council and other noteworthy businesses, it is going to provide some of the much needed social housing by its involvement in the Cherry Tree development. It therefore gives me great pleasure to be here with you this evening to present what I am sure are well deserved awards."

This raised more enthusiastic applause. Brent was clapping again. Knowing a little of Brent's history with the project, Patsy couldn't resist questioning him.

"Are you a fan of Mr Hancock, Mr Brent? Can I take it you'll be voting for him?" To her total and utter surprise Brent's eyes gleamed as he turned to answer her.

"He already has my vote, love." He then turned away to face the stage.

Patsy looked at Meredith whom she knew would be watching and shrugged. Meredith patted the empty seat next to him. Tessa had left the table to usher the winners of awards on and off the stage. Patsy walked over to sit with him. She wanted everything to be right between them. She'd been wrong about his sister, so perhaps she would be wrong about this. She needed to look at his phone and find out who he had been messaging.

Meredith watched Brent, and frowned as Brent cast a casual glance over his shoulder as Patsy left, before returning his attention to the stage. He wondered what had caused Brent to lose interest in Patsy so quickly, and so completely. He knew with certainty that that was not a natural reaction. He placed his arm around Patsy's shoulder as she sat next to him.

"What did you do to him? It's like you kicked him between the legs or something."

"I have no idea, but I'm glad. You're right, he is odd, he seems really excited about this. It's not the Oscars, is it?" She nodded towards the stage as the first recipient collected their trophy for most improved branch.

Stella announced the next award and a round of applause went up. A woman in her late thirties squeezed through the tables. Her own table began chanting her name.

Patsy smiled and nudged Meredith. "She's too excited, she's taken her bag with her. Bless."

Meredith cast a cursory glance in the woman's direction.

"Sally, Sally, Sally," rose the chant as more tables joined in.

Patsy nudged Meredith again. "Look at him now."

Brent was sat on the edge of his chair, clapping in time to the chant.

Meredith shook his head. "I warned you." Meredith looked back to the stage. Tessa was helping Sally climb up the first step.

Patsy nudged him again. Brent was now grinning whilst biting his bottom lip. It gave him a manic air. His hands were held in fists on his knees. Meredith followed Brent's line of sight and frowned. He was watching the woman, Sally.

Meredith leaned forward and focused on her. She appeared perfectly normal, and was nodding an acknowledgement to those on stage applauding her as she made her way towards Hancock. She was a perfectly average looking woman. Nothing to make her stand out in a crowd, not even the low-cut evening gown she wore.

Richard Hancock took the award from one of the organisers, and stepped towards her. He beamed as she neared the centre of the stage. The woman hesitated and seemed to adjust her handbag.

"Fuck!" yelled Meredith, and Patsy slopped her drink as he lurched forward towards the stage.

She dropped the glass as she stood to watch his progress.

Meredith launched himself forward, and belly-flopped onto the stage grabbing the woman's ankles as he landed. She buckled at the knee falling forward. A shot from the gun she had taken from her bag rang out, before clattering to the ground. Meredith roared, realising he had not been quick enough.

The bullet hit Richard Hancock in the leg, and he too fell to the floor clasping the wound as his trouser leg changed colour. Meredith clambered to his feet and picked up the gun as screaming filled the room. People jumped to their feet in horror.

Patsy rushed forward, and hiking up her dress, she climbed to join Meredith on the stage. Laying the woman face down and holding her hands behind her, she looked around for something to secure them with. Seeing a box behind the curtain she called to Stella. Stella moved quickly and handed Patsy one of the identity badges which was attached to a cord intended to be hung around the neck. Patsy tied the woman's hands with the cord and moved her into a sitting position. She stared at Patsy blankly.

Meredith gave Hancock's wound a cursory inspection, and took the microphone. "Sherlock, get your arse up here now, we need a doctor, and someone call an ambulance. The rest of you sit down and shut up!"

A few of the staff did as they were bid. Meredith looked at Brent who was now leaning back in his chair and sipping from an overfull glass of wine. Their eyes met and Meredith pointed at him. Brent shrugged in response. A few women were still wailing and Meredith banged the microphone violently.

"I said shut up! Now everyone take their seats, no one leave the room, and for Christ's sake stop screaming."

Replacing the microphone, he pulled the phone from his pocket and called Seaton. Frankie had reached the stage, and Meredith held out his hand and heaved him up. Frankie went to Richard Hancock and assessed the wound. He took off his belt and tied it tightly around the top of Hancock's leg before looking for something to complete the tourniquet. Patsy knew immediately what he was after and called to Brent to throw her the metal tulip from the centre of the table. Brent cupped his hand to his ear as though he hadn't heard. A woman on the next table grabbed one and raced forward as Brent smirked.

Meredith scanned the room. Nearly everyone had returned to their seats; a few women were crying and being comforted. A low buzz had replaced the shouting and screaming as everyone discussed the magnitude of the event they had witnessed. Meredith dropped down off the stage and held his arms out for Patsy to join him. Removing her shoes, she dropped into his arms.

"What do you want me to do?"

From the corner of her eye she saw Brent move and looked towards him. He'd placed his hands on his hips and his head to one side. He frowned as he realised Patsy was not only assisting Meredith, but was working naturally with him. Meredith followed her gaze.

"Keep everyone in the room." He pointed at Brent. "Especially him. I don't know how, and I haven't got time to explain, but he is involved in the Short, Carter and Franklyn case. You saw how he was a moment ago. He knew that was going to happen."

"No problem. I'll round up some waiters." Patsy stood on tiptoe and kissed him briefly. He smiled at her.

"That's better, my Patsy is back. Now get on with it." Smiling he turned away to ask Frankie how Hancock was.

Patsy jumped down from the stage, and walked briskly towards the table. Brent made to rise. Patsy pulled back her arm and then thrust it forward. The flat of her hand hit him in the centre of the face with as much force as she could manage.

Brent fell back onto his chair, blood spurting from his nose. He grabbed a napkin from the table and held it to his face. Stemming the flow, he removed it, and snarled like an angry terrier.

"I'll have you for that. Police brutality and plenty of witnesses." He waved the bloodstained napkin towards the nearby tables before returning it to his nose.

Patsy stepped closer and leaned in a little. "Good luck with that, since I'm not a police officer. Now you stay there and don't move or I will really hurt you."

Affronted that a woman would make such a threat, Brent jumped to his feet and lunged at her. Meredith was already running towards them. He needn't have worried; Patsy sidestepped Brent's charge, pulled out a chair to throw him off balance, and with a shove in the centre of his back ensured he ended up on the floor. Grabbing Brent's right arm, she twisted it and held it vertically away from his body as she placed one foot between his shoulder blades.

Meredith slowed and grinned at her. "Nicely done, Hodge. Can I be of assistance?"

"This man assaulted me. I'd like to make a citizen's arrest," she replied, returning his grin, and Brent growled at her feet.

"No need, the cavalry has arrived." Meredith nodded behind her as four uniformed officers bounded into the room. He waved one over. "This man apparently assaulted this woman. Deal with him first, probably best you get him straight down the nick. I'll question him once I get there."

The officer pulled handcuffs from his belt and relieved Patsy of Brent. Brent spat at them as he was lifted to his feet. The bloody spittle landed on Patsy's dress.

"You're dead!" Brent's eyes were cold and wide. He sniffed and spat at them again.

The uniformed officer yanked him away as Meredith held his hand up.

"Did you hear that?" He looked around the nearby tables and several wide-eyed staff nodded silently. "Threats of violence. You're on a roll, Brent. Take him away and then come back and get statements from these ladies and gentlemen."

Two hours later Richard Hancock was undergoing an operation, most of Stella Young's staff had been released, having given a brief statement, and Brent was sitting in a cell waiting to be interviewed. Frankie and Patsy watched with Trump as Meredith and Adler interviewed Sally Bainbridge, the woman who had shot Richard Hancock.

"You don't know Richard Hancock?"

"I know of him, but no, I don't know him." The woman looked at the handkerchief that she was twisting between her fingers. "I've seen him in the papers, that's all."

"Who were you going shoot then? And don't lie to me, Sally, I watched you take the gun from your bag. You would be facing a murder charge if it wasn't for me."

"I wasn't going to shoot anyone. Why would I?" Sally gave a sob and looked to Jane Roscoe for support. Jane whispered in her ear as Meredith persisted.

"Then why have a gun?"

"I don't know. It's not mine, I don't know." Her shoulders slumped and she buried her face in her hands. "I want to go home to my babies. Does my husband know?"

Jane Roscoe patted her shoulder and confirmed her husband knew and was trying to find someone to sit with the children so he could come to the station.

"To summarise, Sally, you expect me to believe that somehow someone put a gun in your bag without your knowledge. And that not only did you not notice the weight of the gun, you had no reason to go into your bag during the evening and find it. Then, with this unknown gun you get called to the stage, and rather than accept your award you take out the unknown gun and fire it at Richard Hancock."

"It sounds stupid when you say it. But it's true. It must have been an accident. I must have found it and fired it by accident."

"Would you like to see a film, Sally?" Meredith nodded as she looked at him, her confused expression only matched by Jane Roscoe's. "Tonight's events were being recorded. There were three different cameras rolling throughout the whole evening. They are putting it together now. If I show you exactly what happened do you think it will help jog your memory?" He watched Sally shake her head and shrug, and glanced at his watch. "Suspect has shaken her head in the negative. Interview terminated at eleven thirty-eight."

Leaning forward he switched off the recorder and looked at Jane Roscoe. "I'll go and check how far we are with the film, shouldn't be too long." He jerked his head towards the door. "Can I have a word?"

Standing, he held the door open, and Jane Roscoe followed him into the corridor.

"Thanks for coming." He smiled at her.

"I was working late anyway. But why me?"

"What are your thoughts?" He ignored her question. "Off the record, of course."

"My instinct tells me she had no intention of killing anyone. The evidence would suggest differently, and unlike the Anna Carter case, it is a little more concrete. I'll be interested in seeing the film before passing further comment. It could be argued that it was you grabbing her legs that . . ." Jane Roscoe pointed at Meredith. "That's why you asked for me! Is this connected to Anna's case in some way?"

The door to the room behind them opened, and Frankie stepped into the corridor as Meredith smiled his lazy smile.

"I knew you were the right woman for the job." Meredith looked at Frankie. "Sherlock we're going to have a break now. I want her to see the film."

"I need you to look at something. I think she may have been drugged. It could be shock, of course, but somehow she does ... seem to be fully engaged." Frankie turned to Jane Roscoe. "Do you think she'd agree to a blood sample? We could test and see if she's been drugged in some way."

Roscoe frowned. "I'm not sure about that, you may wish to use it against her. Let me have a word." She opened the door to the interview room and asked Adler to give her a moment alone with her client.

Meredith followed Frankie back into the viewing room. Patsy and Trump broke off from their conversation. Patsy looked at Meredith and he knew immediately that he was in trouble.

"You knew I was going to be testing Brent and why. Why didn't you tell me you thought he was tied up in your case?" As the question left her lips, Patsy knew Meredith couldn't answer her honestly in front of members of his team, and she didn't push him for an answer, but she did share her thoughts with him. "My client believes she was drugged and there is a possibility Brent was involved. Having seen Sally's reaction to your questions, Frankie thinks she may have been drugged. We both saw how excited Brent was when she took to the stage. Perhaps he was involved in that too. Although, I'm not sure why."

Meredith nodded slowly. "Well then, let's hope she agrees to a test quickly." He blew out a weary breath. "Can we get some coffee please, and continue this conversation later?"

Patsy sat in the incident room whilst Meredith updated the Superintendent, and Frankie took blood from Sally Bainbridge. The team had been dismissed for the night as Jane Roscoe had only agreed to the test if her client was allowed to rest. The film had been damning for Sally.

Patsy pulled Meredith's jacket closer and looked down at her stained dress as she pondered the events of the evening, and Meredith's lack of honesty. As though reading her thoughts, he appeared at the door.

"Going to spend a penny, then we can get out of here." He disappeared again.

Patsy stood and walked slowly around the room. She paused at one of the incident boards and squinted closely at the photographs of the practitioners at the clinic. She inclined her head as she wondered again at how small a world they all inhabited. Derek Christie was on Stella's list, albeit with a low probability. She looked up as Meredith returned.

"Can we go to bed now?" By his tone, Patsy knew sleeping wasn't part of his plan.

"Of course." Once again, she put whatever else Meredith was up to at the back of her mind. Tomorrow would be soon enough to deal with that. "There's nothing I'd like better."

Meredith fell onto his back and stared at the ceiling for a moment before pulling Patsy into his arms.

"I think you needed that more than I did." He kissed her on the forehead, his chest still rising and falling from the recent exertion. "Are you going to tell me what's been wrong with you?" He arched forward as Patsy drew an imaginary line down the centre of his chest.

"One question, straight answer?" she sighed and looked up at him.

He frowned, but nodded.

"Do you promise me that there is nothing going on, not with family or otherwise that I should know about," Patsy propped herself upon to her elbow. "No, let me rephrase that. That *I* would think I should know about?"

"This. Again? Has someone said something?"

"No it's . . . I don't know, let's just say I feel like you're keeping something from me."

"Patsy, I'm not. Now let's put this behind us and get some sleep. I have to be up at the crack of dawn. I have the pleasure of interviewing Mr Brent in the morning."

"Okay. I'm sorry. I have your promise, let's sleep." Patsy turned over and snuggled her back up against Meredith and drifted off to sleep.

Meredith lay staring at the ceiling.

CHAPTER TWENTY-TWO

Patsy awoke with a start. Beads of perspiration covered her forehead. Her pulse was rapid and she had butterflies in her tummy. She reached out for Meredith but his side of the bed was cold. Lying perfectly still she listened to the silence, and vaguely remembered him leaving. Lifting her head, she peered at the clock. Seven thirty. Meredith had been gone at least an hour. The mug of coffee he had brought for her stood cold next to the clock. Rubbing her hands over her face, Patsy decided she must have had a nightmare. She kicked off the duvet and headed for the shower.

Even in the shower something niggled away at the back of her mind, but she couldn't pinpoint what it was. Hair dried, makeup on, fully dressed, and sitting at the kitchen table, she sipped her coffee and closed her eyes and searched her mind. Something was in there that she needed to resurrect. She started with meeting Meredith in the bar the night before and worked through the evening in her mind, right up to the point she had snuggled into Meredith. Nothing jumped out at her, so she went back and started the process again. This time she focused on specific time slots, but still nothing.

She opened her eyes, and picking at her toast, she wondered if it was something to do with Meredith, something to do with their relationship, or perhaps her growing paranoia about it.

Clearing the crockery from the table, she emptied her crusts into the bin, and splashed the remnants of coffee into the sink. Pulling down the door of the dishwasher, she pondered her inability to keep to any sort of plan she had to deal with the issues that Meredith threw at her. She was useless, totally and utterly under his spell. A small smile appeared as she thought about the night before. She shouldn't complain about that, it wasn't all . . .

Patsy gasped. Like a bolt of lightning it all fell into place. She threw her hands heavenward and said a silent prayer. A grin on her face, butterflies gone, and cloud lifted, she dashed to find her phone. She drummed her fingers on the table as she listened to Meredith's answer service.

"Hi, only me. I think I know who did it. Well sort of," Patsy glanced up at the clock. "I'm going to check it out. Call me when you have five." She lowered her voice. "Thinking about last night is making me smile by the way."

She hung up and called Linda, another answer machine cut in.

"Hi, Linda, hope all is well with you. Last night was eventful to say the least, someone got shot. Listen, I have an errand to do before I check in with Stella Young. Not sure when I'll get there but call me if needed. Oh yes, and if Chris calls in give him my best."

Patsy terminated the call and collected her coat from the hall. There was lightness in her step as she walked to her car. This is why she did this job. She loved the feeling of reward when she pulled it all together. She crossed the fingers of her free hand as she unlocked the car. She hadn't solved anything yet, she shouldn't tempt fate.

Brent put his hand on Tony Wilson's arm as he made to open the door.

"Hang on a minute. I know her. Bide your time." The pair watched Patsy lock her car and walk towards the exit of the car park. As she walked out of view, Brent jerked his head. "Let's follow her a while."

"Why? I thought it was urgent that we -"

"Humour me, okay." Brent's eyes were cold as he stared at Wilson.

Wilson fell into step. Brent had been at the police station all night and was not in the best of moods. He wasn't going to put his head in the noose by upsetting him.

They followed Patsy to her destination. Brent raised his eyebrows and looked at Wilson.

"Well, that's interesting, don't you think?" Wilson had no idea who Patsy was or why it would be interesting, but he nodded agreement. He hated these early starts.

Patsy pushed open the door and welcomed the rush of warm heat that welcomed her. She walked to the reception desk.

The girl smiled at her. "Hello again. Were we expecting you?" She clicked on the diary and frowned.

"No, not really, but I want to make an appointment." Patsy leaned forward smiling and lowered her voice. "Can I just ask you something?"

The receptionist was only too happy to provide the information that Patsy wanted.

"If that's what you want, we can arrange it." She smiled and nodded towards the door. "Here he is now. Hello Dr Christie, Miss Hodge here was -"

"Yes, I heard. Miss Hodge, please come this way. I can spare you ten minutes." He looked at the receptionist. "Cancel my appointments."

"Really, again? Until what time?" The receptionist looked flustered.

"All of them." Derek Christie stepped forward and took Patsy's arm. He smiled kindly at her. "I'm glad you came, really I am."

Patsy wavered for a moment. She knew it could be folly to go with him, but somehow she couldn't stop herself. She didn't have all the answers, she wanted them and she believed Christie could supply them. She followed Christie to his room. He started talking before she had even taken the seat he offered.

"I know you know." He smiled as he sat. "It all began many years ago when I was in the army. Happened quite by mistake, but isn't that the way of things?" He gave a shrug and shook his head at the thought. "It's a long story, Miss Hodge, so I will give you an abridged version if I may."

Twenty minutes later he placed his elbows on the desk, buried his face in his hands and groaned. Patsy stared at him. If she still had her warrant card she could arrest him. If she made to call the police he could escape. She weighed him up, wondering if she would be able to stop him.

As if reading her mind, he dropped his hands to the desk and stared at her. His weary eyes filled with unshed tears.

"Look around you, Miss Hodge. Do you agree I have no means of escape?"

Patsy had already checked that out, and she nodded.

"Then you go, then make your call, and let me make mine." His chest shuddered as he drew in a breath. "I have always known this would happen. It was going to be by my own hand of course, not some bright spark like you. In that scenario, I would have been able to say goodbye to my daughter, Sasha, in person. Now it will have to be by telephone." He swallowed and pulled his shoulders back. "Still, all my own fault." He nodded towards the door. "If you wouldn't mind, I give you my word I will be here when you need me." Again, he second guessed her thoughts. "No, I am not going to commit suicide. I promise when they arrive, I will be here, waiting."

For the second time in an hour, Patsy overruled her better judgement, and did as the man asked. She pulled the door shut quietly and called Meredith. It went to the answer service again. Irritated, she hung up and called the incident room.

"Hi, Tom, its Patsy. Is Meredith in the station? Because I know who did it and why?"

"Patsy, what the hell are you on about?" Tom Seaton demanded. "He's like a bear with a sore head this morning. Brent's brief got him out again. He's interviewing Sally Bainbridge now. Are you sure you want me to interrupt him?"

"Tom, please," Patsy sighed. "Get him or don't, but get me two bodies down here now." She gave the address and Seaton made the connection.

"I'll have a word, and someone will be with you in less than ten minutes."

"Quicker than that Tom, I'm worried about him."

Trump's car screeched to a halt outside the clinic, and Brent and Wilson watched the two officers rush into the building. Wilson's heart thumped in his chest. Now really was the time to go visit his cousin. He was about to voice this when Brent dug him in the ribs with his elbow.

"Bitch! Come on, let's get out of here." He paused for a moment and pointed at the building. "I'll have her though. Don't care how long it takes." He rubbed his sore nose gently before turning and hurrying back towards the car park. He pulled out his phone and called his wife as Wilson hurried behind. "Don't ask questions, just do as I say. Pack some bags, now, for all of us. We're going on a little holiday . . ." he hesitated. "Get them in the car and then go into my study. There's a false panel at the back of the desk, a button to the right will release it. Get what's there and pack that too."

Brent listened while she explained that James was at his mother's and asked if she should go and pick him up first. Wilson's phone sounded. He waved it at Brent.

"That's weird, I've got a message. I didn't hear it ring, did you?"

Brent turned his back ignoring him, and shouted into the phone.

"I don't need this crap now. Get the bags packed and into the car, get the stuff from the desk, then get over and get him." He glanced at his watch. "I'll meet you there in an hour. I've got to go to the club and get some stuff." He hung up and turned to Wilson. "Tone, you should probably call your missus too. Get me down to the club sharpish, if necessary I'll get a taxi from there."

"No problem, I know where I'm going and they ain't coming with me." Wilson threw his head back and laughed.

Brent shook his head. "You're mad as a box of fucking frogs, you are. It's probably why I like you." They had reached the car. "Right, don't spare the horses, they won't be far behind."

Meredith strode purposefully down the corridor. He opened the door to the first interview room and Derek Christie looked up. Meredith shook his head, closed the door, and quickened his pace. He pushed open the doors to the incident room and his eyes locked on Patsy's. Without releasing them he barked, "Seaton, Hodge. My office now!"

He was sitting behind the desk with arms folded behind his head before they had reached it. He waited until they were seated.

"Let me get this right, because I'm not sure that Trump had all the details. When I interview this bloke, I need to know everything, don't you think?"

The accusation was unspoken, but there none the less. Patsy opened her mouth to respond. He waved it away with a flip of his hand, and began recounting the information he had received so far.

"While in the Army, Derek was a physio for wounded troops. He found that somehow his relaxation techniques put some of them into a sort of hypnotic state. After a bit of messing about with it, he finds that once he gets them there he can suggest things they can do which will lessen the pain. He starts treating soldiers with mental issues as well as physical. Nothing real about it, just mind games, but they work. So brilliant is he that everyone loves him, and his superiors are miffed when he chooses to leave.

"He leaves to marry the girl he loves, and has convinced her that she loves him. He wants to give her a better life off base, and attempts a career in show business. A sort of poor man's Paul McKenna. Am I right so far?" Meredith waited until Patsy nodded. "Good. That career fails, as does his marriage for the best part, and he takes to women, wine and gambling. He does a favour for one of Brent's girls who is recovering from an accident, and an impressed Brent goes to him with an injury, as he has heard that Stella Young also uses him. Christie treats Brent using the relaxation technique." Meredith leaned forward resting his elbows on the desk. "And this is where it gets interesting. Brent realises Christie's talent could prove useful when he catches Christie at it with the receptionist. A pretty young thing, who could only be interested in having sex with Christie if one," Meredith held up a finger, "she was being paid, or two," a second finger joined the first, "she was drugged or hypnotised."

Meredith looked out into the incident room. "COFFEE PLEASE," he bellowed and waited until someone had acknowledged him. "Am I doing all right so far?"

Patsy nodded.

"Brent confronts him, and rather than deny it, he confesses all because Brent has fooled him into thinking he is a good guy. Brent even loans him more money to fuel his gambling habit. Once he has both Christie's secret, and his debt, Brent puts him to work. Am I still on track?"

"Yes, but can I just mention that I have no idea why you're so pissed off," Patsy snapped in response. Seaton sank lower into his chair. "You have a bloke ready to confess down the corridor, another couple you can pick up and charge, and you sit there accusing us of what? What's your problem?"

"Not us." Meredith had a look on his face that most men would have run from, and Seaton wondered if he could nudge Patsy into silence without Meredith noticing.

Patsy was having none of it. "What does that mean? Not us."

"You said accusing us. I'm not, I'm accusing you."

"What? Of what? Sorry Meredith, you're going to have to spell this one out, because I'm missing something here."

"I'm not having this conversation now, we'll embarrass Tom," Meredith turned towards Seaton, "won't we Seaton?"

Tom Seaton held his hands up, in a 'don't involve me in this' gesture.

"Rubbish, he's seen it and heard it all before. Spit it out, Meredith."

"Let's come back to it, shall we? Now back to the story. How did Brent utilise Derek Christie's skills?"

Despite her simmering anger, Patsy was intrigued and amazed by what Derek had told her. She tutted and slammed her eyes at Meredith before picking up where he had left off.

"Brent wanted Stella Young killed. He believed it was her fault he had been thrown off the Cherry Tree development. According to Christie, Brent pretended not to know of her involvement so he could keep track of her movements and habits. That way, when the time was right, it would be easy to put a plan in place. Then, at some party or other, he overhears her telling someone that she was glad she was gay. As it meant that she would never have to bear a child or worse, sleep with a man. Brent forgot about killing her, and decided she would do just that, and to add to his fun it would be her choice. As you mentioned he knew that Christie also treated Stella, and therefore Christie would have access to her."

Meredith tilted his head from side to side, he could see the logic.

"Who was it then? The father, who was he?" Seaton couldn't sit and watch the silent sparring any longer. He needed to move this along so he could escape.

Patsy turned to him and shrugged. "If Christie is telling the truth, he doesn't know. I understand that he told Stella to try and bed the next three men that she met at some bar she frequented. After she had slept with them she would go home and shower and not remember it at all. He swears that all he knows is that Brent would have tried to be one of those she met," Patsy grimaced. "We'll have to await the DNA results. I can't believe she might have to face up to that."

Seaton nodded his agreement. "The other victims, what did they do and why did he want them?"

"Brent had his nose put out of joint when Anna Carter spurned his advances. He was also concerned that she had spoken to Andrew Short about it. He thought it would be ironic if Anna was to kill Short. Christie warned him it was fraught with possible mishaps, but did as he was told. At the same time, he had to set Franklyn ready to sort Anna out." Patsy shrugged. "Set him off by phone apparently. It's scary how easy it all seemed."

"So Brent had someone bump Franklyn off violently? Does Christie know why?" Meredith was back in the conversation.

"Christie swears he wasn't involved in that. He didn't even know Franklyn was dead until I told him. I believe him too. Why confess the rest and deny that, it doesn't make sense?"

"And he gave himself up to you. Just like that. Confessed all." Meredith had captured her eyes again. "You thought, hang on a minute, what if? And without a thought for your own safety you bomb off down there, without so much as a by your leave."

Patsy realised what Meredith's problem was, and bit back a smile. She was surprised that she was glad of his concern on this occasion, rather than irritated by it. She started counting on her fingers.

"Number one, I was only going to see the receptionist to ask if he did hypnotise people. Number two, I left you a message to call me asap. You didn't. Number

Three, you know I can look after myself. Don't forget I'd met him before."

"You had?" Meredith raised his hands heavenward.

"I had. Number four . . ." Patsy left the index finger of her right hand hanging over its opposite number. She turned to Seaton. "Help me here, give me a number four."

Seaton grinned, and pushed himself up out of the chair. "And on that happy note, I think I'll leave you to it. Give me a shout when you're ready to start the interview." He waved and made a quick exit.

When Patsy turned to Meredith his eyes were laughing, although his face remained deadpan.

"Seriously, Meredith, we can't go through this every time I do something on my own. I'm a big girl. I can't believe that's why you were angry." She watched Meredith pretend to scratch his top lip to hide the smile.

"Look, I wasn't in any danger. It was very civilised. He basically said, it's a fair cop, let me confess. It was a relief to him that all I had to do was call the boys to bring him in. I couldn't see how he would get out of the office while I waited."

"Waited for what?"

"He wanted to call his daughter to say goodbye. He had already decided to hand himself in, but thought he had time to sort things out, including saying goodbye to his daughter."

Meredith was impressed with what Patsy had achieved. But he didn't want to show it, so he stood and stretched.

"Do you want to watch the interview then?" He was surprised when she shook her head.

"Yes, but I have stuff I really must do. But I'm glad I could help." She couldn't repress the grin.

Meredith walked around the desk and pulled her to her feet. "So am I." He glanced into the incident room. "Come on, I'll show you out, that lot are watching our every move." He pushed her towards the exit. "Some of us have real work to do." He held the door open for her. "What gave him away, how did you work it out?"

"You."

"Me?" Meredith frowned, unable to think of anything that he had done, which would have led Patsy to Christie.

"Yes you. I was thinking about last night, and how you have me under some sort of spell. I knew I knew something but couldn't get there. When I thought of being spellbound by you, I remembered that the dentist and his patient were waiting for Christie when Stella and I left. Why would a dentist's patient need a physio? Unless, of course, they were nervous, and perhaps wanted to be hypnotised. When Dad gave up smoking he went to see a hypnotist, who also dealt with nervous dental patients. I couldn't pull it together initially because Christie was a physio, not a hypnotist." She tapped her temple. "It was here all along, but you that released it."

"I don't suppose it occurred to you that he could have gone to work on you?"

"Briefly, but I wasn't relaxed enough for him to hypnotise me. You should have seen me pacing up and down outside his door, while I waited for the cavalry." Patsy turned around as Meredith stopped walking. "What is it?"

"How long was he alone? More importantly, how do you know it was it his daughter he called?" Meredith nodded as Patsy's hand flew to cover her mouth in horror.

"You think he may have . . ."

"Exactly. You coming back in, or do I sort this on my own."

"I didn't think. I'm sorry,"

Patsy's shoulders drooped, and Meredith reminded her that if she hadn't been under his spell, Derek Christie wouldn't be in custody.

Patsy pecked him on the cheek. "Go on, you get on. I really do have things I must do. Not least explain to Stella. You can tell me all later . . . in bed."

As she started down the staircase she heard him bellow to Seaton before the door closed behind him.

"Seaton get hold of Christie's calls for today." He held his hand up to stop the protest. "I know, but do it. Give me a shout when you have the info. I'll start the interview." He picked up a note pad from his desk and walked back down the corridor to the interview rooms.

Trump was leaning against the wall outside. He stood upright as Meredith approached.

"He doesn't want a solicitor. I've asked three times now. He wants to talk though. I had to leave the room so he didn't say too much before we started recording." Trump shrugged. "He's a troubled man."

"So I hear. Come on then, let's get on with it." Meredith opened the door, pulled out a chair, and even before Trump had shut the door behind him he had switched on the recorder and was announcing who was present in the room and cautioning Derek Christie.

"Derek, may I call you Derek?" Meredith smiled at the nod. "A few things for the tape to start us off. You have told my colleague here that you don't want a solicitor present, is that still the case?" Again, a nod. "You have to speak for the purposes of the tape." Meredith nodded at the machine.

"I don't want a solicitor. I had already decided to come here today when Ms Hodge turned up. I will admit fully what I have done. I will not attempt to defend myself or my actions, and I will plead guilty to all relevant charges." Derek paused and shrugged. "Where do you want to start? I'm assuming you want the full story, and not the abridged version I gave Ms Hodge."

"Indeed I do, but before that is there anything we should know about before we begin. Anything we may be able to stop."

Meredith watched Derek's face flinch as he recognised the significance of the question.

"No." Derek supressed a smile.

"Are you sure? It seems to me, Derek, that you have carried a burden for far too long. If it's now possible to stop any further harm coming to someone, wouldn't it make you feel better?"

"No." Derek shook his head, and his shoulders rose and fell in a silent sigh.

"Right, and just so I'm straight on this, you haven't set off a trail of events that we may be able to stop."

Meredith watched Derek's eyes move to the clock followed by a twitch of his mouth. He'd suppressed another smile.

"No."

"No, you haven't set something off, or no, we wouldn't be able to stop it?"

"The latter."

"How can you be sure?" Meredith banged the table that separated them. Derek jumped violently, but the look of fear was only momentary. He stared at Meredith with a hatred that was unmistakable as Meredith shouted at him. "Come on, Derek, you can't be sure. Don't let anyone else die."

Derek adjusted his position on the chair and, folding his arms on the table, he leaned towards Meredith.

"It's too late. Don't shout at me, DCI Meredith, it won't work. Never again will I allow myself to be bullied. Now you will be civil or we will stop talking." Derek looked smug with his new-found bravery.

"Okay, I apologise, but you must appreciate this from my point of view. I believe you may have set off another person to kill or injure," Meredith shrugged, "maybe more than one. I don't want to be picking up any more dead bodies."

"I understand that, but as I said it's too late."

"Who?"

"Are we going to discuss what's gone before? I have all the time in the world. I'm not going anywhere." Again, his eyes flicked up to the clock.

"If I were a gambling man, I'd put my money on Brent. He abused your friendship . . . well let's be honest, Brent abused just about anyone he came into contact with. Have you done him one last favour, or has his plan turned back on itself?"

"Ill conceived. I told him the first time he suggested it that it was ill conceived." Derek began to rub his temples with the tips of his fingers. "But when Stella Young fell pregnant, which I am sure you will agree was a long shot, he sought me out. 'Ill conceived', he crowed sarcastically at me, 'I'd say that was well conceived not ill conceived'. He laughed at me. I didn't respond. I never did.

"I repeated the warning, though, when he came to me about poor Anna Carter. And because I am stupid I let my recognition of Short show," Derek shook his head and tutted. "Sorry I need to give you the detail. Short was an extremely nervous dental patient; it took almost twenty minutes at times to get him under. I also later treated him for an injury he sustained playing football. Letting Brent know I knew him made it easier in one way, and more complicated in another. I told Short where to be and when, and it was so much easier for Anna then. I could make sure she got away cleanly. Such a lovely girl. Still, she'll be freed now."

"What have you done, Derek?"

"I hypnotised Anna as I treated her back injury -"

"You know what I mean!"

"Are you shouting again, DCI Meredith? I won't have it you know."

Meredith sighed, this was going to be a long afternoon. He suspended the interview, and jerked his head at Trump.

Once outside he issued his instructions. "He's done something. He made a call that set someone off. Hopefully, to kill Brent. That way I won't feel too bad if we don't get to him on time. I'll call him, and let him know he's in danger. I'll send Seaton or Travers down here to join you in the interview. We'll do it his way now."

Patsy walked out of Stella Young's house and drew the welcoming cold air into her lungs. She was glad that Stella had been at home to receive the information. Whilst there, Patsy had telephoned Frankie for the results of the tests taken the day before. Frankie checked with the lab, and they had processed all but a handful and none of them were a match. This included Brent, which was something to be thankful for. Stella might never find out the identity of Sebastian's father. It was most likely to be someone she met in the bar. Patsy slammed the door of her car and called the office. She got the answer machine again and left a message as she drove home.

"Hi, Linda, only me. I hope you're not answering because you are too busy with another call. The Stella Young case is closed. I'm going to call it a day. I'll give Chris a shout when I get home. It's Saturday so you may as well lock up when you've finished whatever it is you're working on. Did George Tucker come back to us by the way? Look, give me a call when you can. Bye."

Closing the front door, Patsy dropped her keys on the table in the hall and hung her coat and bag over the newel post. She would cook Meredith something nice for dinner. She didn't want to go out. A cosy night in would be most welcome. But first she wanted a long, hot, lazy bath. She hadn't even opened the bathroom door before the doorbell rang. Her first thought was Linda. She'd probably come to collect the gossip from the night before.

Patsy smiled as she skipped back down the stairs. She opened the door and her mouth fell open. It was the woman, or girl as she now appeared to be, that she had seen Meredith with. The girl stepped forward hesitantly.

"Is Meredith in?" Her voice was quiet and she couldn't quite meet Patsy's eye.

Patsy swallowed. "No, but he's due any minute. Would you like to wait?" Patsy saw the hesitation before the girl nodded.

"If you're sure."

Despite her answer, Patsy could see that she was uncertain, so she pulled the door fully open. "Of course, come on in. I'm Patsy by the way."

"Amanda."

"Well, Amanda, I was about to make some tea. Come through." Patsy led the way to the kitchen. "How do you know Meredith?"

Totally unprepared for the answer, Patsy fumbled with the kitchen door handle as Amanda answered her.

~ ~ ~

Brent shoved the last of the money bags into a black plastic sack. He looked around his office, there was nothing here now that couldn't be replaced. He wondered why Tony was taking so long to empty the floats from the tills downstairs. Perhaps he was having a quick drink. God knows he himself could do with one. His phone rang and he pulled it from his pocket. It was his home number. He grimaced as his wife's picture appeared on the screen.

"What? You'd better be ready. I'll be leaving here in less than a minute," he snarled.

Liz looked at the contents of the desk compartment and wondered whether to tell him. She realised that despite what she'd just seen, she was still too scared of him to lie.

"I am almost, but I'm phoning to say the police are on their way."

"WHAT!" Brent kicked the chair in front of him and it clattered to the floor. "What have you told them?"

"Nothing, they wanted me to give you a message."

"Ha! Go on then, what was it?"

"He said to tell you to give yourself up. I told him that even if you'd done something you wouldn't do that. He got quite stroppy and he said to make sure you knew your plan was ill conceived. I asked him what plan. And what does ill conceived mean? He said you'd understand."

"Who did? What are you talking about?" Brent was pacing his office.

"Meredith. DCI Meredith said to tell you your plan was ill conceived, and you..."

Brent didn't hear the rest of the sentence. His phone dropped from his shaking hand. He could hear her calling him as he stared at it. When she had repeated the message, he'd remembered mocking Christie with those words. Was Meredith trying to help him? He kicked the phone across the room, and picked up the black sack. Running down the stairs he called for Wilson.

"Tone, where are you? Change of plan mate, I can't go home, or to my mother's. You'll have to get me to the airport before -"

There was a sickening thud as the metal of the bar stool hit the back of his head. Brent fell to the floor. He looked up at Wilson, and he realised that Meredith's warning was not a trap.

"Tone, don't do this. It's him, Christie. He's got to y-" Wilson's foot found his mouth and Brent began to choke on one of his own teeth. Wilson then kicked him again, and again, and again.

Thirty minutes later a uniformed police officer smashed the lock from the door. Meredith, Seaton and Travers waited outside whilst officers wearing body armour ran in to secure the club. Each second dragged. The all clear was called and Meredith walked to the body on the floor by the bar. He noted the expensive suit, and he recognised the shoes. The face, what was left of it, was unrecognisable.

"Up here. He's still alive, call an ambulance," Seaton shouted, and a uniformed officer called into his radio as Meredith and Travers took the stairs two at a time to join him.

Sitting with his feet up on Brent's desk was Anthony Wilson. His blood had formed sticky pools on each side of the chair. Seaton was pulling on the sleeves of his jacket, and by so doing, was holding his severed wrists above his head. Meredith leaned forward and looked at Wilson's feet.

"I think we know what did for Brent downstairs." Meredith grimaced. "Must have taken a while." He looked up at Wilson's wrists. "Self-inflicted?"

"Looks like." Seaton nodded to the floor. Meredith stepped round the desk and looked at the curved blade of the hunting knife and sighed. He cocked his head to one side as the sound of sirens reached him.

"Here come the good guys. Right, let's see what Derek has to say for himself."

On the way back to the station they took the call advising them that Wilson had died before he reached hospital. Meredith went straight to the interview room and joined Trump. Derek Christie's eyes searched his face for some sign as to what he had discovered. Meredith sniffed. He didn't believe that Brent and Wilson deserved much, if any, sympathy but he didn't believe they should have been murdered in such a way. To him Christie was a coward.

"Derek, you said earlier that you didn't like being bullied, and that confuses me." He frowned at Derek and pinched the bridge of his nose. "Have you never heard the stories about what happens to weak men in prison?"

To Meredith's surprise Derek grinned at him.

"I take it my work is complete. Are they both dead?" Derek leaned forward, eager for the answer. Meredith stared at him for a while, wondering whether to drag it out. In the end, he couldn't be bothered. He wanted to go home, and the longer this took, the later that would be.

"They are." He caught Trump's movement from the corner of his eye, as he too turned for more information. "Brent, if it is Brent, is unrecognisable. Wilson died a few moments ago from self-inflicted wounds. Does that please you Derek?"

"Oh yes. I can rest now." Derek leaned back, interlinked his fingers on his stomach, and closed his eyes. He looked as though he might be preparing to take a nap.

"You're not concerned about prison then?" Meredith was irritated by this man, whose cowardice had ruined so many lives. "You will be bullied you know, and worse."

Derek's eyes opened. "I won't be going to prison."

"Oh, I can assure you, you will."

"DCI Meredith, you are an intelligent man. Do you think my plan was ill conceived too?"

Meredith pondered this for a moment. "What, suicide? How?" He turned to Trump. "Tell me he was thoroughly searched."

Trump looked indignant. "Of course. I did it myself."

Meredith looked back to Christie for an answer.

"I don't think that it would be wise that I share that." His tone was soft and he shrugged at Meredith.

Meredith needed a cigarette. This was going to create extra red tape. There was a tap on the door. Seaton's head appeared.

"Sorry, Gov, we've got Mrs Christie downstairs with his solicitor, David Gage. He's insisting on seeing his client."

Meredith looked at Derek. "Would you like your solicitor to join us?"

"Not much point really, is there?" Derek smiled weakly. "You can tell her to go home though. She should be making sure Sasha is okay."

Meredith suspended the interview for the second time. Trump joined him in the corridor.

"I'm going for a ciggy. Go and tell the solicitor he won't see him, and get rid of the wife. When I've had my smoke, I'll give the prison a ring and explain he needs to be put on suicide watch."

Trump walked in the opposite direction to Meredith, and down to the meeting room where Rebecca Christie and the solicitor were waiting. The solicitor stood as he entered the room.

"Am I right in assuming that you have been questioning my client without legal representation present?" he demanded.

"You are indeed. Four refusals so far." Trump shook his head. "It's not like we haven't tried." Trump turned to Rebecca Christie. "He also refuses to see you. He said to tell you to go home and look after Sasha."

Trump watched as Rebecca's chin twitched. She stood up and looked at the solicitor.

"I'm sorry, David, that's it. I don't care what he's done. I want a divorce. He will not step foot inside that house again." Bending her knees, she scooped up her bag and scarf. She paused at the door. "Tell him he'll never see Sasha again either. Not if I have my way." She pulled the door open. "I'll speak to you later."

David Gage nodded, and they exchanged a smile before she turned and let the door bang shut.

"Now look here. Just take me down to him. I'm sure I can convince him to speak with me. It will look better in court if he has taken advice." David Gage nodded as he spoke.

Trump shrugged. "We can try." He led the way to the interview room.

Christie looked up as he opened the door.

"Your solicitor, Mr Gage, is insisting on having a word"

"Tell him to stop wasting his time."

"Derek, I really must insist. Just give me five minutes and then if you don't need me I'll go," David Gage called over Trump's shoulder.

Christie shrugged. "If he must, but what's done is done."

Trump stepped back and Gage walked into the room, and turned to face him.

"In private if you don't mind," Gage stated, and Trump looked at Christie.

Christie merely shrugged again.

"I'll be back in five minutes." Trump closed the door and went to speak to the custody sergeant.

Meredith frowned as he joined them. "What's happening?"

Trump glanced up at the clock. "You're just in time. Christie agreed to see his solicitor. They wanted five minutes alone. Time's up."

Meredith started towards the interview room, then paused briefly before breaking into a run.

"Shit! Quick, come on!" Skidding to a halt at the door, he flung it open. Both Christie and Gage, appeared to be asleep. "Jesus Christ!" Meredith roared. "Get a doctor in here now!" He rushed to Gage and felt for a pulse, but there was none.

Trump did the same to Christie and shook his head. "Bollocks!"

Meredith cursed. "Do you know how much paperwork this is going to create?"
Trump nodded and pulled a sheet of paper out from beneath Derek
Christie's arm.

He's been having an affair with my wife for two years that I know of.
He also thought I was stupid. It seemed fitting we should end it together.

Trump turned the sheet to show Meredith.

"How? With what? Poison?" Meredith banged his palm against his forehead.
Trump smiled.

"What are you grinning at? I was hoping for an early night. Fat chance
of that!"

"But I can tell you how he, or they I suppose, did it." Trump glanced up at the
camera in the corner of the room.

"You didn't?" Meredith grinned at him. "What, when he was alone with his
solicitor, you recorded him? You do realise that's against the law I suppose?"

"It wasn't so much his solicitor, as anyone." Trump placed the note back on the
table. "When I heard how he'd controlled his victims, I thought better safe than
sorry. I would have told you, but haven't had the opportunity." He stepped to one
side to allow Meredith to lead the way.

Meredith grabbed his hand and shook it. "I've always loved you, Trump."

Frankie Callaghan had arrived with his team to collect the bodies. He removed
a syringe from Derek Christie's pocket, and dropped it into an evidence bag.

"From what I understand Christie had this planned." He looked at Meredith
who was leaning against the door jamb rubbing the bridge of his nose. "You
couldn't have known, you know. You only had him for a few hours."

Meredith grunted. "Yes, I'm aware of that, Sherlock. But I knew how he was
doing it. Come and look at this." Meredith took Frankie to the room next door
and pointed to a chair in front of the central screen. "Take a seat. I've seen it. Just
as well Trump had the sense to do this, although we will still get dragged over the
coals" He leaned over Frankie's shoulder and hit the play button.

Frankie saw Gage step past Trump into the room. As Trump shut the door,
Christie held out his hand and Gage removed what appeared to be a cigar case from
his inside pocket. He passed it to Christie and sat down. Gage then removed his
jacket and rolled up his shirt sleeve and placed his arm on the table. Christie inserted

the syringe into the crook of Gage's elbow. He watched for a second as Gage's body stiffened before his head fell forward onto his chest. Christie moved quickly to the other side of the table and wrote the note. Loosening his collar and tie, he picked up the syringe in his right hand, and with his left pressed his fingers onto his neck until finding the spot he wanted. He then injected himself, and slipped the syringe into his pocket as his body jerked backward. He then slumped forward onto the desk. There was no movement for a full two minutes, and then Meredith appeared.

Meredith leaned forward and stopped the tape. Frankie swivelled the chair around and looked up at him.

"Well, that explains that. I should be able to tell you what was in the syringe within the hour." He stood and patted Meredith on the shoulder. "It took less than three minutes, and it was his solicitor that provided the means. You shouldn't blame yourself."

"I don't. Right, let's call the powers that be, and get that lot off home. No more we can do today." Meredith did blame himself, and he wondered if Patsy would have allowed an unsupervised meeting.

Patsy placed a mug on the table in front of Amanda. "I have to go and sort some things out." She pointed to the remote control. "Feel free to watch television." She forced a smile and glanced at her watch. "Meredith shouldn't be long now."

Closing the door behind her she went upstairs. As she removed her phone from her pocket she wondered whether she should call Meredith. She decided against it, he would be home soon, and that would be soon enough. Having completed the tasks she had set herself, she went back downstairs, and paused at the sitting room door. She could hear that Amanda was talking to someone on the telephone, so turning away she walked to the kitchen. As she picked up her car keys, Meredith opened the front door.

"What a day. Where are you? I need a hug." He hung his coat on the newel post. He frowned at the coat already hanging there.

"I'm in here," Patsy called from the kitchen and he went to join her. She was standing at the sink looking out of the window. She didn't turn to greet him.

He sighed, wondering what he had done this time.

"No hug then." His breath caught as she turned to face him. Her face was pale, and her eyes told him more than words ever could. She held out her arms and he stepped forward to embrace her. "What is it?" he asked as she clung to him.

"You have a visitor. You need to sort some things out. I'll see you soon, I'm sure."

"What? What visitor? Where are you going?"

"Linda's. Not sure for how long. Sod's law, the agents have managed to relet my flat. I'll keep in touch." Her voice broke and she pulled away from him, walking towards the hall. He turned to follow her.

"What visitor? Patsy, don't you dare walk out on me." He was shouting now.

Patsy turned and held her hand up. He stopped walking. "Don't you dare shout at me!" she warned in a harsh whisper. "I asked, and then I asked again. I can't live with a man like you. I simply can't do it."

She turned away and ran up the stairs. Meredith stood stunned in the kitchen, he assumed the visitor was in the sitting room. Well, whoever it was, they could wait. He shook his head realising that at the very least he should know that. But he had so many skeletons it was difficult to choose. He ignored their presence, he wasn't about to invite a third person to this conversation. He walked into the hall when he heard Patsy coming back down the stairs. She placed the suitcase on the floor and removed the holdall strap from her shoulder. Lifting the top two coats from the post, she removed her own, and pulled it on. Buttoning her coat, she looked at him.

He pointed to the door of the sitting room. "I have no idea who is in there, but whoever it is, whatever they've told you, I love you. Please don't do this. Let's sort it out."

He watched the slight shake of her head.

"Bye, Meredith." Patsy slung the strap of the holdall over her shoulder.

He took a step closer. "Patsy, please. Let me get rid of them. Whoever it is, they mean nothing to me. I will be able to explain, I promise you."

He stepped back in shock as her slap stung his cheek.

"You shit." Patsy wheeled the suitcase to the door and reached up to open it.

Meredith rushed forward. He grabbed her shoulders and spun her to face him. "Let's do this together, you come in there with me," he jerked his thumb at the sitting room door, "and I will prove to you they mean nothing to me."

Patsy knocked his hands away and pulled the door open. She lifted the case over the threshold and turned to him.

"Just go and see her Meredith, and hope she didn't hear you."

She rolled the suitcase towards her car.

Meredith called to her as she lifted the case into the car. "Who?"

"Your daughter."

Patsy slammed the boot and opened the door. Before climbing into the car, she glanced at the window. Amanda was watching them.

"The daughter you should have been supporting. The one who just buried her mother without you there. The daughter you should have told me about."

Lifting her hand, she waved at Amanda and smiled at her. She then looked back at Meredith.

"Go and be the man you can be. Go and dry her tears. I can cope with mine."

AUTHOR'S NOTE

Thank you for reading Ill Conceived. I hope you enjoyed reading this story as much as I enjoyed writing it. If you did, I'd be grateful if you would be kind enough to leave a review, or contact me with your thoughts and any comments. Constructive reviews are invaluable to authors. If you would rather contact me personally the details are below.

If you would like to read more of my work, then I would be happy to gift you a FREE e-book from my website: http://mkturnerbooks.co.uk/ Please click contact, and leave your request in the comment section.

ABOUT THE AUTHOR

Having worked in the property industry for most of my adult life, latterly at a senior level, I finally escaped in 2010. I now work as a consultant for several independent agencies, but I dedicate the bulk of my time to writing and, of course, reading, although there are still not enough hours in the day.

I began writing quite by chance when a friend commented, "They wouldn't believe it if you wrote it down!" So I did. I enjoyed the plotting and scheming, creating the characters, and watching them develop with the story. I kept on writing, and Meredith and Hodge arrived. I should confess at this point that although I have the basic outline when I start a new story, it never develops the way I expect, and I rarely know 'who did it' myself until I've nearly finished.

I am married with two children, two German Shepherds and a Bichon Frise, and we live in Bristol, UK.

I can be contacted here, and would love to hear from you:

Website: http://mkturnerbooks.co.uk/
Twitter: @MarciaKimTurner
Facebook: M K Turner

CPSIA information can be obtained
at www.ICGtesting.com
Printed in the USA
LVOW13s1606270617

539544LV00013B/981/P